# MANHATTAN NORTH

## JOHN MACKIE

AN ONYX BOOK

ONYX
Published by New American Library, a division of
Penguin Group (USA) Inc., 375 Hudson Street,
New York, New York 10014, U.S.A.
Penguin Books Ltd, 80 Strand,
London WC2R 0RL, England
Penguin Books Australia Ltd, 250 Camberwell Road,
Camberwell, Victoria 3124, Australia
Penguin Books Canada Ltd, 10 Alcorn Avenue,
Toronto, Ontario, Canada M4V 3B2
Penguin Books (N.Z.) Ltd, Cnr Rosedale and Airborne Roads,
Albany, Auckland 1310, New Zealand

Penguin Books Ltd, Registered Offices:
80 Strand, London WC2R 0RL, England

First published by Onyx, an imprint of New American Library,
a division of Penguin Group (USA) Inc.

First Printing, July 2003
10  9  8  7  6  5  4  3  2  1

 REGISTERED TRADEMARK—MARCA REGISTRADA

Printed in the United States of America

PUBLISHER'S NOTE
This is a work of fiction. Names, characters, places, and incidents either are the
product of the author's imagination or are used fictitiously, and any resemblance to
actual persons, living or dead, business establishments, events, or locales is entirely
coincidental.

*For my sons, John, Dan, and Greg*

## ACKNOWLEDGMENTS

My thanks to Sharon Townley, Emily Cole, and Sue Mather, the "Three Wise Ladies" who keep me honest, encouraged, and on track. Thanks also to David Hagberg, who takes my calls and freely shares his time and wisdom.

# ONE

Luther Robinson sat quietly in the backseat as the gypsy cab navigated the unseasonable sleet storm pelting Manhattan. The weather fit his plan perfectly.

It was early April, but temperaturewise more like the dead of winter. At that late hour and under those conditions, few cars were moving about on the city's slickened streets; New York was one large skating rink.

A frigid gust suddenly whipped in off the Hudson, broadsiding the older Town Car as it moved up Broadway. The vehicle's back end drifted sideways as its balding tires spun helplessly. The driver let out a frightened gasp. Robinson never blinked.

"Jou definitely the last fare tonight, man!" the diminutive driver blurted in Puerto Rican–accented English, his small hands wringing the wheel as he regained control of the two-ton sedan. He reduced the car's speed to a crawl. "Jou ever see anythin' like this in jour life?" he mumbled. "In freakin' April?"

Ignoring the remark, as he had the driver's earlier attempts at idle chatter, Robinson fixed his trancelike gaze on the empty sidewalks. The "hawk"—bitter, cutting wind—ruled this night. Harlem's streets were bare, oddly devoid of life. Even the most hard-core junkies, who normally had nowhere else to go, were missing from their corners. At

161st, he ordered the car to a near stop as they approached Mister Holiday's Lounge.

"Circle the block, driver. Slowly," he instructed, his dispassionate voice muted by the thick woolen scarf that covered most of his face.

The cab turned into 162nd, looped St. Nicholas Avenue, and returned through 161st. Robinson studied every vehicle parked along the curbs. He grinned when just off the corner of Broadway he found the custom Mercedes he was looking for. Beneath the crusty veneer of ice granules he could make out its light-golden champagne color. There was no question about the plate number—he knew it by heart. He had followed that car for three nights last week. He paid the fifteen-dollar fare and stepped out into the night.

Treading carefully on the ice-coated concrete, he measured each step. His Bruno Magli loafers were ill-suited for such mean conditions. He surveyed the dark block. Not a living soul around. He heard only the howl of the frigid wind and the incessant sizzle of prickly particles peppering the street.

Producing a slim-jim from beneath his cashmere topcoat, Robinson leaned against the curb side of the Mercedes and shoved the slender instrument down, past the window's weatherstripping. These newer models could be difficult. Patiently fishing, he methodically probed the passenger door's insides for the lock-rod actuator.

*Bingo!*

Robinson swung the door wide. Typical—no interior lights or alarm. A dope dealer would sooner risk his ride being ripped off than have a faulty alarm bring cops running at an inopportune moment—say, when he was muling a few keys of China White. He was suddenly sickened by the cloying odor of potpourri air fresheners that permeated the car's plush interior, and he held his breath. No-class nigger, he thought.

Removing a Glock 9 from his coat pocket, he smoothly jacked a round into the pistol's chamber and secreted it, butt side up, behind the folds of the passenger-door map pouch. From another pocket he withdrew two slender fourteen-inch nylon cable ties. He curled one into a large loop by starting the narrow-ridged end into its own self-locking ratchet. Careful to leave no telltale bump, he placed the ties, a lead-filled slapper jack, and a pair of surgical gloves flat beneath the passenger-side floor mat. Then he quickly checked the driver's-side map pocket for a weapon—there was none.

Eyes clicking a one-eighty, Robinson stood and relocked the expensive coupe; the stage was set. He walked the few steps to the corner and leaned into the freezing wind whipping along Broadway. Two doors down from Mister Holiday's Lounge he flipped the slim-jim into a lidless trashcan.

His breaths vaporized in the bitter air as his heart rate quickened in anticipation. Sweet rapture. He set his jaw and regained control.

Adjusting his eyes as he entered the darkened, smoke-clouded nightclub, Robinson slowly unwound the scarf from his face and left it draped casually across his wide, well-formed shoulders. Despite the weather and the late hour, Mister Holiday's was rocking. He peeled off his top-coat and suede gloves and handed them to the high yellow clicking gum in the checkroom. He scanned the lounge quickly, then strolled to an open spot at the apex of the large, horseshoe-shaped bar and ordered Rémy. The barman poured, averting his eyes from Robinson's unsettling, surgically reconstructed face. That happened a lot.

From a tightly packed booth nearby, a Barry White–like basso cut sarcastically through the din of the crowd. "Well,

well, Luther Robinson. To what do we owe the pleasure of *your* fascinating company?"

"I'll be damned. . . ." Robinson turned to face the group. "Horace Grimes. What's happenin', bro? And what brings you here on such a godforsaken night?"

"What brings me here? Hell, man. This is one of my damn waterin' holes." Abandoning his multiracial coterie of off-duty hookers, the big man slid from the booth.

As Grimes ambled slowly toward him, Robinson read every bump and bulge in the man's clothing—from the starched shirt collar that pinched at his thick and rubbery neck right down to the pant cuffs that broke smartly across his shoe tops. As he had suspected, the man was heavily armed.

"But," Grimes added, his blacker-than-black face wrinkling into a road map of suspicion, "I'd really like to know what brings Luther Robinson up into our humble midst. How come you ain't down at the Culture Club? Shit, if I owned my own damn saloon, you wouldn't find my ass out on a night like this."

"Hey," Robinson said with a shrug, surveying the crowded room with a bored smile, "sometimes you get tired of your own joint. Sometimes you just gotta break out, get away. Know what I'm sayin'? Let's you and me have a drink together." Robinson raised his snifter in toast. "This is a piece of good fortune, my stopping in here tonight." He lowered his voice conspiratorially. "I've been wanting to discuss something of great importance with you. But"—he glanced again around the room—"we could never talk here."

"Talk what?" Grimes sneered suspiciously. "Business?"

"Business," Robinson echoed. "Business for you. And business for me."

"Yeah? And just where would you suggest we do this

business talkin'? On your turf? Shit! Forget it, man, who you jivin'?"

"I ain't jivin' nobody, Horace. I've just got a straight-up deal to offer. If you're interested, fine. If not, I'll offer it to somebody else." Robinson sipped at the warming cognac.

"Somebody else?" The linebacker-like Grimes stifled a contempt-filled laugh. "Shit! There ain't too many somebody elses left. People in our circle are droppin' like flies lately, or ain't you heard? And a lot of folks be thinkin' Luther Robinson's got him a hand in that shit."

"Let them fools think what they like. I don't give a rat's ass. If they're giving me credit for what's going on, so be it." Robinson shrugged.

"Just what's on your mind, Luther?"

"Expansion."

"Expansion? You mean like takin' over more territory?"

"That's exactly what I mean. More territory, more money." Robinson leaned in tight. "But I can't do it alone. I need to have someone I can trust to pick up the South Bronx and Upper Manhattan."

"Man, look here," Grimes said with a smirk, glancing over both shoulders before continuing. "I'm the brother who's already got most of Upper Manhattan. My operation goes from the top of Harlem clear up to Inwood."

"Yeah," Robinson acknowledged. "But you ain't got the South Bronx, dude." Pausing briefly for effect, he added, "Yet."

"I'm listening." Grimes nodded, greed getting the better of his wariness. "You got my attention."

"Good. I thought I might. But we can't talk here. As they say, the walls have ears and the night has a thousand eyes. Let's you and me go for a ride. The only damn safe place to talk is in a car. Ain't nobody can hear what you say. You with me?"

"Yeah," Grimes said slowly, his deep voice tight with renewed suspicion. "I'm with you."

"Matter of fact, why don't you and me just head on down to Sister Lacy's? They got an all-nighter going. Lotta broads. We could talk there."

"That's all the way down in the damn Forties," Grimes said. "You know what it's like outside?"

"What's the matter, Horace, 'fraid of a little weather?"

"Fuck, no!"

Luther gulped down the rest of the cognac. "Good. I'll pull my ride around and pick you up right in front."

"Hold on, man," Grimes commanded with a faint laugh. "We gonna go for a ride, all right, and we gonna talk. But we goin' in my damn ride or we ain't goin' at all. You dig? Also," he said, reaching both hands beneath Robinson's jacket, "you gonna have to let me give you a little toss, bro'." Nodding confidently toward the checkroom, he added, "I already done had your outer threads searched. I know you gotta be packin'."

"Okay, Horace," Robinson said, allowing the dealer's strong hands to quickly grope his inseam and crotch, and then to work along the inside of his waistband.

Grimes pulled a cheap nickel-plated .32 from Robinson's belly holster and handed it over to the bartender. "Now you nice and clean," he said, smiling smugly.

"And what about you, Horace?" Robinson countered. "You nice and clean?"

"Don't trust me?"

"Trust is a two-way street, bro'."

Grimes nodded and shrugged off his double-breasted suit jacket, revealing a holstered 9mm tucked under his left arm. He slipped from the shoulder rig, wound its straps tightly around the holstered gun, and handed the package across the bar. "But we're still taking my ride," he growled.

"Have it your way; we'll take your car. I don't give a fuck. Whatchu drivin' now, man?"

"Got me a champagne Benz, brother," Grimes said, smiling. "And it's parked right around the corner, so you and me ain't gonna have to worry none 'bout walkin' too far."

"That's cool. You be careful, though, Horace. Them sidewalks is some slick, bro'." Robinson couldn't help adding, "It's treacherous out there."

At Forty-third Street, Horace Grimes carefully steered his new Mercedes west from Broadway toward Eleventh Avenue and Sister Lacy's Lounge and after-hours club. Luther Robinson sat quietly in the front seat beside him, gazing idly out the window as they stopped for the light at Eighth. He was getting sick to his stomach from the overpowering potpourri stench—the damn smell was going to ruin everything. The roads were still slick, but the high winds and the sleet storm had passed. Grimes cut off his wipers.

"Don't get me wrong," he commented offhandedly as they crossed Ninth. "I like Sister Lacy's, but sometimes they got too damn many of them jive-ass pimps hanging around. 'Specially late at night, like this. Never was too much for them flesh-peddlin' motherfuckers."

"I know what you mean, man," Robinson replied angrily. His jaw clenched as memories of one pimp in particular roared through his head like a Category 5 twister. "Ain't too many things in this world I despise more than a damn pimp." He fought off the old thoughts, dropped his hand into the passenger-door map pocket, and gripped the Glock. It was showtime.

"A man's gotta make himself a livin' somehow in this world, though," Grimes said, his brow scrunched in feigned seriousness. Glancing at Robinson, he laughed facetiously. "Just glad I found me a better way."

As the Mercedes sailed through the intersection at Tenth, Robinson turned and pressed the muzzle of the Glock tightly against Grimes' cheek. "The only thing I hate more than a damn pimp is a disloyal son of a bitch who don't know when he's got it good. Make a left on Eleventh, motherfucker."

"Whatchu doin', man?" Grimes shrieked. He pulled his head away, turning in terror toward Luther. "Where'd you get that damn pistol, man?"

"Never you mind. You just head downtown on Eleventh like I said. Make a left on Thirtieth and come back around into Thirty-third. We gonna find us a quiet place and have us a nice discussion. We need to get some damn things straight, you and me. Oh, and one more thing," he added. "Don't even think about making a move to your ankle."

Two minutes later, the champagne-colored Mercedes pulled to the curb on Thirty-third, just off Tenth. "Shut the motor off, Horace," Robinson directed. His right hand shaking, Grimes complied.

"Luther, you wanna talk, that's fine," Grimes started. "But you needn't be pointin' that damn gun at me. We can talk about anything you want, but please put that thing away."

"I look like some kind of fool to you, Horace?" Robinson snarled. "I put this gun away and suddenly you holdin' all the cards with them twenty-five-inch biceps of yours. I can't take that chance." Robinson pointed the automatic directly at Grimes' face. The man shivered and backed away as far as he could go, till he was tight against the driver's door. His eyes crossed as he stared at the approaching barrel bore.

"Fuckin' thing may go off all by itself, Luther. *Please put it away.*"

"That's exactly right, Horace." Robinson felt a rush as he gauged Grimes' palpable fear. "Modified trigger action," he teased, "very light trigger pull. Damn thing just might go off all by itself. I'd be very careful if I was you." He knew that Grimes was ready for any relief. But he also knew that the window of opportunity would not stay open long. He had to act fast, before the big man realized what was really coming down. Maintaining eye contact, Robinson reached beneath the mat at his feet and withdrew the nylon cable ties. "Want me to put the gun away?" he said. "Gonna have to let me restrain them fuckin' hands of yours. We get straight what needs to be made straight, and we continue on to Sister Lacy's—no harm, no foul. We go have us a good time."

"Just don't shoot me, man," Grimes pleaded, still staring at the aimed barrel, sweat pouring from his brow.

"If I was gonna shoot you, fool, I'd do it right now and walk the fuck away from here and be done with it." He offered a casual shrug and a besides, what-choice-you-got? smirk.

Grimes' eyes narrowed to slits of glaring hatred. Apparently accepting his dearth of options, he held out his large mitts.

With his free hand, Robinson quickly draped the looped cable tie around both of Grimes' huge wrists and yanked it as tightly closed as he could. Wrapping the second tie around the first, he looped that one around the bottom of the steering wheel; he cinched it closed. Grimes was his. He felt his excitement growing.

"See," Robinson said soothingly, toying with him, holding out a false hope to the fool. "Now you can't go punchin' my fuckin' lights out, Horace. Now I can put the damn gun away." As Luther pocketed the Glock, he noted that a mild look of relief came to Grimes' face. Fucking moron, he thought. Fool shoulda made a grab for it—that was his only play.

"I wanna know who your main lieutenants are up in Fort George," Robinson said matter-of-factly. He removed and pocketed his suede gloves, and expertly snapped on the surgical ones. He found the rubbery scent and feel of the latex . . . stimulating.

Grimes' eyes grew suddenly wide. The look of relief vanished from his sweat-drenched face, his expression morphing into one of stark comprehension. Sensing a powerful stirring in his loins, Robinson gave a confident smile, knowing he had played this guy just right.

"I wanna know who they are," he repeated. "And exactly where I can find them."

"Hell," Grimes uttered, with seemingly newfound balls. "You know I ain't gonna tell you that."

"I was hoping you were going to say that." Robinson smiled and reached again beneath the car's floor mat and came out with the six-inch flat-sided slapper blackjack. In one motion he clobbered Grimes in the middle of his face, getting his full attention. Damn, it felt good.

"Why you doin' this, Luther?" Grimes cried as smatterings of blood began to run down from his split upper lip and crushed nose. Luther swung again, landing a bone-jarring blow to the man's right cheekbone and brow. More blood—lots more.

"Derek Ogden sends his regards. He knows you've been trying to do an end-around on us. Tryin' to cut your own deal with the fuckin' Dominicans."

Grimes' eyes grew wide and shifted nervously in his head. Breathing hard, he stammered something unintelligible.

"I ain't got no time to fuck around here, motherfucker,"

Robinson snarled. "So you better damn well start telling me where you warehouse, who your damn street bosses are—especially those three assholes who wear them derby hats—and where I can find every last one of their asses."

"I ain't tellin' you shit, Luther," Grimes blurted through bloodied teeth. "I can take all the beatin' you can deliver. Hell, it's only pain. Besides, once I tell you, it's clear that I'm a goddamned dead man. So if you wanna know what it is that I know, you gonna have to keep my ass alive."

"Oh, you're gonna tell me," Robinson said softly, making a show of pushing in the cigarette lighter of the dashboard ashtray. "You are going to beg to tell me. And then I just might not be ready to listen to you. I might not be able to hear you until . . . I'm ready." He cackled. He loved to humiliate his victims. His breaths were getting deeper, more intense. Anticipation of the ultimate gratification again washed through his mind. He fought for control.

When the lighter popped, Robinson plucked it from the dash and waved the glowing circle in Grimes' face, taunting him. He'd seen others like this guy before, tough guys who could stand beatings beyond belief and not talk. But he had never known a dude who didn't cave when the branding iron was pressed into the bare flesh of his face, his neck, his fingertips, or the backs of his hands. The glowing-lighter trick never failed to open up even the toughest guy. Robinson sensed Grimes' bravado slipping a few notches.

"Don't do it, Luther, please," Grimes suddenly begged. Tears welled up in his eyes and streamed down his blood-soaked cheeks. "Please don't burn me, man. God almighty," he screeched, "I don't wanna die. I'll tell you every damn thing you wanna know."

"Not yet, you won't," Robinson said, his voice still soft. As the hint of a deep moan mingled with his breathing, he pressed the cherry-red lighter against the frightened man's upper cheek. A puff of smoke rose as Grimes let out an agonized scream. Robinson casually returned the lighter to its receptacle. He pushed it in for a reheat. Damn, he thought, I could do this for hours. He wished the lighter would heat faster.

Robinson realized that the nasty stink of potpourri that had bothered him earlier no longer dominated the inside of the Benz. His complete concentration had been taken over by the ecstasy of making the grown man agonize and cry— and the sweet aroma of melting flesh. Having extracted every piece of information he needed, Robinson slipped from business into pleasure mode, reaching climax as he jacked Grimes' bloody head and face into a wide-eyed stupor.

With a hint of drool oozing from the corner of his mouth, and breaths of satisfaction coming in staggered gasps, Robinson slumped back in his seat and pocketed the slapper. He rested for a long moment, gazing at the barely breathing and bloodied source of his enjoyment. This, he thought, was one of the best he'd ever had.

Robinson turned the car's ignition switch to ON, lowered the driver's power window, and let himself out of the Mercedes. He stepped casually around to the driver's side, pushed the Glock into the open window, and fired one shot into the left side of Horace Grimes' head. Play over, curtain down.

He carefully tucked the still-smoldering gun into his waistband, pocketed the surgical gloves, and brushed his coat sleeves, checking for blood; he could see none in the dim light. After pulling on his three-hundred-dollar suede gloves, he walked the long block to Thirty-third and Ninth, entered a diner's parking lot, and climbed into his own car.

As always when dispatching scum, he felt good. He couldn't wait to get home and relive it all over and over.

# TWO

Detective Sergeant Thornton Savage breathed a groan of re-signed exasperation, rolled over onto one hip, and turned off the Westclox alarm five minutes before it was set to go off. He felt rotten. He had been awake most of the night blowing his nose and dealing with sneezing fits, and a few more seconds of sack time wasn't going to do him a damn bit of good. And since Murphy's Law was always in effect, this was probably when he'd finally zonk out.

The vicious head cold had made its first appearance last night around ten as he listened to his eclectic collection of favorite CDs and attempted to play along, note for note, on his old fiddle. He had already been through Lloyd Webber's "Memory" and "The Music of the Night"—which always gave him trouble in the bridge. He then briefly visited the Beach Boys and Billy Joel, despite the violin's nostalgic sound never being quite right for "Little Deuce Coupe" or "Piano Man." Like his father before him—whose Guarneri copy he had inherited—Thorn had never taken one lesson on the instrument. Unlike his father, he'd never quite mas-tered it. But sometimes in the evening, if nothing worth-while was on the tube, he'd tune the old fiddle, put on some music, and play along by ear.

He never played in front of anybody—one of the bene-fits of living alone—but sometimes his upstairs neighbor

Mrs. Potamkin would hear him and have a snit. He knew that because she would always find some crafty way to let him know about it. Apparently the old lady wasn't alone in her distaste for his musical talents. Even Ray the cat made himself scarce at the first draw of the bow. Last night—in the middle of Anton Karas' "Third Man Theme"—the bottom string had let loose at the exact instant of Savage's first monster sneeze. Apparently something in the air had triggered his annual mother of a head cold and sinus assault.

Naked, he threw back the covers and dragged his lean form into the john. By seven-thirty he had blown his nose twenty more times without benefit, showered—as hot as he could stand it—carefully shaved, and partially dressed. He resolved to pick up some over-the-counter meds on the way to the office. He swallowed a ginseng, two ginkgo biloba, and a vitamin E, washing them all down with a tall, pulpless OJ—he hated pulp—and took a generous bite from a three-day-old slice of cake Mrs. Potamkin had brought him. Good old Mrs. P knew his weakness for chocolate layer. Every time she baked one with bittersweet icing, she'd send down a slice or two. Too bad he couldn't taste it this morning.

From what he could see through the window of his narrow kitchen, the Village sidewalks still reflected a slick glaze. Last night's freaky sleet storm had passed but all the same, he decided to wear his older military low-cuts. Sensible and sturdy, they were his foul-weather shoes. No point in lousing up the spit polish on any of his dress pairs.

He filled Ray's water bowl and added enough Meow Mix to the food tray to carry his battle-scarred tom for the day. The cat was outdoors doing his thing, dealing with the *Rodentia rattus garbageatus* who dared venture into his private game preserve, the rear yards and narrow alleys of Sullivan Street, over which he reigned supreme. When he finished patrolling, the frazzled-looking smoky-gray would scale the rickety rose trellis out back, take a short leap across to the fire escape, and saunter through the cat door Savage had installed in a missing pane of his second-story bedroom window. The cat would probably spend the balance of the morning sleeping atop the old Kelvinator—he liked the way it vibrated—or curled into his corner of the frayed living-room sofa, recharging aging batteries in preparation for the afternoon rounds. Ray was a piece of work, no question, and, after rooming with Savage fourteen years, still good company.

Savage squared the knot of his charcoal tie against the slate-gray Brooks Brothers button-down, slipped his Fordham College ring on, and pocketed the well-worn case containing his gold NYPD sergeant's shield. The black leather holder had been through the wars with him and looked like hell, but it was like an old friend. As he clipped his holstered Smith & Wesson inside his belt, the phone rang.

"Boss. Eddie Brodigan here. I'm glad I caught you." The voice coming through the line was clear and well-formed. The onetime air-traffic controller was still over-pronouncing his words. "Operations just notified us of a shooting over in the Tenth. Night watch did the initial response, but they're requesting Manhattan South Homicide and your team's catchin'. Marcus and DeGennaro are on their way. Figured it'd be easier for you to head right over rather than coming into the office first."

"What about Lindstrom?" Savage asked, noting a glowing *1* in the digital display of his PhoneMate. A call must have come in while he was in the shower.

"Jack's got a grand-jury appearance this morning; he sends his regrets."

Savage jotted down the info, told the office wheelman to

notify Operations that a team from MSH was en route, and hung up. He pressed PLAY on the answering machine.

"Guess I missed you . . ." The voice was that of Maureen Gallo, his ex–significant other. "Nothing important, honey . . . try you later."

After two more unsuccessful attempts to clear his nose, he belted his topcoat and let himself out of the apartment. It was time to go do *his* thing, in *his* private game preserve: track down the *Homo erectus homicidus* who dared commit their foul deeds within the confines of Manhattan South. The NYPD command encompassed the entire area from the Battery up to Fifty-ninth Street. Above that—to the top of the island—was the bailiwick of the boys from Manhattan North.

The scent of camphor greeted him in the hallway as he left the apartment and set the dead bolt. He turned and found himself face-to-face with Mrs. Potamkin. A survivor of the horrors of Buchenwald, the woman had lived alone in the third-floor apartment since 1950. Orthopedic stockings bunched like doughnuts at her broomstick ankles, and the peculiar growths on her face seemed more apparent today than usual. Despite her off-the-wall appearance and chronic complaining, he was not without affection for the colorful and outspoken octogenarian.

"Oy! Meester Savage. I was just taking out the trash." The surprised tone in her greeting implied that this had been a chance meeting. He sensed otherwise; the trash bag looked suspiciously empty. "What miserable weather for April. Would you believe?"

"Good morning, Mrs. Potamkin." Thorn forced a courteous smile. "Yes, it certainly was a miserable night, wasn't it?" He attempted to move past, but the lady wasn't going to have that. She had a mission.

"It's a terrible thing being stuck inside," she began, and

clicked her tongue. "I don't like being stuck inside, but with the weather like this and all. . . . Maybe, at least, I can hope for some peace and quiet. Maybe read a good book, or something to pass the time in the evenings. Do you understand what I'm saying, Mr. Savage?"

"Yes . . . yes, I do, Mrs. Potamkin." Moving as he spoke, he let the subtlety slide, desperate to get past before she really glommed his ear. "Spring is just around the corner, though," he ad-libbed in afterthought.

*She's subtle like a freakin' atomic bomb,* Savage thought.

The old woman huffed and shrugged, rolled her eyes in exasperation, and headed back toward her apartment, still toting the trash-bag prop.

Savage turned and double-timed it down the stairs.

Guiding the unmarked department Ford uptown on Sixth Avenue, Savage concluded that the day was going to turn out much nicer than he'd originally thought. The morning sun was warm and already evaporating what might be the last vestige of winter weather. Spring, it seemed, had finally arrived.

He hoped the warming trend would hold through the coming weekend. He and Gina McCormick had big plans for Sunday. If the weather was nice, he'd even drag his old T-bird out of storage for the day trip to the Jersey shore. The last time he'd used the car, he was still seeing Maureen Gallo. That six-year on-and-off relationship had crashed for the final time just before he met Gina a year ago.

At Third Street he pulled over and, leaving the car running, quick-walked the few steps to Curley's corner kiosk.

"What's doin', Curley?" he asked with a friendly wink, snatching up a copy of the morning *Post* and pointing out a headline that had something to do with "the Fed." "I've been trying for days to think of those entities presumptuous enough to tack a *the* before their singular name. I already had The Hague, the Bronx, and the Taliban. Now I've got a fourth—the Fed." He knew there were more. He handed Curley a five.

The paraplegic newsstand operator took out for the paper and the usual roll of Wint-O-Green Life Savers that Savage had already pocketed. "What about the Yankees?" Curley said, handing back the change.

"Nah. Plural. Got an *s* on the end. Almost every sports team does."

"Oh!" Curley shrugged, a puzzled look on his face. "Speaking of *the* Yanks, whaddya think of our chances this season?"

"Oh, I think they're good," Thorn replied emphatically. "'Specially with the new guy, Bill Blomberg, at second base. What a terrific trade. Can't believe the Dodgers gave him up."

The bandannaed man in the wheelchair nodded in thoughtful agreement, and Savage trotted back toward his car.

"Hey, Thorn!" Curley hollered after him. "*The* Jazz. *The* Utah Jazz." Savage didn't think it qualified, but he gave Curley a thumbs-up anyhow.

Five minutes later Savage arrived at West Thirty-third, just off Tenth Avenue. The street looked down on railroad staging yards that fed Penn Station on the east and rail tunnels to Jersey on the west. A deserted part of town, especially after dark, it was a great place to hold marching-band rehearsals, primal-scream sessions, or hand-grenade practice.

Last night, someone had also decided it was a terrific place to blow someone else's brains out.

*          *          *

Beads of scented bathwater gave an additional glow to Derek Ogden's mocha flesh as he struck a practiced series of body-builder poses in the mirrored walls. He studied every nuance of his naked fifty-year-old form. Impressive, he thought. His torso started wide at the shoulders with rock-hard pecs, then tapered to narrow hips beneath decently rippling abdominals, with maybe a hint of flab at the waist. More situps and less red meat, he concluded. A smile crept across his face. He was hung like a Tibetan yak. So many bitches left to pole, he mused, so little time. He reached for a towel and sawed it briskly across his back. Five minutes remained before Luther's expected call.

His permanently leased residence, six rooms at the Hotel Carlyle, was a showplace. Radically reconfigured, lavishly decorated, and extravagantly furnished, it was breathtaking. He even had his own gym and workout room.

A bronze statue of the god Mercury, clad only in winged helmet and sandals, stood dead center in the bath suite. The life-size figure was gazing skyward, his right arm raised, pointing to the heavens above. And there *were* heavens.

In a palette of brilliant blues, highlighted with flashes of silver and much gold leaf, the groin-vaulted ceiling had been frescoed with the constellation Sagittarius, Ogden's astrological sign. The arching vaults with their celestial scenes were supported at the groin points by columns of pale alabaster whose bases rested on an Italian marble floor. Every wall was sparkling mirror.

Lifting his foot to the beveled rim of the black onyx spa, Ogden carefully dried between each painted toe. He noted that his fingernails needed attention; the cuticles were ragged. No matter; Helene, his manicurist, and sometimes fifty-dollar blowjob, would soon be arriving with Antoine, his barber and hairstylist. Luther's call would come at precisely eight o'clock; Ogden had ordered them to arrive at 8:10.

Ogden doused himself with Giorgio, wrapped himself in a loose-fitting lounging jacket, and strode barefoot from the bath.

Moving quickly past Picassos hanging on silk-papered walls, Ogden crossed to the reading room on the opposite side of his eighteenth-floor sanctuary. He selected a thick Cohiba from a humidor, drew its length under his nose, and stood at one of the two tall windows that looked down at the morning hurly-burly of Madison Avenue.

Button-down drones, fast-walking to nowhere, moved along the sidewalks in a wave. Workaday jerks of the world. "Fools," he mused, sniffing again at the barrel of the cigar. Vermin, running themselves to death on the hamster wheel of life.

The mantel clock began to chime as Ogden moved to the cherry desk in the center of the room and sat. He reached for the Dunhill next to the phone and lit the Cohiba. Settled, he waited for the arranged call. On the eighth chime, the telephone rang.

"What news have you?" he asked directly.

"The news—despite one disturbing aspect—is good," Luther Robinson reported. "We now control yet another piece of Upper Manhattan."

"Did Grimes know why he was to be eliminated?" Ogden asked coolly. "Did you tell him he was going to die on my order?"

"As per your instructions, yes," Robinson assured him.

"Good." Ogden breathed deeply, nostrils aflare. "Did the bastard beg?"

"Like a sissy child. He promised never to cheat us again."

"What?" Ogden laughed sarcastically. *"Wouldst thou*

*have a serpent sting thee twice?"* he said in a vibrating baritone. *"If you wrong us, shall we not revenge?"*

"Shylock," Robinson announced. *"Merchant of Venice."*

"Correct," Ogden exclaimed. The hours he'd invested educating and polishing the once feral street kid he'd taken under his wing twenty years ago had been well spent. He was pleased with his handiwork. "I thought you'd have some difficulty getting close enough to Grimes," he said. "He was so paranoid and squirrelly. How did you manage it?"

"I was creative. I borrowed from your theories of reverse psychology."

"Excellent," Ogden said, strapping on his watch. "Did he supply the names we needed?"

"After some encouragement, he did," Robinson replied. "The man was not nearly as tough as he thought he was. I'll start getting with his people today and let them know who they're working for now."

"And to whom the shekels from now on go," Ogden said, pausing to enjoy a deep puff from his first Cuban of the day. "We're right on schedule. I like that. You did mention, however, that there was one disturbing aspect?"

"Before Grimes closed his eyes for good, he warned me that I had a price on my head."

"A contract? On you? Bullshit," Ogden scoffed. "I don't believe it. Grimes was buying time . . . trying to curry favor with you. Hoping you'd cut him some slack."

"It's not as if anybody could possibly want Luther Robinson dead." His voice was dripping with sarcasm.

"Did he say who was behind it?"

"I tried getting it out of him. But he couldn't, or wouldn't, tell me. Said it was just the word on the street."

"You believe him?" Ogden asked, resting the cigar in a crystal ashtray next to the Dunhill.

After seconds of dead air, Robinson replied, "It would be imprudent of me to ignore this warning. I've always suspected it was only a matter of time before some ambitious bastard put me in his fucking sights."

"Be careful, then."

"Am I not, always?"

"You have several missions left to go before we're home free."

"Not a problem. Have you decided who's next?"

"Yet to be determined."

"Just let me know."

"By the way," Ogden said, again reaching for his cigar. "I think I've found yet another place to dump some of this cash that's accumulating. If you can believe it, there's a private island in the Caribbean for sale."

"An actual *island?*" Robinson sounded incredulous. "For sale? How did you find out about that?"

"An item in yesterday's *Times*. You know I read it, and the *Journal,* from cover to cover every day. I've advised you to do the same. Knowledge is power."

"Our own island," Robinson mused.

"I'm going to make a few calls later and follow up on this. Besides burying a bunch of cash in an offshore investment, having our own island may also provide a multitude of fringe benefits."

"Sounds great!" Robinson said in an uncharacteristic display of emotion. "Anyway, the money's beginning to pile up here again."

"Must be time for one of my trips south," Ogden said, his concentration split between the intricacies of the Cohiba's delicate wrappings and Robinson's possible response.

"Soon," Robinson affirmed. "Very soon."

A soothing door chime resonated softly in the background as Ogden carefully cradled the antique, Parisian-style phone. He checked his Rolex. It was 8:15.

"You're five minutes late," he snapped at the effeminate hairdresser and the big-chested manicurist standing sheepishly in the hotel's outer corridor. "You know my feelings on tardiness."

"The elevators were very slow this morning, sir," Antoine stammered.

"Save it." Ogden stood back, allowing the pair to enter. He felt good today. He was up. He decided that Helene would stay late this morning.

# THREE

Traffic was still moving through the one-way of Thirty-third, just west of Tenth, when Savage arrived on the scene. Cops in this town did not interfere with the ebb and flow of its busy citizens—not for such a mundane thing as a murder. The cops didn't cordon off streets with radio cars with lights aflashing, or create annoying detours, or drape miles of yellow crime-scene tape around entire blocks. That's the way it would always happen in the Barney Fife PD out in East Cupcake. Hell, most of the NYPD radio cars didn't even carry a roll of that yellow stuff. It was too expensive, and carried only by the sergeants' cars. And sergeants doled it out as if it were gold. There had to be a real special reason to get ahold of a roll of that tape. Murders weren't special. Not in this town. They were just another part of life.

The light-gold Mercedes was parked just off the corner, framed by a handful of blue uniforms, three radio cars, an EMS bus, and a van from the Crime Scene Unit. Inside the expensive current-model coupe was the body of a well-dressed black man, his broad shoulders hunched and deflated, his puffy facial features mashed against the rim of the leather-wrapped steering wheel. Detectives Diane De-Gennaro and Richie Marcus were already on the scene; their unmarked Taurus was parked on the opposite side of the street. Savage dropped his dark-green Crown Victoria just ahead of the double-parked ambulance, blew his nose one more time, and stepped into the game. He was immediately approached by Diane DeGennaro.

Warm and friendly, she and Detective Richie Marcus had been an item for years. Diane's maiden name was Fallon: Blue-eyed and fair-skinned, the pretty redhead was as Irish as the lichen on the Blarney stone. Her current last name—which ended in a vowel—was a holdover from a long-ago marriage to a swarthy longshoreman from Staten Island. For years she had thought Nick DeGennaro's dark good looks and strong arms had been the fatal attraction. Now she was the first to admit that it was probably his green '66 Impala convertible that had sucked her in.

"I've got some bad news, and I've got some *bad* news," Diane said, half-chuckling, half-serious. "Which one you want first?"

"Another pharmaceutical-supplier execution?" Savage asked, raising his brow.

"Yep," Diane said. "That's the bad news. The *bad* news is he's restrained with them same cable straps. Driver's window is open, and he's taken one in the left ear. Sound familiar?"

"Jeez," Savage muttered, digging again in his pocket for his handkerchief. "That's the third one for us this year. And we're only into April." He wiped his nose.

"Third one for us," Diane said. "But there's been others citywide. The Bronx and Manhattan North." Savage nodded.

"Best we can figure is he's been here about four hours," Joe Hayes said, having joined them. Hayes was a patrol sergeant from the Tenth who Savage thought had retired months ago.

"How do we know that?" Savage inquired, his eyebrows contorting as he again blew his nose.

"Sector came through the block just after three. Car wasn't there. And the landlady who lives in the front of five-oh-three"—Hayes turned to point to the small apartment building directly across the street—"remembered seeing the car there when she looked out at about four-fifteen."

"We talkin' to her?" Savage asked Diane. He wiped his nose and stuffed the sodden handkerchief back into his coat pocket.

"Richie's in there with her now, boss," Diane said. "We only got here a few minutes before you did. If you don't need me right now, I'm going back inside to finish taking her statement."

Savage nodded and turned his attention back to the white-maned uniform sergeant. "Heard you'd retired, Joe."

"Did!" Hayes replied with a self-deprecating chuckle. "Put my papers in back in December, but two weeks before my terminal leave was up, I changed my mind. Figured I could eke out another sixteen months before they kick me out on mandatory age." An ironic grin slipped across his deeply lined and weather-beaten face. "Besides," he said, "I missed this shit. Where else can you go and have this kind of fun?"

Savage knew that this was a frequent sentiment of long-time street cops verging on retirement. The truly confirmed ones, like his own father years ago. Men who had The Job so deep in their blood they couldn't trade the blue serge for three-button plackets and a pair of dumb-looking plaid pants. They just couldn't quit the big-balls game to go chase little white ones in some over-fifty-five golf community in Florida, stocked with gray heads and nearly deads. Once a Rollerball player, always a Rollerball player.

"Who actually found him?" Savage asked, popping a Wint-O-Green as the two men walked slowly toward the death car.

"McCarthy and Sanchez. Ten Sector, Charlie," Hayes replied. "Rolled past at six thirty-five. First they thought the guy was sleepin' one off."

"Was the engine running?"

Hayes shook his head.

Savage took a closer look at the body through the open driver's window. "Any I.D.?" he asked Ollie Beyeler, the crime scene specialist, who was standing beside the Mercedes, loading a roll of film into a Canon AE-1.

"Not yet," Beyeler replied, not bothering to look up. "But then again, we can't get near his back pockets till we pry him outta the car and roll him over. We didn't find any I.D. elsewhere on the body, and there was nothing in the glove compartment but an almost empty box of Trojans and an owner's manual."

"For the Trojans?" Savage asked.

Joe Hayes snickered, amused. Ollie closed the back of the camera and shot Savage a disappointed you-can-do-better-than-that look.

Joe Hayes spoke. "We ran the plate and the car comes back registered to a Juanita Grimes: female, black, DOB one/fourteen/sixty-four. And the gigando gold ring on this guy's right hand just happens to have the initials HG encrusted in diamonds. Mr. Grimes," he added with a shrug.

"We been in the trunk?" Savage asked.

Beyeler dug in his pocket and flipped back one page on his memo pad. "Spare tire, jack, coupla dirty athletic socks, a deflated Rawlings basketball, and a stinky pair of size-twelve Air Jordans."

"Valuables?"

"Bundle of benjies in his left front trouser pocket," Ollie replied. "Fifty-two of them to be exact."

"Fifty-two hundred bucks," Joe Hayes announced. He gave an impressed whistle followed by a sarcastic grin.

"Musta been planning to take in a show, have some dinner, and pay for midtown parking."

"He's also got a shitload of gold on his fingers and around his neck," Ollie continued. "Haven't removed those. Your people'll do that over at the morgue. Incidentally," he added, "before you ask, we haven't found any shell casings. Weapon could have been a revolver."

"What's the word on the M.E.?" Savage asked.

"Been notified," Beyeler said. "Ain't got here yet, though. Excuse me, will you?" he said, signaling time out with his hands. "I gotta get a couple of three-quarter frontal shots."

"Do me a favor, Joe," Savage said, turning to the veteran patrol sergeant. "Notify department tow to have a flatbed respond. Once we remove the body, I want this car hauled off for safekeeping ASAP. After I go through it, I don't want anybody else but Forensics touching it."

"Gotcha." Hayes stepped away and began speaking into his portable.

Savage commandeered a plastic sheet from the EMS team and blanketed the death car's blood-spattered front seat. Exhaling in frustration—he remembered when he could spot a pimple on a spiraling pigskin from fifty yards—he reached into his coat pocket for his half-glasses. He set them out on the tip of his nose, pulled on a fresh pair of latex gloves, and carefully slid into the Mercedes from the passenger side.

Up close and personal, the dead man's head and face looked like raw hamburger. Mr. H.G. had had a *real* bad night. His mahogany eyes were partially open and gazing dully out to nowhere, and his toothy mouth was frozen in a grotesque grimace of horror. His pants were wet where he'd pissed himself. Before being executed, he'd been viciously beaten about the head and face. Judging by the fresh bruising and horrendous bump on its bridge, his nose had been broken. The flesh above each eye socket, right at the corner of each brow, had gaping meaty gashes. But the most disturbing aspect was the ratcheted non-releasing nylon cable ties that bound the man's wrists to the steering wheel. Except for the cigarette-lighter burns that dotted his hands, face, and neck, everything else was just like the Escobar case. Same damn M.O.

Six weeks earlier, just before midnight, on a bitterly cold February four-to-twelve, Savage and his team had been called to the end of a lonely Chelsea pier. Ramon Escobar, an up-and-coming merchant of No. 3 heroin—"brown sugar" as it is popularly known—was found DOA behind the wheel of his flashy BMW. His driver's window was down, and the left side of his head looked as if it had been hit by a cruise missile. The young Dominican's wrists had been bound together with similar nylon cable straps. Before being shot, he had also been extensively tuned up, blackjack style, by someone who really knew how. The spatterings of brain tissue and dried blood that draped the once-pristine interior of Ramon's ride had reminded Savage of a Williamsburg live-poultry butcher's slaughter apron. The M.E. figured that Ramon had been dead over twelve hours. Because of rigor mortis and the arctic chill, Ramon's rigid body had to be hefted to the meat wagon in an almost cartoonish sitting position. No way those impossible-to-straighten angles were going into a body bag. The sole advantage of that bitterly cold night was the lack of DOA stench. Ramon was frozen solid like a pork chop. Savage's team was still carrying that open case. There were no leads. He snorted, wondering if Ramon had yet thawed out.

"Can ya imagine?" Richie Marcus' gravelly voice came from over Savage's shoulder. The paunchy homicide detective leaned into the Mercedes. "Fuckin' guy's got a hundred-thousand-dollar ride, and he's got it all stunk up like a fi'-dollar whorehouse with them cheesy, fifty-cent air fresheners. Piss and potpourri—what a freakin' combination!"

"Unhh," Savage mumbled, stifling a sneeze.

"Where's the boy wonder this fine spring morning?" Marcus inquired, letting loose with one of his involuntary snorts.

"Your buddy's got a grand-jury date," Savage replied dully, preoccupied with the car's ignition switch and key. The switch was set to the ON position, just the way it had been in Ramon Escobar's BMW. "Probably won't see Lindstrom till around noon."

"Son of a bitch is like a friggin' blister," Marcus grumbled. "Always showin' up after all the damn work is done."

Hiding a smile at the neverending Richie-Jack antagonism, Savage leaned down for a glance at the victim's lower extremities. He estimated the Allen-Edmonds lightweights on the DOA's feet to be about a twelve wide, which would jibe with the sneakers in the trunk. Made of soft woven leather, they were good-looking shoes. He decided to check his Edmonds catalog at home and see if they were available in his ten EEE, in a lighter shade; brandy maybe. A fleeting twinge of guilt hit him—hell of a way to find a nice shoe. Raising the slightly bulging cuff of the man's left pant leg, he uncovered a snub-nosed .38 clipped into a Jay-Pee ankle holster. He turned and pointed out the find to Marcus.

He moved his attention to the victim's facial wounds. "Look at these cuts above each eye, Richie," he said, indicating the thick trails of drying blood that had run down the victim's swollen cheeks and collected in shimmering clumps on the lapels of his leather coat. "They bled for a long time. Looks as if he'd gone through some tough Q & A before being put to sleep."

"That's blackjack work at its finest," Marcus announced.

"And look at them bracelets. Just like the Ramon Escobar job back in February. Same deal. How much you wanna bet this guy's a purveyor of happy powder, too?"

"Not anymore," Savage muttered, muscling the dead man's static bulk to an upright sitting position, then forcing the wide shoulders back against the seat. The victim's arms—his thick wrists still lashed to the steering wheel—extended fully. Turning the man's head to the right, Savage began to examine the entry wound made by the bullet. The hole was just forward of the man's left ear, hidden in his bushy sideburn, slightly more than an inch beneath the temple.

"Lot of damage to this cheekbone," Savage observed thoughtfully. "Must have slowed the bullet down. I'm not finding any exit wound. The round's gotta still be inside his head."

"Diane and me'll be ringside at the autopsy," Marcus assured him. "We'll have it by this afternoon."

"Citywide, I think this makes five with the same general M.O. in the last ninety days," Savage mused, speaking more to himself than to Marcus. Using the tip of his penlight, he opened the lid of the dashboard ashtray. Except for the cigarette lighter—whose element was crusted with burnt flesh—it had probably never been used. H.G. wasn't a smoker.

"With the Ramon Escobar case and the one found dumped in Battery Park," Marcus said, "this makes the third one in Manhattan South. But didn't one also go down in Manhattan North?"

"Yep," Savage acknowledged. "And another one was found last week behind the wheel of a car in the Bronx Terminal Market."

"That the dingy produce market next to the stadium?" Marcus asked.

"Just a soft line drive away," Savage confirmed, thinking that no other ballpark in the major leagues could be identified simply as *the* stadium. Hell, every baseball fan in the country—or the world for that matter—knew *the* stadium could only mean Yankee Stadium. And what about *the* Bronx? There was no such place as *the* Brooklyn, or *the* Detroit, or *the* London. There was *The* Hague, he remembered. He wondered for just an instant how some people, some places, and some things achieved the *the* status. He would make a point to look that up sometime.

Savage readjusted the glasses on the tip of his nose and leaned over to study the clear nylon tie that bound the victim's wrists together, palms out. It had been pulled extremely tight, cutting deep ligature marks into now-swollen flesh. Another tie—looped through the one encircling the wrists—was lashed tightly to the bottom of the steering wheel.

"Damn things cut right into him," Marcus commented.

"Judging from the scuffs on this steering-wheel leather, looks like he really struggled to break free."

"Yeah," Marcus grunted flatly. "But them goddamned nylon ties is strong."

"Make sure Ollie gets some good close-ups on these wrists. Especially the way they're lashed to the wheel."

"Ten-four," Marcus replied. "By the way, the M.E. just pulled up. Looks like that bookish little douchebag, Harding."

"'Bout time," Savage said, massaging his forehead. His sinuses were pounding like the hammers of hell. "Once Mr. Harding gets done eyeballing this guy and telling us he's dead, let's get the body out on the sidewalk and you and Diane finish the search. Then, before they bag him, get hold of a pair of scissors from EMS and cut these ties off. I want them compared right away to the ones we took off Escobar and the guy down in Battery Park. Get with Manhattan North and Bronx Homicides for a comparison on the ones taken from their victims. Also, run that .38 on his ankle through NCIC."

"Gotcha."

"Another thing. Besides the cigarette lighter, make sure we give this ignition switch and key very special attention for possible prints."

"Think we'll get that same surgical-glove residue, like Escobar's?"

"Possibly," Savage said. "But maybe we'll get lucky this time. Maybe our shooter lost his mittens. Besides, there was a horrendous sleet storm last night. I'd bet a week's pay that this dude wouldn't be sitting here with his driver's window wide open, allowing all his nice leather to get drizzled on."

Marcus nodded. "I see where you're goin'. You figure the ignition key was turned to ON, and the driver's power window lowered, only after our victim had his hands lashed to the wheel. Only the shooter could have done that."

"You're learning, Marcus," Savage teased. "You're gonna go places in this job."

As Savage slid from the car's front seat, Marcus snorted self-consciously and asked, "Any word yet on getting a partner for Lindstrom?"

"Not yet," Savage replied. "I know we're the only team in the office that's running one man short," he added apologetically. "And I know that puts extra work on us all."

Marcus shrugged. "Been that way for a long time, boss. Ever since Bert Marshall retired. I know you don't want to settle for just any bozo that might come down the pike, but . . ."

"Believe me, I've been working on it, Rich. I proposed

somebody to Lieutenant Pezzano, and if he can swing the guy I'd like to get, we'll all benefit in the long run."

"Anybody I know?"

"Abe Hamilton," Savage said huskily, snapping off the latex gloves. "I'm heading back to the office. My freakin' head's killing me."

# FOUR

Trapped on Twenty-third Street behind a soot-belching tour bus with Quebec plates, at the height of Manhattan's morning rush hour, Savage inched across town from the scene of the latest candyman snuff toward the Thirteenth Precinct. Breaking free from the noxious cloud just before he choked to death, he pit-stopped briefly at Walgreen's for a twenty-four-pack of Sine-Aid, and then ran next door to Minton's Health Foods for a sixty-day resupply of vitamin C. While there he also picked up some echinacea and decided to try a new brand of ginseng.

As was his practice, when Savage got to the East Twenty-first Street station house, he ignored the elevator and took the stairs to the third floor two at a time. Once inside the offices of Manhattan South Homicide, he made directly for the water cooler, busted open the bubble pack of sinus-relief tablets, and quickly downed two. For good measure he also took two tablets of vitamin C.

"You got a call from Maureen Gallo, Sarge," Eddie Brodigan whispered as Savage leaned across the wheelman to sign himself present in the command log. "'Bout ten minutes ago. I wasn't sure what you wanted me to say, so I gave her the old 'you were out in the field' routine, and didn't know when you'd be back in the office today, if at all." Grimacing, he added, "I don't think she believed me."

The burly Irishman handed Savage a folded Post-it. "She left this return number."

The "wheel" in any police unit was the office hub. The wheelman answered the phones, maintained the command log, knew where everybody was at any given moment, and took and dispersed all messages—official and private. He knew everything that was going on—official and private: who was warring with his wife, who was behind in child support, and who had a slinky mistress on the side. He knew what bars the cops could be reached at, and how to handle "Plan B"s. A good wheelman was practiced in the ways of discretion, and Brodigan was an expert.

"Thanks, Ed," Savage quietly answered. He pocketed the Post-it and walked through the desk-filled squad room to the cramped office space he shared with the unit's two other sergeants, Billy Lakis and Jules Unger. Lakis headed up Team One and Julie ran Team Two. Neither was there. Lakis had signed himself out to the M.E.'s office, and Team Two was due in at four o'clock. Savage quickly spun the combination on his locker and hung the Burberry topcoat alongside his chevroned blue uniforms. He hadn't worn "the Bag" in years, but it was there, pressed and ready to go at a moment's notice. In this job one never knew. Today a prestigious homicide investigator in tailored pinstripes. Tomorrow a uniformed patrol sergeant assigned to midnights in Midtown South. Such was life in the Big Apple.

After filling his oversized coffee mug with a jolt of Brodigan's high-test, Thorn returned to his quiet office, closed the door, and peeled open the little yellow square. He really did not want to return the call to Maureen Gallo. Their relationship had died a year ago. In what might have been a posturing move, she'd dumped him. But hell, after all that time with the lady, he couldn't just ignore her—he owed her that much. Maybe she needs something, he thought. Might as well get it over with. He picked up the phone and dialed.

"Maureen?"

"Hi, honey," she greeted him warmly.

No one would ever suspect by her intimate tone that it had been more than a year since they'd shared a bed. It was ten months since he had begun dating Gina McCormick exclusively. Once Maureen found out that he had taken up with Gina, she was suddenly back out of the woodwork, calling and contacting, looking to reestablish herself in Savage's life. The calls had tapered off, but were still coming. No deal. Gina was his lady now.

"What's doin'?" he opened casually, fearing what was coming.

"Nothing important, really," she said. "Hate to bother you on the job—I know how you dislike that. Tried to catch you at home this morning before you left for work, but missed you. There'll be a message on your machine. Just thought I'd call and touch base. How have you been?"

"Fine." Then, only for the sake of conversation, he added, "My sinuses are killing me, and I've got a terminal headache, but other than that. . . ."

"Sounds to me like you could use some taking care of."

"Unh," he grunted, sorry for having mentioned it. He'd opened the door for her.

"Why did you go into work?" she asked incredulously. "One of the only benefits of that miserable job of yours is that it allows unlimited paid sick time. You should be home in bed. I could come over and brew you some hot tea or make you some chicken soup."

"You know I haven't taken a sick day in over twenty years."

"Yeah," she responded curtly. "Like the mayor or police

commissioner are going to give you some kind of medal for that."

Thorn didn't respond.

"You probably need an antibiotic. Have you gone to see a doctor?" she queried. "Guess I know the answer to that. After almost seven years, I know you better than anybody does, Thorn Savage. And better than anybody else ever will."

Here it comes, he thought.

"You wouldn't go see a doctor even if your head was falling off."

"Unh."

"If something else was falling off," she said, laughing, "I bet you'd go see a damned doctor."

"Unh," he grunted again, thinking, here we go with the subtle—and not so subtle—messages. Next, he knew, she'd take some sort of oblique shot at Gina.

"Isn't your friend Ginola, or Gineeta, or whatever her name is, looking after you?"

"You know her name's Gina," he said quietly. "Leave her out of it. You don't have to bring her up."

"You need someone in your life to look after you, Thorn. You won't do it for yourself, and apparently no one is doing it for you."

"I'll manage."

Maureen Gallo was a good lady, a damn good lady. A looker, she always turned heads by walking into a room. She was highly principled, smart as a whip, and fiercely protective of people she cared about. And there was no question that once upon a time they had loved each other beyond reason. When things had been good between them, they had been very good. But there had been too many down times. She was in many ways a perfectionist, and things never seemed quite satisfactory to her. They'd made several attempts at living together, but each of those attempts had failed miserably. It was nobody's fault. It just didn't work. The love saga of Thorn Savage and Maureen Gallo had been a six-year ride on Coney Island's Cyclone, and he'd finally decided to get off.

Thank God he'd found Gina.

"You'll manage to wind up in a hospital if you don't start taking better care of yourself," Maureen chided.

"Listen," Thorn broke in gently. "I appreciate the offer, but I'm really doing okay. Was there something specific that you called me for?"

Her tone softened. "I'm having a little get-together at my gallery next Friday night. It's not an exhibition, and it's not a showing of any artist in particular. It's just a party to celebrate my tenth anniversary of being in business. Thought you might like to drop by."

"What," he chuckled, "for some wine, cheese, and fruit cakes?"

"And me," she breathed suggestively.

"I don't think I'll be able to make it, Mo," he said softly. "But congratulations on the milestone. I'm proud of you. I know how hard you worked to make that place go. You've earned every bit of your success." He meant every word.

"I didn't think you'd say yes. But I had to ask anyway." There was a pause. "And if you should change your mind, that'll be fine. Just show up."

"Okay," he muttered, knowing he'd never go.

"I miss you terribly, Thorn," she blurted. "Just remember, honey: anytime, anyplace. You know we belong together."

Thorn sat silent.

"And," she added, "I'll always be there for you."

"I know that."

Savage exhaled deeply and dropped the phone into its

cradle. He took a sip of his coffee and stared down at nothing. Eddie Brodigan broke into his reverie as he leaned through the doorway.

"Line five, boss," the wheelman said. "It's the chief of detectives," he emphasized with wide eyes. Thorn nodded and reached for the receiver.

"How's the chief this morning?" Savage asked, familiarity and warmth in his voice. Chief Raphael Wilson was an old friend.

"Things are fine, Thornton, but they could always be better, right?" Wilson said. "I'm having a sit-down in my office this afternoon with Roland Chauncey. He's got information on those dope-dealer homicides that've gone down in the past several months. I understand there was another one this morning over in the Tenth."

"You heard right, boss."

"If I know Chauncey, the info'll be good, but he says it's highly sensitive. He's asked to see me privately, but I want you to attend."

"Two questions, chief. What time you want me there, and what do you want me to bring?"

"Spend the next few hours putting together an overview report on all these killings. Names, dates, locations, M.O.'s, links, et cetera. Be here at fifteen hundred."

Cambria Heights certainly wasn't the best part of Queens County to live in, but neither was it the worst. NYPD detective Abe Hamilton had always considered it to be the best of the worst. It was the best he could do. Neighboring St. Albans, another enclave of black strivers, it was one of the easternmost communities in New York City's easternmost borough. Beyond it lay Nassau County, the start of Long Island and the 'burbs.

Almost fifteen years ago, two years after the birth of

their only child, Little Abe, Abe and Tammi Hamilton had managed a down payment on a small three-bedroom on 226th Street, just off Francis Lewis Boulevard. Smack-dab in the middle of Cambria Heights, and only five minutes from Belmont Racetrack, where Abe frequently moon-lighted, it got them away from South Jamaica, where they had both been born and raised.

If there was a worst in Queens, Abe had always thought, South Jamaica had to be it. Poverty and crime, the Siamese twins of urban blight, had ruled South Jamaica when he grew up there. Never academic—Tammi was the Catholic-school and community-college brains of their outfit—Abe had squeezed by and graduated from public high school. Amazingly, surrounded by the South Jamaica junkies, pros-titutes, and ever-present violence, he never fell prey to the street. After a stint in the Eighty-second Airborne, he mar-ried Tammi and joined the NYPD. It was there that he met and formed a friendship with Thorn Savage.

Abe Hamilton vowed that his one and only child would never know the horrors of ghetto life. If he and Tammi had to exist on peanut-butter sandwiches and chicken-noodle soup, if he had to work five jobs in order to afford it, his son would attend private schools. Abe vowed that Little Abe would one day know the fullness of the American dream and be able to live in Forest Hills or Malba, the *best* of the best in Queens.

"Well?" Abe said, as his seventeen-year-old let himself into the passenger side of Abe's sputtering, rough-idling Camaro. "How did it go?"

"Okay," Little Abe replied flatly, slowly dragging the shoulder harness across his narrow chest and fastening the clasp.

Detecting tentativeness in his son's voice, Hamilton

pressed, "Okay? How do you mean, okay? SATs are no piece o' cake, but did it knock your damn socks off?"

The long lean teenager answered with a slow shrug and a timid grimace.

"Speak to me," Abe said. "Tell me how it was. If you got bad vibes about this one, maybe we can schedule you for another."

"Yeah," Little Abe said. "And if I do worse on that one, they'll average the two scores." Clearly frustrated, he added, "I'm never going to get into a good college."

"And if you do better next time," Abe reminded gently, "they also average the scores. Maybe you were a little uptight today. Next time you'll know more what to expect."

His son sat in dejected silence as Abe aimed the car toward home.

"Your mama's roasting a bird with all the fixin's for dinner," Abe said, breaking the quiet. "But we won't be eatin' till after six o'clock. Whaddaya say you and me stop for some lunch? Knowing you, you must be hungry as a bear."

"Okay."

Abe reached across the space between them and touched his boy's shoulder. "Son," he said quietly, "it *will* be okay. Everything will work out."

# FIVE

Ever true to his Eleventh Commandment, "Thou shalt not keep the chief of detectives waiting," Savage left extra time for the afternoon drive downtown. At ten to three he parked his department Ford in the cavernous garage beneath One Police Plaza. Situated like a red brick sentry at the foot of the Brooklyn Bridge, surrounded by Manhattan's financial district, Chinatown, and Little Italy, NYPD headquarters had once been in the shadow of the World Trade Center. Coming here, so close to the wretched absence of the Twin Towers, never failed to increase Thorn's pulse rate. And, he often thought, probably caused a spike in his blood pressure as well.

Toting the reports Chief Wilson had requested, Savage popped a Wint-O-Green and waited several minutes for an elevator at the building's sub-basement. When one finally arrived, he boarded and pressed the button for the thirteenth floor. The sluggish car made thirteen distinct stops, one at each level. There was nobody waiting at most of the stops. Savage felt his nostrils begin to flare after stop seven. He impatiently chewed the inside of his cheek and rocked on his heels. One P.P. had the slowest elevators in the world. During the enforced inactivity, he realized that the sinus misery he'd awakened with had subsided and he was sneezing less. The self-prescribed remedies were kicking in.

Striding along the corridors of the thirteenth floor, Savage exchanged courteous nods with familiar faces among the headquarters staff. Some were "Remington Raiders," an old-time cop expression for men and women who entered the police service and then wormed their way into cozy clerical slots to become career paper-shufflers who made all the rules but who never had to play the game. He squared the knot of his tie before letting himself into Room 1312.

"Good afternoon, Sergeant Savage," Chief Wilson's chunky receptionist, Darlene Dolan, cooed from behind her desk. Her big brown eyes flashed to the wall clock. It was 1500 hours. "You're right on time, as usual," she added, cocking her head and narrowing her gaze suggestively. "I bet your timing's perfect in everything."

"Hello, Ms. Dolan." Savage grinned at the moon-faced woman. Thorn liked Darlene; she was a sweetie. "How're things in Sunnyside?"

"Great," she bubbled, making warm eye contact. "Just finished redecorating my bedroom—new wallpaper and carpet. Oh, you've just got to see it to believe it; it's absolutely gorgeous! And my new waterbed . . . *umm,* divine. Have you ever slept on a waterbed, Sergeant?" She drew out the last few words for effect.

"Owned one years ago. Got seasick—had to get rid of it. The chief ready to see me?"

"He's still busy; he'll be with you in a few." She pointed to the folder tucked under his arm. "If that's the report the chief's waiting for, he wants me to bring it in to him right away."

Savage handed over the file. Darlene darted into the chief's private office. Smiling her tough Irish-broad smile when she reemerged, she moved to the sputtering Mr. Coffee in the alcove behind her desk. "I knew you'd like some nice fresh coffee while you waited. It just finished brewing."

"Thanks."

"Dark, half teaspoon of sugar . . . just the way you like it." Darlene held out a steaming mug. Her fingers brushed his as she relinquished the cup.

Maybe it was the weather, he thought. This morning, from out of nowhere, Maureen Gallo had called to express her undying love. Now Darlene Dolan was sending out all kinds of signals. Jeez, even if Gina weren't the only woman in his right life now, he'd never had any fantasies about Darlene. He was relieved when the desk intercom came alive with a short buzz.

"The chief'll see you now, Sergeant," Darlene announced, batting her big browns.

Chief of Detectives Ray Wilson was the highest-ranking African American in the forty-thousand-member NYPD. A dynamic and likable man—and an ex-Airborne trooper—he was known for running a tight, but fair, ship. Having himself risen through the ranks the hard way, Wilson knew every pitfall of The Job. Because of this he had the true regard—if not the utmost respect—of virtually every investigator in the bureau. Seated behind his wide desk when Savage entered, Wilson gestured to a round-faced, balding black man of about sixty. "Mr. Roland Chauncey, I'd like you to meet Sergeant Thornton Savage."

Rising from one of the two soft chairs facing the chief's desk, Roland Chauncey half-stood and extended a ham hock of a right hand. "Sergeant Savage," he said with a mild West Indian accent. "Chief Wilson speaks highly of you."

One of the early conservative voices in the black community, Chauncey had been a public figure for many years.

"I've taken a quick look through your report, Thorn," Chief Wilson said. "What the hell's goin' on in Dopedom?"

"Looks as if they're downsizing," Savage speculated coldly. "Offering early retirements."

"Early retirements? Jesus!" Wilson grunted sarcastically. "The Marquis de Sade must have packed the golden parachutes. How'd you go about putting the Bronx and Manhattan North cases together with those you're carrying in Manhattan South?"

"Checked M.O.s citywide," Savage answered, sitting in the empty chair next to Chauncey. "In every case, the victim—a black or Dominican male in his thirties—was a known high-echelon dope dealer. Each one of them ran his own narcotics fiefdom. The dots weren't hard to connect."

"According to your report, the victim in the Bronx and the one in Manhattan North were not trussed up with those cable straps. Nor were they found to have been beaten in any way."

"That's true, Chief," Savage replied. "But both were found behind the wheels of parked cars. And both were headshot through open driver's windows with a nine-millimeter. Gut feeling is, pending ballistics, gotta be the same guy."

"How about the victim near Battery Park?" Wilson asked. "That guy wasn't found in a car, nor was he shot. He'd been stabbed. Different M.O. there, no?"

"Slightly," Savage agreed. "He wasn't found in a car, and he hadn't been shot, but he'd been beat up real good and was wearing a set of those same plastic bracelets. Each has been a variation on a theme."

The chief of detectives nodded.

Roland Chauncey cleared his throat. "Sergeant, I've known Chief Wilson here since he was a skinny kid growing up on Lenox Avenue. I trust him completely. I also know that his faith in you is complete, so I feel that what-

ever we discuss here today is in *total* confidence."
Chauncey emphasized his words with a cold glare. "Let me
put it another way. I've never been here, and we've never
had this discussion. Are we all together on that point?"

Savage looked at Chief Wilson.

"I've already given Roland my word on that, Thorn."

Savage nodded and sat back in his chair, carefully studying Chauncey, measuring him.

"We have a plague up in Harlem," Chauncey began
thoughtfully. "And, for that matter, in many neighborhoods
throughout this city: the plague of drugs. That, of course,
comes not as a surprise to you, nor is it a new problem. My
people have suffered under the unbearable yoke of drugs
and drug dealers for a long time. But now we may have
been given the chance to break the back of the drug business, and we need your help. I promise community support
regardless of the tactics you need to use against these
bums."

Savage sensed sincerity; Chauncey's heart was obviously in the right place. But the sudden quaver in his voice
revealed an underscore of distress and, unless Thorn missed
his guess, more than a hint of fear.

"We'd never break the law in order to effect an arrest,
Mr. Chauncey," Savage explained patiently.

"I know that," Chauncey said. "Your reputation for in-
vestigative ethics, and your belief in the sanctity of our
criminal-justice system, are well known. But I'm also told
that you can be quite creative within those limits when you
wish to be. Isn't that so, Chief Wilson?"

Ray Wilson cleared his throat and shrugged noncommit-
tally.

Chauncey, still clearly nervous, went on. "I have information from excellent sources—sources that I will *never*
divulge—that what we are experiencing is a Pac-Man-like

situation at work in the city's drug trade. Where once there were anywhere from eight to ten major dope kingpins, we now find that virtually all these operations are being gobbled up. Taken over by one man. Entire operations: importing, warehousing, cutting, packaging, and street distribution, all absorbed by one operation . . . and one operator."

"And who might Pac-Man be?" Savage said, narrowing his gaze directly into Chauncey's eyes.

"Derek Ogden," Chauncey replied after a long and uncomfortable pause. "His name is Derek Ogden."

"Name mean anything to you, Thornton?" Wilson asked.

"Uh-huh," Savage said, taking a quick sip of his coffee. "He's the rags-to-riches black guy who supposedly made his fortune dealing in fine art and rare antiquities. Very high-profile."

"Anything else?" Chauncey queried, testing.

"Basically," Savage responded with a shrug, "he's arrived."

"You're up on your current events, Sergeant. I'm impressed." Chauncey nodded approvingly to Chief Wilson and continued. "He owns and operates a place called Ogden World Galleries up on Madison in the Seventies. Besides dealing in antiquities and paintings, he also considers himself to be a patron of the arts. He frequents the Met, Carnegie Hall, the Guggenheim. . . ."

"He's the latest darling of New York's polite society," Ray Wilson agreed. "On the outside, at least, he appears to be a highly successful, cultured businessman."

"And he's politically well connected," Chauncey broke in. "No doubt about it. He hobnobs with some pretty powerful people."

"Suffice it to say, Thorn," Wilson interrupted, "Ogden's been busy building a lot of momentum in establishing himself as, among other things, a black role model. This guy really loves himself."

Chauncey's look turned angry. "That's right. But if my information turns out to be true, role models like this man our children do not need."

Savage sat quietly and took another sip of coffee.

"If you could see beneath Ogden's flamboyant, self-serving veneer," Chauncey grunted in disgust, "you'd find an enormous ego wrapped around a treacherous criminal. One who would make the likes of the late John Gotti appear as an introverted shoplifter." Words came rapidly and the big man seemed almost to be running out of breath. He dabbed his moist brow with a crumpled handkerchief plucked from a back pocket.

"Mr. Chauncey," Savage interrupted, "you're telling us that Derek Ogden deals not only in objets d'art, but also objets d'dope?"

"Big time, Sergeant. Big time. This man is quickly becoming the largest single distributor of poison in New York, if not the entire United States." Chauncey alternated his troubled glances between Savage and Wilson. "Derek Ogden is a runaway megalomaniac who has come to consider himself some kind of god. And woe be to anyone—a point that was stressed over and over to me by my sources—*anyone* who dares get in his way."

"Thorn," Chief Wilson interrupted, "if Ogden is behind all these executions, if he's systematically killed off all or most of his competition, he now *is* the drug trade in New York, or soon will be. Quite frankly," he added with an amazed smirk, "his knocking off these other dealers and assuming sole leadership of their entire operations allows us to put him in the crosshairs and blow him right out of the water. That'd put a major hurtin' on the drug trade, at least for a little while."

"Do we have anything that ties Ogden into these homicides?" Savage asked. "Anything that can be brought into a courtroom?"

Wilson leaned forward in his chair. "So far there's no link, Thorn, nothing except Roland's information. But he's an old friend with extremely good sources, and I put great stock in anything he brings my way." The chief made a show of glancing at his watch. "Gentlemen, I have a meeting with Police Commissioner Johnson in ten minutes. I'm afraid we'll have to adjourn." He stood and extended his hand to Roland Chauncey. Chauncey said a quick good-bye and let himself out through the office's back door.

Wilson spoke in measured words. "What we have to contend with here are some political facts of life. Ogden is a well-known, and, for now at least, a very highly regarded man in some parts of this city—a hero to some people, if you will. Our department cannot be seen to be besmirching this guy's reputation with an investigation based solely on hearsay or rumor. I won't allow this matter to become a political nightmare for the PC or the mayor."

Politics, Savage thought scornfully. What he said was, "I get your drift, Chief. If we conduct a very discreet preliminary, and Ogden comes up clean, end of story. We drop it, and nobody knows we've ever been there to take a look. But if he's anything like Chauncey says he is, surely the administration can take the heat when we follow up."

"If he's dirty, yeah. But if we blow this thing, or fuck up any part of this investigation, we're gonna wind up with a handful of shit and risk losing any goodwill we might still have in these communities. Fucking Sharpton'll organize an *Angry* Million Man March, and hold it right in front of fucking City Hall."

Savage nodded.

"You're the only one I'd trust with something this sensitive, Thornton. If we move on this guy, it absolutely must be airtight. I don't want any room for allegations of police conspiracies. No fucked-up chains of evidence. I don't want Ogden or any of his attendants, friends, or employees approached. Not even for any oblique questioning which could possibly raise him up. Ogden is not to suspect in any way that he's being looked at. Not unless, and until, we have something concrete." Wilson glared into Savage's eyes. "And if this matter ever does wind up in a courtroom, the goddamned glove better fit. You reading me, Thornton?"

"Five by five, Chief."

The chief of detectives spun in his chair and gazed out through the huge window behind his desk. For a long minute he seemed to be contemplating the bright afternoon sunlight and the resultant dark shadows that played off Lower Manhattan's cathedrals of capitalism.

"How would you proceed?" he asked finally, turning to face Savage.

"I'd like to put a man on Ogden—the right man. Have him see where he goes, what he does. Follow him into the can if necessary. If Ogden's tied up with heavy-duty dope, sooner or later he'll tip his hand."

"Any one man in mind?"

"Abe Hamilton. He's black and he's sharp, an ex-undercover. We go way back and I trust him completely. If we gotta get in real close, he's the guy who can do it."

The chief peered down his nose at Savage. "Weren't you and Hamilton partners, as cops, back in the old Street Crime Unit?"

"Long time ago," Savage admitted. "Worked our asses off there to earn our gold shields. Went our separate ways in The Job when I got promoted to sergeant. But personally we're still close."

"How close?"

"I'm godfather to his only child."

"Where's he currently assigned?"

"Seven-five Squad. My lieutenant and I've been itchin' to have him make a move into Homicide, and my team just happens to be one man short. . . ."

"Good a time as any to fill that open spot," Wilson agreed. "When can you begin?"

"Glad to get this thing rolling first thing Monday."

"What else you gonna need?"

"Surveillance vehicles. At least two. One should be a taxicab. Stevie Wonder could pick out our squad unmarks as PD."

"Done. I'll contact Brooklyn North and see that Hamilton gets the weekend off. He'll be assigned to you effective Monday morning. I'll also contact your boss, Pete Pezzano, and square things with him—let him know you'll be on special assignment." Wilson dropped his voice an octave. "I know that Hamilton's your main man, and I know he's probably damn good. But this one is a heavy. There's absolutely no room for fuck-ups in this case, *Capisce*? If Ogden's bad, we'll sink him. But if not, we gotta back off right away. I'll give you seven days to come up with something."

Savage nodded and rose from his chair.

"And," the chief reminded him, "you heard Chauncey. You saw how scared shitless he was—and that man don't scare easy. This Ogden just may be some kind of real maniac. You and Hamilton be *real* careful out there. Cover each other."

# SIX

The throaty rumble from the black '57 Thunderbird's twin exhausts was constant as Savage drove south on Jersey's Garden State Parkway. The masculine purr from the dual-carbureted 312 intensified each time he goosed it to pass a Sunday-morning dawdler. Nearing the small town of Lakewood, he reached across the front seat and gently caressed Gina McCormick's left knee.

"It's such a beautiful day, Thorn," she said, peering at him over the top of her wire-rimmed Ray-Bans. "After what happened during the week, who'd have thought it would turn out so nice on the weekend?"

The crazy weather that had lashed the metropolitan area with paralyzing sleet storms and unseasonably bitter cold had disappeared as suddenly as it had arrived; so had his sinus misery. As he had hoped, Sunday morning's sky was clear and a dazzling blue, and the temperature had climbed into the low seventies. What a perfect day for their plans.

It was going to be a big day for Gina. But only he knew the full extent of what lay ahead. Smatterings of conversation had punctuated the comfortable silence of the hour-long ride. He sensed her nervousness. It was understandable. When they had spoken, she had kept it light. It was her way of dealing with her mounting apprehension.

"Must have taken a long time to restore this little car,"

Gina said, smoothing her hand along the dashboard. "Every little detail is so perfect. Where did you do it? You don't have a garage to work in."

"Old friend of mine's a car dealer. He let me use space in his shop. Took three years of days off and vacation time." Thorn glanced at her and said lamely, "He was *very* patient with me."

"You did all the work yourself?"

"Me and Abe."

"He's really your best friend, isn't he?"

"Yup. Met at the police academy. Been best friends ever since."

"You've told me that Abe's wife Tammi was very close with Joanne before she was killed."

"They went everywhere together—they were like sisters. They were as close to each other as Abe and me."

"And . . . Maureen?" Gina said. "What did they think of Maureen?"

"Whaddaya mean?"

"Did they like her?" Gina pressed. "After all, you dated her for six years."

"Yeah," Savage responded, finally seeing where all this was heading. "They loved Joanne, and they liked Maureen—and they really *really* like you a whole lot."

"Really?"

"Really," he assured her. "You okay?" he asked gently. "You certain you want to go through with this?"

"Positive. I'm gonna be just fine." Nodding resolutely, apparently trying to convince herself, she slid over and kissed him softly on the cheek. "I love you," she whispered. Tweaking his ear, she added, "Later on, I'm going to show you just how much."

The car's mellow drone remained constant as the silence between them settled in again.

Five minutes after paying the toll at the Lakewood exit, they pulled into the remote private airstrip that was home to Felicity Parachuting. There they were greeted by Armand DeCaprio, Felicity's always-smiling, gregarious owner.

"It's about time your skydivin' pals finally got to meet the lovely lady you're always bragging about." The swarthy former Navy SEAL looked Gina up and down, obviously liking what he saw.

"Gina, meet Armand," Savage said, unlocking the T-bird's trunk. "Pay absolutely no attention to anything this man has to say, unless it's about piloting or parachuting. He's the world's best in both those departments. He doesn't know a helluva lot about anything else, though."

"Gina, my dear." Armand reached out with sinewy arms, took her hand, and made a show of kissing it. "You're every bit as beautiful as Thorn said you were. I understand your maiden name was DiLeo. Neapolitan . . . Calabrese?"

"Told you," Savage interjected. "Gotta watch out for this guy. He's gonna try to steal you away. He's always had a thing for Italian chicks." Facing his longtime friend, he added, "She's Sicilian."

"Hey!" DeCaprio countered with a palms-out shrug of exaggerated helplessness. "What can I say? I'm one of those hotblooded Mediterranean types." Savage rolled his eyes in mock exasperation.

"I'm flattered, Armand," Gina said with a faint laugh. "I'm glad we finally got to meet. Thorn thinks the world of you."

"And me of him, lovely lady. I don't suppose he's ever told you how he saved my wretched life one fine day."

*"Armand . . ."* Savage said as Gina's questioning gaze shifted back and forth between the two men.

"'Nother jumper slammed into me during a ten-man formation," DeCaprio quickly related, ignoring Savage's red light. "And I was knocked unconscious—totally out of it. I would never have had a chance to open my chute. If it hadn't been for Thorn—"

"Told you not to pay any attention to this guy," Savage interrupted, lifting a blue nylon duffel from the trunk. "He don't know what the hell he's talking about."

"Well, I know what I'm talking about," said Gina. She turned and faced DeCaprio. "I don't suppose Thorn's ever told you the circumstances of how we happened to meet?"

DeCaprio shook his head.

"He saved my father's life. If he hadn't been there, and been so much on the ball, my father would have been murdered right in his own hospital bed."

DeCaprio's darkly tanned brow furrowed into full attentiveness. "Tell me the whole thing."

Gina cleared her throat and began, "It was about a year ago—"

"Some other time," Savage snapped impatiently, throwing the duffel bag across his shoulder and slamming the car's trunk.

DeCaprio's bushy jet-black eyebrows skewed in a mix of mild disappointment and understanding. "Suffice it to say, lovely lady," he drawled, "that it seems we both owe this lug quite a bit. And, for the moment, we'll leave it at that."

Gina nodded and grinned.

"But now," Armand bellowed excitedly, "it's down to business. I understand that you've journeyed here today to make your first jump out of an *air-o-plane*."

"I've run down all the information on that island," Derek Ogden announced into the phone.

"Does it have a name?" Luther Robinson asked.

"Rudder Cut Cay," Ogden replied, blowing a smoke

ring. "It has a total of three hundred and sixty-three acres. It's got a sheltered harbor. And listen to this, a twenty-four-hundred-foot private airstrip."

"We could fly in or sail in. Nice. Who's actually selling it?"

"Florida Department of Insurance. They got it in a settlement of a failed life-insurance company that had been too heavily invested in high-risk junk bonds. It's going off at auction, in Tallahassee, on Wednesday the twenty-sixth. They expect it to bring a minimum of three point five mill. Which, mind you, must be paid in full at the time of auction."

"Shit," Robinson responded. "That's chump change."

"It's got a thirty-two-hundred-square-foot main house, water storage tanks that hold more than a million gallons, a caretaker's house, a laundry facility, a staff house. It's fucking unbelievable."

"What did you say the place was called? Ruh . . . Rutter Key?"

"Rudder Cut Cay," Ogden corrected. "It's in the Exuma chain between Little Darby Island and Musha Cay, one hundred and five miles southeast of Nassau. No range problem for the *Slavedriver,* and perfectly situated for our needs. Aside from its being an excellent location for drops and storage, I can stock the place with gorgeous bitches and use it as a playground."

Without comment on Ogden's last remark, Robinson asked coolly, "How do we go about making the acquisition?"

"I'll be at the auction bidding," Ogden purred. "With a letter of credit from the new subsidiary of our holding company in the Caymans. They will be the purchaser of record. It will be, as the wops say, a piece-a-cake."

"You're a genius," Robinson said, his voice brimming

with awe. "I remember, as a kid on the street, perfecting ways to break into parked Audis to snatch Blaupunkts for a big twenty-five dollars a pop. I thought that was the way to go. Now . . . buying an island. That's class."

"Just be grateful that I recognized your, shall we say, special talents," Ogden interrupted. "I've steered you right since you were a child, Luther. You stick with me, my boy, and one day we'll be putting a down payment on *Manhattan* Island. And," he quickly continued, "speaking of your talents, I'm working on some additional 'retirement' decisions."

"Who?"

"Spencer Baldwin, probably. Then possibly his portly cohort."

"Tyrone Boone? The Fat Man up at Feathers?"

"If we do Baldwin, it'll give that fat bastard something to think about. It should get him back in line."

"I hope the fat fuck *doesn't* get back in line. Never liked him. Could never stand being near him. He smells. When do I get the green light?"

"I'll get back to you on that. Oh, and by the way, *Madame Butterfly* is opening Thursday at the Met. I presume you'll be joining me?"

"Who's conducting? Rizzi?"

"Armiliato. Rizzi is doing *La Bohème* this season."

"Black tie?"

"Of course."

"I'll be there."


Under Armand DeCaprio's personal tutelage, Gina and two other student jumpers—an in-shape octogenarian from Hoboken who had made his most recent jump on June 6, 1944, and his not-so-in-shape accountant son—spent the entire morning and early afternoon sitting through lectures, watching training films, and leaping from a four-foot wooden platform into a pit of fine sand. They practiced parachute-landing falls—PLF's—in preparation for the big step. Gina somehow managed to keep her nerves under control, praying to see the day through. And, during a quiet coffee break, when she and Armand found themselves briefly alone, she got to confide the story of the attempt on her father's life and how she and Thorn had first met.

Finally, the three students were outfitted with jump suits, boots, helmets, goggles, and main and reserve parachutes. Even *Gina* couldn't make this ensemble look provocative.

"Let the games begin," Thorn declared with a Caesarean flourish as Gina haltingly made her way from the equipment shed. She feebly acknowledged his greeting.

She knew he'd already completed two ten-thousand-foot freefalls that day while she was making four-foot jumps into a sandbox. But her moment of truth had arrived. Constricted by the tight parachute rigging, she waddled after Thorn to the waiting plane.

Armand's blue-and-white Beechcraft had been extensively modified for sport parachuting. All cabin seating, as well as the cabin door, had been removed. The last to climb on board, Gina knew she would be the first to exit. Seated closest to the gaping hatch, she would be most exposed to the three demons that would soon enter: noise, wind, and numbing fear.

The engines coughed, sputtered, and burst into raucous life. A blue-gray cloud belched briefly from the exhaust pipes and then disappeared in a rush, blown away by prop blast. From her position, seated against the rear cabin bulkhead and facing forward, she could see Armand at the cockpit controls. The engine noise became deafening as it filled the plane's hatchless interior. Any attempt at conversation from this point on was futile. She glanced at Thorn and reached out. He clasped her hand and squeezed. His touch gave her strength.

She trusted Thorn totally. But aside from her lifelong dread of violent electrical storms, with their startling flashes of lightning and explosions of rolling thunder, she had never known this level of fear before. She had also never thrown herself out of a perfectly good aircraft at twenty-five hundred feet—twice the height of the Empire State Building. She shivered.

There was a firm tap at her shoulder as the jumpmaster reminded her to keep both arms securely wrapped around her chest-mounted reserve chute. She released Thorn's hand and hugged the bundle as tightly as she could. If the reserve accidentally deployed within the doorless craft during flight, it could have tragic consequences for everyone.

Armand revved the engines and the plane began to move along the rutted hardpan that led to the paved runway. She studied the other jumpers. They were certainly colorful. Nested together in rows, some had lightning bolts emblazoned on their helmets or stitched onto their jumpsuits. These, she thought, were the real psychos—the ones, like Thorn, who'd made hundreds or perhaps thousands of jumps. They were all loonies, she thought. Their helmeted heads bobbed in unison as the light craft reacted to the bumpy field beneath its wheels. This was truly a ship of fools.

The bumping stopped; they were on the runway. Full power. Immediately, G-forces pinned her against the bulkhead. The thunderous roar from the wing-mounted engines numbed her senses and diminished only slightly once the plane became airborne. Trees and buildings, which moments before had been at eye level and life-size, now took on the dimensions of toy-size miniatures as the plane rapidly gained altitude.

"Is everybody *happeee?*" The jumpmaster bellowed the question at the top of his lungs, and all the crazies, including Thorn—and the crusty old WWII vet—responded in gleeful unison:

*"Yessss!"*

Everyone, except Gina and the accountant son from Hoboken, was ecstatic. *What in God's holy name am I doing here?* she thought. Why did I ever tell him I've always wanted to know what it's like to jump out of a damned plane?

The Beechcraft leveled at twenty-five hundred feet and assumed an elliptical path above the airport. After factoring in wind speed and direction, Armand would signal the jumpmaster to have the students exit. Theoretically, this ensured their descent onto the drop zone, an enormous expanse of sandy land that from this altitude looked the size of a beer coaster.

Did Thorn know what she was experiencing? Could he see it on her face and in her eyes? Her senses of sight and sound were becoming overwhelmed, her faculties incapacitated by the same sickening fear she'd felt as a child, cowering beneath her blankets during a monstrous nighttime storm.

Thorn reached over and gently squeezed her hand. She looked back at him and struggled to smile.

"I'll be right behind you," he yelled.

The jumpmaster signaled and, with exaggerated motions, hooked the static line from her main parachute to the large steel ring bolted to the plane's frame. He pulled the connection forcefully, demonstrating to all that it was securely fastened. He motioned her toward the open hatch.

Gina's heart pounded. She felt each beat thumping from deep within her chest.

The plane's engines throttled back: It was time. Not

knowing what was driving her, insanity maybe, she slid along on her butt and sat, feet dangling, in the huge opening where the door used to be. Fighting a hundred-mile-per-hour gale greatly amplified by the violent turbulence of prop blast, she planted her heavy-duty jump boots on the small platform just below the gaping hatch. The wind, the noise, *the whole fucking idea,* was terrifying. Seated in the opening, moist palms clutched in a death grip on each side of its frame, she heard the jumpmaster holler the second most frightening words she could think of:

*"Stand by!"*

Her mind, like a computer gone haywire, filled with unconnected thoughts. Somehow, through the mental blizzard, she heard the jumpmaster's supreme command:

*"Go-ooo!"*

Without a second to reconsider, she sprung upward with her legs and thrust outward with her arms. She dived into the violent whirling mass of prop blast, hurtling toward earth, remembering to arch her back and spread her limbs. Her desire to soar with Thorn stronger than her fear of death, she felt herself fly, tethered only briefly to the plane by the umbilical of the static line. The runaway reel-to-reel of her mind, which had been headed toward tangle city, stopped short. Instantly, it clicked forward again at a slow, controlled pace. The fear was gone. Opening shock had occurred, and the fully deployed canopy above her was a marvel to behold. She reached up and firmly grabbed the steering cables. The menacing thunder of the Pratt & Whitneys diminished to nothing as the Beechcraft quickly became just another distant bird in the unbounded heavens.

Alone, dangling thousands of feet above earth with no sensation of falling, Gina felt her wits return in a flash. Adrenaline filled her. She let out a wild *"Ya-hooo,"* and felt a surge of wonderment and exhilaration that she knew she could never describe to anyone . . . except Thorn.

"Will you marry me?"

Was she was hallucinating? Hearing things? Here, out of this incredible silence, her thoughts were invaded by a familiar voice.

"Will you marry me?" Thorn hollered out again as he soared around her, gracefully maneuvering his chute in a large, lazy circle. A mild breeze played between them as he hovered nearby, escorting her as she gently descended to earth.

"Will you marry me, Gina?"

The day, the moment, was unbelievable. She'd done more living and felt more emotion within the last two minutes than in her whole life. . . . And now this—an airborne proposal of marriage from the finest guy she'd ever known.

Suddenly, a sensation of falling was coming on. This, Armand had explained, was "ground rush." The ride was nearly over. As she neared the earth, her peripheral sight took in less of an expanse. Trees and buildings suddenly became larger and larger, moving closer with increasing speed. She brought her legs together, slightly bent at the knees, and looked out at the horizon. She tried not to anticipate the landing. Her PLF was perfect; she fell to the sandy earth as her not-yet-collapsed canopy, pulled by the mild breeze, dragged her slowly along on her back.

Then Thorn was there, taking control of her chute. Still on her back, she beamed as he knelt beside her, a delicate yellow band with a Tiffany-set diamond pinched between his fingers. She looked up into his eyes, those eyes that she always felt looked so lonely and alone, and so beautifully unhappy.

His voice, a tender whisper. "Will you marry me, Gina?"

*    *    *

As Thorn wheeled the little T-bird back into Brooklyn across the Verrazano, he thought about the magic-carpet fantasy the day had been, and the exhausted sleeping woman next to him who had turned his life around. Never would he go back to the unfulfilled existence that he once thought of as okay.

All their tomorrows were going to be wonderful. Gina had said yes.

# SEVEN

It was no gentle April shower, Savage thought. It was an out-and-out monsoon, as much a damn sidepour as it was a downpour. Raincoat notwithstanding, there was no question that he was going to get wet this morning. The question was, as he rolled slowly through East Twenty-first Street—searching for a spot near the Thirteenth Precinct station house—how wet? The closest parking space he could find was almost a block away, off the corner of Third Avenue. He tossed the PD plate onto the Crown Victoria's dash and, covering his head with the morning *Post,* stepped out into the weather.

Utilizing moves developed as a Fordham running back more years ago than he wanted to think about, he hop-scotched the deeper puddles and zigged past the mounds of garbage-swollen Hefty bags piled along the sidewalk for the Monday-morning collection. Somewhere ahead, above the gusting wind, he heard the dull thud of trash being chucked into a sanitation truck's whining hopper. That, along with the loader's whistle and "Yo!," was a typical city sound effect. It played on every street of every borough, twice a week, rain or shine.

Soaked at his pants cuffs, Thorn let himself through the big station-house doors just as two uniformed rookies were leading a herd of manacled prisoners to a paddy wagon

idling at the curb. Last night's arrests were being transported down to Centre Street. Cuffed among the daisy chain
of unsmiling street mopes, burglars, dopers, and hung-over
drunks was a pair of miniskirted, heavily made-up he/she
hookers in lamé go-go boots. Muscular, sinewy, and liber-
ally tattooed, both blond-wigged gents went six-six or better. Loud and animated, laughing and jiving, one would
think these two were off to a Dennis Rodman look-alike
contest rather than a morning arraignment at Manhattan
Criminal Court.

God, he loved this job.

Nothing, not the torrential rain, nor the traffic he'd just
faced, could screw up Savage's extraordinary state of mind
this morning. He was still riding yesterday's incredible
high, unable to get Gina off his mind. He'd stopped trying;
he just kept grinning.

The bleakness of the day, coupled with the blunted illumination of tired ceiling fluorescents, gave the squad room
the dark and dreary feeling of a cave. The few windows that
looked out onto the sooty brick side wall of the adjacent
School of Visual Arts begged for ammonia and a squeegee.
They did little to add any natural light. The miserable
weather also left the cave dank and damp. Fortunately,
someone had been thoughtful enough to turn on the heat.

From behind his desk in the middle of the room, Richie
Marcus greeted Savage. "Mornin', boss. Believe the friggin' weather out there? Weekend was beautiful. Today I'm
gonna start buildin' an ark."

"Today we've gotta get out to Motor Transport and pick
up a couple of surveillance vehicles," Savage responded,
pulling the wet trench coat from his shoulders. "A nondescript Cadillac and a yellow taxicab, as a matter of fact.
Where are Diane and Jack?" he asked, looking about the
unusually barren office.

"Dropped Diane off at Forensics on the way in," Marcus replied. "She's picking up that semen-analysis report on the hooker dismemberment in Midtown South. Jack had to make a stop at the M.E.'s office. He shouldn't be long; his ferry's due any minute."

"We get a positive I.D. yet on Friday's West Thirty-third Street victim?" Savage asked.

"Yeah," Marcus said, looking down at a yellow pad on his desk. "Name was Horace Grimes. His wife—one Juanita Grimes—I.D.'d him at the M.E.'s on Saturday. Guy had three pages of rap sheets. Mostly drug-related. No surprise there. Also, got a no-hit from NCIC on his thirty-eight."

Savage noticed that Richie's hair was still wet and freshly combed, and a soggy *Daily Racing Form* was simmering nicely on a heat register beneath one of the windows. No wonder the heat was on.

"You almost get drowned out there too, Rich?" Savage asked.

"Yeah," Marcus growled, the lone syllable more of a blunt instrument than a human response. Flipping the switch of his Swintec word processor to ON, he added, "I moored my sub to a bell buoy around the corner and swam the rest of the way. But hey, what the hell, I'm here."

A tattoo of Dennis the Menace, its once-bright blues and bold reds faded by time, squirmed on Marcus's beefy right forearm as he began banging away on the keyboard. Cynical and suspicious, yet oddly sensitive, Marcus had been raised in St. John's Home for Boys. A court-ordered stretch in the Marines had kept him out of jail as a kid and accounted for the difficult-to-distinguish *Semper Fi* on his other forearm. After graduating from the Corps he joined the NYPD and became a highly decorated detective. Along the way he met Thorn Savage, who, he'd always said, was one of the few people he'd ever completely trusted.

Richie's professed expertise ran a wide gamut, from topics as mundane as fishing and football all the way to the heady stuff of racehorse handicapping, craps, and pinball philosophy. As a result he'd been sarcastically dubbed "the Swami" by his coworkers. He had a few other names, too: Marcus was a notorious ballbreaker.

"Abe Hamilton's been transferred here on a Telephone Message," Brodigan announced to Savage. "Spoke to him ten minutes ago, said he'd be a little late getting in this morning. He's over at Brooklyn Criminal Court on an old collar. I put a memo on your desk to that effect."

"Did you put one on the C.O.'s desk?"

"I notified Lieutenant Pezzano when he called in at oh-eight-hundred," Brodigan said, then reminded Thorn, "He's attending a management seminar down at One P.P. We're on our own all this week."

Savage nodded in recollection. He hated those mind-numbing cover-your-ass seminars. He knew he'd probably be scheduled to attend one in the coming weeks. He'd squirmed out of the last two; maybe he could find a way to squirm out again. He hated being pulled away from his work.

"Hamilton *is* coming into Team Three, right?" Richie Marcus inquired, a please-say-yes look on his ruddy face.

"We're the only team that's short-handed," Savage said.

Marcus' eyes glinted for an instant, and he stifled a grin of malicious humor as he rose from his desk. He stepped casually to the window and deftly flipped the *Racing Form* over. "Well done on that side," he said with a sheepish shrug.

Always able to read Marcus' mind, Savage knew perfectly well what had triggered the detective's suddenly devilish expression. Poor Abe, he thought.

"Send Hamilton in to me as soon as he gets here," Savage

told Brodigan. He turned and walked to the sergeants' room, plopped down at his desk, and dialed the phone.

"Ballistics. Hoolihan." The voice that answered was agitated and surly.

Savage hated that kind of attitude in a cop. "Davy Ramirez available?"

"Hold on . . ." the man groaned, annoyed at having to answer the phone. "Hey, Ramirez," he hollered, "pick up on six."

"Detective Ramirez. How can I help you?"

"Now, that's how a cop should answer a damn telephone!"

"Thorn," Ramirez said breezily. "How've you been, man? I was talkin' about you just last night. Your ears was ringin', right?"

"Hope you were saying nice things about me, Davy. Lord knows I've always spoken well of you."

"Oh, yeah, I'll just bet you have," Ramirez said. "Listen. I was just about to give you a call. Got my hands on a great pair of Yankee tickets for the fourteenth of May—Mother's Day. Can't use 'em. Gonna be outta town. Interested?"

"Of course," Savage replied without a second's hesitation. The Yanks were starting a homestand that Friday against Boston.

"I'll get them out in department mail," Ramirez said. "You'll have them by tomorrow."

"By the way," Savage asked, "who was that charming guy who answered the phone? He always so friendly?"

"Oh, you mean Hoolihan," Ramirez whispered. "Man, you picked up on him right away, didn't ya? Yeah, he's a real asshole. Always complaining about something. You know the type: 'Oh no-o-o-o . . . it's Tuesday.'"

"Guy needs a charisma transplant."

"Needs more than that," Davy confided. "He's a rubber

gun being surveyed out of the job on a psycho. Meanwhile, they sent him up here to answer phones. It's good they pulled his guns and got him off the street where he can't fuck over innocent civilians. But whadda they do? They put him up here, where he can fuck over other cops."

Savage grinned at Davy's assessment of the office wacko. Their opinions of the losers in The Job had always jibed.

"Listen, Davy. I need some of your expertise."

"I just knew this wasn't a social call," Ramirez sighed. "Well, it's gonna cost ya."

"Yeah? How much?"

"A cold *cervesa, por favor.*"

"I can handle that."

"Course ya can; homicide boss getting supervisor's money? Now that that's settled, what can I do for ya?"

"There's been a string of public-service homicides. Four in Manhattan and one in the Bronx. Victims were all heavy-duty dope dealers, and they all went bye-bye within the last hundred days. Last one went down Friday in the Tenth. Four of these cases supposedly involved the same kind of weapon, a nine millimeter. . . ." Savage stopped, hoping Ramirez would quickly recall the cases.

"Yeah, somebody's been real busy lately. I haven't personally worked any of those cases. But I've heard some buzz about them in the office. Whaddaya need to know?"

"It was you people at Ballistics who established that the rounds recovered in these cases were fired from a nine. That right?"

"That's the rumor."

"What else can you tell me?"

"For example."

"Was it always the *same* nine?"

"Boy, you're gettin' right to the easy ones, ain'tcha?"

"I know you can handle it, Davy."

"Yeah, we're pretty sure it was always the same one."

"Was that gun used in any earlier homicides?"

"Going back how far?"

"All the way. Five, ten, a hundred years."

"You wouldn't believe what I'd have to do to find that out. Open homicides stay on file here forever, and we got a million of them. I'd have to do an exhausting, very time-consuming hand search to determine that."

"Well, you'd do that for me, wouldn't you, Davy?"

"If you insist. But you're gonna have to spring for more than one cold one."

"You drive a hard bargain, Rammy. Okay, you got it. We'll bounce Manhattan one Friday night and the Bud's on me. Answer me this now: What make are we looking for? Can you guys determine manufacturer? Or model? Can that sort of information be extrapolated from marks on spent rounds?"

"Sometimes."

"Educate me."

"Some manufacturers use a right twist to the barrel rifling; some use a left. Width of the rifling lands and depth of the grooves are also signatures of a given manufacturer."

"Ballistics 101. That much I know."

"If we get a decent spent round and, more important, a shell casing to work with, we can usually determine the maker, and sometimes the model. Or at least narrow down the possibilities."

"Good. Now tell me something I don't know, like has your office made any determination in these cases yet? Have they been able to identify make and model on this nine?"

"Not sure. But my guess is no. We're running short-handed up here, and public-service homicides get a pretty

low priority. I can find out, though. It may take a little time.
What else would you like to know?"

"Guess that's all for now. But I may need more later,"
Savage said, nodding to Abe Hamilton, who'd knocked and
slipped quietly into his office, followed closely by Richie
Marcus. Diane DeGennaro had also arrived and was signing in at the wheel desk.

"Well, that would be just like you, wouldn't it," Davy
chided. "Always wanting more." His tone softened. "Hey,
no problem. I'm off the next two, I got a week's vacation,
and then I come back on midnights. You believe we've finally got most of our records swung over to computers? But
a lot of this may still have to be hand-searched. The midnights'll give me plenty of time to dig out anything we've
got on this piece. I'll get back to you as soon as I've got
something positive."

"Ten-four and thanks," Savage said, signing off. He
dropped the receiver into its cradle, quickly stood, and
reached out for Abe Hamilton's huge right hand. Hamilton
took it with the grasp reserved for a special friend and old-
time companion. "Good to have you aboard. Get drowned
coming in?"

"Not really." The slender black man, never known for
good looks or bad temper, shrugged. "Rain's kinda let up."

"Happy to get outta Brooklyn?" Savage asked as he slid
back into his chair.

Hamilton ran spidery fingers through his unintentional
Don King coif. "Oh, yeah. You know what precinct squad
work is like; it can wear you down. Know what I mean? I
really welcome this change, Thorn. Thanks. How'd you
arrange it?"

"Hey," Marcus growled. "Ain't you heard? The boss is
connected with the chief of D. Anything Sergeant Savage

wants, he gets. In this case he wanted somebody who was black, ugly, and not too fuckin' smart."

"You're gonna start in already, eh, Cartoon Arms?" Hamilton frowned. "I ain't here two fuckin' minutes and already you're on my case."

"No point in wastin' any time," Marcus said, shrugging. "Besides, it's been years since I've had a chance to break your nuts. And you were always so damn easy. By the way, you comb your hair with an M-80 this morning, or what?"

"Some things never change, eh, Thorn?" Hamilton sighed, turning his back on Marcus, who was still beaming at him.

"So, what happened in court this morning?" Savage asked.

"Ahh, yessss!" Hamilton drawled in his practiced W. C. Fields. "I'm glad you asked that ques-*chun*." He shot a smile at Savage. "The street-corner pharmacologist, whom I took into custody for the improper vending of a nefarious white powdery substance, wisely entered a plea of *nolo contendere* to an E grade felony, and was forthwith remanded to the penitentiary where he will be incarcerated for a period of not less than eighteen months."

As Abe talked, Savage's glance shifted up to the man's wild-looking hair. It stood straight up, as if he'd just played footsie with an IRT third rail. Thorn knew Abe had often been accused of training it that way. But the truth was that it was completely natural. The unusual hairstyle added to the incongruity of Abe's Marcus-baiting impression.

"So." Savage played the straight man. "The street dealer copped out and took eighteen months. Good. I'm glad that matter's closed."

"In more ways than one," Marcus sneered, rolling his eyes as he left the small office. "A black Jack Benny . . . for crissake. . . Hey, Hamilton! Get a fuckin' life, will ya?"

"Go take your Ritalin, Marcus," Abe hollered after the ex-Marine, then mumbled to Savage, "That man's depriving a village somewhere of an idiot."

Hamilton and Marcus never stopped playing the baiting game. But it was a harmless battle of wits they'd played for years. Savage knew they liked and respected one another.

Hamilton quietly asked, "So tell me, Thorn. What's this all about? Why my sudden transfer? What's an old narcotics undercover doing here at Manhattan South Homicide?"

"Let's wait till Jack Lindstrom gets in. Once the whole team's here, I can bring everybody up to speed at the same time."

Hamilton nodded.

"Meanwhile, get yourself fixed up with a locker and a desk," Savage suggested. "Brodigan'll show you where. Then tonight you and I are going out to give somebody a real good eyeball."

"Ahh, yessss," Hamilton commented. "This is beginning to sound like some old-time fun and games." He stood, bowed with a flourish, and grinned broadly as he left the room. "Always glad to be of service, my liege."

Leaning back in his squeaky chair, Savage surveyed his cramped office. A constant hum—a form of external tinnitus—came from the dim fluorescents above. Beside his desk was a wheeled table that supported a well-worn electric typewriter shared by the three sergeants. The shelves above his desk brimmed with legal publications and the most recent case law. His desk was well organized. A blotter calendar with tear-off monthly pages bore daily notations of significant activities within his command and provided a chronological record of unit matters at a glance. Also, there was a framed photo of Joanne and Jennie. It hit him suddenly that in two weeks they would be dead twenty-three years.

After they were killed, he'd sold the split-level on Long Island and completely wrapped himself up in The Job. He moved into the Manhattan apartment he now shared with Ray, the gritty smoke-colored cat who'd appeared on his fire escape one night during a blizzard. The small flat was all he needed. It was warm, comfortable, and convenient to his work. Then Gina had come into his life. Her picture was on the desk too, right next to Joanne and Jennie's.

"Good afternoon. Gulf Stream Marina." The voice at the other end of the line was soft and feminine. "This is Kim. How can I help you?"

"This is Derek Ogden from New York. Put Reed on."

"He's out in the yard, sir. One minute; I'll page him."

Tinny taped music, dragging badly from age and over-use, blared across the line. Ogden rolled his eyes at the insufferable noise. Finally, a man's husky baritone replaced the racket.

"This is Reed."

"Derek Ogden here. How's the weather in Lauderdale?"

"Great, Mr. Ogden." The boatyard operator's tone instantly shifted to one of clear subservience. "It's eighty-two degrees, winds out of the southeast at ten knots, and waves about two feet—a perfect day for being out on the water. Are we going to see you soon, sir?"

"Very soon. Earlier than anticipated, as a matter of fact. I plan on being down in about a week. What's the status of my *Slavedriver*? Have those new props been installed?"

"No sir, Mr. Ogden." The boatyard owner fumbled nervously for words. "The new props are, well, ah, here, but we haven't had a chance to haul her and fit them as yet."

"Haven't fitted them yet?" Ogden yelled into the phone. "What the hell do you mean, you haven't fitted them yet? You've had a fucking month."

"Sir, I had no idea that you would be coming—"

"Bull*shit!*" Ogden scowled. "Now hear me good. I don't care what it takes, but you get it done ASAP, which spells *now*! Do you read, *Reed?*"

"I do, sir. Be assured that everything on the *Slavedriver* will be completely shipshape when you get here."

Ogden smirked. He knew the marina owner hated kowtowing to him, but he dropped more bucks there than any ten others combined. Twenty maybe. And he always paid in cold, hard cash.

"I'll see that she's all fueled and ready to go for your regular Bahamas run. I'll even have Bobby oil all the teak."

"Wonderful," Ogden said, moderating his wrathful tone to one of cloying indulgence.

"My pleasure, Mr. Ogden."

"Good man, Reed. *Ciao.*"

Dropping the phone into its cradle, Ogden spun his chair and thought about his absolute need to have it his way, always. About never having to bow to anyone, ever, for anything. Certainly, he'd never bow to no damn white man he could buy and sell fifty times over.

Ogden knew he could demand almost anything, from almost anybody, at any time, and get it. But, of course, he reminded himself, he had started life with great raw materials: innate talent, superior intelligence, fabulous good looks, and a charismatic, controlling personality. That, coupled with years of hard work, persistence, and skill, had elevated him to the life he knew today: a life of hobnobbing with the rich and famous, the glitteratti—the beautiful people. But surely he was the most beautiful of all.

Yet despite all his successes he would never forget the abject poverty of his fractured youth. And the pain of hopelessness and despair that poverty brought. He was on top now, and he owed it mostly to the ability to make tough decisions that came so easily to him. Life-and-death decrees, as it were. He reached for a fresh cigar and speed-dialed Luther Robinson at the Culture Club. Life, he thought, was good. It was time for another decree.

"Yes?" Robinson's voice, as empty as it was terse, came on the line.

"You need to see to that Baldwin retirement we discussed yesterday," Ogden said. "Take care of it immediately."

"Consider it done."

# EIGHT

Monday night's preliminary surveillance of Derek Ogden had been a success. When Savage arrived at Manhattan South in preparation for Tuesday night's second round of urban peekaboo, Richie Marcus followed him into the otherwise empty sergeants' room.

"How'd it go?" he asked. "You able to connect with Ogden?"

"We connected," Savage said, then quietly closed the office door. "Considering it was our first attempt at him, we did great. Abe drove the cab and I kept the backseat warm. At five o'clock, Ogden's chauffeur pulled the Bentley up outside Ogden World Galleries on Madison. At ten after, Ogden came out and was driven directly over to the Carlyle Hotel."

"He lives at the Carlyle?" Marcus whistled. "I'm impressed."

"Supposedly maintains a suite of rooms there," Savage mumbled, hanging his glasses on the tip of his nose and shuffling quickly through a stack of completed DD-5 forms left in his IN box for review. "Gonna have Jack Lindstrom look more closely into that."

"Did he ever leave? Go out anywhere?" Marcus asked, crushing a half-smoked cigarette into the full ashtray on Jules Unger's desk.

"Went to some kinda do over at Carnegie Hall. Abe and I stayed with him till midnight when he was dropped off back at the Carlyle. Speaking of Abe," Savage said, craning his neck and looking through the window wall into the squad room, "I bet he's not in yet."

Abe Hamilton had not yet arrived for work. He'd make it on time—1500 hours—but unless Savage missed his guess, just barely. It was now only minutes to.

Savage had always considered himself blessed with the best team in the office. And now, with the addition of Abe Hamilton, they were probably the best, most well-rounded homicide investigation team in The Job. Thorn knew he could take a powder for a month—go fishing in the Azores—and the team would continue to work every bit as efficiently as if he were standing there with the whip.

"Forensics came up with no usable prints from the Horace Grimes car," Marcus announced. "Whoever knocked him and the others over must have a cleaning contract with Merry Maids."

Savage moved to his locker and spun out the combination. "Not surprising. What about that powdery residue like they found in Escobar's car?"

"They came up with the same microscopic residue on the interior door handle, ignition switch and key, driver's power-window button, and cigarette-lighter knob," Marcus said in his nicotine- and bourbon-tattered rasp. "All indicating that the last hand to touch them was prob'ly wearing a fresh surgical glove."

Savage snatched his coffee mug from the top shelf of the locker. "What else?"

"Them plastic ties we cut off Grimes were identical to the ones used on Escobar. They had the same tiny logo embossed on them: the capital letters TB inside a circle."

"TB?"

"Thomas & Betts Corporation, Memphis, Tennessee. Spoke to the home office. They told me those things come in a variety of lengths, eleven- and fourteen-inch being the most popular. They make 'em in black or clear."

"All our boys were wearing the fourteen-inch clear models," Savage mused under his breath.

"They're called Cat-Pak Cable Ties," Marcus said, tossing a bundle of fourteen-inch clears onto Savage's desk. "They run seven-fifty for a hundred-pack. They're used for tying, bundling, securing, fastening. Strong as a son of a bitch."

"Where did you get them?" Savage asked, handling the rubber band–wrapped bundle.

"Available just about everywhere. They're distributed nationwide through a variety of wholesalers and jobbers. Probably every hardware, building, electric, or plumbing supply store on the East Coast carries them. Forget tracing 'em."

"Gonna hold on to these." Savage dropped the ratcheted nylon strips into his top desk drawer. He grabbed his mug and headed to the squad room coffeepot with Marcus tight on his heels.

"Gotta be more than one guy doin' these snuffs," Marcus said as Savage stirred a half-teaspoon of sugar into the steaming brew.

"Tell me what you're thinking, Richie," Savage said genially, knowing he was going to be told anyway. He eyeballed the lone chocolate doughnut in the Entenmann's box on top of the coffee table. If somebody didn't eat it, it'd probably go stale, he reasoned. He started to reach but fought back the temptation.

The husky detective flipped a new Winston between his lips, ignited it, and began to growl out a theory. "No traceable fingerprints, except the victim's, were found on either car's outer door handles, passenger *or* driver side. No glove residue at those locations either. That tells me that our killer pulled the surgical gloves on after entering those cars, or already had them on beneath regular gloves."

"I buy that," Savage responded. Carefully steadying his overfilled mug, he walked back toward the sergeants' room. As he passed Jack Lindstrom's desk, the detail-oriented detective pointed at the telephone receiver at his ear and mouthed the initials *IRS*. Savage acknowledged with a nod. As he passed the wheel desk, Eddie Brodigan handed him a sealed piece of department mail.

Marcus trailed him back into the small office and casually seated himself half-assed at the edge of Jules Unger's desk. "Grimes was a pretty big boy," he said, sucking in a deep drag. "And Escobar was no slouch either." Smoke escaped in staggered bursts from his nose and mouth as he went on. "I'm thinkin' maybe they both got double-teamed."

"Go on," Savage said, opening the mail envelope. It contained two Yankee tickets and a brief note from Davy Ramirez. He dropped the tickets into his desk drawer beside the bundle of cable ties.

"I figure it had to take at least two guys to bind them up with them plastic gizmos. Neither one o' them tough fucks'd stand still for one guy tryin' that shit."

"Even one with a nine millimeter aimed at their hearts?"

Marcus offered an unsure shrug.

"Go on," Savage urged, not totally discounting Richie's two-man scenario. He'd already been there and didn't like it. But maybe Richie had a new slant.

The tip of the Winston glowed a bright orange. "Okay," he said, slowly exhaling more smoke. "Now they got the victim—Grimes or Escobar—trussed up like a Christmas turkey, right?"

"I'm with ya," Savage drawled, sipping tentatively at the still-steaming coffee.

"Then they lash the poor bastard's wrists to the steering wheel."

"Which leaves the victim pretty much defenseless," Savage said, nodding to Jack Lindstrom, who slipped into the office and leaned against the tall file cabinet in the corner.

"Right. Then," Marcus argued, "one guy stays in the car with the victim, tunes him up real good—to get the information he wants, or whatever—while the other one stands guard outside."

Savage, expressionless, took another sip.

"And," Marcus continued, "once the inside guy finally gets what he needs, or determines he ain't gonna get what he needs, he reaches over and turns the car's ignition switch on. He lowers the driver's power window, then lets himself outta the car via the passenger door. That accounts for the glove residue being at those locations in either car."

"Then," Savage finished the scenario, "the guy standing guard, or the beater, walks around to the driver's open window and lets the victim have it in the left ear with a nine."

Marcus shrugged hopefully. "Whaddaya think?"

"It works," Savage acknowledged. "But I still gotta go with the idea of a single hitter."

"Boss." Diane DeGennaro strode into the office, smiling. "Got some interesting stuff back on Ogden's limo." Waving yellow rap sheets, she added, "I've also managed a very discreet criminal-records check on him. What would you like to talk about first?"

The springs squeaked as Savage rocked back in his ancient chair. He noticed how the smattering of freckles around Diane's tiny nose gave her an almost adolescent charm. "Tell me about the car first," he replied.

"Supposedly, it's one of only two Bentleys custom-stretched by Rolls-Royce back in the mid-seventies. Both were armored and fitted with bulletproof glass. One went to the Shah of Iran. Ogden picked the other one up at a collector-car auction out in Scottsdale, Arizona, three years ago. Get this," she said, gawking individually at each man with a wide-eyed stare. "He paid three hundred and fifty big ones. You believe that?"

Jack Lindstrom let out a muffled "Whoa!"

Savage whistled through his teeth.

Marcus replied with a blasé "Whaddaya expect, for crissakes? It's a damn bulletproof Bentley. That's what they go for."

"Nothing impresses you, hah, Marcus?" Lindstrom asked. "You who ain't got a goddamned pot to piss in stand here and act as if you're current with the numbers on the exotic-car market. Jeezus," he mumbled, shaking his head.

"I happen to know prices," Marcus snapped indignantly.

"Yeah," Lindstrom said. "The price of everything, and the value of nothing."

"What about the criminal background, Diane?" Savage interrupted.

"Frankie Birnstill down at BCI ran these off on the q.t. for me," she replied, her voice hushed. Handing Savage a copy, she read aloud from the Bureau of Criminal Investigation original. "Derek Maximilian Ogden, AKA—"

*"Maximilian?"* Marcus blurted out. "Ain't no wonder that son of a bitch thinks he's a freakin' god."

"Derek Maximilian Ogden, AKA Ogden Daniels, Daniel Ogden, and Danforth Hudson, has got himself a nasty history here," she said. "Bit of a naughty boy in his youth. Back in the late sixties and early seventies he got himself sent down to the principal a few times," she added breezily.

"Assault two in 'sixty-eight," Savage said. "Possession of stolen property in 'sixty-nine. Assault one in 'seventy-one. Possession loaded gun and manslaughter in 'seventy-two." He looked up, fixing his eyes on Diane's. "He did a bullet at Riker's for the manslaughter."

"One solid year," Diane affirmed. "But he's been spotlessly clean ever since."

"Who said Riker's can't rehabilitate a man?" Marcus croaked sarcastically, scratching his underarm.

Weary from a hectic ten-hour-plus day, Gina McCormick left the Maiden Lane offices of Kearney & Dunton, where she headed up the firm's appraisal department, and walked to the IRT station on Wall Street. Rush hour was over and she easily got a seat on the 3 train. She could go home now and turn her full attention to wedding and reception plans. This, she thought, with a sublime smile on her face, was the happiest time of her life.

As the train plowed through the blackness of the East River tunnel toward Brooklyn, she eyed the other homeward-bound straphangers. Most seemed worn out, spent. For the thousandth time that day she allowed her thoughts to drift back to Thorn, and felt herself being enveloped by a warm sense of contentment.

The train screeched to an ear-bending, jerking stop at Clark Street. Gina smoothed the skirt of her pale-gray linen business suit and picked up the letter-sized leather attaché that did double duty as a purse. When the doors slid open she got off, took the crowded elevator to street level, and began the six-block walk to the Brooklyn Heights home she had been housesitting for the last twenty-two months.

It was a perfect spring night to enjoy the sycamore-canopied quaintness of the quiet area. The Heights was a cultured old neighborhood with an artistic, intellectual aura, sort of an upscale Brooklyn version of Manhattan's Greenwich Village. It was expensive, safe, and secure, and just a short hop from her downtown job. When her widowed boss, Harrison Kearney, hit seventy-five, he had retired as CEO of the firm and immediately set out on a two-year around-the-world jaunt. He had recruited Gina to housesit his fashionable nineteenth-century town house, which overlooked New York Harbor. It was sumptuous and rent-free. Divorced and living alone—in a drab apartment building soon to meet the wrecker's ball—she had jumped at the opportunity. Two months from now Mr. Kearney was scheduled to return and she would have to vacate. Six weeks from now, however, she and Thorn would be married and living in his place in Manhattan. The timing was perfect.

She made a quick stop at the Starbucks on Montague for a blend of the French roast coffee that Thorn liked so much. He'd promised to take this coming Saturday night off from the special assignment he'd been working. It was her birthday, and they were going out to celebrate. If they stayed at her place Saturday night, she'd make an old-fashioned breakfast for them on Sunday morning. She had already laid in extra-lean bacon and a dozen eggs. Fresh rolls and a crumb cake could be picked up from Claussen's after seven o'clock mass. She'd have to attend church alone—Thorn always slept in. Once they were married, she would work on getting him reacquainted with religion. He hadn't darkened the doors of any house of worship since he lost his wife and daughter in that terrible car wreck so long ago.

Gina descended the slight grade of Hicks Street and turned into Grace Court Alley. A century ago this cobbled cul-de-sac probably didn't even have a name; it was merely a narrow mews of attached two-story carriage houses. Horseflesh had occupied the ground floors in those days, and stable help lived in the garrets above. Each unit's ground floor, once storage for saddles, harnesses, and other tack, was now partitioned into decorator kitchens, dining areas, baths, and high-ceilinged living rooms. Stalls, once home to teams of hardy Scottish draft horses, had become kitchen-accessible single-car garages housing German sedans, American SUVs and, in Gina's case, a four-year-old red Miata with a tan convertible top.

Gina fished out her keys and unlocked the front door of the first town house on the right. Once inside, she quickly punched the five-digit code into the alarm keypad. Kearney had installed a state-of-the-art alarm system even though this was one of the safest neighborhoods in Brooklyn. She ascended the wrought-iron spiral staircase to the master bedroom. A few minutes later, snug in her favorite terry robe, she returned downstairs to the kitchen.

She removed a covered plate of penne pasta from the fridge, popped it into the microwave, and punched three minutes on the timer. Waiting for the food to heat, Gina picked up the list of wedding invitees and studied it. The list included her parents, Tony and Connie DiLeo; her favorite aunt, Chickie; Cousin Lauren and her husband, Chris, and Joe Mistretta, a bachelor uncle. Also there was Morgana Feldman—her maid of honor—and two other women friends from the office. Thorn's brother, Brian, and his wife would be there, along with his sister, Emily, and her two teenaged kids—and several cops and their wives. Most prominent among them were Thorn's oldest and best friend Abe Hamilton and his wife, Tammi. So far they were up to twenty-nine names; she hoped they weren't forgetting anyone.

At first, and surely only for her benefit, Thorn had suggested renting a hall, hiring an orchestra, and inviting half of Kings County. She'd convinced him otherwise. She didn't need a crowd; it wasn't her style, nor was it his. At this stage in their lives they didn't need a big shindig. A small group of intimate friends and close relatives to share their special day would be ideal. And if they could manage to keep the list to around thirty, Mr. Kearney's Brooklyn carriage house, though small, would do perfectly well for the reception.

As the massive grandfather clock opposite the stairs began sounding the quarter-hour notes of the Westminster chimes, the telephone rang. She guessed at the caller.

"How's the bride-to-be?" The voice was upbeat and animated. "This is your maid of honor calling."

"Hi, Morgie," Gina said, not surprised that her guess had been right.

"Where've you been?" Morgana asked. "I've been trying you for the past hour. Work late?"

"Yes. Didn't have much choice. Had something that absolutely had to go out today."

"You're so damn conscientious, I can't stand you," Morgana teased. "When are we getting together for lunch?"

"I'm loaded up with work this week and next," Gina said. "But I'm taking the following week as vacation. We'll do it then."

"I'm going to hold you to that," Morgana announced. "So, you teach that policeman to dance yet?"

"Eh," Gina said. "Poor man's got two left feet. He'll never be Fred Astaire, but I gotta give him credit, he tries. I keep reminding him step-two-three, step-two-three. All I want is one waltz on my wedding day."

"It's good he's trying," Morgana said. "Thorn sure looks athletic, but he certainly don't look dainty—know what I mean? But if he's gonna be married to you, he needs to at least know how to waltz—oh," Morgana said, suddenly shifting gears, "by the way. I thought it would be a wonderful idea to place your engagement announcement in the Sunday *Times*."

"What?" Gina gasped with a disbelieving laugh. "We're hardly what anybody might call society people. I don't want—"

"So," Morgana went on, "I went ahead and did it."

Gina hesitated. "I don't think so. . . ."

"Don't worry about it," Morgana said. "Anyway, I've already called it in. It'll run Sunday after next. You're about to be famous," she bubbled. "Everyone will know who you are. You can clip it out and save it for posterity."

Gina hung up the phone and retrieved dinner from the microwave. She felt the sublime smile slipping back across her face. After ten years of false starts, mismatches, and loneliness, everything was finally perfect.

### Wednesday, April 12, 10:00 P.M.

Luther Robinson focused mother-of-pearl opera glasses on Spencer Baldwin's fourth-floor windows. Baldwin's tacky, over-customized Cadillac was parked just around the corner. Robinson had not missed him. Any minute, he thought, extracting a small glass vial from the pocket of his dark windbreaker. He took a quick blow of coke, exhaled slowly, and snapped on a fresh pair of surgical gloves.

As the finale of *Romeo and Juliet*'s *Fantasy Overture* faded to silence, he selected a Yo-Yo Ma disc. Soothed by the cellist's brilliant rendition of "Le Cygne"—the lamentation of a dying swan—Luther settled back in the bucket seat, half-closed his eyes to savor every note of his favorite piece, and waited.

His mind drifted back to his first contract murder. The experience of thrusting the long, hard barrel of a pistol into a man's ear and pulling the trigger to deliver the supreme payload had been an awakening, a coming of age. As Derek always said, killing was just like sex—you never forgot the first time.

It was, he remembered, a cool autumn night in Harlem in the early eighties. Looking like any other fifteen-year-old ghetto kid of the time, he had casually walked up on a mink-clad dude lounging behind the wheel of a big Lincoln. The target was dining on greasy wings in front of a rib joint on Eighth Avenue with his driver's window halfway down and his radio blasting Gladys Knight. Without a word Luther had pushed the barrel of a cheap Saturday Night Special into the guy's ear, pulled the trigger twice, and walked away. He'd immediately gone home to Aunt Lucy's tenement, stashed the gun beneath his bare mattress, and jerked off, over and over, until he could orgasm no more. Exhausted by the incredible emotional and physical release, he collapsed and slept for fourteen hours. When he awoke, he knew he'd found his life's calling. He was a killer.

By the age of sixteen he had completed five contract hits and been paid handsomely for them. Obsessed by his chosen discipline, and nurtured like a prize hothouse orchid by his mentor, Derek Ogden, Robinson discovered himself to be a virtuoso of death. Derek said virtuosos were born, not made, bestowed with special skills and talents that destined them for greatness in their fields. Some were put on earth to become composers of timeless classical music, others multi-octave sopranos, and still others Hall of Fame shortstops. Luther had been born to make an art form of efficiently terminating inconvenient human life.

Through the years Luther had honed his talents with careful study and much practice. Each new assignment brought an unrivaled thrill, each new hunt an unparalleled stimulation. The stalking of prey became libido-tickling foreplay that, because he was always in control, he frequently prolonged. Getting there was half the fun. But the kill was the thing. The kill was the climax.

Luther's thoughts were pulled back to the present as the lights of Spencer Baldwin's apartment suddenly went black. As expected, the man was headed out to his usual late-night revelry. Luther Robinson knew better. Spencer Baldwin was headed out to die.

# NINE

Derek Ogden, slick as a snake in handsomely tailored semi-formal evening wear, emerged from the Carlyle's front entrance. He was a big man, tall and broad, and had a bald spot at the crown of his head. Pausing beneath the hotel's marquee, he produced a fifty-dollar cigar and, with well-practiced panache, fed it into the corner of his mouth. His private chauffeur—a no-neck in his forties, built low to the ground and fire-hydrant sturdy—leapt from behind the wheel of the Bentley and held the rear door open. With the hotel's doorman fawning in his wake, Ogden swaggered to the waiting limousine.

Seated behind the wheel of a Chevy cab parked fifty feet away in the hotel's East Seventy-sixth Street hack stand, Abe Hamilton announced, "That, my friend, was the picture of a dude who has a very secure grip on the world's short curly ones."

"Got that right," Savage drawled from the cab's backseat.

Abe pinched his wide nostrils and, like a nasal TV announcer doing a show-ending voice-over, rattled, "Transportation by Rolls, tux by Valentino, and monstrous ego by Trump."

Trump! Savage thought. Of course—*the* Donald. He jotted his new *the* on the clipboard.

Abe started the Chevy's engine, put the car into gear, and engaged the meter. Up ahead, the Carlyle doorman stepped into the street to play traffic cop. He made a show of holding up the nonexistent traffic as the Bentley lumbered slowly away from the hotel's loading zone. The limo made a right at Park, looped the block, and headed uptown on Madison.

"Wonder what Cinderella ball we're off to tonight?" Abe said.

"From the way he's dressed, I'd say it's gonna be another night at the opera."

"Damn," Abe groaned, and clucked his tongue. "Don't this guy ever do anything that's fun?" He looked into his sideview and drifted the cab into the shadow of a wide van two vehicles behind the Bentley.

"Fun like what?" Savage asked.

"I don't know." Abe shrugged. "Go for a cocktail. Take in a porno flick. Do something . . . interesting. Know what I mean?"

"What you're saying is," Savage said, "if he went for cocktails at some swell East Side saloon, we would have no choice but to follow him in."

"You are correct, sir."

"And in order for us to blend, we again would have no choice but to order up some cocktails ourselves."

"At the city's expense, of course," Abe quickly pointed out.

"And," Savage continued, "if he opted instead to visit some porno palace . . ."

"We would have no choice but to get some tickets. Make sure he doesn't slip out the back door."

"He had fun last night," Savage said. "A charity ball. Two grand a throw, remember?"

"Oh, yeah," Abe agreed. "How could I forget? Mister O

was chowin' down on juicy prime rib—rubbin' shoulders with the mayor and the cardinal in the Waldorf—while you and me sat outside dining on petrified doughnuts and cold coffee inside the yellow room of Chez Taxi."

"While forty blocks away," Savage reminded him, "Spencer Baldwin was getting his brains rattled by a nine millimeter."

"Our boy couldn't have been in two places at one time," Abe said. "And I gotta say, so far Ogden's looking pretty much like the saint all his press releases say he is. If we were looking for fire, we ain't seen so much as a puff of smoke."

The Bentley glided smoothly up Madison. Two-tone gray, the living room on wheels dwarfed everything in the traffic around it. By contrast, even the biggest Cadillacs seemed plebeian in size. It was a whale schooling with minnows, and a cinch to follow.

"Can you imagine how much damn money it costs to live full-time in the Carlyle?" Abe asked, an equal mix of awe and ire in his voice.

"Prob'ly couldn't count that high," Savage said, reaching for the binocular case next to him. "Wonder if the Kennedy clan still maintains a suite there. I know they did back in the sixties—the so-called days of Camelot."

"Gotta figure the cheapest room prob'ly goes for two-fifty, three hundred a night, right?" Abe speculated.

"Probably couldn't get a broom closet in there for that."

"And this guy don't have just *a* room—he's got himself a whole damn suite of rooms. I bet if you wanted to book that suite on a daily basis it would bring, what? A thousand? Two? Jeez!"

"Ogden's got a five-year lease on that suite," Savage said. "But anything comparable would cost thirty-five hundred a night. Lindstrom already checked it out."

Abe shook his head angrily. "Two weeks of this guy's rent would cover a semester at Harvard Law for my kid."

"He's gonna make that light at Eighty-sixth, Abe," Savage warned. "The DON'T WALK sign's starting to flash. Better close the gap a little."

Abe goosed the accelerator, and the yellow cab slipped through the intersection just as the light broke against them.

At 110th Street the Bentley made a left and cruised along the top side of Central Park. Without even breathing hard, it flattened the steep hill that runs alongside the Cathedral of St. John the Divine. At Broadway it turned downtown. Its speed never exceeded twenty-five, and it never changed lanes. At Seventy-ninth the car pulled ponderously to the curb like a great liner gingerly maneuvering into a narrow berth. Leaving the driver's door ajar, the uniformed chauffeur stepped out onto the street. He stood, adjusting his belt, slowly turning to take in a sweeping three-sixty scan.

"Dude sure looks like he's watchin' out for a tail," Abe said, pulling the yellow Chevrolet to a stop one block back.

Savage focused the Bausch & Lombs through the Plexiglas partition. "Look at him. He's eyeballin' everybody on the corner and every car in sight."

"Didn't even give us a peep," Abe crowed, pulling the Chevy's gear lever up into PARK. "That's why I love these cabs for surveillance."

His close-cropped head swiveling constantly, the chauffeur disappeared behind the newsstand on the corner.

"Dude's either got a painfully large prostate," Abe observed, commenting on the man's peculiar, side-to-side waddle, "or he's a direct descendant of Donald Duck."

Moments later, the odd-walking chauffeur returned to the Bentley. He handed some magazines through the rear window.

"Probably *Screw, Hustler,* and *Penthouse*," Abe mumbled.

"Doesn't that head of yours ever come out of the smut locker?" Savage asked, binoculars still pressed to his eyes. "That all you ever think about?"

"It's not the *only* thing I live for anymore," Abe said dolefully. "There's still my Hummel collection . . . and my pressed flowers."

The chauffeur unbuttoned his jacket and did another scan before reopening the driver's door. The tough-looking man with the funny walk hitched up his left shoulder and slid back behind the wheel.

"See that move, Abe?"

"Saw it," Hamilton replied, slowly pulling the Chevy's gear lever back into drive. "Unconscious shoulder hitch. Sucka's packin'. Looks like Duckie Boy's got himself a shoulder rig on the left side."

Savage set the binoculars down on the seat beside him. His adrenaline valve had opened. The hairs on the back of his neck jumped to attention. That same feeling he got every time he stood in the open hatch of a jump plane at ten thousand feet. His street instincts had sounded their silent alarm. This was not going to be just another boring night at the opera. He reached in his pocket for a Wint-O-Green.

"Now, what would a peace-loving guy who deals in oil paintings and old rocking chairs be needin' with a gun-totin' chauffeur?" Abe asked.

"Don't know," Savage muttered. "But I think we just saw our first puff of smoke."

As was his nightly ritual, just before eight o'clock Calvin Dempsey shuffled the short half block from his fleabag on 148th to Matt's, on Broadway, for his evening libations. He took his usual place on the shaky stool in the back corner, at

the far end of the well-worn bar. Corners made him feel secure. He never liked sitting with his back to the action, especially in a dive like Matt's.

Calvin's black-and-Kelly-green-checkered flannel shirt—
more appropriate for a brawny Canadian woodsman than an
inner-city black man—was faded and wrinkled, and stuffed
haphazardly into unpressed gray pants that were two sizes
too big; his bony ass was lost in the baggy seat. The loose
trousers were cinched sausage-like at his narrow middle by
a worn belt into which a number of extra holes had been
crudely punched. The belt's extra length dangled freely
from the buckle.

Calvin was quiet. The only word he ever uttered to the
bartender was "Gin." He rarely engaged anyone in conversation, and, if addressed, responded in as few syllables as
possible. The Matt's regulars thought him just a sullen old
man and knew little about him. Calvin Dempsey was waiting out his life. He was in no particular hurry to die, but
possessed little enthusiasm for continuing.

Calvin's stringy body was bent and frail, but it was in his
tired face that his age was most amplified. He had the appearance of a man whose sleep account was seriously over-
drawn. Weary lines roamed everywhere, mostly around
basset-hound eyes that had witnessed too much meanness
in their sixty-eight years. His watery eyes had long ago
mastered the art of feigned indifference. Calvin was a con-
summate people-watcher. He chain-smoked his Kools and
missed nothing that occurred in his orbit.

Thirty years ago, overwhelmed by a rage he'd been
powerless to control, Calvin had carried an innocuous-
looking Bohack's shopping bag into a smoke-filled pimp
bar on Eighth Avenue. Completely concealed in the brown
paper sack was a ten-gauge shotgun with barrels and stock
sawed down to a stub. He walked up behind a beanpole of

a man decked out in a bright-yellow jumpsuit and a gaily plumed porkpie hat who was seated at the middle of the bar. The slickass was laughing, shuckin' and jivin', amusing the barkeep and some other gaudily costumed, no-class flesh peddlers with his flashy, look-how-cool-I-am act.

Calvin's fifteen-year-old daughter was lost, gone down the tubes. She'd been stolen, violated, and put on the street with a hundred-fifty-a-day smack habit by the pimp in the yellow getup. It was payback time.

Calvin jammed the mean end of the Remington between the pimp's shoulder blades and pulled both triggers. Puréed heart and lungs, containing minute shreds of yellow polyester and bits of sternum, oozed like a thick pudding down the booze bottles behind the bar.

Satisfied at having done his deed, Calvin laid the weapon on the bar, blue smoke still curling from its abbreviated barrels, and ordered a triple of top-shelf from the horrified bartender. With the dead man at his feet, he savored the gratis drink and waited stoically for cops from the local precinct to arrive. Calvin pleaded guilty to murder two and spent his next twenty-four birthdays in Greenhaven. He was never sorry for what he'd done. The jive-ass had deserved to die.

These days the better part of Calvin's life was spent in Matt's Bar. Parkinson's tremor had left him with little control over his gnarled and arthritic hands. He couldn't pee worth a damn, and he'd long ago lost all interest in pussy. He sipped quickly at the brimming glass, trying not to spill any of the precious gin. As he drank he was aware of the noisy humanity that swirled all about him, an assortment of unruly street mopes and junkies, dealers and hookers, who drifted constantly through his field of vision. They were a loud and obnoxious crowd, all talking at once, nobody ever listening. Jabbering monkeys. These assholes always have so much to say, he thought. Just like in prison.

It was business as usual in Matt's tonight. The bartender was augmenting his income by peddling stolen DVDs he kept under lock and key in the back room. Junkies, high on cheap wine and heroin, mingled with the bottom-line hookers who sat around hoping to turn a quick trick for a few bucks. Calvin just shook his head and took another sip of gin, numbing his mind, wondering what he'd done to deserve this life he had.

Street-corner dope dealers dashed in and out. The bartender quickly resupplied them with glassine-packaged heroin and banked their earnings. One never stood out on this part of Broadway holding too much dope . . . or too much money.

Nope, Calvin didn't miss much.

Ogden's Bentley veered off Broadway at Columbus and became part of a feeding frenzy of stretch limos, private cars, and taxicabs, all jockeying for discharge spots in front of Lincoln Center. The crowd, most in formal dress, streamed toward the main entrance of the complex, past the erupting fountain and beneath purple banners lettered in gold with the single word BUTTERFLY. The huge banners briefly took Thorn's eye. He watched as they rose and fell, inhaling and then exhaling the mild evening breeze.

The Bentley finally wormed its way into a spot, and the dutiful chauffeur waddled around and opened the door for his passenger. Derek Ogden stepped out. He passed a few words with the driver; then, with a strong gait, he strode swiftly away into the funneling throng.

"For the life of me," Abe said, making eye contact with Savage through the rearview mirror. "I just don't understand no black man sittin' still for hours listening to a bunch of *I*-talians screaming at one another."

"Such is life," Savage said, summoning up his best Barry Fitzgerald brogue as he bailed from the taxicab's backseat. "You be a good lad now, Abe, and don't be losin' sight of that fine English carriage, or the husky lackey who's drivin' it. I believe I'll be stayin' with Squire Ogden for a wee bit."

"Ten-four," Abe acknowledged, switching on the Motorola portable. "I'll be on the air if you need me."

Savage fast-walked his way through the crowd and into the lobby of the Metropolitan Opera. Derek Ogden, however, had disappeared, swallowed up by the opening-night swarm. Flashing his shield to an usher, Savage got directions to the Met's security office. There he identified himself to a mildly attractive, bottle-blond receptionist who was all tits and teeth. She announced him over a desk intercom.

Seconds later an inner office door swung open and a solidly built, well-dressed man in his early fifties appeared.

"Bob Moeser, head of security," the man said, extending his right hand. "What can I do for you, officer?"

There was something familiar about the sandy-haired security boss. Iceberg-blue eyes that seemed capable of seeing through lead walls added a cold intensity to his smoothly shaven and intelligent oval face. He wore a conservatively cut pinstripe with razor-sharp creases. His cordovan wing tips were carefully shined. The man had an undeniable police bearing.

"I'm Thorn Savage from Manhattan South." They exchanged a quick, firm handshake. Savage cocked his head. "Didn't we attend the Police Academy together? About a hundred years ago?"

"At least a hundred." Moeser's stoic face relaxed into an

easy grin. "You took the Masbach Trophy at graduation. Impressive, considering it was a class of over six hundred."

"How'd you remember that?"

The grin stretched an inch wider. "I came in second."

Savage grimaced.

"Curtain just went up, Mr. Moeser," the busty receptionist broke in.

Moeser acknowledged her with an abrupt nod.

"Okay, Thorn. I know you're not here to see *Butterfly,* so step into my parlor and talk to me." Moeser led the way into his small private office, leaving tits-and-teeth to file her nails.

*Butterfly*'s first intermission came at exactly 9:20. Wearing the scarlet blazer of a house usher, Thorn Savage stood next to the complex's security boss at the top of the Met's sweeping staircase. From that vantage point, he watched as the opening-night crowd swelled from the auditorium at both the grand tier and orchestra levels. Most of the tuxedoed men ambled casually to refreshment bars to order blush wines or Perrier. The ladies, in their latest de la Rentas or Chanels, made straight for the powder rooms. Savage studied the bustling activity, hoping to see Ogden's balding crown appear. He wondered where Abe might have been led by the chauffeured Bentley. The audience below snacked on coffee and light sandwiches. Thorn's stomach growled; he hadn't eaten since breakfast.

"It's been a while since I've been here," he said, scanning the cavernous lobby. "I'd forgotten just how big this complex is. There's plenty of places my guy could be, and I might not ever see him."

"True enough," Moeser agreed, glancing at his watch. "But there's still time during this intermission to visit all the areas he could be. No sign of him yet?"

"Nope. He's definitely not in these groups."

"If he's not out here, then he should still be in the auditorium. Let's take a look." Sidestepping the many small groups clustered in conversation, Moeser navigated and Savage followed closely, mildly self-conscious in the ill-fitting jacket.

"We'll go to the dress circle and grand tier and see what we can see from there," Moeser said, talking as fast as he walked. "Now's a good time. The houselights are up and most of the audience is in the lobby."

They entered the grand tier through a side portal, marched down the right aisle to the front row, and turned to scope the faces of the audience. They also had a topside rear view of the seats below in the orchestra.

"No black guy with a Saint Anthony," Thorn mumbled.

Moeser shrugged. "Might be takin' a leak. We could wait a few more minutes, then try the balcony level and family circle. But from what you tell me, I don't think we'll find your man in those seats." He grimaced and shook his head. "They're kinda like the upper deck at Shea."

"Nah, he wouldn't be up there," Savage sighed. "This guy would have the best seat in the house, and"—his eyes went wide with dawning awareness— "the most private." He gestured toward the private boxes that dotted the auditorium's side walls. "He's in one of those. Bet my life on it."

Moeser's face lit up with an approving smile.

"Can you park me where I can get a clear look at the faces of everyone returning to those boxes?"

"Probably the only place that'll give you that perspective is up on stage," Moeser quipped. "Want me to get you a kimono and some makeup?"

The houselights flashed, calling the audience for the start of Act II. Conversational clusters disassembled, powder rooms emptied, and opening-nighters began moving in orderly chaos back to their seats. Savage, usher-like, rocked on his heels inside the corridor that accessed the private boxes on the auditorium's right side; Bob Moeser was covering those opposite.

As the crowd ambled slowly down the narrow hallway, peeling off at their respective boxes, Savage finally saw Derek Ogden come into view. He was in animated conversation with a younger black man who, by virtue of his easy, fluid strut, Savage figured to be in his mid-thirties. The man was athletically lean and dressed as expensively and impeccably as Ogden, but that was where the similarities ended. Ogden was thinning at the crown, but the younger man was totally bald. Ogden was handsome, if not rakishly so, where the younger man's face looked somehow distorted. As the pair drew closer in the dimly lit corridor, Savage saw that the face was a creation of many surgeries, a mask pulled together to create a whole from fewer than enough parts. The original injuries must have been horrendous; he could have been a survivor of a plane crash.

In muted conversation, the two men breezed past Savage without even glancing in his direction. He got a good closeup of both, and then trailed behind as an usher might, following them to the most forward box. Hovering there momentarily, he overheard only snatches of muffled discussion as the pair settled into their high-priced seats. They were talking about a fat man.

The houselights dimmed. The conversation ceased.

The rookie usher disappeared back up the access corridor as the curtain began its ascent. He needed to contact Abe Hamilton, and he needed one more favor from Bobby Moeser.

# TEN

Taxicabs and gleaming limousines again crowded along Columbus and Amsterdam avenues, siphoning off the departing Lincoln Center crowd. Thorn Savage and Abe Hamilton sat in their idling cab, watching Ogden's unmistakable Bentley inch forward in the Amsterdam Avenue queue.

"Good thing you stayed with the car," Savage said from the backseat. "Might never have figured Ogden getting picked up on the opposite side of the complex."

"This guy'll keep you guessin'," Abe agreed. "We gonna stay with him?"

"Only if his handsome buddy joins him," Savage responded, studying the exiting crowd through binoculars. The Bentley was now front and center of the west exit. "We can pick up on Ogden anytime we want; he's a cinch. But I'm more curious about this new guy. He made the hair on the back of my neck do a jig."

"His face was really that fucked up? You know, like a wax figure?" Abe asked in disbelief.

"Like a Madame Tussaud's work in progress," Savage said. "Guy's had more plastic surgery than Zsa Zsa and Michael Jackson put together, and he's still hideous."

"Whew, baby!"

"But he's obviously a money guy," Savage said. "Carries himself like some kind of prince, for crissake."

Derek Ogden and his companion suddenly appeared within an opening in the milling crowd. Oblivious to the finger-pointing and hushed whispers of those backing away from them, or—Savage chose to believe—brazenly disdainful of the negative attention they were getting, the two men chatted amiably beneath the floodlit marquee of Lincoln Center's west gate.

"Get a good look at this guy," Savage said, passing the field glasses up to Abe.

"Holy jumpin' shit," Abe slowly breathed, adjusting the focus. "Dude's right up from central casting. Reminds me of the damn Scarecrow from *Oz*."

"Title works for me."

"Looks like his skin has been, you know, shrink-wrapped against his head bones—his face and skull—without any cushioning tissue in between." Abe made a gruesome face and passed the glasses back. "Fucker's cadaverous."

Across the street, Derek Ogden was animated. Wagging his index finger, he gesticulated to his seemingly spellbound sidekick. At the conclusion of the brief conversation, Ogden climbed into his waiting ride, which quickly faded into a sea of taillights. The Scarecrow moved off on foot in the direction of upper-level parking.

"Didn't go with Ogden," Savage said. "And didn't try to hail a cab. Must have his own wheels."

"Upper-level parking's got a bunch of different exits," Hamilton murmured in frustration.

"Let's just wait."

Three minutes later Savage's cell phone rang, breaking the tense silence. It was Bob Moeser.

"He's driving a low-slung BMW coupe, silver, with New

York State license plates. Can't make out the number. He's gonna exit on the north end, the down ramp that comes out on West Sixty-fifth. Happy hunting!"

"Thank you, Bobby," Savage murmured into the Nokia. "Owe ya one, buddy."

Abe Hamilton floored it. With the V-8 screaming, the cab peeled rubber as it blew through the light at Sixty-fourth. At Sixty-fifth he hung a right, drove midway down the block, and stopped seventy feet back from the parking garage's north exit.

"There's our boy," Hamilton mumbled as the silver BMW's gleaming snout, headlights aglow, emerged from the exit ramp. "Nice car," he added. "That's an 850 CSI. Man, I'm impressed. You don't see many of them. They were a limited edition—went for about ninety grand. How tight you wanna stay on this guy, Thorn?"

"Close enough to avoid surveillance interruptus." Savage scrawled the BMW's now-visible license plate number across his clipboard, just below "The Donald."

"I'll try. But if this dude decides to run, just remember, he's the guy with the V-12."

As the sleek machine crossed Broadway, Savage radioed its plate number in to Central. The moderate-to-heavy traffic along Central Park West proved no obstacle to the BMW's aggressive driver, who made all the lights as he sailed uptown. The taxi barely kept up. At 110th Street the Scarecrow headed east to Lenox, and then turned north again; at 137th he U-turned and pulled smoothly into the empty parking space directly in front of the Culture Club Lounge. Carrying a dark attaché case, he climbed from the car and quickly disappeared into the street-level nightclub.

"Manhattan South unit requesting information on New York plate DBY-079," the portable crackled.

"Go ahead, Central," Savage responded.

"That plate comes back registered to one Lucy Robinson. Female, DOB 5-7-30, residing at 318 West One-thirteenth Street, New York City, apartment 3B as in Boy. Vehicle should be a '96 BMW two-door, silver in color. You copy?"

"Ten-four, Central. Thanks," Savage acknowledged, jotting the info onto his clipboard. Glancing up, he mused, "Don't look like no Lucy to me."

"Nah," Hamilton said. "Certainly don't look like no Lucy Robinson who's in her seventies. Could you imagine an old lady tooling around in a ride like that?" He adjusted the rear- and sideview mirrors to keep the silver coupe in frame, and shifted in his seat to make reflected eye contact with Savage. "Could it be he's just one of those nefarious types who don't like having their names on any official records?"

"Could be."

"Looks to me like the old *if the ninety-thousand-dollar ride is not registered in your name, then the IRS cannot ask where you got it* ploy."

"Lot of that going around lately," Savage replied, thinking Abe was right on the money.

"Well, what's the game plan?"

"Let's wait him out," Savage said, slouching into a comfortable recline. "I've got a feeling about this guy."

Just after midnight, the Scarecrow, dressed casually in dark shirt and tan pleated slacks, and still carrying the attaché case, emerged from the Culture Club. He triggered a keyless remote that popped the BMW's rear hatch, placed the leather case in the trunk, and closed the lid. He then climbed gracefully into the road machine's cockpit.

"Now, there's an interesting concept," Abe said. "Keeping a change of clothes at your local saloon."

"Methinks our friend is more than just a mere patron of

that fine establishment," Savage murmured as he watched the BMW U-turn and roar past them, speeding uptown on Lenox.

Hamilton reset his mirrors and smoothly resumed the tail. The roadster headed west on 145th and, after a series of lefts and rights, fell into a line of cars slowly working their way through an incredibly crowded 144th between Broadway and Amsterdam. Allowing a three-car cushion, Abe followed.

"Holy shit," Abe exclaimed. "It's like freakin' *Where's Waldo?* Talk about a work-free drug zone."

"Busy night on One-four-four," Savage said. "How many mopes you put in here right now? Two-three hundred?"

"Easy," Abe agreed, inching the cab through the block, maintaining his distance from the BMW. "And they're all either buyers, sellers, or lookouts."

"Or heat."

Abe waved off a bone-skinny but hard-looking black chick who tapped on his window hawking "Coke!" She was one of several on the block who wore bright yellow bandannas. Right next to her, a Dominican kid in an orange cap hawked "Classic coke." They were the street codes for straight and crack cocaine. Other entrepreneurs moved about like flies, darting from car to car, their color-coded caps or scarves denoting variations in purity and price of heroin, grass, ecstasy, ups, and downs.

"Ballsy bastards," Abe drawled with a slight chuckle. "Wonder what the color of the day is for grass?"

"Gotta be green."

At first glance, the bustling activity seemed to be chaos. But every dealer's move was choreographed; there was no lost motion. Each knew exactly what he was doing and where he should be. It was a ballet. It was also a gauntlet for the unsuspecting who inadvertently entered 144th and got caught up in the dope-dealing flea market.

"There's not a single soul in this block that's correct." Savage observed. "I wonder if the Scarecrow's aware of just how close he is to the center of the drug universe?"

"He knows," Abe hissed. "I've been watching him. He ain't bought a thing. He's just here checkin' the herd on the lower forty."

After looping the block and slowly making two more passes through 144th, the BMW headed uptown on Broadway. It passed through Washington Heights and Fort George, and then crossed Dyckman Street. At 204th the coupe made a right turn, traveled two more blocks, and pulled over between Sherman and Post Avenues, where it dimmed its lights. One block back, Abe parked the taxi behind a debris-filled demolition Dumpster set curbside.

"Heavy Dominican up in these parts," Abe said. "These apartments house a lot of well-to-do Hectors that live nice, have nice families, and send their kids to Catholic school. Trouble is, a lot of them are making their tremendous fortunes in sidewalk pharmaceuticals."

"Look at this group," Savage said, nodding toward three darkly dressed men walking abreast, who had suddenly appeared on the set. Simian in their movements, each sporting a derby, they had appeared out of Post Avenue. The man in the middle carried a leather attaché case.

"The Nairobi Trio," Abe murmured.

The three walked directly toward the idling Bimmer. The two flankers had their heads on swivels, and each kept one hand under his jacket.

"Bulges?" Hamilton said.

"Too dark, can't tell for sure," Savage replied, forcing the field glasses against his face and straining his vision.

"But I bet they've got more artillery than we do. Man," he added in a whisper, "that is one tough-looking trio."

As the three neared the back of the BMW, its rear hatch suddenly popped open. With each sideman scanning a different one-eighty, the huge middleman placed his case carefully into the car's trunk. He exchanged it for the one that was inside and slammed the lid. Without a word, the men turned and, walking slowly, disappeared into Post Avenue whence they had come. The three never looked back.

As soon as its trunk lid slammed, the BMW pulled away. It made a quick right on St. Nicholas and a left on Dyckman. Then, winding through the gears like an Indy racer, it headed south on the Harlem River Drive.

"This guy's gonna be a son of a bitch to stay with," Abe called out over the roar of the taxi's engine as they raced full-bore down the Drive's entrance ramp. The BMW's low-mounted, horizontal taillights shone, disappeared, then shone again as the mark threaded itself through a pack of cars half a mile ahead. "If he ever gets an open field, I got a feelin' he's gonna go like a fuck."

"Just do the best you can. We really need to see where he goes."

The taxi's speedometer climbed rapidly as Abe kept his foot nailed to the floor. Savage strained his eyes ahead; the horizontal taillights were fading in the distance. The Bimmer had picked up the pace.

"Why do people drive in groups?" Abe hissed angrily, slowing to work through a traffic cluster before finally breaking free from the pack, and again standing on the gas. "Must be some form of basic human insecurity. You look down the road and there's a group of six or eight or ten cars traveling all in a pack. If one gets a blowout, they're all in fuckin' trouble." Abe's voice was rising; he was losing his patience.

"Not positive, but that could be him in the middle of that next pack . . . same kinda taillights . . . *shit*!" Savage hated the uncertainty. "Let's hope we get lucky."

Horizontal brake lights suddenly flashed from the middle of the pack ahead as a low-slung job made a dangerous move to the right lane. Cutting off two cars, it barely negotiated the exit ramp at Ninety-seventh Street and dropped out of sight. Abe spun his head and gave Savage another "what now?" look.

"Go with him," Savage said.

The taxi moved into the off lane and left the Drive at Ninety-seventh. The silver coupe they'd seen make the hair-raising exit was stopped for a red light at Second Avenue.

"That ain't him." Savage angrily slapped the Plexiglas partition. "Son of a bitch, that ain't him. It's a silver sports job. But it's not the fucking Scarecrow. Look at the plates: Connecticut. Damn it all, we've lost him."

Back to the drawing board, Savage thought, exhaling loudly. "It's a wrap," he said, frowning. "Let's go home."

"What do we know?" Abe asked, turning left onto Second Avenue for the slow mope back to the barn.

"Well, we now know Ogden and the Scarecrow are buddies."

"We also know Scarecrow is up to his bulging eyeballs in the dope trade," Abe offered. "And that he's somehow connected to the Culture Club."

"That place is definitely significant," Savage said, smothering a sneeze. "I'll have Marcus and DeGennaro do a license check on it first thing tomorrow. I'll also have them get a line on Lucy Robinson. But what I'd really like to know is where Scarecrow was taking that satchel."

"Or *who* he was taking it to."

"I'm thinking that circle eventually comes right back to Mr. Derek Ogden."

"I'm thinkin' you're right," Abe said. "What about tomorrow? Same bat time, same bat channel?"

"Wear your slickest threads," Savage said. "Maybe you should have a few cocktails at the Culture Club tomorrow night, give the place an eyeball. You use the flash Caddy; I'll stay close with the cab."

"I knew I was gonna like this assignment. What about Saturday night?"

"I'm not working Saturday night; I'm gonna do a day duty. Gina's birthday, remember?"

"Oh, yeah," Abe moaned, turning to make eye contact. "Right. I'd forgotten."

Savage discerned some disappointment in Abe's voice. "Don't worry," he said. "I'll assign you to work on Saturday night. You'll still make the OT."

"Thanks."

"I ain't doing you no damn favor, Abe," Savage said with a faint laugh. "I'll expect you to spend that night putting everything we've done up to this point down on paper. I know how much you're gonna like that."

"Ouch!"

Savage fought off the irritation of losing the hard-earned tail. Tomorrow was another day, he tried telling himself. But that didn't cut it. He was still angry for making the wrong call on the Drive.

"Let's play Police Jeopardy," he said, attempting to lighten his own mood. "For a hundred dollars and control of the board, what do you think was in that attaché case the Nairobi Trio flipped into Scarecrow's trunk? Dope or money?"

"Money," Abe quickly replied.

"Don't forget to phrase your answer in the form of a question."

"*What is* money?" Abe corrected with feigned excitement.

"You are correct. You get to pick again. What will be your category?"

"I'll take Attaché Cases for two hundred, Alex."

"For two hundred dollars, what was in the attaché case that the Nairobi Trio *removed* from Scarecrow's trunk?"

"What is dope?" Abe asked haltingly.

"Oh, I'm sorry. The answer we were looking for is, 'What is *nothing*?'" Savage's voice became serious. "That attaché case was empty; it was going back for a refill of cash, probably to be picked up tomorrow or maybe the next day, when that trio of goons will no doubt again do their thing." As traffic slowed for a red light at Seventy-ninth, Savage thought out loud, "But I'd be surprised if they do it at the same time and place every night."

"Think they prearrange the drop location by phone?"

"I wonder."

"I wonder where they got them derbies," Abe said. "They were cool."

It got quiet again as they drove the rest of the way back to the office. As Abe parked the taxi up the block from the station house, he broke the silence. "Maybe tomorrow we can pick up on the Scarecrow again."

"Yeah," Savage said. "But if we do, we're gonna have to find a way to stay with him." Suddenly an old idea struck him. "You still have that miniature cordless drill?"

"I do," Abe replied, a knowing look forming on his face. "Why don't I charge its battery and bring it to work with me tomorrow?"

"Good idea."

# ELEVEN

**Friday, April 14, 8:45 A.M.**

When Detective Jack Lindstrom arrived at Manhattan South on Friday morning, he was greeted with a message to contact Harriet Clayberg, the Internal Revenue investigator in Minneapolis he had telephoned on Tuesday. The message specified that he call her at home. Allowing for the two-hour time difference, he could still catch her before she left for work. Harriet was an old personal friend, and one of his better ins with the IRS.

Lindstrom's association with Clayberg had begun twenty years ago when, as a young plainclothesman assigned to a hooker detail in midtown, he campaigned to prevent Harriet's runaway teenage daughter from being totally flushed down the streetwalker/doper toilet. Harriet junior was shacking in a Times Square flopper with a lanky six-six pimp who went by the name of Floyd Blue. She was underwriting Floyd's fancy tall-man threads and custom Eldorado by peddling her charms along Eighth Avenue, which was known at the time as the Minnesota Strip.

Mr. Blue was known to keep his stable of ladies in line with a curious mixture of tender affection and brutal beatings. Ever mindful of the bottom line, he used only body blows or well-placed kicks to discipline—he once broke three of Harriet junior's ribs. He rarely struck his ladies in the face, and never around the mouth. "To do so," he once

said, "would be counterproductive, like smashing a surgeon's hands."

Empathizing with Harriet senior's tearful pleas for his
intervention—she being a fellow Swede whose telephone
voice and presence reminded him of his dear old aunt
Gert—Lindstrom had dogged the pimp, making his
gentleman-of-leisure life miserable with constant arrests
for promoting.

Whenever Lindstrom pulled Blue's car over and took
him into custody, he would impound the gaudy two-tone
purple pimpmobile. Not so much for evidence as for safekeeping. During the subsequent drive to the Manhattan impound yard, he would be sure to pull reverse a few times at
sixty; that was all it usually took to smoke the Eldorado's
delicate gears. When Blue finally managed to get his ride
out of impound, it would invariably need a new transmission, or worse. Jack was never sure whether it was the arrests and lawyer fees or the impoundments and expensive
tranny overhauls that ran Blue off. He suspected it was
screwing with the man's ride that had finally done the trick.

At any rate, Lindstrom eventually succeeded in breaking
the pimp's Svengali hold on Harriet junior. He got the
seventeen-year-old off the Strip and into rehab for the heroin
jones Blue had saddled her with. She now lived outside St.
Paul with her CPA husband and two daughters, and headed
up the local PTA.

"How's my favorite IRS person?" Lindstrom asked genially when Harriet's voice came on the line.

"As if there could possibly be such a thing," Harriet
Clayberg said, chuckling. "Anyway, tomorrow's April fif-
teenth; it's about as busy as it ever gets around here. I'm up
to my fat you-know-what in work."

"You have time to look into that matter I called you
about the other day?"

"I made time."

Lindstrom reached into his desk drawer for a fresh legal pad. "Whaddaya got?"

"For the last six years Derek Ogden has filed federal tax returns listing himself as sole proprietor of Ogden World Galleries. During that period he's reported annual incomes of between seventy-five and one hundred thousand dollars."

"Hmmn? Any other incomes besides World Galleries?"

"That was the only income source he reported to us."

"What about before six years ago?" Lindstrom posed. "Is there anything that could account for this guy's wealth? Did he hit the lotto? Big inheritance? Did he invest in Microsoft before Windows?"

"Before six years ago, he never once filed a tax return—ever. Before six years ago, he doesn't even show on our screen."

"Never had taxes withheld from wages?" Lindstrom asked, incredulous. "Paid into Social Security? FICA? That sort of thing?"

"Never. No record."

"I know," Lindstrom announced, tongue in cheek. "Mr. Derek Ogden must have been working off the books all those years. Scrimping, scrounging, and saving his hard-earned pennies until he amassed this fabulous fortune."

Harriet offered a brief laugh, but then got serious. "Because the kind of income he's reported couldn't possibly support the lifestyle you described to me, and because you asked me to take the extra step, I tapped into several other lines."

"They are?"

"Don't ask. Just sharpen your pencil. We got lots to talk about."

\*     \*     \*

Richie Marcus started looking for numbers as soon as he
steered the silver Taurus off Frederick Douglass Boulevard
into West 113th Street.

"Worked up here in the Two-eight years ago," he said,
glancing momentarily over at Diane DeGennaro, "when I
was in Street Crime. Looked a lot different in those days.
Looked something like a war zone after a freakin' blitz."

"Area looks pretty nice now," Diane said, pointing at a
brownstone-faced tenement with a three-step stoop up
ahead of them on the left. "There's three-eighteen over
there, and there's a big space right in front."

"Most of these places up here were roach traps back in
those days," Marcus said, mounting the curb and scuffing
both left tires as he pulled the Taurus to a bouncing stop in
front of the building. "Those that weren't boarded up or
burned out, that is. And come dark, almost everybody on
the damn street was packin' a piece, and ready to use it. It
was like freakin' Dodge City."

The aroma of fresh enamel greeted them as they entered
the foyer of 318. The building seemed neat and squared
away. The narrow hallway beyond had new tiles on the
floor, fresh paint on the walls, and new light fixtures above.
The handrails on the staircase were also new. A WET PAINT
sign hung from the forest-green newel post. There was a
row of twenty mailboxes set into the hall wall. They too
were shiny and new, with sturdy-looking steel doors. Diane
and Richie studied the names on each one. Apparently there
was no Robinson living in the building. The name Davis
was neatly printed on 3-B's mailbox label.

"Can I help you?" an older man in well-worn coveralls
said, descending the staircase. He carried a paint bucket in
one hand and a brush that had been dipped in forest-green
paint in the other. He was in his late sixties, but Marcus
could tell he was still with it and limber.

"Hello," Marcus said, reaching in his pocket for his shield case. "I'm Detective Marcus, and this is Det—"

"I know you the po-leece," the man interrupted, waving Marcus off with the brush. "I don't need to see no I.D. What can I do for ya?"

"And you are?" Diane asked as the man placed the paint bucket on the floor and laid the wet brush carefully across its top.

"Booker T. Jefferson," the white-haired man replied, wiping his hands with a thinner-soaked rag. "My momma give me that name back in the thirties, before people started calling boys things like Shaq-*eel,* and girls things like Eu-*reen* and Chlo-*reen*." He shook his head.

"You a hired painter?" Marcus asked, fighting off a laugh. "Or do you live here?"

"I'm the super. Been livin' in this here building twenty-five years." He pointed to the first door on the right in the hallway. "That there's my 'partment."

"Could we ask you a few questions, Mr. Jefferson?" Diane asked. "Maybe you can help us out."

"I'd like to help you out. Which way did you come in?" the man said with a straight face. "Just kiddin,' " he quickly added with a wide smile. "Been dyin' to use that line on somebody. Couldn't help myself. Heard it on TV the other night."

"We're looking for a Lucy Robinson," Marcus said. "Supposed to live at this address in Apartment 3-B."

"Used to."

"Moved out?" Marcus said.

"Year or so back. Got sick. Put in some kinda mental institution, or sumpthin. Too bad. Nice lady, kindhearted—do anything for ya."

"Did she own a car?" Diane asked.

"Didn't own no car that I ever knowed about. I don't believe the lady even had her a driver's license. Leastwise, I never saw her drivin' no car."

"How long did she live here?" Diane asked.

"Already here when I got here. Her and that damn bastard nephew what lived with her years ago."

"She had a nephew living with her?" Marcus said.

"What she had was the devil himself livin' with her, man," Booker T. said with disgust. "A real bad boy—straight from hell, you might say. In the time he lived here with his aunt, I used to find dead dogs and cats in the basement. And they wasn't just dead . . . them po' things had been tortured."

"Remember the boy's name?" Marcus asked.

"Luther," the man said, shuffling toward the door marked SUPER. "Come on into my 'partment. It's time for my coffee. I'll tell you anything you wanna know 'bout them people."


When Savage arrived at Manhattan South shortly before five-thirty on Friday evening, Richie Marcus and Vinny Pagano—the nighttime wheelman—were debating what was, and what was not, a "soft hand" in blackjack. Jack Lindstrom was deep into a lengthy report at his typewriter, and Diane DeGennaro was taking notes over the phone. Unger's team was on RDO, and Lakis' crew was somewhere out in the field. There was a we-need-to-talk look on Lindstrom's face. Savage wondered if the look had anything to do with Jack's problems at home—maybe he needed some time off. The whole process of going through a divorce—a divorce that he did not want—was taking its toll on the usually staid and stoic man. He'd been bummed out now for months.

After half-filling his coffee mug with overbrewed dregs from the squad-room pot, Savage motioned Lindstrom into the sergeants' room. He set the coffee in the center of his desktop calendar, eased into his creaky swivel chair, and quickly organized a small stack of reports left on his desk. They concerned a rape-homicide of a thirteen-year-old that Diane DeGennaro had cleared the week before. He would study them later. There was also a plain white envelope, addressed to him in Lieutenant Pete Pezzano's scrawl, tucked into the calendar's corner flap.

"So?" he said genially when Lindstrom ambled into the small office, closing the door behind him. "What keeps Jack here so late on a Friday evening?"

Lindstrom sat down heavily in Jules Unger's chair. In a voice almost completely devoid of emotion or enthusiasm, he said, "Heard back from my source at IRS."

Savage looked for an easy corner on the commanding officer's hermetically sealed envelope—there was none. "And?" he said, sliding the unopened envelope back under the corner flap.

"Apparently Derek Ogden is, and has been for some time, under investigation by the international banking authorities. Seems he's got myriad holdings throughout the Caribbean. My sources are certain he's dumping untold gazillions into a couple of banks in the Bahamas, and at least one, possibly two banks in the Caymans. This is all very hush-hush, and whatever particulars my source can get on those banks will be e-mailed to me at home."

"Don't tell me Ogden's doing all this under his own name?"

" 'Course not. His identity is hidden behind a slew of gobbledegook names and fronts in at least several dozen accounts."

"How's he able to get the banks to go along with that bullshit?"

"In some cases, he owns them."

"As a matter of record?"

"Nope. Sort of a . . . silent partner."

"If your sources know so much, why haven't they jumped this guy? Put him out of business?"

"Supposedly, they had a good case under way. But their only witness, a former manager of one of the Bahamian banks that Ogden's purported to control, turned up DOA. What remained of his shark-nibbled body washed up on one of their first-class resort beaches last year. Dental records made it a positive I.D."

"Bullet holes in his head?"

"Two, as a matter of fact," Lindstrom said with a stunted, sarcastic chuckle. "As a result, the investigation into Ogden's finances is now completely stalled, and will probably have to go back to square one."

"How so?"

"Without that bank manager's testimony, they've got nothing to hang their hats on. No paper trails. No wire transfers of monies. That whole episode has caused all of Ogden's other confederates on the islands—who were probably not gonna talk anyhow—to now develop total amnesia about anything related to him. Plus, Ogden is very well insulated. He's connected with some very powerful Bahamian government officials."

"Your sources are saying that somebody's just walking into these banks and depositing raw cash into all these bogus accounts."

"They're quick to point out that it's hardly an uncommon practice. The sunny Carib is considered the cash Laundromat to the world."

"How is he getting the money onto those islands in the first place?" Savage asked. "Past customs?"

"The million-dollar question. Literally."

"I want you to work on the answer," Savage said, opening the top drawer of his desk. "Take as much time as you need, but be thorough."

Thorn fished the two Yankee ducats from beneath the rubber band–wrapped bundle of nylon cable ties and held them up invitingly. "First-row boxes, right behind the Yankee dugout. They're playing Boston on Mother's Day. You and me?"

"You're on!" Lindstrom said. For the first time in weeks, Thorn saw the hint of a smile come to Jack Lindstrom's face.

Richie Marcus and Diane DeGennaro let themselves into the office just as Lindstrom let himself out.

"Anything on Lucy Robinson?" Savage asked, again fumbling with the sealed envelope and having no luck.

"Confined to some laughing academy upstate," Marcus said. "A real ritzy, private laughing academy, I might add. Ten Gs a month, and all the Depends you can use."

"Scarsdale Oaks," Diane said. "We thought we'd take a ride up there first thing tomorrow morning. I've already talked with the facility's administrator, a guy named Carruthers."

As Abe Hamilton squeezed into the tight office, Savage nodded to Diane and looked to Marcus. "Anything on that club's licensee?"

"State Liquor Authority licensing division lists a Culture Club Lounge at 3707 Lenox. According to their records the licensee is—guess who? Lucy Robinson of 318 West 113th Street, Apartment 3-B."

"Lucy Robinson!" Abe murmured. "That's the same lady who supposedly owns our boy's high-dollar Bimmer."

"One and the same," Savage replied.

"Man," Diane remarked, looking Abe up and down. "You certainly are dressed to the skies tonight. You off to see the wiz, or what?"

"Funny you should ask that," Abe said, shooting Savage an ironic glance. "Actually, I'm off to see his buddy the Scarecrow."

"Where'd you get that awful tie?" Marcus asked Hamilton, shaking his head and clicking his tongue. Then, with a surly edge, "Somebody give it to you for Kwanzaa?"

While Abe and Marcus exchanged nasties, Savage figured out the combination to Petey Pezzano's envelope.

> *Thorn,*
>    *Chief Wilson wants an update on the Ogden*
> *matter ASAP. Needs to know if we've got anything at*
> *all to go on yet. Apparently, PC Johnson and the*
> *mayor are both up his butt about the matter . . .*

By eight o'clock, arriving patrons had already created a double-parking condition outside the Culture Club. Eager to get a jump-start on the weekend, or perhaps to dull the memory of the week past, the Friday-night crowd was already two deep at the bar. With every booth in the lounge nearing capacity, the three hard-as-nails bartenders were pouring serious cocktails with all hands.

Loaded with CDs ranging from Marvin to Dr. Dre, the space-age jukebox stood right at the club's front window, affording a panoramic view of Lenox. It too was doing a land-office business. Several pretty young things busied themselves feeding it fistfuls of cash while gyrating booty to its bass-heavy, funky rhythms. The music, piped through a dozen high-powered speakers, was loud and would get louder as the night progressed.

Beyond the smoke-filled and raucous lounge area, behind the soundproofed reinforced walls and armored door to his immaculate rear office, Luther Robinson ground his perfect teeth together as he digested what he was hearing from Ernie Atkins, the muscle-bound ex-con who managed the day-to-day operations of Robinson's popular nightspot. Atkins had a lot of street connections, and also served as Robinson's liaison with some of Harlem's lesser drug echelons.

"Nobody knows for sure who the contractor is," Atkins said. "Possibly an Italian, more likely a Dominican."

"My guess is it's one of our own kind," Robinson said, scowling.

"In that case, he's probably an import from Detroit or Baltimore, maybe Philly or Newark."

"Yeah, maybe," Robinson hissed, anxiously rocking in his desk chair. "But I need to know who's responsible for putting that fucking contract out in the first goddamned place."

The strong odors of ammonia and bleach, laced with the overpowering scent of full-strength Pine-Sol, filled the lavishly decorated back room.

"Who has the most to gain by your being dead?" Atkins asked, his eyes beginning to water from the chemical assault.

"Who has the most to lose by my staying alive?" Robinson barked back. No sooner had he gotten the words out than his thoughts jumped to Tyrone Boone, the Fat Man who owned Feathers Bar over on St. Nicholas.

Robinson turned and peered through the one-way glass immediately beside his desk. The security window afforded a clear view of almost every face in the place. For close individual looks, he picked up a remote and put the lounge security cameras into sweep mode. He scanned those on the dance floor, studying each face in the desktop monitor. Then he zoomed in on every face at the bar. The Friday-night crowd was building, but he saw nothing out of the ordinary. No new faces. But it was early yet. His thoughts centered again on Tyrone Boone. *That motherfucker!* That fat bastard. He knows he's marked. He's gotta be the one.

"Leave," Robinson snapped, feeling his blood about to boil.

Ernie Atkins about-faced and quickly left the office, pulling the steel door tightly closed behind him. Using the security remote, Robinson engaged the heavy door's solenoid-operated dead bolt.

He dialed the number of Derek Ogden's cell phone. As expected, there was no answer. After the beep, he punched in 666 and hung up. Sitting upright in his chair, long-fingered hands clasped in his lap, Robinson listened to the unremitting whirr of the ceiling-mounted air purifier. It was the only sound in his soundproofed office. The return call came within minutes.

"You caught me just as I was arriving at the Pierre for that Urban League thing," Ogden said directly. "They're giving me some kind of humanitarian award. Talk freely; I'm on a pay phone in the lobby."

"Sorry to trouble you," Robinson replied. "But something important has come up."

"Your numbers told me that. What is it?"

"I've just gotten additional information on that contract we discussed the other day. The one that's supposed to be out on me."

"Oh!" Ogden said, his voice dropping an octave. "And?"

"Word on the street seems to confirm it."

"Any suspects?"

"One," Robinson snarled. "Gotta be the Fat Man."

"Tyrone Boone?"

"Yeah."

There was a brief pause on the line until Ogden finally spoke. "That fits," he said. "It's just come to my attention that since his main man, Spenser Baldwin, so abruptly left us, our rather large associate has been having discreet discussions with some of our Dominican and Asian American friends. Perhaps he wishes to do business directly with them rather than remain in the fold."

"When and how do you want this handled?"

"I think you should pay Mr. Boone a visit, soon, and inquire as to his intentions. I think he should clearly know of our disappointment and concerns. Be ever mindful that as a maverick, he would control fifteen percent. That we simply cannot abide."

"I'll see to it immediately." Luther's voice was a frigid monotone. "But he's sure to lie."

" 'If thou speak'st false, upon the next tree shalt thou hang alive. . . .' *Macbeth*. Do be careful, my boy. The whale is not without teeth."

"I don't intend to stick my head in his mouth."

"Good. Carry on. Oh, by the way, if retirement *is* called for, do we have a suitable replacement who can step right into that slot?"

"I have several candidates from which to choose."

*"Ciao,"* Ogden said.

Robinson rose from his chair and stepped into the private bathroom off his office. He locked eyes with the image that stared back from the medicine cabinet's gleaming mirror. Like two burning coals, his eyes amplified the fuck-the-world sneer stitched permanently into his visage.

Grasping the medicine cabinet top and bottom, Robinson carefully withdrew the entire unit from its snug, pressure-fitted recess in the white-tiled wall. He set the cabinet aside. Reaching into the narrow space behind the wall, he felt a cold hardness through a pliant and protective wrapping. His breaths now came in short rapid currents.

He unwrapped the Glock 19 from the zippered freezer bag and, holding the pistol at high port, ejected the ammo magazine. Ensuring that it was completely full with fifteen rounds, plus one in the chamber, he jammed the clip back into position and holstered the gun at the small of his back.

Robinson again reached into the wall and plucked out a Teflon-blackened French stiletto. Derek had bought him the serious killing tool several years ago on a business trip to Marseilles. He snapped the glint-proof blade open and carefully ran his fingertip along its precision edge. Refolding the weapon, he dropped it into the pocket of his blazer hanging behind the bathroom door, and then turned to the sink and reached for the surgical soft soap. Almost taking off skin, he scrubbed his hands, wrists, and lower forearms. After drying with paper towels, he returned to his desk.

It was only a little after eight. The Fat Man, he knew, would not arrive at Feathers any earlier than ten or any later than eleven. He sat back in intense contemplation, his gaze alternating between the one-way security window and the high-resolution monitor. He would study any new face that appeared in the mingling crowd. He would do that every night from now on, looking for the face that didn't quite belong, the face here on serious business, not for pleasure. Like a pathologist at a microscope, he would search for the deadly germ infiltrating a slide of otherwise benign bacteria.

# TWELVE

The taxicab moved anonymously within the flow of evening traffic as it passed the Culture Club. The sleek BMW was parked directly in front of the lounge, blocked there by a double-parked older-model Grand Marquis. Savage squared 136th and 137th streets, then swung back onto Lenox and pulled into the parking lot of Harlem Hospital Emergency. He eased the cab into a narrow spot beside a parked ambulance, shut off the motor, and reached for the binoculars. Not that he really needed them. The Culture Club was directly across the avenue. From this vantage point he had an unobstructed view of the location and of the mystery man's car.

"Scarecrow One to Scarecrow Two, *K*," he said, holding the portable below window level. "How do you read, and what's your location?"

"You're five by five, Scarecrow One." Abe's response was loud and clear. "I'm in One-four-one, off Lenox."

They could communicate point-to-point on Manhattan South Homicide's private frequency. Their messages would not interfere with those of other police commands, nor would they be monitored by the Communications Division. If assistance of any kind became necessary, a flip of the radio's frequency switch would instantly reconnect them to the rest of the department.

"Our boy's ride is on the set," Savage announced. "But guess what? It's already blocked by a double-parker."

"Friday night's boogie-down time up here," Abe responded with a faint laugh. "And double-parkin's the name of the game. May as well break out the crossword puzzles."

"That's not the worst of it," Savage groaned. "Damn thing's parked directly in front, right outside the joint's huge picture window. I'm thinking it's a bit too close for comfort."

"When the double-parker moves, let's set up anyway and play it by ear," Abe suggested. "Meanwhile, I'll stay out of sight up here. Just ring when ready."

Savage slid the portable under the front seat. They would have to be patient. He hoped the guy who owned the Grand Marquis wasn't a party animal intent on making a night of it. He popped a Wint-O-Green onto his tongue and slumped back into a comfortable slouch. He'd forgotten to bring a crossword.

Harlem soon became tented in darkness. A street lamp on the near corner flickered nervously, then came to life, illuminating the sidewalk below, where brown-skinned girls with tightly braided hair shrieked and giggled as they played at double Dutch. Savage always likened the game to attempting a stroll through a spinning eggbeater. He watched, fascinated, as one by one, sometimes in pairs, the children jumped in and out of the whirling ropes being twirled in machine-like unison by older girls with seemingly tireless arms.

On the opposite corner a fidgety junkie with darting, frightened eyes paced like a caged cat, waiting, no doubt, to make his evening score. He wore a Chicago Bulls cap two sizes too large, and his loose-laced Reeboks had seen better days. He was soon joined by another equally tortured-looking soul. Without exchanging a word, both men slipped quickly into the corner building.

Not far from the double Dutch crowd, a bone-weary part-Dalmatian appeared. Swollen teats hung beneath her protruding ribs. She had a litter waiting somewhere. The starving animal sniffed along the sidewalk, moving with great effort into an alley and beyond Savage's view.

Savage recalled the winter afternoon, many years ago, when he and Abe were young partners in the old Street Crime Unit. Assigned that day to patrol the Twenty-eighth and Thirty-second precincts, they responded to a "shots-fired" run only blocks from here. A man lay on the corner, gut-shot and unconscious, his still form outlined by a rapidly expanding sea of bright red. No time to wait for an ambulance—a severed artery was draining the poor bastard dry—they scooped him up, stuffed him into their unmarked, and raced him here to Harlem Hospital, where precinct detectives took over the investigation. Savage and Abe never did find out if the guy made it. But it had taken hours to scrub away the blood that had congealed in every nook and cranny of the old Plymouth's interior.

On that same day—and only hours later—they responded once again to the same corner, to the very same spot, where yet another shooting had occurred. That victim had been seen arguing with a second man, who had gone to the trunk of a car and produced a .30-06 hunting rifle. The second man fired point-blank, hitting the victim square in the chest. He was DOA before he hit the ground. Savage could still visualize the great volume of flowing blood, steaming in the wintry air. It spread along the sidewalk like an incoming tide, engulfing the dessicated crimson stains spilled on the same spot only hours earlier. So much for the theory of lightning never striking in the same place twice. In Harlem, in those days, it sometimes did.

Savage's recollections were interrupted by sudden activity in front of the Culture Club. Three sharp dressers had exited. They talked and laughed briefly, and then, after slapping hands and bumping knuckles, separated. Two of the men climbed into the Grand Marquis as the third walked away. Savage watched the Mercury pull from its double-parked slot, roll slowly down the avenue, and turn right at the corner.

"Abe . . . you're on. If you don't like the setup, we'll go back to the drawing board, okay?"

It was eight forty-five.

Detective Abe Hamilton hopped from behind the wheel of the Cadillac and stepped quickly around to the car's right rear tire. Crouching, he loosened the inflator valve until he heard air begin to slowly escape. Back behind the wheel, he squared his collar in the rearview and raced off. Moments later the white Sedan deVille "flash" car—with its untraceable Jersey license plates—double-parked in front of the Culture Club, right next to the Scarecrow's silver coupe.

Fashionably dressed for the part, Hamilton blended right into the Harlem street scene. His looks, clothing, and carriage belied the fact that he carried a badge for a living. All that anyone on the street saw—if they even cared to look— was a middle-aged black guy double-parking his ride in front of a Lenox Avenue saloon on a Friday night, a perfectly natural scenario hereabouts.

Abe stepped from the car, locked the door, and strutted into the nightspot with just the right amount of uptown panache. Taking a mental snapshot as he entered, he noted that the place's roomy interior was divided into three general areas. Plushly padded stools, upholstered in medium-gray leather, encircled a large oval bar being tended by three very big men in red vests and matching bow ties. Elevated one step, and further separated from the bar by tubular railings of polished brass, was a dimly lit lounge section with randomly placed cloth-covered four-tops and, along the far wall, a number of comfortable-looking booths also upholstered in medium-gray leather. In the back, beyond the bar and lounge, a mirrored ball spun slowly above an intimate dance floor. Damn thing must be an antique, Abe thought. He hadn't seen a mirrored ball in years. Cigarette and cigar smoke wafted through the air, and grooving music pumped loudly through speakers that seemed to be everywhere. A state-of-the-art jukebox was off the bar, only steps from the entrance alcove. It stood beneath a wide window that looked out on Lenox. Two young things gyrated there, pressing buttons, laughing, and seemingly keeping a watchful eye on outdoor events. Thorn's "too close for comfort" was certainly no exaggeration.

The place was nowhere near capacity, but it was busy. Abe figured the head count to be somewhere around sixty. It was early yet, and the place was sure to get much busier as the night went on. He slipped into an open spot at the bar, mildly concerned how the Cadillac and, more important, the ass end of the Bimmer, were plainly visible to the jukebox sentries.

"Walker Black, rocks," Abe ordered brusquely, and did a quick survey of everyone in the room. No Scarecrow.

Drowning a scoop of ice with the dark amber liquid, the barman poured generously into an oversized old-fashioned glass etched with a silhouette of a dapper gent in top hat and tails. The opposite side of the thick glass bore the name *Culture Club* etched in bold script. After returning the bottle to the top shelf, he dragged Hamilton's twenty across the bar with a huge left paw and set the drink down with his right. From the shape of the man's nose and the condition of his knuckles, Hamilton made the guy as a well-seasoned ex-welterweight and decided *never* to irritate him. The man returned with change. Nine dollars a rap, Abe calculated. Talk about keepin' the fuckin' riffraff out . . . damn good thing the city's payin' for this. Laughing indignantly to himself, the detective hoisted the glass. He looked around some more; still no Scarecrow. The exotic car was here, but the driver was not. Patience, Abraham.

"Hey, sugar. I ain't never seen you here before." She was a snake-hipped honey with big brunette hair and a slightly turned, chipped front tooth. Sidling right up to him, she asked, "Where you been hiding?"

The lady was one of the jukebox gyrators. She was tall and black-eyed, with narrow shoulders and a slinky slim body. Abe could tell—by dint of thirty-some years policing in shithouse commands throughout the city—that she was also a lounge-working pro, and a certifiable hundred-a-day junkie. She was wicked pretty, but another year or two of the Life and she'd be bouncing the bottom, streetwalking the West Thirties, hustling the late-night slimers from Jersey who slip through the Lincoln Tunnel looking for quickie five-dollar blowjobs before heading home to wifey-poo and the kiddies. Abe saw it all, and more, reflected in eyes slowly losing their ability to reflect. He read it too from the long sleeves that came all the way down to tightly buttoned cuffs. The sleeves probably concealed enough track to make Albany. The little girl was all of twenty, maybe twenty-one, but she was just another fading hooker with more stop-and-go miles than his Camaro beater.

"I come by for a taste now and then," Abe replied. "You just ain't been lucky, sweet thing." He winked, smiled, and took another sip of Johnnie Walker.

"Buy me a drink?"

"Sure. . . . Bartender, set me up for another, and see to the lady as well." He peeled another crisp twenty from a

Murphy thick with singles. The gyrator's glintless eyes widened at the sight of the wad. She looked him up and down.

"What is *your* name, big boy?" she said, staring directly into his face. As an aside to the hulking bartender, "Champagne cocktail."

Hamilton flipped the twenty onto the bar and sipped his scotch while thinking of an alias. He decided to stay with the one he'd used years ago as a Narcotics Division undercover.

"Humphreys," he said. "Abe Humphreys. Who're you, sweet thing?"

"Carla Williams. But my friends call me Buzz."

Hamilton immediately bought "Buzz." The little hooker probably had a reputation for dynamite hummers, he quickly concluded. But he didn't buy "Carla Williams" for a second. No hooker ever voluntarily offered her real name.

The next hour saw a steady stream of new arrivals. The bar crowd swelled to three deep, the music went up at least another fifty decibels, and the dance floor came alive. The evening's party was quickly gathering a good head of steam. Abe almost wished it were a night off. He was on his third scotch. His small talk with the hooker continued, and despite the strong drinks, he kept his mind tightly focused on the business at hand.

Finally, like a ghostly apparition emerging from the blackness at the back of the lounge, the unmistakable Scarecrow sauntered into view. His eyes, reflecting the millisecond flashes of light that spun from the ceiling's mirrored ball, gave the appearance of a pair of high-speed cameras shooting a thousand frames a second. They seemed to take in everything while looking at nothing. He skirted the crowded dance floor, acknowledged the bartenders with a nod of his ugly head, and then slid into a corner booth in the lounge area. The Scarecrow sat opposite a hard-looking guy whose massive deltoids and biceps—probably constructed in a prison workout room—were bursting the seams of his intentionally undersized lime-green short-sleeve. Abe could tell by the intensity of their body language and expressions that their conversation was more than idle chitchat. The men were kicking around a heavy.

Despite his severely screwed-up face, Scarecrow was in every other way the picture of big-time success. His clothes were impeccable and expensive, his jewelry was unquestionably custom, and his alligator loafers must have cost at least a grand.

"Whoa, man," Abe whispered conspiratorially, hoping to get Carla to respond. "Look at the face on that dude. Damn, he is hurtin'."

"Hey," Carla whispered back, her eyes bulging. "I'd be careful what you say 'bout that man. He owns this place, and he's one bad motherfucker."

Carla probably figured that if Abe Humphreys was no stranger to the Culture Club, he should have known that. "Oh, so that's him," Abe quickly covered. "Heard about that dude, just never did actually lay my eyes on him." In his most sincere voice, with just the right mix of casual indifference, he asked idly, "What's his name again?"

"Man . . . where you been?" She shot Abe the fish-eye. "That's Luther Robinson."

"Oh, yeah!" Abe acknowledged with an exaggerated grimace, as if embarrassed by faulty recall. "Lucy's nephew."

"Huh? Say what?"

It was clear that Carla didn't know what the hell he was digging for. And there was that goddamned fish-eye again.

With the Scarecrow involved in a deep discussion and, for the moment at least, no gyrating going on at the juke-box, Abe decided it was showtime. He took a studied look at his watch and then, as if late for an appointment, downed the rest of his drink.

"Well, darlin' "—he nodded to Carla—"it's been nice. But I gotta run. Got me some business to see to." He scooped his change from the bar, dealt out another twenty as a showy tip, and moved off through the partying crowd.

"Hey, baby," she called after him, raising her glass in toast. "Thanks for the cocktails. Sure hope I'll see you here tomorrow night." She sipped her drink and headed back to the juke.

"Was that an invite?" he asked, his head cocked and his eyebrow raised.

"Mmm-hmmm!"

"Then I'd have to say it's a very good possibility, sweet thing."

Abe was sure Buzz, AKA Carla Williams, had some reservations about this newcomer, Mr. Humphreys. He also knew it would probably take him another meeting, or two, to adequately cultivate her. She was a heroin-addicted hooker, no question, but he felt certain he'd made a knowledgeable connection inside the Culture Club. A connection that might get him a better look behind Scarecrow's scrim of legitimacy.

The Sedan deVille wasn't going anywhere. It was disabled, down on the right rear, its whitewall Michelin completely flat. Aware that curious eyes might be watching his every move, Abe feigned surprise and anger at the unhappy discovery. He opened the car's trunk and, still shaking his head in mock disbelief, made a show of dragging out the spare—one of those hateful space-saver types—the jack, and the wheel wrench. Crouching in the narrow space between the Cadillac and the BMW, out of sight of jiggling sentries, he set to work.

Ever so faintly, above the sounds of passing traffic, Abe heard the opening bass notes of "My Girl." He hummed along as the classic rode gently on the still evening air, reverberating through the nightclub's brick walls, booming from the high-powered sound system inside. It was their song, his and Tammi's, when they were courting. It would always be their song. Aware suddenly of a nagging libido, triggered possibly by Johnnie Walker, the Temptations, or both, Abe found himself looking forward to the end of the night. He couldn't wait to get home to Cambria Heights, and his always-affectionate wife and lover. Moving quickly, he wrenched off the old tire and wheel and set it aside. About to hang the space-saver, he noticed that "My Girl" had become momentarily louder. The club's front door must have been swung open. He heard the approach of footsteps.

"Appears you have me blocked in." The voice was deep and refined, but the tone was somber and cold. "How much longer are you going to be?"

Still in a squat, hand-tightening the lugs, Abe turned to his left. Starting at the alligator shoes, he raised his glance slowly, past the pleated slacks and tailored blazer, all the way to the hideous waxen face.

*Oh shit!*

"Just a few more minutes, bro'," Abe said. "I'll be outcha way." Jesus H. Christ, he thought, you believe this?

The Scarecrow was close. So close that Abe detected an aroma of . . . something—something antiseptic, something sterile. The man's coal-black eyes, set deeply in his horror-mask of a face, appeared to be glaring, yet at the same time eerily expressionless. Abe felt a shiver course up his spine as he tightened the final wheel nut.

The club's music again became momentarily louder, and

two seconds later the black Schwarzenegger in lime appeared.

"Mr. Robinson," he announced in a Mike Tyson squeak. "You have a phone call. I believe it's . . . the Man."

Scarecrow, now AKA Luther Robinson, offered no reply. His cold eyes locked intently on Abe's, he raised his expensively shod foot and stepped down firmly on the old tire lying in the road. The deflated sidewall compressed easily under his weight. Without a word or a change in demeanor, the Scarecrow wheeled and walked quickly back to the nightclub.

Abe blew out the breath he had inhaled a week ago and prayed that the Man, whoever that was, was a gabber. Hoping too that Carla had by now gyrated herself away from the window, he removed the Dremel Minimite from his jacket pocket and quickly made his play. He drilled two neat holes, each about the diameter of a fine pencil lead, an inch apart, into the base of the BMW's left taillight.

As the white Cadillac disappeared down Lenox, Savage kept the binoculars trained on the entrance to the Culture Club and the Scarecrow's car. He allowed several minutes to elapse. No one entered or left the bar. No one came out to inspect the BMW. He keyed the radio.

"Abe, you okay?"

"Yeah. But he got a bit close there for a minute."

"Saw that. Think you got made?"

"Negative."

"Sure?"

"Positive. He figures I'm just some schmuck who got a flat. But he sure did check me out. He's not at all the trusting type, I can tell you that."

"Where you at?"

"I'm on One-thirty-five, east of Lenox. I'm thinkin' he's

getting ready to leave out of there soon. Let me know when he moves."

"Ten-four. Once he starts rolling, you lay back. I'll hang close. White Sedan deVilles are pretty much generic, I know, but I'd rather he didn't see that one again tonight."

"Ten-four."

"Abe!"

"Yeah?"

"Ya done good."

# THIRTEEN

**Saturday, April 15, 12:05 A.M.**

The light was red. Interminably so, but it made no difference anymore. For Luther Robinson, the night had been a complete waste of time. He'd been uptown to Feathers, traveled all the way downtown in heavy traffic to Sister Lacy's Lounge on Forty-third, and then, on the slim chance that he'd find Tyrone Boone at El Sid's, another of the Fat Man's haunts, jackassed all the way back up to Fort George. There he found out, almost too easily, that Boone was away for the weekend. Robinson wasn't at all sure he was buying into that bit of bullshit. One thing was for certain, word of his inquiries was now sure to find the Fat Man before he did. Keeping one eye on the mirror, he saw that traffic was stacking up behind him at the light.

Robinson's hands, graceful as the Pieta Christ's, almost effeminate—yet strong like the bone-crushing talons of a flying flesh-eater—wrung the leather-wrapped steering wheel as he released a pent-up sigh of frustration.

He wanted the Boone confrontation to go down while he was still in that wonderfully heightened, blissful state. It was always best that way, always far more exciting. To have watched as Boone squirmed beneath the true extent of his wrath would have brought enormous pleasure; after all, they'd always disliked each other intensely. He would have made the slovenly creep beg for his miserable swinish existence. When done toying, he would have dispatched the fat slob to that big sty in the sky where he could wallow for all eternity.

He felt himself coming down. Damn it all! Too much time had elapsed and the delicious stimulating anger quotient was on the ebb. Not that he ever really required much in the way of anger or rage to be capable of extreme violence. Violence, he'd always known, was his passion, a passion ever ready for intercourse—anonymous or otherwise.

Resigning himself to forget the Fat Man for the night, Robinson forced himself into a more placid state. The time of confrontation would eventually come. Boone was living on borrowed time, the target of an implacable avenging angel hellbent on his destruction. But for the moment he was safe, unavailable to meet his inevitable fate.

Robinson powered up the CD player, selected *Piano Greats*, and hummed along to Chopin's "Polonaise No. 6 in A flat." The traffic light finally switched to green.

As the BMW moved along Broadway's gauntlet of neon, Robinson saw that its highly polished body and crystal-clear glass shone like a luminary, reflecting moonlight and the spectrum of colors that struck it from every angle.

The car was meticulous. It had to be. After all, it was just another extension of him. Each day, as soon as he arrived at the club, he would have Atkins get some down-and-outer to rub hard wax on the graceful fenders and scrub the tires and wheels. Every week the cockpit-like interior underwent a complete cleansing. The leather was carefully shampooed with mild disinfectant, and the dashboard recesses were toothbrushed and Q-tipped. His apartment, his car, and his office were antiseptic. Germs were one of the few things that Luther Robinson ever feared.

He was contemptuous of tobacco users—Derek Ogden and those foot-long Cubans notwithstanding—and so no one had ever smoked in his car. He did not permit it; the ashtrays were pristine. The foul breath and nicotine-stained fingers of cigarette smokers nauseated him.

Robinson's eyes flashed again to the rearview. It was an absolute imperative to be aware, at all times, of who, or what, was near him. He was always on guard, but never more so than when he neared home. No one, except Derek, was ever to know where he actually lived.

Everything seemed normal, but tonight he would be extra-vigilant. Who knows, he thought, maybe Boone isn't out of town. Maybe he's gunning for me. His eyes again flashed in the mirror. Wouldn't that be a bitch? I'm out hunting his black ass and can't find him because he's out hunting mine.

He squirmed purposely in the seat, feeling the reassuring bulge of the nine tucked securely in the custom holster at the small of his back. "Yeah. Wouldn't that be a bitch." He burst into raucous laughter at the irony, and then took another studied glance in the rearview.

"Looks like he's given up, Thorn." Abe's voice crackled over the portable.

"You may be right," Savage responded nasally, stifling a sneeze he'd felt coming on for the last five minutes. "He's definitely slowed down. But I'd give a week's pay to know what his game has been."

"Hey. He's been lookin' for somebody, man," Abe said. "No question."

"Yeah, but he looked like he was really pissed—a man with a mission. I wonder who he was looking for, and why?"

"Prob'ly his plastic surgeon."

Scarecrow's coupe seemed to have taken on a new personality. It cruised passively along Broadway past Fort

Tryon Park, no longer running lights or cutting in and out. At Sherman it made a right, followed by another at Dyckman. As it committed to the Harlem River Drive, going downtown, Savage eased off and gave the Scarecrow a bit more slack. He checked his mirror and picked up the headlights of Abe's Caddy following two blocks behind. The three-car caravan was in its second hour.

Earlier tonight, as it wove in and out of heavy traffic, ran lights, and segued sharply through darkened side streets, the high-dollar roadster had been easy to follow. Because it was almost undetectable at close range, the earmarking was rarely discovered by the subject of a tail. But when seen from a distance, the tiny tunnels of white light bleeding through the red tail lens glowed brilliantly, making the fox highly visible to the stalking hounds.

"I think this guy may be calling it a night, Abe," Savage said. "Maybe he'll lead us to his crib."

"Think so? It's not even midnight. That's a bit early for a big boy like this to call it quits on a weekend night. You'd think he'd wanna do a little bouncin'."

Quickly falling outside temperatures, accompanied by a damp wind whipping in off the river, had turned the cab's interior into a mobile meat locker. Savage was still fighting the remnants of the damnable head cold that had lingered from last week, and the last thing he wanted was a relapse settling back in his sinuses. He reached over and switched the cab's heater on.

Downtown traffic was light to moderate, and soon the Harlem River Drive became the FDR Drive. To Savage's left was the East River. Beyond, in the dark distance, he saw the suggestion of the Triborough Bridge. The cable-supporting towers of the sweeping span that fed Queens were outlined in sparkling lamplight. Gracie Mansion came into view, quickly dissolving, as the roadway snaked beneath the riverside knoll on which it stood.

Maintaining fifty-five, Savage's taxi was buffered from the BMW by a Lincoln Town Car and another rattling taxi. Abe, a quarter-mile back in the Cadillac, still brought up the rear. As the loosely knit clutch of cars approached the Seventy-third Street exit, the BMW slowed. With much advance notice, it signaled to get off.

"Looks like he's getting off at Seventy-third, Abe. You believe this? He's actually signaling. . . . What's wrong in this picture?"

Savage's internal alarms wailed like an air-raid siren as he let off the gas and slowed to forty-five.

"We've been on him all night," Abe said. "And never once did he telegraph his intentions. This guy ain't suddenly signaling cause he's worried about the vehicle and traffic laws."

Savage knew the exit at Seventy-third and pondered the unusual variety of options it offered. Scarecrow could go west on Seventy-third toward York, or he could parallel the Drive along the narrow service road to see if anybody got off behind him. If everything was cool, he then still had the option of going west on Seventy-first or jumping right back onto the Drive. No doubt about it, it was a good place to clean up a tail.

"Abe. If he's being slick, this could be a ploy to see if he's being followed."

"Seems like our boy might be paranoid," Abe said. "Which'd surely fit."

"Unhh. Let's lay back as long as we can, and hope he commits before we have to."

The BMW swung off the Drive, ran the service road for several hundred feet, and then pulled over and stopped.

"Ohhh . . ." Savage groaned, the utterance tinged with

grudging respect. This prick is shrewd. . . . "Abe, he's decided on the service road, but the son of a bitch pulled over and stopped."

"You called that shot."

"Got no choice now. I'll get off and take the service road too. I'll have to pass him, then go west on Seven-one. You stay on the Drive so you can pick him up in case he jumps back on."

"Ten-four."

Savage took the exit and passed the idling BMW at fifty. At Seventy-first Street he turned west one avenue and stopped for the light at York. Please stay red, he begged silently, not wanting to be seen sitting at a green.

"Thorn," Abe's voice crackled. "Just rolled past him. He's still sitting on the service road eyeballin' everything that goes by."

"Ten-four. He's gotta make a right and come up behind me, or get right back onto the Drive behind you. In either event I'll—" The headlights of the 850 CSI suddenly appeared in Savage's rearview. "Abe, he's made his decision. He's comin' up behind me."

"Just jumped off at Sixty-third. I'm heading back your way on York."

Savage's only option was to make a right turn on York as the light he'd been sitting at turned green. York was a two-way avenue. If Scarecrow made a left there and headed downtown, Abe could pick him up. If he continued westbound on the one-way of Seventy-first, Savage could quickly U-turn and follow. The question became moot as Robinson's car swung uptown on York, falling in behind Savage's cab at the light at Seventy-second.

"Abe. We're north on York; he's right behind me."

"Ten-four, foot's on the floor," Abe rhymed. "York Avenue's clear, and this old Caddy *flies*. Be back with you in a heartbeat."

"Hey," Savage cautioned. "Don't forget, that little doughnut spare you're riding on ain't designed for speeds over fifty." Despite the admonition, he knew Abe's flounder foot was standing on the Caddy's gas pedal.

On the green Savage continued north at a restrained pace, hoping to buy time for Abe to close the gap. He knew the lights along York would break progressively and they probably wouldn't see another red until Ninety-sixth. The 850 CSI, unhurried, paced Savage's cab as they rolled through the intersection at Seventy-seventh. It made no attempt to pass.

"Gotcha, man," Abe's voice announced. "I just passed Seven-five, and there's no mistaking those little white beacons about two blocks ahead of me. Beyond that I can make out the ass end of your cab. We got him sandwiched."

"Great. As long as you're back in the act, I think I'll pick up the pace. A moping cab can look out of place."

"Ten-four."

As Savage approached the intersection at Eighty-fifth, the roadster behind him suddenly made a sharp left and disappeared into East Eighty-third Street.

"Howdya like that for a Harlem left?" Abe said.

"I'll spin around," Savage replied. "But you'll have to stay on him till I can catch up and leapfrog you."

"I'm on him," Abe bellowed. "But he's maxing all twelve of his cylinders. . . . Jesus, that thing can fly. . . . He's at First Avenue already. He just made a right and headed uptown."

"Shit!" Savage cried. "Don't lose that son of a bitch."

"Thorn," Abe responded seconds later. "I'm north on First, man . . . but the fucker's nowhere in sight. He's gone. He could've ducked into Eighty-fourth or maybe Eighty-

fifth. Who knows? With that fuckin' rocket ship he might
have made it all the way to Eighty-sixth."

"Our only hope now is if he comes back towards me on
the one-way of Eighty-fourth. I'm on York between Eighty-
four and Eighty-five. I'll squat here and wait for him to
come out. If he don't show . . . we're screwed. He's gone."

"I'm looking into Eighty-fourth now, man," Abe answered. "Don't see no traffic in there."

"Shit!"

"I'm gonna roll through," Abe said. "See if he's parked
anywhere along the curbs."

Savage ground his teeth, defeat gnawing at his gut. "I'll
pick him up if you push him out."

Abe's white Cadillac finally appeared at York and
Eighty-fourth. He was shaking his head in wonderment.


Robinson again checked his mirror. All seemed safe.
There was a taxicab ahead, and only one set of headlights
behind. He would soon be home. The apartment was his secret refuge from the madness of the game, his escape from
the liquor-swilling losers at the club and their stinking tobacco smoke. Away from the lowlifes and decadence that he
was better than, and wished no part of. A world that needed
purification, a delousing, an antiseptic bath—and, frequently, even a mercy killing or two.

He steered the high-powered Bimmer into Eighty-third
and checked his mirror. The lone car that had been behind
him on York, though probably benign, followed him onto
Eighty-third as well. Just to be on the safe side, he sped
through the long block and made the right at First Avenue.
Floor-boarding it one block north to Eighty-fourth, he made
another quick right and pulled immediately into the serpen-
tine, shrub-concealed driveway of the Southview, his high-
rise residence. He closed the headlights and went on

hyper-alert, alternating darting glances between his side-view mirror and the security gate ahead that was *so-o-o* slow to lift. These few critical seconds were dangerous. If another car were to pull tightly behind his before the gate completely rose, he would be trapped.

Finally, the sluggish gate was open. Rolling forward, he took one last check in his mirror before the concrete drive began its steep descent. His twisted mouth dropped and his eyes snapped wide at the image conveyed. In disbelief, he spun in his seat to watch a white Cadillac move haltingly through the block. It was a Sedan deVille minus its right rear wheel cover; the tire was one of those space-saver baloney spares.

Robinson's mind swirled into a spiral of anger and fear. The BMW lurched forward awkwardly and then wound down the ramp into the garage levels beneath the thirty-three-story Southview.

*That's the same damn car that went past when I pulled off the Drive.*

He steered sharply into one of his two reserved spots immediately adjacent to the private elevator marked PENT-HOUSE ONLY.

*And it's got to be the same damn barge that just tried stayin' with me on Eighty-third.*

Robinson climbed from the locked BMW and strode the few steps to the penthouse elevator. He looked twice over each shoulder and, sensing his jaw tighten to a molar-busting crush, stabbed the six-digit code into the keypad.

He knew that preemptive attempts on his life were to be expected. There was never any doubt that the day would come when he would be the prey centered in someone else's crosshairs. Within his chosen field, that was simply a fact of life. Enemies and would-be competitors would love to see him dead and buried, removed from the scene, emas-

culating Derek and leaving him bereft of his mighty sword
of justice. Those same enemies would then turn the indus-
try back into the multi-headed chaos that it once was.

The elevator opened. Robinson stepped in, and the door
closed slowly behind him. The penthouse car began its
smooth ascent.

That's the same Caddy that jive motherfucker was fixin'
a flat on. That son of a bitch is working for Boone.

"Goddamn! Goddamn moth-er-fucker!"

# FOURTEEN

Diane DeGennaro thought Harold Carruthers had a strangely big head. She figured it to be about the overall size and shape of a teenage mutant watermelon. The short-legged, roly-poly man had big moon eyes like those of a weary saddle horse and, starting about a millimeter above his right sideburn, the wildest combover she had ever seen. The administrator of Scarsdale Oaks was on the wrong side of fifty and the wrong side of handsome, and his breath wasn't so hot either. She shot a get-a-load-of-this-guy glance at Richie, who kept a straight face. Compared to Carruthers, she thought, handsome Richie looked like a movie star.

"Her long-term memory is phenomenal," Carruthers said, leading them into the wide, arched corridor that led to the facility's west wing. "Like most with her condition, it's absolutely incredible the minute details that she can recall from many years ago. Just don't ask her what she had for breakfast. Or what her name is."

"Alzheimer's?" Marcus asked.

"Yes, that," Carruthers said, "compounded by many years of severe alcohol and drug abuse."

"She in a private room?" Diane asked.

"This is Scarsdale Oaks, Detective," Carruthers replied

haughtily, approaching the door to Suite W-18. "Every one of our residents has a private suite."

"This is a very fancy place," Diane said, stopping Carruthers before he opened the door. "And," she said, gesturing all about her, "I would suppose, a very expensive place. I'd like to know, for the record, what it costs to maintain this patient here?"

"That specific information is privileged," Carruthers responded. "However, let me say that, depending on the individual patient's requirements, it can run upwards of eight to as high as fifteen thousand dollars per month."

Richie Marcus let out a muffled whistle. "Boy, you didn't even blink when you said that."

"We'd like to know who's footing the bill for this particular patient," Diane asked.

"I can't tell you that, Detective," Carruthers said. "Not only would that be against our corporate policy, but it would also violate our patients' expectation of, and right to, privacy."

"We can subpoena that information," Marcus interjected.

"I suppose you could try." Carruthers shrugged. "But this *is* a medical facility—a psychiatric medical facility at that—and absent a subpoena, or the patient's express written approval, we will not divulge such information. However," he offered with a smirk, "if the patient wishes to share that information with you voluntarily, go for it."

Lucy's spotless room was large and nicely appointed. Diane recognized the burnished brass lamps as Stiffle, and the furniture—head and footboard, dresser, and two nightstands—as upper-end Pennsylvania House. The four walls were papered in a country pin dot, and the window valance and side drapes matched the thick Croscill comforter draped across the neatly made full-size bed.

Lucy Robinson was a rail-thin, rawboned old black woman rocking slowly in a non-rocking chair beside a wide picture window. The matte dark flesh on her face looked dried out and leathery, almost mummified. She reminded Diane of a member of her grandmother's collection of apple-head dolls.

Hugging a floppy-eared toy rabbit, the old woman gazed dully in the direction of the nearby Metro-North Railroad station and the surrounding Westchester hills. It was a sunny morning, and everything in the wide, unobstructed panorama seemed to be greening up.

"Lucy is always looking out the window," Carruthers remarked, gazing intently at Diane. "She stares down at that train station for days on end."

"She waitin' for somebody?" Marcus grunted, this morning's voice more slagheap than usual. Diane recognized the hoarseness: he'd been out too late last night and had one too many. They hadn't talked yet today.

Carruthers cleared his throat, ceased his eye contact with Diane, and replied weakly, "Couldn't say."

Oddly evasive of you, Diane thought. "Maybe it's impossible for you to know what's in her head, but don't tell us we're going to need subpoenas to find out if she has visitors. Because that is not privileged information." Diane was not at all sure if she was on firm ground with that statement, but figured she'd wing it.

"She only ever has one visitor," Carruthers revealed reluctantly.

"What's the visitor's name?" she said.

"Don't know," the suddenly nervous man replied.

"Male or female?" Marcus broke in.

"A man," Carruthers said, turning to face Richie.

"Describe him," Diane pressed.

As if he were judging a badminton tournament, the man's head jerked back to look at her. "Black . . . mid-thirties," he stammered. "Bald."

"What else?" Marcus quickly grunted.

"Eerie. His face looks like that of a wax figure that had been left too close to a heat source. Like it was partially melted and runny. Know what I mean?"

Diane made a millisecond's eye contact with Richie.

Carruthers leaned close to the old woman. "Lucy," he said gently, "you have some visitors. They came all the way up from New York City just to see you. Isn't that nice?"

Lucy ceased her rocking and turned to face Diane. She seemed to be analyzing her through eyeballs whose jaundice had moved well beyond yellow to a muddy brown. She did not speak, but when she saw Marcus, she clutched the long-eared toy tightly to her sunken chest.

"Would you like to talk to these nice people, Lucy?" Carruthers said, still in a gentle voice. The old woman shook her head and frowned defensively.

"Is that your baby, Lucy?" Diane asked softly.

"Yeah," Lucy said, "and I won't let you take my baby." Her voice was weak, as old things are weak, but her tone was firm, as casehardened things are firm.

"I'd love to see your baby," Diane wheedled. "What is your baby's name?"

"I won't tell you," Lucy said, turning again to look dully out the window. "You'll take my baby away from me, again."

"Again?" Diane shared a quizzical look with Richie. "I wouldn't take your baby away from you, Lucy," she assured gently.

"He will!" The old woman sneered, nodding toward Marcus. Again she pulled the toy tightly to her chest.

"I won't let that man take your baby," Diane assured her, motioning Marcus away with her hand.

"My baby needs me," the old lady said, clearly talking to the doll. "I'm the only one he has."

"He?" Diane said. "Is your baby a little boy?"

"My sister is so bad to that boy."

"How is she bad?" Diane asked.

"Jest bad. She make him do those terrible things all the time."

"Terrible things? What things, Lucy?"

"It wasn't his fault. She made him do it all the time—for damn money." Lucy resumed her rocking and lovingly kissed the toy rabbit on the face. "My baby used to be so handsome," she said to no one in particular, then angrily turned toward Marcus, who was standing by the door. "Before *he* hurt him."

Diane shared another quick look with Richie. "What happened to his face, Lucy?" she asked, hoping to ride the old woman's stream of consciousness before it evaporated. "How did his face get hurt?"

"He did it!" the old lady snarled, glaring still at Marcus.

"Who is he?" Diane pressed gently.

"Messina." The old woman scowled. "Detective Messina." Lucy hugged the bunny and crossed her broomstick legs. "He'll take my baby away again."

"Lucy. Did Detective Messina come and arrest your baby?"

"Yesterday," Lucy said with a nod.

"Yesterday?" Diane repeated.

The old lady's eyes glazed over. She did not answer.

"Lucy," Diane whispered. "Did Detective Messina hurt your baby?"

"I'm tired now. I want to go to bed."

\*     \*     \*

Just because Savage had been plucked from his usual duties to go run the nighttime streets on a special assignment for Chief of Detectives Wilson did not mean that his many other obligations as a team boss at Manhattan South Homicide went away or were being seen to by others in the interim. They did not, and they were not. The unit's two other sergeants, Unger and Lakis, had more than enough headaches of their own. Though homicide numbers throughout the city had gone down over the last several years, work never stopped coming in.

Without even stopping for lunch, knowing he was going to eat a big dinner that night, Savage used most of the Saturday day tour to catch up on existing case reports that had collected in his IN box during the week. He also had Jack Lindstrom run Luther Robinson's name through BCI. The result came back quickly: NO RECORD.

At one-thirty, Diane DeGennaro returned to the office. She set her bag and a folder full of loose papers on her desk in the squad room, removed her springtime blazer, revealing a 9mm holstered tightly against her narrow waist—just beneath a perfect chest—and entered Savage's cramped office.

"Just got back from Scarsdale," she said.

"Where's Richie?" Savage inquired, surprised not to see Marcus welded to her finely shaped hip.

"Dropped me out front. He's looking for a spot."

Longtime partners, Detectives Diane DeGennaro and Richie Marcus always traveled together. They always slept together, too. Nobody in The Job was supposed to know that, but the sixteen detectives, three sergeants, and one lieutenant commander at Manhattan South Homicide all did.

"How'd it go?" Savage asked.

"Lucy Robinson's a borderline veggie," she began. "No

way is she capable of owning or operating a nightclub, or a high-powered sports car. This guy Luther, who's probably her nephew, is just masking ownership by using her name."

"Jack ran him through BCI this morning," Savage said. "Came back No Record."

"Maybe he's carried under an alias?"

"Maybe. And maybe he's never been collared."

"You ever know anybody on The Job by the name of Messina?" Diane asked. "A detective?"

"Don't sound familiar. Why?"

"Eh." Diane shrugged. "Just something the old lady mumbled."

"Sergeant Savage," Eddie Brodigan interrupted, calling out from the wheel desk. "Pick up twenty-three. It's Abe Hamilton." Savage acknowledged the message, picked up the phone, and nodded to Diane as she left the office.

"Wanted to remind you to wish Gina a happy birthday from me and Tammi," Abe Hamilton said. "She also wants you guys over for dinner as soon as we get back on a regular schedule."

"Okay, and okay," Thorn replied.

"So how does it feel working a day tour?" Abe teased. "Stuck in the office like some jive inside lob."

"Terrible," Savage said. "But I've been catching up on a lot of paper. Which brings us to what you're gonna do tonight, Detective Hamilton. You're gonna catch up on *yours*. It's gonna take some time to put down on paper what you're carrying around inside your head on this Ogden matter. In particular, I want a five on the time you spent inside the Culture Club and any information you got from that little hooker with the bent tooth . . . what was her name?"

"Carla Williams, AKA Buzz."

"Carla Williams, right. She's the one you figure you can pump about Robinson?"

"Uh-huh."

"Think we can put any trust into anything she might tell us?" Savage asked. "Hookers come in pretty low on the honor scale. Just a shade above gypsies and lawyers."

"I get the sense we can," Abe said. "She's really not a bad kid."

"She's a hundred-a-day junkie. Fact is, with her being a hooker *and* a junkie, I'm surprised that she hangs out in a place as classy as the Culture Club. Or that they even allow her to."

"She can still trade on her personality and appearance. My guess is Carla Williams hangs out in better places hoping to snag her a man. I'm guessin' she realizes her only hope in life is to contract a husband before she contracts the fucking plague."

"Pathetic, hah?" Savage exhaled hard. "You gonna be in at six?"

"Yeah, but first I gotta stop in at the Seven-five Squad and pick up my paycheck. Officially—because of administrative lag time on transfers—I'm still assigned there. It'll probably start comin' to Manhattan South next pay period."

"Don't you use direct deposit? Department's offered that option for years."

"Don't believe in it. Still like getting a check put in my sweaty little hand."

"You probably won't be able to cash it," Savage said. "Banks'll be closed till Monday. You gonna need some bucks to tide you over?"

"No. Believe it or not, I'm in good shape this week," Abe replied. "Tammi'll deposit it on Monday."

"Okay. When you get to the office, write up your fives and call it a night. Tomorrow we'll do the Culture Club and see if we can't reconnect with Robinson. If he does his rounds, we'll be there with him. Also, it'd be nice if he leads us back to his crib."

"Ten-four," Abe responded. "But if I knock out my paper early enough, I just might make a stop up at the Culture Club. I'd like to make another inside observation. That Carla broad practically begged me to show tonight."

"Marcus might start a rumor that you've got somethin' goin' uptown with Carla baby," Savage teased. "You wouldn't want that gettin' around the office, would you? Just think what kind of field day the Swami could have with that."

"Hey! Fuck him *and* the arthritic horses he throws his money away on," Abe said, bristling. "You know, I used to think the Swami was a prick."

"Then what?"

"I remembered that a prick has a head on it."

Savage threw his head back and roared. "He's certainly a bird of rare plumage. But don't you guys ever get tired of the ranking game? Shit's been goin' on for years, for crissakes."

"Nah," Abe drawled. "We just like to beat up on each other. But," he added quickly, "what about tonight? After all, this little broad invited me up there. I'd hate to miss an invitation to pick some brain."

"Without backup?" Savage said, hedging. "The chief'd have my ass if anything went wrong."

"What could go wrong?" Abe groaned persuasively. "Hell, I'm a big boy. I've got the right to stop for a cocktail on the way home. Why not at the Culture Club?"

"I refer you to Murphy's Law."

"It's important I get inside that place tonight," Abe pressed. "Shit's goin' down in there, and Carla baby is tuned in. Hell, *you* can't do anything anyway. You show that Rob Roy mug of yours around there, and everything's gonna' grind to a halt."

"You sayin' I look like a cop?" Savage asked, answering his own question with a faint laugh.

"Besides being white, you got every damn thing but a numbered cap device screwed into your forehead." Abe snickered. "If you showed up, it'd be just like in the old westerns when the sheriff pushes through the swingin' doors—the piano goes off key, and everybody in the joint goes mute."

Savage pondered in silence.

Abe continued to press. "Hey, I'll just go and have a few tastes and a little chitchat with Carla. I'll be like a fly on the wall; nobody'll even know, or care, that I'm there."

"Awright," Thorn agreed reluctantly. "Observations only. I don't want you gettin' involved in any bullshit."


Diane dialed the number and listened to the phone on the other end ring eight times before it was picked up. Several long seconds elapsed before a weak voice finally breathed, "Hello." The voice did not sound healthy.

"Sam Messina?" Diane asked.

"This is Sam."

"Sam, this is Detective Diane DeGennaro, NYPD."

"Yeah?"

"Are you the Sam Messina that used to be on The Job? Worked up in the Three-two Squad back in the seventies?"

"Uh-huh. Got out in '85 on the Heart Bill. Got emphysema now, too. How'd you find me?"

"You do get a pension check."

"Unh," the man grunted, understanding. "What can I do for ya?"

"Sam, do you remember locking up a guy named Robinson?"

"When?"

"Whenever."

"I worked in the Three-two, detective. Smack-dab in the middle of Harlem." The man stopped to take several staggered gasping breaths. "There was an awful lot of Robinsons up there," he went on. "I think the only one I probably never collared was Jackie. But all he did was steal bases. Besides, he was long dead before I got there."

"We came across some information that a *Luther* Robinson may have been arrested by a Detective Messina once upon a time."

"Where'd you say you worked?"

"I'm a First-grader in Manhattan South Homicide."

"Homicide!" Messina wheezed. "Figures."

"You remember a Luther Robinson, Sam?"

"If it's the same one I'm thinkin' of, he was a twelve-year-old kid. Tried escaping from me in the Family Court Building down on Lafayette. Revolving doors in the lobby were clogged with people coming and going, so he tried for one of the plate glass side doors. Hit it at full gallop thinkin' it would swing open. It was locked. Took his whole friggin' face off."

"Certainly sounds like our boy. Remember what he was charged with?"

"Murder. Double homicide."

"Whoa."

"Killed his own mother. Blew her and her pimp away while they slept in her bed."

"Jesus!"

"Mother was a real piece of shit. Alcoholic hooker. Worked right out of her own apartment over on Eighth Avenue. Her and her pimp used to force the kid to participate in kinky three-ways whenever some john with those little-boy 'proclivities' was ready to duke up the bread. Apparently, that night the kid balked and the john walked. The sloshed mother and the bully pimp beat the living shit out of him. Guess the kid had had enough. When they finally fell asleep, he found a piece among the pimp's pile of clothes. He forthwith put them both to sleep, permanently."

"Oh, man," Diane drawled in disbelieving belief. Now, she thought, she'd heard it all. "We're working a case where we desperately need a comparison of Luther Robinson's fingerprints, but we've been unable to locate any records that could even give us this guy's DOB. If you did in fact collar him, we can't find any of those arrest records, fingerprints, nothing."

"And you won't."

"How's that?" Diane asked.

"He was a juvenile; twelve, maybe thirteen. Whole case was processed through the Family Court. You must know what that was like before they started treatin' kids as adults in capital crimes. Talk about revolving doors . . ."

"He committed murder," Diane said. "Surely he was fingerprinted."

"Printed him myself," Messina wheezed deeply, as if he were becoming excited. "But it don't make no nevermind. The print cards, court documents, arrest records, the case disposition . . . everything got sealed by the Family Court. You'll never see any of it."

"What did the courts do to him?"

"Not a goddamned thing. Released him to the custody of some aunt. His mother's sister—Lucy, I think her name was. I remember that because of the similarities between their names—Lucy, Luther. Hardworkin' decent sort, though. Not at all like the kid's fucked-up mother. It was at his aunt's place where I eventually found the kid hiding when I first locked him up. His aunt Lucy tried to cover for him, but I found him in a bedroom closet under a mound of quilts. He told me later it was his aunt Lucy's place he was heading for when he made his, shall we say, ill-fated escape attempt. She was the only one ever watched out for him."

"What a horror story," Diane breathed.

"There's eight million stories in the naked city," Messina announced callously. "But don't go frettin' too much; the kid was bad. Complete sociopath."

"And it's your belief that this . . . 'Cadillac Man,' as you refer to him, never saw you—or that very distinctive automobile you drive—entering your building's garage?" Derek Ogden was slouched comfortably at his desk at Ogden World Galleries, half-smoked third cigar of the day in hand.

"That's what I'm telling you," Luther Robinson replied. "He did not see me."

"How can you be so certain?" Ogden said, unconvinced. He swiveled his chair in a one-eighty to eye the soupy afternoon from his office window. It was only three p.m., but somebody had shut off the outside lights. It was getting dark. New York was about to get wet.

"You know how my building's situated, right on the corner of Third Avenue, with its circular drive and portico entrance on the Eighty-fourth Street side."

"Yes, I know."

"When this Cadillac-driving motherfucker decided to swing into Eighty-fourth, it was only a guess on his part. He was only groping. He didn't know what the hell had become of me and my ride. I was *gone,* and he had no idea where the hell I'd gone to. He was a full half-block behind me when I turned up Third Avenue. By the time he got to Third, I was nowhere in fucking sight. He never saw me make the turn into Eighty-fourth. For all he knew, I might have been beamed up by goddamned Martians."

"But when he did turn into Eighty-fourth, didn't he see your car in the portico drive?"

"The only car in that drive, under the portico, was some big-ass stretch limo with a gaggle of old white rich bitches getting out of it. My ride was nowhere in sight. In fact, I was already behind his dumb ass, concealed in the garage cut that splits off right at the beginning of the portico drive. He couldn't see me, but I could sure see him. He just continued through the block, gawking all the cars parked along the curbs."

"I know what you're saying about that basement driveway. It gets lost behind all that thick landscaping," Ogden murmured in thoughtful agreement. "I've missed it myself."

"You almost have to be a resident of my building to know that cut is there. It was probably designed that way deliberately . . . security reasons . . . aesthetics."

"Hmm."

"He figured he lost me. What else could he have thought?"

"We shan't speculate on that," Ogden said. "But I sincerely hope that you're correct." He brought the cigar to his mouth and took a shallow puff.

"I'm correct," Robinson said forcefully. "Besides, if I deal with this motherfucker appropriately, the question becomes moot. Does it not?"

Pursing his lips, Ogden slowly released a narrow stream of smoke, and then answered, "True enough. But we don't even know who this man is. Or, for that matter, from whence he came."

"Oh, I know from whence he came." Robinson spat out the words. "He was sent by our obese associate up at Feathers."

"Ooh!" Ogden stretched the syllable. "There's an undeniable edge to your voice, my boy."

"And well there should be."

"Let's talk about something else for a minute," Ogden said. "You need to calm down. Emotions must always be kept under strict management." He reached for a heavy silver tray that had once belonged to Diamond Jim Brady. He recalled having paid three thousand for it at auction. He also remembered the early days, when he didn't make that much in a whole year. Now he could spend that much on mere trinkets without even thinking about it. He rotated the Havana's tip along the tray's ornately etched rim, neatly rolling away the gathered ash.

"That island auction is coming up," he said in a calming tone. "I'll have to be heading south. Are you going to have some bundles ready to go?"

"A lot of bundles."

"Wonderful."

"I'm being lined up for the kill," Robinson said, his voice rising. "There's no doubt that this guy's a contract player."

"Suppose not. Let us suppose that he is his own entity. A new player."

"I'll just have to find that out, now won't I?" Robinson snarled.

Ogden puffed and paused. Then, in his most paternal tone, he cautioned, "At this point, do you really think you can? If you don't know who he is, you will have great difficulty finding him, no? In the past we've always known where to locate the people we needed to deal with. May I remind you, my son, we don't have that luxury in this instance."

"Then I will wait for him to find me. I will be patient. He will come again. When that happens, I will be prepared."

As droplets began to pelt the diamond-shaped panes of the Madison Avenue window, Ogden's gaze slowly panned his collection of richly framed oils, which hung from the vast office's rosewood-paneled walls. His favorite, a Rembrandt copy, *The Slaughtered Ox,* hung directly opposite his desk. It was an exceptional example of representational art; the original hung in the National Gallery in Washington D.C. After many seconds of consideration, he took another shallow puff of the Cuban and admonished his surrogate son with carefully chosen words.

"It is imperative not to have any unfortunate incidents occur at the club. That place has always maintained a low profile. It has the reputation of being a trouble-free spot and, as such, receives little attention from the local police precinct and—to the best of our knowledge—none from NYPD Narcotics or the DEA. Which in turn gives us a sound base of operations. I do not want that image adversely affected."

"Nothing will happen there. Or even close to there. I assure you." The icy smoothness of Robinson's emotionless tenor was back.

Derek Ogden smiled. "Then I will leave the entire matter in your hands. Do what you think is right."

"I know what's right. *He's a walk-in' mo-ther-fuck-in' dead man.*"

Except for Detectives Carmen Delgado and Herbie Shaw from Team Two, who were working a four-to-twelve, and Police Officer Vinnic Pagano, the nighttime wheelman, all was quiet in the Manhattan South office when Abe Hamilton arrived there a little after six. Everybody else in the unit was on RDO or had worked a day tour.

Carmen Delgado had revealed the secret of the office's temperamental Newco two-pot coffeemaker—jiggle the

ON/OFF switch and use only the right-hand burner—and Abe brewed himself four cups of high-test open-eye. Using Jack Lindstrom's clean desk and faithfully maintained Swintec word processor, he spent the next three hours inhaling caffeine and typing DD-5s. The confidential case file on Derek Ogden and Luther Robinson was rapidly expanding. He also opened a monthly expense report to recoup his out-of-pocket over-the-bar expenses, which he calculated to already be fifty-eight dollars.

# FIFTEEN

"Sergeant Savage. So wonderful to see you!" Freddie Forlini greeted him with a wide grin. "Allow me to show you to the table we've prepared just for you and your lovely lady." Freddie eyed Gina up and down, bowed, and then led them through the restaurant's crowded, and somewhat noisy, front dining room to the smaller, quieter dining room in the back. The room was a light pink. Alabaster cherubs posed in niches set into the walls every few feet.

Located at 93 Baxter Street, just below Canal and only a block from the 100 Centre Street courthouse, Forlini's was Thorn's favorite Italian restaurant. He had been coming here since he was a rookie. Freddie was one of the three brothers who owned and ran the place.

Freddie sat them at an intimate semicircular booth in a remote corner of the dimly lit room. After carefully placing gilt-edged menus on either side of a single red rose that lay in the center of the linen-covered table, he turned to a retinue of black-vested busboys and waiters. "This is Sergeant Savage," he said, lifting bushy brows over alert, deep-set dark browns. "He is a very special friend. And this is a very special evening for him and his lovely lady." The staff nodded deferentially. "Enjoy your dinners, sir and lovely madam."

"Would sir and madam care for some wine or a cocktail before ordering?" the headwaiter asked.

"Yes, Rico," Thorn answered. "We'd like a bottle of lightly chilled Bardolino."

Rico acknowledged with a nod and a murmured *"Excellente."*

As the waiter moved off with swift strides, Savage placed a small gift-wrapped package and accompanying card beside the long-stemmed flower.

"Oh, Thorn." Slowly, sensuously, Gina lifted the rose to her face and inhaled the delicate fragrance before removing Thorn's card from the unsealed envelope.

> *Where would I be without you in my life?*
> *Happy Birthday, darling.*
> *All my love . . . always.*
> > *Thorn*

He prayed that Gina wouldn't think the handwritten sentiment too corny, or even worse, contrived. He'd always worried about things like that. But he meant every word. Throughout his life he'd known he was a closet romantic. Even in the early days of his marriage to Joanne, he'd felt those thoughts but was always too self-conscious to say or scrawl them. His usual card sign-off had always been simply, *Love, Thorn.* He wished he had been better able to express himself in those days; Joanne would have liked that.

His life was coming together once more. He'd been given another shot, with another good woman, and he wasn't going to blow it. He would say what was in his heart, no matter what.

Gina peeled away the bow and wrapping from the small package. Her face lit with delight at the sight of the golden bracelet inside. Eagerly, she removed it from the box and slipped it onto her wrist. "I love it," she said, bubbling. She held out her arm and Thorn set the clasp.

Almost unnoticed, Rico returned to the table, poured the ruby-red wine into two crystal wineglasses, and quietly retreated.

Gina hunched her shoulders and leaned forward, revealing her cleavage. "You know, don't you, that I can't wait to get you back to your apartment. You're not going to forget *this* night, Sergeant Savage."

Thorn didn't know she was capable of such bold seduction, but he wasn't complaining. "I love you," he whispered, saluting her with his glass. She raised her wine; their glasses clinked.

The dinner was Forlini's at its best. The pasta and veal were prepared to perfection. The dry red was delicious and heady. The spell was broken only momentarily when Hugo Forlini sent over complimentary after-dinner snifters of Grand Marnier.

Dessert would come later.

By ten-thirty Abe had finished typing the last of the DD-5s. It was shortly after eleven when he parked the white Cadillac on Lenox and dropped a fresh twenty on the Culture Club's mahogany.

The soft jazz of Sade—unquestionably his and Tammi's favorite female vocalist—filtered through the lounge's sound system. Abe thought it just a few decibels too loud. Luther Robinson's roadster was parked in its usual spot, right out front, but the gargoyle himself was nowhere in sight. And so far Carla Williams was not among the bumpers and grinders force-feeding crisp U.S. currency into the money-gobbling music machine by the front window. With his first drink in hand, Abe circulated slowly through the large, loud, and crowded room. Carla was not on the dance floor, nor was she at one of the many candlelit tables or perimeter booths. For a weekend night, it was early yet. She was, he concluded, still out making hay while the sun didn't shine. Like him, she was getting in a little Saturday night OT.

Abe looped the bar's oval and captured an end stool offering a broad view of the club's interior. He watched the boogeying crowd, kept an eye on the front door for Carla's arrival, and sipped the Walker Black double. When the smooth sound of Sade ended, some raucous hip-hop horseshit came on. He rolled his eyes.

Luther Robinson spun casually in his office chair and peered through the one-way security window next to his desk. From the lounge side, the glass panel appeared as one of many randomly placed mirrors decorating the Culture Club's back wall.

"He's here!" Robinson bellowed, both hands slamming the polished desktop. "That motherfucker's here!" Cadillac Man's presence at the bar, and his brazen nonchalance, stung Robinson like root canal without Novocaine.

"Where?" Tyrone Boone asked. "Let me see." The obese man waddled to the glass and stared out at the lounge crowd. "Which one?"

"The jive-ass turkey in the cheap double-breasted pinstripe. The one sitting at the far end." Robinson worked the security camera's controls and brought the man into tight focus on his monitor.

"I don't know that man. I ain't never seen that man before." Pleading, Tyrone Boone continued. "Mr. Robinson, I swear to you. I ain't never put out no contract on you, man. You gotta believe me."

"Then who *is* that motherfucker out there?"

"I don't know. God be my judge . . . Mr. Robinson, I just don't know." The Fat Man was in a borderline panic.

"Curious . . . I just happen to spot him in my place twenty minutes after you have the balls to come in here, kissin' my ass. You know you're in big-time fuckin' trouble, don't you, motherfucker. You know you're on my list." Fighting to govern escalating anger and to keep from slipping too soon past his point of no return, Robinson was staring holes into Boone.

"I know you wuz lookin' for me," Boone stammered, nervous sweat boiling at his rubbery brow. "But what you heard 'bout me tryin' to deal direct with the Dominicans is all wrong. It jest ain't so. They came to me, tryin' to sell me on that idea, and I flat turned them down, man."

Luther held Boone in his ice-cold glare.

"Look, I knows what happens to people who fuck around on you, Luther. I'm not a stupid man. I don't wanna die."

"Hmm."

"Mr. Robinson, I came here tonight to plead for my life. I knew if you found me first, I wouldn't stand a damn prayer. I done nuthin' wrong, Mr. Robinson. Nuthin'."

"How in the hell do I know, for *sure*, that you're loyal, and that I can trust you to remain in my organization?" Robinson snarled the words at the groveling man.

"Anything, Mr. Robinson, anything at all. I'll do anything to regain your trust."

His manicured fingertips steepled together, thumbs and forefingers cradling his bony chin, Luther leaned forward in his chair. He turned away from Boone and stared out through the clandestine viewing window in brooding contemplation.

"Perhaps we can work out a way for you to redeem yourself, Mr. Boone."

\* \* \*

Fifty watts, the lowest setting of the three-way bulb, oozed yellow through the pleated shade of the simple night-stand lamp. The dim glow produced soft variations and slender shadows at raised and curled wallpaper seams all about the room. The mellow sound of Coleman Hawkins carried lightly from the living room's Bose speakers. Savage had his back against the headboard, basking in the *après-amour.*

Sitting beside him, Gina was naked. Her narrow shoulders were lost in the deep plush of pillows propped pell-mell against the headboard. Her brunette hair was in mild disarray.

"Do you realize that this . . . is the first time . . . we're spending the entire night together in your apartment?" she asked, mildly out of breath.

His head now resting against Gina's pile of pillows, his legs tangled in the wildly rumpled sheets, Thorn was tripping in a twilight zone of extreme contentment. He made no attempt to answer her question, lazily choosing instead to interpret it as a statement.

Gina's gentle hands rubbed his bare chest. "Thorn," she prodded softly, just above a whisper, "we need to finalize a honeymoon destination with the travel agent."

"Uh-huh," he mumbled, wishing the talk could come later but knowing he'd have to answer that one. "I thought we were leaving that choice up to you."

"I know," she said. "But I'm having trouble deciding. Help me out. Where would you like to go? What would you like to see?"

"You," he murmured. "When I wake up in the morning, and when I go to sleep at night. It won't make much difference to me if we're on the *QE 2* or a rowboat in Central Park. Anywhere you are is fine."

"Bermuda," Gina sighed. "How about Bermuda? I've

heard it's so romantic. And they have really good weather in June."

Thorn looked up to see her awaiting his response. "Bermuda's great," he agreed. "The Job owes me plenty of days, so getting the time off won't be a problem."

Gina smiled contentedly. "You always going to be that easy?"

Kissing her on the shoulder, he said, "Let's plan Bermuda."

"Great!" She turned and hugged him. "I can't wait." Energized, she hopped from the bed. "I'd like a cup of tea. Would you like some? I'll put the kettle on."

"This late?" Thorn asked, looking at the windup on his nightstand. It was almost twelve-thirty.

"Why not?" she said, searching through their clothing, which had been hastily piled on the side chair.

He studied her lean solid body as she pushed her arms into his Brooks Brothers pinstripe. She did a middle button and rolled up the long sleeves. The shirt completely covered her petite, size-six frame. What an incredibly sexy sight, he thought. Not only is she smart, but she's gorgeous. Did I luck out or what?

"Well?"

"Well, what?" he mumbled, his mind preoccupied with his vision of her.

"Tea, do you want some tea?"

"I'll pass on the tea, sweetie," he said, untangling his legs from the sheets and stealing another one of her pillows to put between his back and the old mahogany headboard. "Fact is, I don't believe I even have any."

"You do. I brought some up two weeks ago. It's in the pantry next to the fridge."

He watched Gina glide barefoot through the living room and fill the kettle at the kitchen sink. What a picture, he thought, knowing it was her looks that had originally attracted him. He also knew it was her steady style, her imperturbable grace, and her evenhanded approach to the whole world that kept him attracted—more and more as time went by. Gina was a hell of a woman. In many ways she and Maureen—and Joanne before her—were very much alike. It was that thread of consistency he seemed to seek in women. All were stand-up and solid, totally trustworthy and loyal. In some ways, however, they differed. Where Joanne could often be rigid and inflexible, Gina was more pliant, agreeable, and accommodating, without being subservient. Where Maureen could frost a room over if she disliked its occupants, to the point where everyone in it needed fur coats and mukluks, Gina was diplomatic and tactful. What a woman, he thought.

"Ray. There you are. How's my little bud?" The crusty gray cat, just in from midnight rounds, weaved back and forth between Gina's bare legs, looking up and purring. "He likes me, Thorn. He does." Ray rubbed his scarred and whiskered head firmly against her naked ankles.

"Sure he does. He's no fool," Thorn answered, swinging his legs over and sitting naked at the edge of his bed. "Besides, he's got the best view in the house."

Abe was on his second scotch, and somehow the music that had been so loud when he came in now seemed mellow and at just the right volume. The annoying hip-hop had finally ended, and the large room now echoed with some good down-and-dirty B. B. King. Swiveling the stool and peering through the crowd, he caught a glimpse of a redesigned Carla Williams as she breezed through the Culture Club's front door.

He almost didn't recognize her. Gone was the shoulder-length mane of brunette curls. Tonight's do was deep blond

with frosted tips—very short. She had looked better with
the big hair. Abe stood up and concentrated his stare, making himself more visible as Carla exchanged animated
greetings with a cluster of cocktail-sipping pals. It worked.
She looked in his direction for just an instant and they made
eye contact. Carla acknowledged him with a friendly wave
but stayed among the group for several minutes, chatting
and giggling. Finally she broke away, sauntering provoca-
tively to Abe's corner of the bar.

"Well, how you doin', big boy? Fixed any flat tires
lately?" Carla's cockeyed front tooth was prominent as she
teased with a broad smile.

"Yeah, wasn't that a bitch," Abe said, putting a laugh in
his voice. "That was the first damn flat tire I've had in
years," he lied. "Ruined a real fine shirt fixin' it, too."

Carla batted heavily made-up eyes, and then, with mild
indignation, said, "Well . . . how long you gonna let me
stand here without a damn drink?"

"Damn," he said, "you are one forward lady, ain't you?"

"No, I'm one thirsty lady," she countered, still grinning.

Abe motioned and the big bartender nodded. Seconds
later, a champagne cocktail—whatever the hell that was—
was set before Carla.

"You seem to know a lot of folks in here," Abe said casually. "You must be comin' to this place a whole lot."

"Baby, I know every damn fool in this place, but right
now I'd really like to get to know you . . . Abe
Humphreys."

"Well . . . Carla Williams, you remembered my name.
I'm flattered as all hell." He raised his drink in toast.

"Ooh, and I'm flattered too, you remembered mine."
The good-natured kid struck a haughty pose and patted her
goldilocks. "Well, Mr. Humphreys, how you likin' my new
look?"

The fat man, they knew, was the key. Unlike the other perp, whose tall and slender description could easily fit many black males throughout the Upper West Side neighborhoods, the fat man would stand out from blocks away. If the two perps were locals, he was the one they had the best chance of finding. Fat men—morbidly obese fat men— were not that common uptown. If someone happened to be an obese man on a Manhattan North street, then he would eventually be leaning on a wall surrounded by plainclothes cops.

At four o'clock Saturday morning, when the streets finally became all but deserted, Savage excused DeGennaro, Marcus, and Lindstrom. Over their strong objections, he sent them all home for rest and recuperation. They were to report back to the Manhattan South Homicide office at three p.m. and await orders. He raced home, showered and changed, put down fresh food and water for Ray, and went right back to the Manhattan North offices, determined to review every report turned in thus far. By one o'clock he was bleary-eyed.

"We're comin' up totally dry, Thornton," Pete Pezzano said with a perplexed look, and then added a softener. "But you know that can sometimes happen in an investigation. Just when you think you've exhausted your every option, something pops up, and you're on your way again. Right?"

Savage gave him a halfhearted smile. He already knew that a little divine intervention wouldn't hurt.

"We can hope that somebody'll dime these bastards out," Pezzano mused. "One of them is eventually gonna piss off a girlfriend, or somebody else, who'll run right to a phone and give the sons of bitches up."

Savage grimaced and nodded in dispirited agreement. He reached in his pocket for a Wint-O-Green. He was fresh out.

Pezzano kept on talking. "We don't get any medals for great detective work when that happens, but we'll take it every time. Right, Thornton?"

"Right."

"Hey," Pezzano said, glancing at his watch, "it's way past lunch time. Let's go get a bite." The size-48 lieutenant stood, and with forced enthusiasm intended to elevate Savage's somber mood, suggested, "We'll go over to Mama Joy's for a sandwich. Whaddaya say?"

"You go, Pete. Howie Bender's bringing witness number nine back in again. Nine and six are the only two of the ten I haven't personally interviewed. I don't wanna miss this guy. Besides, I got sandwiches comin' outta my ears."

"Nine's that rickety-lookin' old man," Pezzano said. "Calvin Dempsey. Which one was number six, again?"

"Blond female, Deborah Brown."

"Right. She's the little broad who said she was in Matt's drinking because her boyfriend had beat her up earlier in the night."

"Unh!" Savage grunted bitterly. "She also gave a bogus address, and nobody's been able to locate her since. I wish I'd been able to get a whack at her before she was cut loose."

"Can't hold these witnesses indefinitely," Pezzano said. "Besides, you were all tied up with the funeral them first few days."

"Yeah, well . . ." Savage groaned. "Anyway, I'm gonna stick around. I wanna review the fives again. Somebody had to see something more than ski masks and dark clothes. Hell, we don't even have decent descriptions on the goddamned weapons." Savage leaned forward in his chair, nostrils flaring, barely able to control the overwhelming anger that was eating away at his insides.

"You're absolutely right, Thorn," Pezzano agreed, his

lantern jaw set, the upbeat enthusiasm gone. "But look what we got for witnesses. Them junkie bastards ain't gonna tell us shit even if they know. Every one of them's got a damn 'B' number and a yellow sheet a fuckin' mile long. We're gonna have to start prayin' for a goddamned informant." Pezzano snatched his jacket from the hook on the wall. "I'll bring you back a ham and cheese."

Savage drew a mug of awful coffee and returned to his desk. He pinched the top of his nose, the exercise giving momentary relief from pile-driving sinuses, and then snapped on the desk lamp. The gloom of the day had brought little natural light to the borrowed office. Again he pored over the mound of field reports, reports that he now knew verbatim. Pezzano was right. Nobody knew nothin', and if they did, nobody was sayin'.

At three o'clock he slid the pile of reports off to the side and picked up the envelope marked AUTOPSY. He took a deep breath and opened it. Medical-examiner records with accompanying photos taken during various stages of Abe's autopsy were clipped neatly together. He stared at photo number three: Abe's naked body supine on a cold metal table, his chest separated at the sternum and pulled wide apart, revealing a hollowed-out, empty cavity. All internal organs had been removed. Abe's face looked so natural . . . as though he were sleeping. Biting his upper lip till it hurt and breathing through his nose in short staggered snorts, Thorn slid the gruesome photographs into a separate envelope and clipped it to the file. After regaining his composure, he turned to the pathologist's report and forced himself to read.

Victim died from massive cardiac hemorrhage, the result of a single gunshot wound. Bullet entered right breast at a point three centimeters above right nipple, first striking victim's right thumb, severing trapezium at proximal phalanx. Believe victim was standing and assuming a defensive posture, probably turning to his left and elevating his right arm when fatal shot was fired. Projectile continued through R/S pectoralis major and intercostal space between second and third costae. Projectile abraded, but did not penetrate, the ventral aspect of right atrium. Projectile passed through the aorta, entered the ventral aspect of left atrium, and exited dorsal aspect of same, at a point two centimeters above left ventricle. Projectile: a 9mm bullet, recovered from thoracic cavity. Heavy concentration of barium on dorsal aspect of victim's right hand, and outer clothing in area of right breast, consistent with fatal shot being fired at extremely close range.

His head bowed, Savage folded his hands into his lap. In mumbled prayer he spoke to his friend. "I'll get these bastards, Abe. I swear I will fucking get them."

Considered swell in its time, the six-story apartment house on West 144th started life back in the late twenties, achieving full occupancy just hours before the stock market suffered the crippling stroke that ushered in the Great Depression. With its winding staircase that accessed all floors and a modern Otis elevator, the building originally housed families of the area's white middle class, many of whom were tenured educators at CCNY, situated only blocks away. Once proud, the now-abandoned building was a fetid, stinking, charred shooting gallery for the area's dope fiends and drug addicts. It swarmed, twenty-four/seven, with heroin junkies and crackheads idling away their miserable lives hovering in and out of varying states of euphoria and unconsciousness.

The structure's electric supply had been disconnected years ago and, day or night, its interior spaces were pitch-black minefields of dry-rotted floorboards strewn with broken glass, discarded needles, and raw human waste. For years rain had swept past its shattered and missing windows, and sieved into its core through fire-blackened openings in its partially burned-out roof, accounting for the clammy dampness. All that remained of the elevator was a black abyss that plummeted from the roof to the trash-scattered, rat-infested basement. Rotted treads of the winding staircase demanded careful negotiation by those seeking the penthouse retreat of Dopedom's undead.

The place was a haven to those who had the price of a fix and needed a place to flop. Lighters glowed like fireflies in the mine-like darkness as crack smokers fired up and heroin hopheads cooked their spoonfuls. The city had sealed the building many times, but before the mortar had ever set, junkies, like concrete-eating termites, had tunneled their way back in.

Carla Williams's head rested on a soggy mound of fallen plaster, her skinny body curled into a tight fetal position atop a stubborn remnant of green linoleum. She was awakening. Her ragged-edged acrylic nails lightly scratched a rotted floorboard in what had once been a family kitchen. Painfully forcing apart swollen eyelids, sealed shut with mucus and dirt, Carla blinked at the crackhead light show that flared in the blackness all about her. Outside, it could be high noon or midnight; in here there was no way of telling. She remembered nodding after her last hit of smack, but had no earthly idea of how many hours—or days—had since passed. At the next plateau of consciousness, she discovered that her hair was wet, matted, and stinking from urine, as was the left shoulder of her Saks jumpsuit.

"Moth-er-fucker," she spat wrathfully. Had she laid her head down in a puddle of piss? "No way." She scowled. In the darkness some junkie had relieved himself, not knowing or not caring that she lay there.

"Hey, what time it is?" Carla called out the syntax-skewed question, hoping someone would respond.

"What time you want it to be?" The deep voice that whispered from the darkness belonged to Leon, her regular dope connection. A lighter flashed and she saw his face eerily illuminated above her.

"I want it to be quittin' time," she moaned. "I don't want to be soundin' like no wuss, Leon, but I just can't take the Life no more." As she dropped her chin to her chest, her thoughts flashed to her infant daughter and how much better off the sweet child would be if she was raised by a non-junkie, non-hooker, non-alcoholic piece of shit.

Carla shook her head vigorously. The horrible execution of poor Abe Humphreys—whom she now knew to have been a plainclothes policeman—and the role she'd played, no matter how reluctantly, in bringing it about—was creeping back into mental focus, chilling her. It would only be a matter of time until the cops came looking for her. And she knew that Luther would never allow that to happen. She couldn't hide out here forever, but she dared not show her face on the street.

"Whatchu doin' here, Leon?" Carla asked pointedly. "You don't never come up here." The skinny mulatto was no different from any of the other street dealers. Like zookeepers holding the supply of raw red meat, they never wandered into the cages of the big pacing cats.

"Just checkin' things out," Leon breezed. "How ya'll doin', anyway, sugar? You doin' all right?"

"My life is *shit,* man." She coughed and gagged, then hawked a lob of thick phlegm across the room. "I'm out suckin' dicks all day so I can take care of my child, and maybe come here at night sometimes to get high. Then some jive-ass junkie pisses all over my goddamned head. Damn," she whined. "Mother*fucker!*"

Carla spit another green glob and continued on a roll of self-pity, but she knew no one was listening. The zombies within the sound of her voice were off somewhere on another planet. All except Leon.

"Hey, Buzz," he said sympathetically. "It ain't all that bad. You likes gettin' high, don'tcha?"

"It's my only damn escape." How did I ever wind up like this? she thought. If only there was a way to turn back the clock, and this time to listen to her momma's wise words. She "harrumphed" ironically.

"Let's you and me get high right now, sweetie," Leon said, his voice velvet.

"Say what? Hell, I'd love to get high, man, but I'm flat-ass broke, you dig? Anyway, I gots to get home to my child. My momma been watchin' her, and I ain't seen my little baby for days."

"You broke, baby?" Leon murmured with uncharacteristic concern.

"Sold my damn hair to get money to buy my child a birthday present. Y'hear what I'm sayin'? Now I ain't got my hair or the damn hundred. I done shot it all into my arms." Carla cocked her head and looked up at the man through burning eyes. "So we ain't gettin' high together, Leon, unless you offering the easy payment plan."

"Hell, your baby's with your momma," Leon said reassuringly. "She as safe as safe can be. Now, if you wanna get high, I'm buyin', sweetie. This one's on Leon," he said with a soul-brother flourish, *"your main co-neck-shun!"*

Carla stared at the man's blurred outline, giving him the fish-eye.

Leon held a lighter's flame beneath a spoon as the white powder dissolved into clear liquid. He filled a syringe, and then depressed the plunger until several drops appeared at the needle's tip. "Here, baby. I'll be right behind ya."

As Leon held the lighter, Carla searched up and down her puny left arm, looking for a spot on a usable vein; there were very few left. Finally finding one, she inserted the needle. Looking resignedly to Leon, she allowed herself a rueful smile and pressed the plunger home. Within seconds she felt herself floating into a blissful dream world.

It was a warm sunlit day there, and it smelled good. And it was clean. Very clean. She was wearing a pretty flowered skirt and a beautiful silk blouse with short sleeves that puffed at her shoulders. Her momma was there. Sharika was there too. Momma and Sharika were together. Momma was smiling—she seemed somehow very content—and sweet Sharika giggled happily as Momma gently pushed her, back and forth, in a baby swing. It was a park playground, filled with toys and games and all manner of wonderful things. There were shady green trees and plump little bumblebees, butterflies and puppy dogs, and helium-filled balloons that raced to the sky.

Carla watched herself as if watching a movie—a silent movie. She saw herself pick a flower from a garden, lush and beautiful, and then turn and hold it up for Momma and Sharika to see. They both liked her choice; they both smiled. The park was so beautiful. Suddenly, she knew it was time to leave. Carla passed through the playground's gate, turned, and looked back. Momma was still swinging little baby, and both were still smiling. Carla saw Momma nod assurance to her and blow her a kiss. The picture faded to dark.

\*     \*     \*

Leon quickly cooked up another batch from a specially marked glassine and reloaded the syringe. He knelt beside Carla and jabbed the needle into her arm. As Carla's uncontrolled bladder began to drain onto the green linoleum, Leon slipped unnoticed from the building.

# NINETEEN

**Saturday, April 22, 3:00 P.M.**

Still poring over the fives, Savage was startled by an
"Ahem!" and a sharp rap on the office doorjamb. It was Detective Howie Bender. Behind him was a scruffy old man in
a green flannel shirt.

"Sarge," Bender said. "This is Calvin Dempsey, witness
number nine. Did you want to speak with him in here, or
in one of the interview rooms?"

"Come on in, Mr. Dempsey," Savage said casually,
standing up and gesturing the rumpled old-timer to the
chair that faced his desk. Savage saw that the detective
only partially closed the door behind him.

Despite his bird-like frame, Calvin Dempsey ambulated
on big feet—easily 12 wides—and had leathery hands the
size of catcher's mitts. And though the years had left him
with shoulders severely stooped, they had once been tape-
measure wide. Must have been one tough son of a bitch in
his day, Savage thought. He addressed the man in a gentle
and reassuring tone.

"Mr. Dempsey, I'd like to introduce myself. I'm Thorn
Savage." He reached across the desk and held out his hand.
Savage felt wariness and distrust telegraph through the old
man's halfhearted grip.

"I hope you don't mind talking to me for a little while,"
Savage said. "Somehow I think that you may be able to

help me." He raised his wiry eyebrows and stared at the man with a look of hopeful anticipation. "Am I right?"

The old man blinked again, his eyes seemingly unable to maintain direct contact. He shifted nervously in his seat and crossed his legs tightly before responding. "I done already told the other gentlemen, over and over, I don't know nuthin' more than I already said."

Savage stared back in silence, and then sifted through the pile of interview reports that littered his desk. He located Dempsey's statements and studied them again. Carbon copies of all the others, they began and ended with dark clothes and ski masks.

"Calvin, it says here that you're sixty-nine years old. That right?"

"Yessir. That's right. I was put on this here earth a long time ago."

"Where were you born?" Savage asked genially.

"Greenville. Greenville, South Carolina."

"Nice city, Greenville. I've got me some friends that live right next door over in Spartanburg."

"Yeah, it's nice," Dempsey said. "Hell, I wish I could go back there. And I would too, if I had the price of a damn bus ticket."

"Tell me." Savage cushioned what he was about to say with a respectful and understanding tone. "How many years did you spend in prison, Mr. Dempsey?" The question was direct, but nonjudgmental. Savage wasn't fishing; he knew the look hard time puts on men's faces. Calvin had the look in spades.

"Served twenty-five years. My time was split 'tween Attica and Greenhaven. . . ." For the first time the old man made solid eye contact and, without having to be asked, offered, "I killed a man who flat-out deserved to die."

"But you're not a junkie, Mr. Dempsey. I can see that just by lookin' at you."

"Like you could see that I been to prison?"

"Something like that, Calvin. May I call you Calvin?"

Hesitant and still distrusting, the old man finally nodded.

"My point, Calvin, is this: If you're not a junkie, what were you doing in Matt's? That place is a total junkie hangout. A man like you shouldn't be rubbin' shoulders with street junkies. I know you can't like doing that."

"Where else can I go? I can't be goin' too far from where I lives 'cause of my arthritis. My room's jest 'round the corner from there. Besides, it's the onliest bar 'round that I can afford. I'm a po' man, Mr. Savage. Hell, all I been eatin' lately is dog food."

"You strike me as an honorable man, Calvin. You may have killed a guy a long time ago, but I get the sense that you're an upright man. A man of principle. Someone with the courage to do the right thing when it needs doing. Am I right?" Thorn maintained a low and reassuring voice.

"I dunno." Calvin hesitated for a moment, then leaned forward and added, "Mr. Savage, if you chitchattin' wif me thinkin' that I'm gonna change my story, then you best fo'get about it. 'Cause I ain't."

"Is that because you can't change your story . . . or because you won't change your story, Calvin?"

"Mr. Savage, let me explain somethin' to ya." The old man stared squarely into Thorn's eyes and spoke. "I gots to live here. I gots to deal with these motherfuckers each and every damn day. Y'all picked me up in a po-leece car, and you gonna give me a ride home in a po-leece car. Everybody on the damn street gonna see that shit. Then, tomorrow, if they arrests the boys that done shot that po-leece man, everybody might gonna say that it was 'cause of what Calvin Dempsey done said."

"Calvin, I know that you can help me. I know it as sure as I know my own name." Savage's mind began to swirl as he contemplated ways in which he could break down the old man's defenses and get to what he needed. But he knew the old man was right to protect himself. If word got out on the streets that he'd cooperated with the police, his life could well become more miserable than it was now, if that was possible. Savage stood and tightly closed the office door. He would make his bid.

"I know that you need to protect yourself, Calvin. I know that if you're seen with the police just before an arrest is made, it could result in problems for you. But most of all I know that your greatest fear is that someday you'll be called upon to testify in court as to what you saw that night and what you told the police."

Thorn sat next to the old man, his voice just above a whisper, persuasive, sincere. "I'd like to make a deal with you, Calvin. You're an honorable man, and I'm an honorable man. Now, speaking as an honorable man, I make the following promises. First, when you arrive home today, it will not be in a police car. Second, I give you my absolute word of honor that nothing you tell me will be put down on paper. I will carry it around inside my head, and no one will ever know that I heard it from you. If pressed, I will swear that I got it from an anonymous phone caller. You will not be called down here again. And you will never be called to court to testify to anything beyond dark clothes and ski masks. The officer that was killed was my friend and my partner for some thirty years. He was a good man. He was a man who did not deserve to die."

Calvin sat still in his chair, biting the callused skin

around his quarter-sized thumbnail. Savage could almost
see the wheels turning.

"Calvin, when was the last time you had a big, thick,
juicy steak?"

"Huh? Say what?" The old man tried to hide the temptation but his brightened eyes gave him up.

Savage persisted. "You know, the kinda steak that flops
over both ends of the platter. I happen to know a place
downtown that has those kinds of steaks. I'd like to treat
you to dinner. We could talk a little bit, then I could send
you home in a cab." Savage leaned close and spoke in a
whisper. "I've also got five hundred-dollar bills in my
pocket that're lookin' for a new home." He'd withdrawn
the cash from his savings in the event he could buy some
information on the streets. He decided to spend it now, all
in one place. He wished it were five thousand.

"You wantin' me to sing for my supper?"

"That's what I'm wanting. Can you do it, Calvin?"

"Just s'posin' I wuz to tell you every little detail that I
seen. Hell, it ain't gonna help you none, anyways."

"You let me worry about that. Whether it helps me or
not, a deal's a deal. The steak and money are still yours."

"I would never want it to come back to me," Calvin
said. "'Cause if it did, I would deny ever sayin' anything,
y'understan'?"

"I hear what you're sayin', Calvin. And I give you my
word. I will never reveal you as the source of any information."

The old man turned in his seat and stared at Savage
through jaundiced eyeballs. "No tape recorders?"

"No tape recorders."

"I believes that I can trust you, Mr. Savage."

"Are you ready for that steak, Calvin?"

"Yessir . . . I believe I'm ready."

\*      \*      \*

This was the last Saturday three-to-eleven that Patrol-man Tommy Finneran would ever have to work. He had been marking time for the last three months, and in three more days he could finally call it quits from the Scarsdale PD. He'd finally have his time in, and he and Patti could make the move out to Lake Havasu, where he could boat and fish and Patti could join up with her older sister, whose family had made the big move three years ago. No more long tours of duty, he thought. No more leaf-raking and bit-terly cold blizzards. No more court appearances. No more paperwork. No more freakin' bullshit.

As he did every Saturday and Sunday afternoon imme-diately after turning out from the station house, Finneran picked up a coffee and drove his radio car to the Metro-North lot, where he parked alongside the well-landscaped berm at the northernmost end. He liked the spot because he could sip his joe and read his paper in private and not be bothered by nosy passersby. He only used this place on weekends, when the trains were running off peak and the station's parking lot was virtually empty. On weekdays the lot was always filled to capacity. On those days he had his coffee at the fire station.

Finneran opened the Dunkin' Donuts bag and removed the maxi-size container. He carefully peeled off the lid and set the container into the dash-mounted cupholder to allow the lava-hot black-no-sugar to cool. It was then that some-thing began nagging at him. He took a studied look around the vast lot. Finally it struck him.

Parked not fifty feet away—all by its lonesome—was a dazzling blue Mercedes. It was the same purplish-blue sedan that he'd seen parked in the very same spot last week while he enjoyed his Sunday coffee. The car's front wheels were turned hard to the right, just like last week. And the windshield wipers were still at half-mast, as if someone had shut the key off while they were in midstroke. Finneran knew the car hadn't been moved since he'd last seen it a full seven days ago. Possibly a stolen/abandoned, he thought, unhappily realizing the mountain of paperwork that would bring.

"Dammit," he growled, picking up the handset and calling in the sedan's New York plate number, which he could clearly make out. Sundays were quiet in Scarsdale; the response from the radio was almost immediate.

"Unit four-oh-seven, be advised your plate number comes back 'no hit.' Vehicle registered to a Clarice Boone, female, black, DOB twelve/twenty-two/seventy-five, residing 1066 Audubon Avenue, New York City. No wants or warrants on vehicle or registered owner at this time."

"Hmmm." Finneran recapped the coffee and slipped the patrol car into gear. Without stepping on the gas, he idled the short distance over to the Mercedes and swung alongside. The car had that abandoned look, no doubt about it, he thought. He noticed a small puddle of fluid that appeared to be leaking from the left rear quarter-panel drain hole. When he threw his car into park and stepped out to investigate, the abominable stink almost made him puke. There was no question about that odor either, he thought, again picking up the handset.

"Dispatch. Unit four-oh-seven requesting patrol supervisor respond to Metro-North parking lot, north end. Possible DOA in trunk of auto parked thereat."

"Ten-four!"

Finneran put the radio down and shook his head. "Fucking paperwork," he snarled.

As the green Crown Victoria rolled slowly down Broadway, Calvin Dempsey began to relate what he had seen in

Matt's Bar on the night Abe Hamilton was murdered. Savage listened without interruption, formulating questions to be asked later.

"There was sumpthin' real wrong with that whole situation, Mr. Savage. . . . Real wrong."

"Go ahead, Calvin. Tell me what you think. Don't hold nothin' back."

"Matt's Bar is like you say, a real junkie hangout. It don't seem right that them boys would want to rob a damn junkie bar for a lousy few dollars. You know what I'm sayin', Mr. Savage?"

"I know what you're saying."

"Hey, you be goin' to the penitentiary for the same amount of time whether you be doin' a armed robbery for five thousand dollars or fifty dollars. Couple of smart boys knockin' over Matt's jest don't make no damn sense."

"There's desperate dudes out on the street, Calvin. They'll waste you for a buck, for crissakes."

"That's jest it, Mr. Savage. I don't believe them boys was desperate."

"How do you know that?"

"Most everybody that's desperate's a damn junkie, and I ain't never seen no super-fat junkie before. Besides, that man was wearin' fine threads and a solid-gold watch. His pants had a sharp crease, like they just come in from the dry cleaner. Know what I'm sayin'?"

"Go on."

"Now, the other guy, the slim dude, he wasn't desperate neither. His clothes was sharp and 'spensive, too. I could smell money on that dude. Shit." Calvin shook his head. "The man was wearin' genuine alligator shoes. Hear what I'm sayin'?"

"Alligator shoes?"

"Damn right. Them kicks musta cost a ton o' bread."

"Tell me more about the guy in the alligator shoes, Calvin."

"He be about six-three. You know I couldn't be seein' his face or hair 'cause of the ski mask, but he was wearin' him a real expensive suit."

"How expensive?"

"The kind what got a comma in the price tag—you dig what I'm sayin'? And he was the damn brains of the outfit. You could tell that he was in charge. He was the one who shot the po-leece officer."

"Did the policeman identify himself or try to stop the robbery in any way?"

"Couldn't do it. The slim dude kep' a real close watch on everybody all the time."

"What did the fat guy do?"

"He went behind the bar and took all the money out from the cash register."

"What did he do with it? Put it in a bag?"

"Jammed it all into his pockets."

"Then what did he do?"

"He started going down the line to rip everybody else off. First one he come to was the plainclothes officer. He started goin' through his pockets, taking money and shit, and puttin' it all in his own pockets."

"Then what?"

"That's when the slim dude stepped in. He pushed the fat boy aside, and *he* started searchin' the officer. When he found a gun and a po-leece badge, he dragged the officer off to the side and begin talkin' to him."

"What was said?"

"Couldn't hear what was bein' said, but it was intense. The slim dude was really in the officer's face. He beat on him a bit, then shot the officer full in the chest with his own damn gun. Then the two boys ran right out, and was gone."

"What kind of guns did these guys have?"

"The fat dude had him a thirty-two revolver. Looked kinda old. It was probably a Smith and Wesson, maybe a Colt. I didn't see that gun real clear, except that I know it was blue with wood grips. Now, the slender feller had him the baddest-lookin' nine I ever did see. Damn."

"Tell me about the nine."

"It was a Glock. It had a dull, blackish-gray finish."

"How do you know it was a Glock?"

"One thing a man learns, hangin' out on my end of Broadway, is guns. That there Glock is the gun that every-body be wantin', but they hard to get."

"How long were you in Matt's before the robbery went down?"

"Coupla hours."

"When you got to Matt's, was the police officer already there, or did he come in after you did?"

"He come in way after me, jest befo' the robbery. He come in there a minute or two behind that woman who was all beat up. He sat right next to her."

"You mean the short-haired blonde whose face was all swollen?"

"That's who I mean."

"In her statement, Deborah Brown never said anything about coming into Matt's with the officer, and nobody else has put them together, either."

"Nobody gonna tell ya that. But I'll tell ya, she come in first, hear what I'm sayin'? Then he come in right after her. I'm tellin' ya, they was together. They was talkin' and everything. Seemed to me that he couldn't be the boy who beat her up; she was bein' too nice to him."

"What else you know about this Deborah Brown?"

"That her real name? People on the street just calls her Buzz."

Savage felt every muscle in his body tighten and contract as if he were performing all-over isometrics. He forced his best poker face to conceal the impact of Dempsey's last statement. A disturbing theory was developing as each piece of information brought the scenario of Abe's killing more into focus. Why hadn't he seen it sooner?

Savage parked on Fifty-fifth, just east of Third. The old man continued to talk as they slowly walked the short distance to P. J. Clarke's, Savage's favorite saloon. After nodding a discreet ask-me-no-questions hello to the white-haired bartender, Frankie McBride, Savage and Calvin Dempsey were shown to a small table in the most obscure corner of the back dining room, well beyond the bar.

"Order whatever you like, Calvin. I'll be right back." Savage excused himself and went to the bar. "Frankie, let me use the phone."

Frankie McBride had been tending bar at Clarke's as far back as Thorn could remember. Clarke's was Thorn's favorite watering hole, and Frankie was not only his favorite bartender, but also one of his closest friends. Frankie could always sense Thorn's mood, even before Thorn himself realized it. Frankie also made a killer martini.

Modulating the esophageal speech mastered years before, after losing his vocal cords to cancer, McBride sounded like a whispering robot as he cupped his left hand over his ever-present bow tie and croaked, "What are you doin' with Uncle Remus?" as he set the telephone on the bar.

"Jesus, Frank. Just treat him right. *Capisce?*"

"I'll see he's treated like a fuckin' king."

Savage dropped his Visa card on the bar. "Take an imprint of that. Whatever his total comes to, add thirty percent for the waiters." Savage dialed the number to his office.

"Manhattan South Homicide. Detective Marcus."

"Richie, Thorn Savage. Get Jack and Diane on the line with us."

As soon as DeGennaro and Lindstrom picked up, Savage provided the three members of his team with a quick synopsis and immediate assignments.

"Jack, get right down to Centre Street and find Judge Rothmann. If he's not there, go to his house if you have to. We need eavesdropping orders for Ogden World Galleries and the Culture Club. Richie, I want you to put on your telephone repairman duds, get your little bag of tricks, and, in anticipation of the court order being issued, begin setting up the wire at Ogden World Galleries right now."

"Who's gonna cover the other joint?" Marcus growled.

"I'll get Pezzano to supply somebody from Manhattan North," Savage said. "Diane, you there?"

"I'm here, boss," she replied.

"Get the 'B' number for witness number six—Deborah Brown."

"The little blonde who looked like she'd caught a good beating?"

"Uh-huh. Then I need you to run right down to Photo Unit. Get Chet Dibzitzki to run us off some eight-by-tens of any and all photos of her that we may have on file."

"From what I remember seeing of her, my guess is she's probably been collared a few hundred times," Diane said. "Probably got a bunch of booking photos on file . . . but what are we looking for?"

"We know what she looks like now," Savage explained, "when she's all beat up. I wanna see some old pictures of her. I'm bettin' that little bleach-blonde has sometimes been a brunette with hair down to her shoulders. And I'm also bettin' she used to have a slightly turned and chipped front tooth."

"Abe's description of Buzz," Diane muttered. "The hooker he was working at the Culture Club."

"Exactly," Savage said. "Also, while you're down at Photo, I want you to get Chet to process eight or ten official photos of uniformed members of the department. Pick 'em at random. Black, white, it doesn't make a difference. But it'd probably be best if they were all males. Another thing, I want those photographs left absolutely virgin. Nobody's to touch 'em."

"Anything else?" Diane asked.

"Start polishing your acting skills."

"By the way," Richie Marcus broke in, "I got a message here from your friend Davy Ramirez, over at Ballistics. He called to leave some information on a gun you spoke to him about a coupla weeks ago. He said for me to tell you it was a—"

"Don't tell me," Savage interrupted. "It was a Glock, right?"

"Right. That mean anything to you?"

There was a long pause as Savage exhaled heavily into the phone.

"Yep. Sure does," he sighed. "Was he absolutely certain?"

"Positive. Among other things, he said the Glock leaves a very distinguishable firing pin mark on the cartridge primer."

"Anything else?"

"Says that gun was used in a ton of homicides, going back almost ten years, and that all the cases are still open. All the cases were clearly dope-related, and—"

"Thanks, Rich." Savage hung up, cutting Marcus off in mid-sentence. He immediately dialed Manhattan North.

"Lieutenant Pezzano, Manhattan North Homicide task force."

"Petey, this is Thorn. Don't talk, just listen. Get as many bodies as you can out on the street and find our number-six witness: Deborah Brown, now AKA Carla Williams. She also goes by the street name of Buzz. She's been holding out on us. We know the perps had ski masks on, but I'd bet a year's pay she knows who was under them. I don't want to go into detail right now, but trust me. I think we're gonna find this whole robbery business was nothing but a ploy to single out Abe Hamilton and kill him."

"Sweet Jesus! You really think so?"

"Yeah. If they can't find that Buzz bitch on the street, have them stake out the Culture Club over on Lenox. That's one of her playgrounds; she may show back there."

"We'll find her. We'll get her ass back in here."

"Few more things, Pete. Get a wire set up at the Culture Club—a court order's on the way. Then get a surveillance team down to the Carlyle. I want a discreet tail reinstated on Derek Ogden." Savage checked his watch. "I'll be back uptown in a little while. Meanwhile, call an emergency meeting of all the pertinent brass for first thing in the morning."

"Chief of D? Borough bosses? Everybody?"

"Everybody."

Savage pushed the phone back across the bar, winked at Frankie, and with hasty steps returned to the old man in the rear dining room.

"You've been very helpful to me, Calvin. You're a stand-up guy." He folded the five hundred-dollar bills and slipped them into the old man's shirt pocket. "Here's an extra twenty. When you're finished eating, grab a cab. I can't stay, but your tab is covered."

"You a man o' your word, Mr. Savage! You jest be careful now, y'hear, dealin' with them crazy motherfuckers up dere. They'll hurt ya. They will." As Savage turned to go, Frankie McBride arrived with a tall glass of gin and addressed the old man.

"Your cocktail, sir."

# TWENTY

Robinson's private elevator went to only three floors of the Southview. It serviced an isolated corner of the basement garage—with its PENTHOUSE ONLY reserved parking spots—the building's main lobby level, and his thirty-third-floor penthouse apartment. Standard call buttons at the lobby and garage levels had been replaced with digital keypads. No six-digit code, no elevator. The garage and lobby areas were scanned continually by security cameras, with a series of monitors in Robinson's apartment and a miniature one in the elevator cab itself. He did not like surprises.

Though compact, the elevator car was done out like a first-class compartment on the Orient Express. Ebony paneling was polished to high gloss, all metal trim was plated in 24-karat gold, and subtle lighting was provided by a pair of antique Tiffany sconces done in a dragonfly pattern. The rare fixtures had been a gift from Derek.

When the elevator settled to a gentle stop at his top-floor residence, Robinson locked the door in the full open position. He strode through the apartment to the dining room, where he quickly selected the smallest of the three remaining tightly wrapped bundles of cash.

Back in the elevator, he studied the miniature security monitor as he remotely scanned the garage level thirty-four floors below. Manipulating a tiny joystick, he zoomed in on

Derek's Bentley, parked immediately beside his own roadster. The garage was all clear. Why not? he reasoned. It was
half past four in the morning. Robinson checked his Glock;
it was cocked and locked. He released the door and pressed
the call button for SUB-BASEMENT/GARAGE.

Thirteen bundles of cold hard cash were already stashed
inside the reinforced compartment hidden between the
Bentley's backseat and its trunk. The bundle he held would
make it fourteen. As the elevator smoothly descended, he
recalled that they'd never before moved more than eleven
bundles of this size. But business was getting better. Derek
would have to begin making more frequent trips or have another compartment installed. As to the two bundles still remaining in his dining room, Robinson decided, no problem.
He'd simply hold them for next time.

Standing at the head of the long table in the war room of
Manhattan North Homicide, Savage related what he'd uncovered the afternoon before and the reason for the Sunday-
morning meeting. Chief of Detectives Ray Wilson sat
opposite him, at the far end of the table. Captain Hough,
from the borough office, and Lieutenant Peter Pezzano each
sat on either side. Savage carefully relayed every detail
given him by "an anonymous phone caller," and how that information all jibed with the ballistics report from Davy
Ramirez. Reading Wilson's face, Savage knew the chief
wasn't buying the old "anonymous phone caller" bit. He
also knew that Wilson would never admit that to anyone.
But there was something else, something unmistakable. The
chief was distant . . . angry.

"What have you put in place so far?" Wilson asked
coolly.

"I've arranged for camera surveillance to be set up on
Ogden World Galleries, not only for keeping tabs on

Ogden, but also for photographing Luther Robinson if he makes any visits there. The day may come when they deny any association with one another."

"Are we onto their phones yet . . . Sergeant?"

The chief's formally phrased question and icy demeanor were just additional indications to Savage that he'd fallen into disfavor with the man since Abe's killing. He wasn't happy about that, but he understood completely.

"Judge Rothmann issued wiretap orders for the art gallery and the Culture Club," Savage said respectfully, glancing at his watch. "I'm sure they've already been activated." He looked around the table for any additional questions. There were none. "Our situation is this," he continued. "We're morally certain that Ogden runs both the Manhattan and Bronx dope empires, and we also believe that Luther Robinson is his front and enforcer. We can't prove it yet, and the D.A.'s office says we don't even have enough to make an arrest, but we know it was Robinson who executed Abe Hamilton. Until we make our case, we're gonna stay right on top of them."

Captain Hough broke in. "How much do we know about this guy Robinson?"

"He operates the Culture Club, a nightspot over on Lenox," Savage replied. "We believe it may be the base of their operations. We've set up a camera team inside Harlem Hospital across the street. They'll also be monitoring the phone lines. We'll know when Robinson arrives, when he leaves, and what he says on the phone."

"Aside from squatting on these locations with cameras and wires, have we got tails on both these guys?" Hough asked.

"I don't want a tail on Robinson," Savage cautioned. "That son of a bitch's got rearview mirrors on a swivel head, and now he'll be more paranoid than usual. He'd know we were on him in a minute. I don't want him seeing so much as a uniform directing traffic until we've got enough to snap the cuffs on."

"What about Ogden?" Hough quickly followed up.

"Last night we set up a surveillance team at the Carlyle," Savage said. "No sign of him yet, but the team is standing by there. Normally, we wouldn't expect to see him much before ten a.m. One problem, though," Savage added. "The big Bentley has gone missing."

"Think that has any significance?" Chief Wilson asked.

"Don't really know, boss," Savage said with a grimace. "Maybe the Bentley's in for a fifty-thousand-mile checkup. But it will be somewhat more difficult to tail Ogden without it."

"We have addresses for these guys?" Hough asked.

"Ogden maintains a suite at the Carlyle not far from his art gallery—walking distance. Again, this guy is usually highly visible. And if the Bentley was there, he normally would be too."

"What about Robinson?" Hough again.

"The surveillances were inconclusive. We believe he may live somewhere on the East Side, possibly in the Eighties."

Chief Wilson eyed Savage critically. "Beyond the 'anonymous tip,' what evidence do we have against these guys? Is there any way we can actually prove Robinson was the shooter?"

"When you first gave us this investigation, Chief, you told me that we had 'everything and nothing' on Ogden," Savage said.

"I recall telling you a lot of things, Sergeant."

"Well, Chief," Savage continued, feeling the barb, "unfortunately, nothing's changed. These two have fully mastered the art of covering their asses." He peered over the top of his half-glasses at Pete Pezzano. "Lieutenant, would you be good enough to update the chief and Captain Hough as to witnesses and informants?"

Pezzano opened a file folder and cleared his throat. "One of the eyewitnesses to the Hamilton shooting—witness number six, Deborah Brown—was a known prostitute, who we now believe could have positively identified both perps."

"Could have?" Wilson snapped, a frown twisting his face.

"She was found DOA last night, overdose, in a shooting gallery off Broadway," Pezzano said with a shrug.

"Accidental?" Captain Hough asked.

"Summary toxicology showed her blood contained a massive amount of pure heroin." Pezzano glanced briefly at the faces around the table, and then went on. "Also, the body of a black man in his thirties, whose height and substantial weight easily fit the general description of perpetrator number one, was found late yesterday afternoon in the trunk of a car parked in a railway station up in Scarsdale. . . . He'd been shot twice in the head. It's estimated he'd been dead about a week."

"Hey, so he was a fat man. It's gonna take a lot more than that to tie him to the killing of a cop in New York City." Hough looked to Chief Wilson, apparently expecting support for his premature observation. Wilson sat stone-faced.

Pezzano continued, "This obese man was trussed up with nylon cable ties and gagged. It's believed that the victim was already inside the trunk when he was dispatched. When the body was searched at the scene, officers recovered approximately fifty dollars crumpled up in the victim's jacket pocket." Pezzano paused for effect, and then delivered the blockbuster. "Mixed in with those bills was a City

of New York paycheck . . . payable to Detective Abraham
D. Hamilton."

"Well, gentlemen," Thorn said flatly, "now you know
the latest developments. As far as witnesses and informants
go, I think you'll agree that we've suffered some setbacks.
Anybody that could have positively implicated Luther
Robinson in the shooting of Abe Hamilton is now DOA."

Pete Pezzano closed the file folder.

Wilson folded his arms across his chest. "Where to from
here?" he asked, glaring back and forth between Pezzano
and Savage.

"Not certain, boss," Savage responded. "Right now
we're just groping."

"Has the car they found the fat man in been gone over
for prints?" Wilson asked.

"As we speak, Chief," Savage replied. "But we have
nothing to compare them to. The currency recovered from
the fat man's pockets, along with Abe's paycheck, has been
forthwithed down to Latent. We're waiting to see what they
come up with. They'll do a comparison check for Abe's
prints on file, and we have a complete set of prints from the
DOA perp. Any additional unaccounted-for prints will ulti-
mately be used for comparison to Robinson's. If we could
get a latent print belonging to Robinson on that check, or
somewhere on that car, we could start strapping the bastard
into the electric chair."

"Robinson have an arrest record?" Wilson asked.

"Collared for murder when he was a kid," Savage said.
"But all those records are sealed."

"Son of a bitch was fingerprinted and we can't use those
prints for comparison in these major homicides?" Captain
Hough asked, incredulous.

"No sir," Pezzano informed him.

"If the only time Robinson's been arrested was as a juvenile, and his fingerprints taken at that time are sealed and unavailable to us, how're we gonna get a full set of his prints so that Latent can look for comparisons?"

"We're workin' on that, Chief," Savage said.

The voice-activated recorder suddenly clicked on. Richie Marcus snuffed out the remnant of his Winston and set aside *The Daily Racing Form.* Adjusting the headphones, he set the volume level. The tapes were turning. He noted the time, 1436 hours.

"Good afternoon, Gulf Stream Marina."

"This is Derek Ogden. Put Reed on."

"One minute, sir. I'll page him to the phone."

Marcus heard cheesy canned music come on the line as the caller was put on hold. Before he could forget, he reached over and circled the four-horse in Wednesday's third race at Aqueduct.

"This is Reed." The man's preoccupied voice put a merciful end to the static.

"Derek Ogden here, Reed. How is the weather in Fort Lauderdale today?"

"Just fine, Mr. Ogden," the man replied. "It's eighty-two degrees, a perfect day for being out on the water. Are we going to see you soon, sir?"

"A few days. I plan on leaving New York tomorrow afternoon. I have a business stop to make Wednesday morning in Tallahassee, and I expect to arrive dockside that evening. Is the *Slavedriver* shipshape?"

"Yes sir, Mr. Ogden. The new props have been installed and we put her back in the water last night."

"All fueled and ready?"

"Yes, sir. Since you're probably making your usual Bahamas run, I made sure to top off the auxiliary tanks as well."

"When I get there, I intend to unload the Bentley and get immediately under way. No hitches."

"There will be no hitches, sir."

"Good. *Ciao*."

Diane DeGennaro pulled the brown Plymouth sedan to the curb directly in front of the Culture Club. The car was the embodiment of the unmarked, yet totally obvious, department automobile. She set the police I.D. plate on the dashboard and stepped from the cruiser, carrying a zippered vinyl folder. The Scarecrowmobile was in a lot next to the building. The expensive roadster was being hand-polished by a rangy black guy in his twenties. Inside the bar, and outside on the curb, heads turned. Everyone knew she'd arrived.

Aside from the jukebox being silent, the lounge was precisely as Abe had described it in his reports. Late-afternoon patrons, in scattered conversation around the large oval bar, hushed when she walked in.

"Can I help you?" The huge bartender's attitude was defensive and suspicious.

"I certainly hope so. I'd like to speak with the owner of the place, or somebody in management . . . if I could." Diane tried to make her voice and stance convey an almost sheepish personality. Right now she needed to be greatly underestimated.

"What about? Who are you anyway?" the bartender growled, as if he didn't know the answer to part two.

"Pardon me for not identifying myself," she said, flipping open her shield case. "I'm Detective DeGennaro from the New York City Police Department, Internal Affairs Bureau."

The bartender shrugged. "What do you want?"

Maintaining the unthreatening air, Diane said, "My reason for needing to speak with the owner is confidential in nature. Our records indicate that the licensee is a party by the name of"—she opened the vinyl folder and glanced at a typed list, and then muttered—"Robinson . . . Lucy Robinson. . . . Is that so?"

"Yeah . . . well . . ." the bartender stuttered, seemingly unsure how to respond.

"What can I do for you, Detective?"

The voice behind her was almost cultured, and had a definite edge of arrogance. "I'm Mr. Robinson, and I run this establishment for my aunt." The Scarecrow, dressed in dark pleated slacks and an ivory turtleneck, stepped from a darkened corner of the club.

"How do you do, Mr. Robinson?" Struggling to control vengeful urges, Diane reached out and offered her hand. She also made sure to suggest a momentary reaction to Robinson's terrible face. "I wonder if you could spare a few moments of your time." She looked around at those seated at the bar, and added, "In private, of course."

"Of course." Luther led the way to a four-top in the far corner of the lounge. "We can sit over here. By the way, you do have identification with you, Detective . . . DeGennaro, is it?"

The nerve of this bastard, Diane thought, as again she flashed her shield and photo I.D. Robinson glanced and nodded, satisfied.

Still assessing her with cold and penetrating eyes, Robinson sat opposite her. "How can we be of service to the New York City Police Department, Detective?"

Trying to stay on script, but realizing she had to wing it, Diane began. "Well, sir. Matters of this nature are sometimes embarrassing to the department, but complaints of corruption against our members must always be vigorously followed up. I do hope you understand."

"I understand completely, Detective," Robinson replied. "We mustn't allow any bad apples to corrupt our police department. However, we've not made any complaints against any policemen."

"Well, I know that, sir," Diane said with a timid nod.

"Ours is a better-class establishment," Robinson went on, "and we experience very little in the way of trouble here. Consequently, the police, to my knowledge, have never even been called here."

Diane could see that Robinson still appeared unsettled about the purpose of the impromptu interview. She could also tell that the man's curiosity was maxed.

"Quite frankly, sir," Diane said, "the owner of another establishment in the area has come forward with a serious allegation against a uniformed member of the local precinct. Our investigation would be incomplete if we failed to speak with other bar owners in this area, to see if they've also been approached and thereby possibly able to shed additional light on this matter."

"Just what sort of complaints are you referring to, Detective?"

Taking exaggerated glances over both shoulders, Diane leaned across the table, allowing her voice to drop. She looked directly into Robinson's soulless eyes and tried her best to sound like an IAB hump with a mission. "It has been alleged that a uniformed police officer has gone into several local establishments, shaking down the owners or licensees. These owners are alleging that the officer is demanding money from them in return for not reporting them to the State Liquor Authority."

"Reporting them for what?" Robinson asked intently, beginning to buy into the charade.

Still whispering, Diane confided, "Drug-dealing being permitted within the establishment."

"Oh, well," Robinson countered, a pathetic excuse for a grin forming on his ugly face. "That accounts for the reason that no one has approached us, Detective. There are no drug sales being made in our establishment. We would never tolerate that sort of activity here at the Culture Club."

"All the same, sir, I wonder if you'd be good enough to look at some photographs I've brought along." Diane dug into the folder and placed an envelope on the table. "There are photographs of eight different uniformed police officers in there. All are full-face enlargements of official department file photos. The investigation that I'm conducting may center on one of the officers in that grouping. Please look them over slowly; take your time. Remember too that it's quite possible the officer visited your lounge while off duty, and not in uniform. Perhaps to just size your place up."

Diane watched as a bewildered look spread across Robinson's skeletal face. She could see the infinite possibilities beginning to dawn on the man; now he'd have to look at the photographs.

She slid the envelope across the table. "Just tell me if you recognize anybody."

Robinson removed the photographs from the packet. One at a time he studied each picture, slowly considering each face. Diane sensed his relief that Abe Hamilton's photo was not among the grouping.

His curiosity assuaged, Robinson appeared to be tiring of the ersatz Internal Affairs investigator. "No . . . no one," he declared curtly. "I don't recognize any of these men."

"Well, in that event, would you be good enough, sir, to turn the photos over and look at the names that are printed on the reverse sides? Please tell me if you recognize any of those names."

Clearing his throat in a display of boredom, the monster complied. "No. I don't recognize any of these names. Now,

if that's all, Detective?" Robinson shoved the pictures back
into the envelope, apparently unaware that virgin glossy
photographs were a magnet for prints, even from finely
manicured fingers.

"Oh, yes, sir. That's all. Thank you for your time." Diane
smiled, returned the packet of photos to the vinyl folder,
and stood. "Sorry to have troubled you, sir. But you've been
most helpful. Good day."

You ugly bastard, she thought as she moved past the
jukebox, pushing against the door that led her out. We'll be
back.

# TWENTY-ONE

"Your Honor," Savage implored, "this bastard's getting ready to move tons of dope money out of the country. He's going to literally ferry it on board his own yacht."

"You know that for certain, Sergeant?" Judge Harold Rothmann asked in a tone of terse preoccupation, without so much as looking up. Leaning over the desk in judges' chambers behind Arraignment Part Two at Manhattan Criminal Court, the robed man was vigorously stirring a precise amount of Metamucil into a tall glass of water.

"As certain as we ever can be, Judge."

"Has somebody informed you of this fact, Savage? A registered C.I. perhaps?"

"No sir," Savage admitted. He was not about to lie to Rothmann, no matter what was at stake. He had known the judge for twenty-five years, and the man had always treated him right. "There are no confidential informants, sir, registered or otherwise. But we know that Ogden owns several banks in the Caribbean. In the Bahamas and the Caymans."

The judge shook his white mane and exhaled loudly. "That, in and of itself, Sergeant, does not criminal behavior make. It does not mean that he's dirty, or tied up in the killing of a policeman."

"He's dirty, Judge."

"I'm constantly seeing Ogden's name mentioned in the

papers. I've caught him on TV talk shows. He's one of the beautiful people, Thorn. He's a millionaire who's big into charities, fund-raisers, that sort of thing. He's a real up and comer." Lifting the tall glass, the judge smirked and added, "He's even had photo-op sessions at Gracie Mansion, for God's sake." In four long gulps he downed the entire Metamucil mixture, made a face, belched, and sat down behind his desk.

"He's the proverbial wolf in sheep's clothing, Judge," Savage pressed. He quickly peeled back the foil on a Life Saver roll and popped a Wint-O-Green. "He comes on like some kind of great humanitarian, but he's a gifted manipulator and string-puller. And right now he's got to launder an awful lot of cash. We know from informants, whose identity we're sworn to conceal, that Ogden cleans up his money by running it through his banks on the islands. Based on a telephone conversation overheard last night— on an eavesdropping order that you issued—Ogden is about to make a move. He's leaving the city today. Heading to Fort Lauderdale in his goddamned bulletproof chauffeured Bentley. He intends to board his private yacht there and immediately sail off to the Bahamas. What a perfect way to get dirty cash out of the United States and into his Bahamian banks. He probably makes landfall at some obscure location, avoiding any encounter with customs, and hand delivers the cash."

The judge was listening intently. "You know," he said, grimacing in exasperation, "I've got to get myself reassigned. Stop working the arraignment parts. Start getting Saturdays and Sundays off like everybody else in this frigging building. Shit, I've earned it."

Savage offered a perfunctory nod of sympathy, took a deep breath, and sailed on. "This guy is so well insulated from his dope empire, and from Hamilton's murder, that we'll probably never get the goods on him. But if we hit him today, we may catch him at his most vulnerable time—when he's holding tons of dope money. If we can use that as leverage, maybe he'll want to make a deal. Then maybe we can get him to give up his boy Robinson. Judge, it's our only shot."

The longtime jurist stared from beneath bushy eyebrows, pondering Savage's argument. "You want me to issue a warrant that will permit you to search his entire automobile?"

"Yes."

"Stem to stern?"

"Yes."

"What specifically will you be looking for?"

"Cash proceeds from illicit drug transactions, and possibly weapons."

"Even if you find something, Savage, your search may not survive at a hearing. Without revealing the identity of your informants and having them testify to show probable cause, this whole thing may wind up in the toilet. You know that?"

"I know it. But I'll have to cross that bridge when I get to it. If we don't move now, and in this manner, this thing could be stalemated for a very long time. Possibly forever."

The judge scowled thoughtfully. As Savage sat quietly opposite, a uniformed court officer knocked at the chamber door and stuck his head in.

"Are you about ready to reconvene, Your Honor? We're still holding fifty-two cases."

"Give me five minutes," Rothmann replied, holding up the film-coated glass. "Gotta take care of this case first." The court officer nodded and disappeared.

Without a word, the judge slid back his big leather chair

and, robe flowing, strode directly to the small bathroom off
the chamber. He pulled the door closed behind him.

For the next five minutes Savage paced the office, hoping the judge would see things his way and wondering if
anybody had actually ever read any of the hundreds of law
volumes that lined the chamber's walls. Finally, Judge
Rothmann reappeared.

"I'm probably the only judge in New York that would
approve such a warrant," he said, adjusting his robe.
"Based, that is, upon what you've got in the way of probable cause. But I'm going to issue a search warrant for
Ogden's Bentley. Off the record, my decision is based less
upon lawful considerations than upon my regard for your
police instincts."

Savage nodded a silent thank-you.

"But you damn well better be right," Rothmann added
sternly. "Or I'll be working weekends for the rest of my
life."

The Bentley was back; so was Donald Duck. The big car
was parked right in front of Ogden World Galleries on
Madison Avenue at Sixty-seventh. The no-neck chauffeur,
his thick arms folded defensively across his chest and his
head on a nonstop swivel, leaned casually against its massive front fender. Savage's Crown Victoria sat idling at
Sixty-eighth and Madison. Jack Lindstrom was behind the
wheel, Savage beside him. Lieutenant Pete Pezzano and Detectives Marcus and DeGennaro waited at Sixty-sixth Street
in a second unmarked car, a blue Taurus. It had been two
hours since they had set up. It was two-thirty and traffic
moved past them at a good clip. By three o'clock, however,
it would be a different story. Madison Avenue would become choked with vehicles in the afternoon rush hour.

"Team Two to Team One." The portable on Savage's front seat crackled with Richie's raspy voice.

"Go ahead, Team Two," Savage replied into a hand-held.

"Just a radio check, boss. How're you reading us?"

"Five by five, unit. You're loud and clear. How do you read us?"

"Loud and clear, boss."

Five minutes passed before the radio crackled again.

"Subject is moving, Sarge. He just came out of the location and got into the back of the Bentley."

"Ten-four. Remember, I'll keep him in sight and see where he goes. You guys keep me in sight. I don't want him stopped until we're sure that he's actually headed out of the city. That will be our signal that he's loaded everything into that car that he intends to bring along with him."

"Gotcha, boss."

The Bentley saloon pulled away from Ogden World Galleries, blending smoothly into traffic. As it passed Savage's location, Lindstrom steered in behind at Sixty-eighth Street. They followed at a discreet three-car distance to Seventy-second, where the elegant British motorcar headed west toward the park.

"Think they're going crosstown, Sarge?"

Savage keyed the radio. "Looks that way."

The Bentley crossed Fifth Avenue at Seventy-second and entered Central Park's transverse road. It was unmistakable in the one-lane flow of traffic. Minutes later it emerged from the park on Manhattan's West Side.

Let the games begin, Savage thought.

Derek Ogden made a selection from the CD player's controls and carefully set the system's graphic equalizer. As the colorful orchestration from Puccini enveloped him, he melted comfortably into the buttery softness of the Bentley's kid-leather seat, closed his eyes, and listened for every note.

He welcomed these periodic long motor trips to Fort Lauderdale. They allowed him days of total and uninterrupted relaxation, surrounded by his favorite music.

"Mr. Ogden, sir," Bruton, the stocky chauffeur, announced through the intercom as he committed the Bentley to the Thirty-ninth Street Lincoln Tunnel approach. "I believe we being followed."

"Pardon?"

"Them two cars behind us . . . they come racin' up soon as I turned off Ninth Avenue."

"What two cars?" Ogden turned in his seat and looked through the Bentley's rear glass.

"That there Crown Victoria and that dark blue car behind it. They jest come outta nowhere."

"Let's just wait and see what they do. Another minute and we'll be in Jersey."

"I don't think we's gonna has to wait," Bruton said. "They pullin' up aside now. . . . Shit . . . they be the po-leece. They motioning me to pull over. What should I do, Mr. Ogden?"

"You sure they're the police?" asked Ogden, flustered. He slumped back into the seat and peeked through the side window as the green Crown Victoria roared past and pulled immediately in front of the Bentley. The blue Taurus then pulled alongside. The driver of the Taurus sounded a short *whooop* of the siren as a heavy-set Italian-looking man flashed a police department sign and motioned for the Bentley to pull over.

"They be the police, all right," Bruton lamented. "And they got us completely boxed."

"Damn."

\*          \*          \*

Suspects arrested in New York County are photographed and fingerprinted, and then arraigned on the charges before a judge who may set bail. The holding cells behind Arraignment Part AR-1 at 100 Centre are the bullpens where prisoners wait for their cases to be called. It is a zoo, a cage overflowing with the dregs of humankind.

Loud and obnoxious tough guys collared for serious robberies and assaults were mixed in with ridiculous-looking strapping transvestites arrested for prostitution. Stinky winos smelled up the place and passed time scratching their body lice. Wackos, weirdos, and full-blown psychos who'd made countless trips through these holding pens frightened the bejesus out of those souls making their first.

A bespectacled accountant, hung over from the night before, cowered in a corner, avoiding all eye contact. The delirium tremens, with its terrifying visual hallucinations, could never equal the freak show of career criminals and social outcasts that surrounded him. He had good reason to be afraid. Being beaten, robbed, or sodomized by one or more of the other prisoners was a very real possibility. It wouldn't be the first time such had occurred in these cages, located only steps from a sitting judge.

The apathetic turnkey from the Department of Correction opened the iron door each time an arresting cop came to collect a prisoner to bring before the bench. The lock would be twisted again on the return run if the prisoner failed to make bail or was remanded by the court.

Derek Ogden and his chauffeur stood in the far corner of the dirty concrete cell, leaning against the graffiti-scarred block wall. Ogden was deep in thought; anger played across his carefully groomed face. Hatred simmered within. His ordered world had been invaded and thrown into troubling disarray. He had a new archenemy—the source of his humiliation—Sergeant Thornton Savage of the NYPD.

"Ogden and Bruton." The corrections officer swung the door wide as he called the names. "Ogden and Bruton, let's go!" The two men stepped from the crowded cell into Savage's custody.

"You don't have any idea who you're fucking with, cop." Ogden's voice trembled with barely controlled rage.

"Correction," Savage hissed, fixing him with cold gray eyes, "you don't know who *you've* fucked with. But before we step out in front of the judge, let me assure you of a few things."

Ogden surveyed his adversary: chiseled features without being thin, good dresser for a cop, and harder than hell. There was something else. This wasn't business—it was personal.

"I am going to crucify you," the cop said in a loud whisper. "I am going to spend every hour of my day to put you away, *and* I am going to destroy your whole miserable empire. You hear what I'm saying, *Derek?* You lowlife bastard."

Ogden contorted his face in defiance. "Don't threaten me, motherfucker. I can have the mayor on the phone in five minutes. I'll have you shoveling horseshit at the Mounted stables. I'm a well-respected man around this town . . . *cop!*" His black eyes shone with contempt as he added, "I'll bury you."

Savage sneered, thrusting his face a few inches from Ogden's nose. "By this time tomorrow, all your big-time friends—and everybody else in this town—are going to know what a dope-dealing, coldblooded killer you are. Ain't nobody gonna come to your rescue. You're gonna be a pariah. You're a piece of shit, and I'm going to make it my personal business to take you down."

Ogden's survival instincts kicked in. His mind raced. The cop had a definite agenda. Whatever was motivating this guy to be such a prick was not idle bullshit. He would have to reckon with this man.

The female bailiff with a Sister Wendy overbite called out the docket numbers and read aloud the charges as Savage led his two prisoners into the crowded courtroom. Ogden and his waddling driver were met by high-profile defense attorney J. Harry Kornbluth. He stood with them before the bench. Savage took his place beside A.D.A. Alan Goldberger.

Judge Aloysius Cromartie scanned the court papers, his massive head bent so that the port-wine birthmark just below his thinning hairline stood out like a map of Uzbekistan. With beady blue eyes, canopied by bushy white eyebrows, he examined Derek Ogden briefly before turning his attention to Kornbluth.

"The charges have been read, Counselor," he said. "How do your clients plead?"

"Not guilty on all counts, Your Honor," Kornbluth replied firmly.

"So noted." Cromartie scribbled on the court papers. "I'm sure you wish to be heard on bail, Mr. Kornbluth. Please proceed."

"My client, Mr. Derek Ogden, is a well-known and highly respected pillar of the community. He has had no involvement with the law in almost thirty years and was en route to a brief vacation in Florida, traveling lawfully along a public thoroughfare, when his chauffeur-driven vehicle was forced to the side of the road and unlawfully searched by detectives. It is our contention that the police had no probable cause to stop, or subsequently search, Mr. Ogden's car. Therefore—"

"Your Honor," Alan Goldberger broke in, "the police officers were acting under color of a warrant issued by Judge

Rothmann of this court when they conducted the search of Mr. Ogden's vehicle. I would therefore ask that you direct Mr. Kornbluth to cease characterizing that action as being 'unlawful.' "

"I understand that, Your Honor," Kornbluth said. "But the officers had no grounds for arresting Mr. Ogden. They found no contraband or weapons on him—"

"Mr. Kornbluth," the judge advised, looking over the top of his black horn-rims. "The search warrant specifically enumerated: 'weapons and contraband U.S. currency.' One gun and an incredible amount of currency were found within your client's vehicle."

"Yes, I realize that, Your Honor. However, the weapon in question was found on the person of Mr. Thomas Bruton, Mr. Ogden's chauffeur. Not on Mr. Ogden himself. There-fore—"

"Therefore," the judge interrupted, holding out his hand in a *stop* motion, "only Mr. Bruton was charged with the weapons possession, Mr. Kornbluth. . . . What about the money recovered from Mr. Ogden's automobile?" The judge was matching the attitude of the notoriously pushy lawyer. "Does that money belong to Mr. Bruton as well? Or does that money belong to Mr. Ogden?"

"That money belongs to Mr. Ogden, Your Honor. My client is an extremely wealthy man. He often brings large sums of cash with him when he travels. My client was going on vacation—"

"Your client must have had quite a vacation planned." The judge rolled his eyes and turned his attention to Savage. "I want to make sure this isn't a typo, Officer," he said. "How much money was recovered from the defendant's auto?"

"Just short of one point seven million dollars, Your Honor. The cash was all carefully wrapped in fourteen waterproof bundles, containing approximately a hundred twenty thousand dollars each." Thorn looked to his left and made brief eye contact with Ogden, who stared back menacingly. Savage also shot an antagonistic glance at J. Harry Kornbluth, the overfed defense attorney, whom he disliked. Since he was a kid he had always gotten intensely bad vibes from anyone whose name started with an initial.

"One point seven million in cash? Stuffed into plasticwrapped bundles?" The judge looked cynically back at Ogden's lawyer. "The felony complaint before the court states that these bundles were recovered from behind hidden panels in the trunk of your client's Bentley automobile, Mr. Kornbluth."

"That's true, Your Honor, but—"

"It also states that your client was in possession of a five-million-dollar letter of credit from some savings institution in the Cayman Islands." The blue eyes flashed. "Are you trying to insult the court's intelligence? Do you really expect the court to believe that your client was bringing that amount of cash and credit into Florida for walk-around money? Maybe he was going to make a down payment on Disney World." The remark brought smothered gasps of laughter from the court personnel and from two hookers seated off to the side, awaiting a recall of their cases.

"How much cash my client chooses to travel with is his business, Your Honor. Is it not?"

"Tell me about this offshore five-million-dollar letter of credit drawn to the state of Florida, Department of Insurance, that was in your client's possession," the judge said to Kornbluth with an inquiring frown. Kornbluth stood mute.

"Judge," the A.D.A. interrupted, "the officers looked into that. The Florida Department of Insurance informed them that Mr. Ogden, representing a firm called Regal Holdings, out of the Caymans, had been registered with them to bid at auction this Wednesday on the purchase of an island somewhere in the Caribbean."

"An island?" The judge harumphed and zeroed his frosty gaze tightly in on Kornbluth. "Your client was set to buy . . . *an island*?"

"My client sits on the board of Regal Holdings, Your Honor. He was merely going to conduct a matter of business on their behalf."

"Counselor," Judge Cromartie drawled, "methinks something stinks in Denmark. If your client wasn't engaging in money-laundering in the first degree, as charged, tell me why he had so much cash secreted in his car."

"Fact of the matter is," Korbluth recited, straight-faced, "my client was carrying that very substantial amount of cash in order to transact a purchase of several valuable paintings. It is not unusual for pricey art transactions to be conducted on a cash basis—"

"Nor," the judge broke in, "is it unusual for thousands of drug transactions to be conducted on a cash basis—the allegation that underlies the people's conspiracy in the second degree charge, Counselor."

"We deny that allegation as well, Your Honor," Kornbluth said respectfully.

Savage noted that the lawyer's tone was becoming more conciliatory; he was obviously beginning to recognize the need to take a different tack with the judge, who was becoming irritated.

"Is that why he offered the police sergeant a two-hundred-forty-thousand-dollar bribe, Counselor? If your client was so pure of heart, why would he make such an offer?" The judge shook his head, a wide grin painted on his disbelieving face.

Kornbluth responded. "Your Honor, we emphatically deny any such offer ever being made. The allegation of a bribe attempt is an out-and-out fabrication on the part of the police." Ogden turned with a smirk and glared over at Savage. Savage cupped his mouth and whispered briefly to the assistant district attorney.

"Your Honor," the A.D.A. said, "I am informed by Sergeant Savage that the bribe offer made to him by Mr. Ogden was, in fact, recorded on tape. Mr. Kornbluth will have a difficult time attempting to convince a trial jury that such allegation was a fabrication."

Kornbluth turned to Ogden with a questioning look on his face. Ogden angrily shrugged and looked menacingly at Savage.

"Counselor, let's move on," the judge said. "Are you also representing Mr. Bruton on the weapons charge?"

"Yes, Your Honor."

"Mr. Bruton's rap sheet is somewhat lengthy, and it indicates a number of prior felony convictions. If convicted, he could be looking at considerable time, Counselor." Shifting his glance to the chauffeur, the judge asked, "Are you aware of the severity of the charges against you, Mr. Bruton?"

"Uh, yes, Judge."

As the chauffeur spoke, Savage strained to hear Kornbluth's whispered conference with Ogden, who was fast losing his much-heralded poise and was shuffling around before the bench in exasperation.

"Stand still and take that angry look off your face, Derek," Savage heard Kornbluth warn him. "The judge isn't liking it."

"Fuck the judge," Ogden whispered through tightly clenched teeth. "I'm Derek Ogden, dammit. This whole thing is bullshit. It's a jive humbug, that's what it is! It's all because of this fucking cop. Who is this fucking guy, anyway? And why the fuck does he have such a big hard-on for me?"

"Shhhh!" Kornbluth murmured from the side of his mouth. "Dammit, don't let the judge hear you."

Assistant D.A. Goldberger addressed the court. "Your Honor, in the matter of *People* versus *Bruton*, the defendant is a convicted felon charged with possessing a deadly weapon: a fully loaded handgun. In view of the defendant's lengthy record of violent crimes, the People ask for bail in the amount of one hundred thousand dollars."

The judge scribbled notes on Bruton's case jacket and addressed Kornbluth. "Do you wish to be heard on the matter of bail as it pertains to Mr. Bruton?"

"I believe the bail amount asked for by the People to be excessive and request that Mr. Bruton be released on his own recognizance."

"Nice try, Mr. Kornbluth," the judge said. "Bail for Mr. Bruton is set at fifty thousand dollars, cash. If Mr. Ogden wishes to see his employee's bail, he should be able to cover that amount from his watch pocket. Now let's discuss Mr. Ogden's predicament." The judge faced the A.D.A. "Mr. Goldberger, let us hear from the People."

"Your Honor, the People request no bail in this case. The arresting officer informs me that an investigation conducted by his office has revealed evidence that Mr. Ogden is a major narcotics-trafficking figure in New York City. He stands before the court charged with the Class-B felonies of conspiracy in the second degree and money-laundering in the first degree. Those charges are compounded by the C felony of attempting to confer a two-hundred-forty-thousand-dollar bribe upon the sergeant at the time of the arrest. The People intend to present considerable information to the grand jury, and fully expect a multi-count indictment to be handed down. It is clear that the defendant could, and would, be able to meet any bail amount the court might set. The People would argue then, based on the severity of the charges, coupled with the likelihood of a conviction that would result in considerable jail time, the defendant would be likely to skip the jurisdiction if given bail."

The judge turned to Kornbluth. "Counselor?"

"We disagree, Your Honor. Mr. Ogden is a long-standing resident of the city. He has his roots here in New York. He is a businessman who owns and operates a highly respected, world-renowned art gallery. He is not some common criminal. We ask that bail be set by the court so that my client can be free to operate his business, which requires his presence on a daily basis in order to properly function. Your Honor, my client has a right to bail!" Kornbluth was again coming on strong.

"Mr. Kornbluth, bail is a tool the court may use in order to ensure a defendant's appearance," the judge replied. "It is not a right." The judge paused to let the information sink in. "In this case it is clear that the defendant has practically unlimited financial resources. When weighed against possible long jail time, the forfeiture of considerable bail monies may be but a small price to pay for one's freedom. Also, I must factor in the attempted bribe offer, involving several hundred thousand dollars, that is alleged to have occurred at the time of arrest. That charge particularly disturbs me and strongly enhances the probability of guilt in this case. Therefore, I am binding this matter over to the grand jury and order that Mr. Ogden be remanded to the custody of the Department of Correction. No bail. Since he likes islands so much, let him spend a week on Riker's." The judge scribbled notations on the case jacket and slid the papers over to Sister Wendy. "Put this matter down for Tuesday next. Bailiff, call the next case."

After Ogden exchanged a few angry words with his attorney, Savage escorted him and Bruton back through the doors that led to the Tombs and cold iron bars.

"Okay, Savage." Ogden scowled as the turnkey slammed the Remand cell door. "Obviously you're going for my throat, so now I'm going to go for yours."

"You threatening me, Ogden?" Savage asked icily as he passed the commitment papers to the corrections officer.

"No threat, cop. Just a plain, out-and-out fucking promise." Ogden's tightly focused eyes could have burned away the bars. "*Nobody* does this to me."

Savage turned his back on the dope dealer and walked away. As he moved down the long concrete corridor, he could hear Derek Ogden screaming after him at the top of his lungs. "You bastard! You fuck with me, and you invite disaster that you cannot imagine. *'Seize on him, Furies, take him to your torments!' Bastard!*"

# TWENTY-TWO

**Tuesday, April 25, 11:00 A.M.**

"Sergeant Savage." Nubby, large-knuckled fingers clutched the jamb as Marcus, the Swami, leaned his less-than-svelte bulk into Thorn's office. "Phone call from the D.A.'s office. Said her name was Marilyn Pankow."

Savage anxiously lifted the receiver. "Good morning, Ms. Pankow, Thorn Savage here. I appreciate your returning my call so quickly."

"What can I do for you, Sergeant?" The voice was feminine but conveyed the unmistakable self-assurance of a hard-nosed prosecutor. As a bureau chief in the Manhattan District Attorney's Office, Pankow had probably booked more people into Attica than Conrad Hilton ever did into his hotels.

"A lot," he replied firmly.

"Uh-oh. Just what is it that you have in mind?"

"How about we discuss it over lunch, Ms. Pankow? You name the time and place and I'll be there. Lunch is on me."

"Can't do it today. Booked up. Besides, if you're treating to lunch, you must want a heavy."

"Not so heavy," he said. Then, hedging, "Well, maybe just a little heavy." Savage had never met the prosecutor, but so far he liked the woman's quick style. She was upfront and flexible.

"You like Cantonese, Sergeant?"

"Never leave home without my chopsticks," he lied tactfully. He didn't do Chinese—too damn many veggies.

"Seventeen Mott, tomorrow, one o'clock. Bring your appetite."

There was much to discuss with the bureau chief who oversaw the prosecution of all major narcotics cases in New York County. Thorn wanted to meet with her informally, not on his turf or hers. Lunch on neutral ground was perfect, even if it meant suffering through a bowl of wontons.

He glanced at the clock, and for the first time in what seemed like forever, he felt in a playful mood. Alone in his office, he dialed Gina at home. She was taking a much-needed vacation this week.

"Hello?" she answered.

"Ummmm, hmmm," he drawled in a lecherous nasal whine. "This is an obscene phone call. Will you accept the charges?"

"Absolutely," Gina replied. "Please, go ahead."

"If you are scantily clad, wearing lace underthings, or not wearing any undies at all, please press one now." He knew Gina was amused by these silly games and was probably delighted that his spirits had improved. A single beep came over the line.

"Ummmmm," he moaned again. "Let us continue, my dear. If you would like to engage in degenerate fornication with a wildly handsome stud, often described as 'well endowed,' please press two now." There came another immediate beep.

"I must say," Gina said through a stifled giggle. "Your modesty reminds me a lot of someone I know. To what, sir, do I owe the pleasure of this pornographic phone call?"

"Your caller wishes to know if you can come out and play, little girl?"

"When, well-endowed one?"

"Tonight, of course, my dear."

"Your offer does sound very attractive, Mr. Caller, but I'm staying home tonight."

Undaunted, Savage quickly parried. "Not to worry, my dear. We have a mobile unit that can swing by and see to your every need, no matter how bizarre the lady's wishes may be. What time shall I pencil you in for?"

"Eight would do nicely, sir. Whatever should I wear?"

"Madam need not worry about garments." Savage was now beginning to stifle his own welling laugh. "Our operative will bring along a complete line of our latest costumes for madam's selection."

"You nut! What are you doing?" she asked through her laughter. "Things must be really slow down at that office."

"Just thought I'd call and talk dirty. We haven't done that in a while."

"You mean I'm not gonna get a chance to try on some of those wonderful outfits?" Gina clicked her tongue. "I'm disappointed."

"Yeah, me too."

"Listen, Mom just called," Gina said. "We've been invited to my folks' for dinner tonight. Lasagna," she sang temptingly. "Think you can break away?"

"No way. I'll be lucky if I get outta here by midnight. But I promise I'll make it an early one and come by tomorrow."

"Okay. I've got something I want to run by you anyway."

"What's that?"

"I want to talk to you about Abe's son," she announced excitedly. "I'd like to organize a benefit for him. Set up a scholarship fund. I've got some friends out there who'd fully support it and help me get the thing off the ground if I asked them. You know, the public outpouring to the NYPD after 9/11 hasn't yet stopped, I just know that people would contribute to the family of a fallen cop. We might be able to raise enough money to help cover his tuition, books, living expenses. . . . What do you think?"

"Uh, yeahhh . . ." he said unenthusiastically, the sensitive topic quickly darkening his mood. "I love you for thinking of it. . . . But we'll talk more tomorrow, okay?"

Gina and her circle of charitable friends might possibly raise enough to help underwrite Little Abe at some community college, he thought. But they'd never—no matter how well-intentioned—make a dent in what it would cost to realize Abe's dream of his son one day attending Harvard. Nor was it their responsibility. It was his responsibility.

"See you tomorrow, sweetie," Savage signed off.

Sunlight splayed through the foot-thick opaque glass blocks that allowed the only natural light into Section 60-B at the Riker's Island House of Detention for Men. Lying on his cot, Derek Ogden flipped another page of last Sunday's *Times*.

The cavernous, multi-tiered, concrete-and-steel interior of the cellblock amplified every sound. One man speaking sotto voce could be heard throughout the block. Instead there were hundreds of loud feral men, going about their jailhouse routine: talking, yelling, laughing . . . all at maddening high volume. These sounds of men, crammed like pigeons into a massive and inescapable coop, all blended into the nerve-racking jailhouse chorus that played all day and most of the night. Booming rap with its thunderous bass competed endlessly with excited Latino salsa for supremacy over the truly captive audience. The daily cacophony was unbearable. The only escape from this tyranny of sound was his tapes and earphones. He wore them always. He had to. Compared to here, Bedlam, he thought, would seem an oasis of tranquility.

Sensing movement, Ogden shifted only his eyes and

watched as a lumbering cockroach stutter-stepped and disappeared into a vent next to the wall-mounted stainless-steel toilet. He'd found a way to cope with the unbearable noise and was becoming inured to the odors of unwashed and toileting men, so noticeable on day one. His next court appearance was still six days away. Kornbluth, the brazen attorney known for successful defenses in high-level drug prosecutions, would then argue for bail, which, even if an indictment were forthcoming, the dashing lawyer assured him would be granted.

Situated in the East River dogleg that separates the Bronx from Queens, Riker's Island is accessed only by a narrow causeway that passes within a stone's throw of LaGuardia's runways. Members of the prisoner population—overwhelmingly black and Hispanic—await trial in the city's courts, or have already been convicted and sentenced to a term of one year or less. Anything more and they go upstate.

Derek Ogden was no stranger to Riker's. He'd done a bullet here back in '72, after copping a plea on manslaughter and weapons possession. He was well acquainted with the systems and day-to-day operations within the Men's House of D.

Nothing much had changed in the intervening years. Favors could still be had. A prisoner of Ogden's repute could expect to be treated to many of those favors—at a price, of course. In a clear violation of prison rules, the last four editions of *The Times, The Post, The Daily News,* and *The Wall Street Journal* had been hand-delivered to his cell. Bennett, one of the jailers regularly assigned to 60-B, was a neighborhood boy whose father operated a dry-cleaning business up on 125th Street. Bennett delivered the papers and would see to many of Ogden's needs during his seven-day stay. In return, Ogden had an envelope containing five thousand dollars delivered to the elder Bennett. It was chump change, but it would ensure some degree of comfort. No cash ever changed hands inside the jail; Bennett's integrity could never be brought into question.

Ogden leafed through the Styles section of the paper, absorbing anything he considered of note. His eyes widened at an item on page seven, and he jerked to a full sitting position. An engagement announcement, "McCormick-Savage," brought his blood to a boil. *Savage* . . . that hateful name had haunted him these past days.

His mind spiraled into an all-consuming rage. Nobody *ever* humiliated Derek Ogden—and lived. More than anything, he needed to bring that arrogant bastard-cop to his fucking knees. Make him hurt like only Derek Ogden could make him hurt! Forcefully controlled, the rage finally settled into a stone-cold hatred. Ogden read on.

> *Gina McCormick of Brooklyn Heights and Thornton Savage of New York City announce their engagement. Ms. McCormick is a senior executive for the public adjusting firm of Kearney and Dunton. Thornton Savage is a highly decorated member of the New York City Police Department. The couple plan a June wedding. . . .*

He sat, transfixed, gnawing a polished thumbnail.

"Mr. Savage, you are about to learn what pain is really like." He sprang from the cot, grabbing the bars with both hands.

"Bennett . . . Bennett!" His deep voice reverberated throughout the cellblock. "Let me out of here; I have to make a call. . . . Bennett!"

# TWENTY-THREE

**Wednesday, April 26, 11:30 A.M.**

The automobile was not the conveyance of a burglar, or a bad guy, or some lowlife slimer who bore watching. It was the carriage of a gentleman. It did not stand out at all in this upscale part of town. Even the cops in patrol sector Henry of the Eight-four had driven by and not given the roadster or its blur of an occupant—shadowy behind the dark window glass—so much as an eyeball. After all, it was just another moneyed person, sitting in a very expensive sports job on a tree-lined side street in fashionable Brooklyn Heights. What else was new?

Having remained virtually motionless all morning, waiting for his target to appear, Luther Robinson exemplified the quiet perseverance these endeavors always required. He needed to get a good look at this bitch, so he had to wait. All day and all night, if need be: Anyway, he didn't mind. He was especially fond of this type of situation, which permitted extended observation of the intended.

What a rush, to watch from on high as the victims blithely engaged in mundane activities—hosing down the car, or putting out the garbage—unaware they were living out the final few seconds of their lives. The intense rush always culminated in that moment of bliss when he stepped forward, drew his gun, and sent them to Hell. He uttered a surly grunt as death scenes of victims past flashed across his mental screen.

He switched his thought back to how and where he could best accomplish this latest mission. It had already started out so easily. He couldn't believe the bitch actually had her address listed in the Brooklyn telephone directory.

"A.D.A. Pankow?" Savage asked guardedly, approaching a tall brunette who seemed to be waiting for someone beneath the weathered and mildewed awning at 17 Mott Street.

"Sergeant Savage?" the handsome woman in her late thirties said, reaching out to shake his hand.

What a terrific-looking district attorney, Savage thought. Pankow was wearing a conservative gray suit that pretty much concealed her long legs. She needed, and wore, minimal makeup.

"Please," she said, "call me Marilyn." Her eyes were a variation of green that flashed as she spoke. "Have you ever eaten here, Sergeant?"

"Long time ago," he replied, still partially caught up in her eyes. "Call me Thorn."

"Well," she offered, with a glib roll of the hazels, "it doesn't look like a whole helluva lot. But the food's really good, and the price is right."

They took the short flight of grimy concrete steps down to the basement eatery and were hustled to a deuce in the corner by a wrinkled, bony Asian woman. Behind the constantly swinging kitchen doors, waiters could be heard rattling off their orders in high-volume Chinese, trying to keep up with the demands of the fully packed and noisy dining room. It was lunch hour in Chinatown.

The dining room's decor consisted of peeling bamboo-motif wallpaper above dingy dark wood paneling. Overhead, dust-laden water and steam pipes crisscrossed the yellowed acoustic tile ceiling. The carpeting under their feet had once been red. They got through the small talk and ordered their lunches, and Savage began.

"I'm the arresting officer in *People* versus—"

"*People* versus *Ogden*," she cut in. "After your call yesterday, I looked through all the new cases that've come in, and I found your name among them."

"Well," he said, "then you know basically what we're gonna bring to trial."

"If it goes to trial," she clucked with a doubting sideways glance.

"That's my point," he countered. "We know the conspiracy case could be stronger in terms of hard physical evidence. Fact is, we'd be in real trouble with this matter if that car wasn't loaded with money and he hadn't made the bribe offer."

"Two-hun-dred-and-for-ty-thou-sand-dol-lars!" Her pretty face scrunched in disbelief. "This guy actually offered you that much money?"

"He offered me two of his fourteen bundles of cash to let him and his chauffeur ride off into the sunset. He could have offered all fourteen; it still wouldn't have made any difference, he was going. But thank God I was wired. The recording of the offer is as clear as a bell."

After the look of amazement faded from her face, Pankow spoke. "Ogden may have certainly incriminated himself on a bribery. But whether we can prove a conspiracy to distribute narcotics is quite another matter. If the tape is everything you say it is, we should be able to prove the felony bribe offer. And"—she blew across a spoonful of steaming wontons—"that one he did to himself, the schmuck."

"I'm afraid this case goes much deeper than narcotics dealing, Marilyn. I need to bring you up to speed."

She held the next spoonful of soup halfway to her lips and looked quizzically across the table. "Go on."

Savage carefully laid out every aspect of the case to the prosecutor. Speaking in a loud whisper above the din of the room, he wove the story from start to finish. When he was done, the restaurant was nearly empty.

"Let me see if I'm reading you correctly, Sergeant." The A.D.A. paused as she worked a toothpick between two upper molars. "You would like to parlay this weak conspiracy case into a first-degree murder charge against Luther Robinson for the killing of Detective Abraham Hamilton."

Savage nodded. "It's the only way we're ever gonna get Robinson out from under his rock."

"You want my office to play up the conspiracy, laundering, and bribery charges we have against Derek Ogden in order to convince Ogden's lawyer, J. Harry Kornbluth, that his client is facing hard time. And if we succeed in doing that, you're hoping that Ogden will consider looking to make some sort of a deal. At which point, you feel that we could get his attorney, Kornbluth, to persuade Ogden into handing up Luther Robinson on the homicide. Have I got it so far?"

"So far."

"You're also telling me that confidential informants who provided the basis for much that we now know might never testify."

"Right," Savage acknowledged. "But Ogden and Kornbluth don't have to know that. At least not yet."

"Look, Sergeant. I'll concede that the People might never have another shot at Ogden. I also understand your frustration in attempting to build a case against Robinson because every witness gets dead. . . ." Pankow shrugged and a lopsided expression formed on her face. "But the fact is, if we went ahead with what we currently have against either man, they may both walk."

"I know that," he conceded. "But with your help we can squeeze Ogden to the point where he *believes* that his case will be vigorously prosecuted by your office, and that he *could* do some heavy-duty jail time."

"We'd have to go through Kornbluth."

"If we can convince his lawyer that we have informants ready and willing to testify, it just might shake them loose."

"Hmm," Pankow muttered. "Permissible deception . . ."

"Law says we can use it."

"Yeah, as long as an innocent doesn't get hurt, and the subject is enough of a schmuck to bite. Are you thinking Ogden's a moron, or that his attorney will even let us talk to him?"

"We can try. If your office assures Kornbluth that you're going for his client's throat unless they have something to trade, it may be all we need to get Robinson handed up for Abe's murder."

"For something that heavy, I'd probably have to offer a walk."

Savage nodded ruefully. "Quite frankly, Ms. Pankow—Marilyn—I want both Robinson and Ogden. But it's clear that we'll never get them together in our sights. So I figure we've got to prioritize. If we don't put heavy pressure on Ogden, and then act as though we're gonna cut him some slack in exchange for information, we may never get Robinson."

"You may be right, Sergeant, but I'm afraid this scheme of yours has only a slim chance of working. If I know Kornbluth, he'll delay this case with unimaginable postponements and push it right to the brink. There's really big bucks involved there, and that venal bastard won't miss out on the chance to drain some deep pockets, especially very deep ones like Ogden's." She checked her watch, stood, and made a show of reaching into her purse. "Give me a coupla days to sort this all out. I'll get back to you. Here," she offered, holding out a fiver. "Let me at least get the tip. Besides, you didn't even touch your food."

Savage waved her off. "I've got it, Marilyn." He stood and shook her hand. "I appreciate your time. Please get back to me as soon as you can. I've gotta keep punching, and try to get 'em on the ropes."

Thorn felt the meeting with the prosecutor had gone okay. He'd pushed all the buttons he had to push and she had responded well. He left cash on the table, slipped a cellophane-wrapped fortune cookie into his jacket pocket, and drove back to the office.

Proper field logistics, that's what is called for here, Luther Robinson thought. I must ensure that the element of location is totally in my favor. First and foremost I must always remember to cover my ass. I must get her alone. I must be swift . . . and silent. His breathing came more deeply; it was rapid and sensual. *Too soon, too soon.* He needed to shake the urges that were prematurely rising in him. He turned on his music and allowed the sound to gently soothe. He refocused his eyes and thoughts on the town house just inside the narrow alley a half-block away.

The dwellings in this neighborhood of big-time haves were like miniature fortresses. People with this degree of wealth knew well how to protect their homes. Wrought-iron bars—ornate yet functional—capped many ground-floor windows. Exterior doors bore multiple locks, and sophisticated alarm systems probably sold very well locally. He watched intently as nannies with their toddler charges in tow exited, then later re-entered the same residence, observing the series of locks they dealt with to get inside and picturing the electronic security systems they no doubt had to quickly disarm once in.

Pondering that, Luther realized he did not fear the strong possibility of an alarm, silent or otherwise. Hell, he wouldn't have to be in there long enough to worry about one. He wasn't going to boost a large-screen Sony like some burglar with a dolly. What he had to do would take but seconds. Getting *into* that town house without keys was the problem. He resigned himself to following her and becoming familiar with the places she frequented. There would be a proper place, of that he was certain, and once that location was found, he could carry out another mission for Derek.

Day eased into night and there was still no sign of the bitch. Lights began to glow from most of the apartment windows, but not from hers. She wasn't home; she must've been out all this time. So be it. He would now be vigilant for her return. Removing a small glass vial from his jacket pocket, he took a quick blow of coke. He shifted his position, readjusted the headrest, and settled back. He would wait for days if need be. Derek required that this matter be handled right away, before his release from Riker's. Derek is still the master, Luther thought. The man really knows how to cover his ass. The coke began to take effect and he turned up the music, accompanying it with animated, forceful drumming of his thumbs against the leather-wrapped steering wheel. Another hour passed.

Gina's parents had celebrated their fiftieth wedding anniversary back in March, and despite their many years together, they still adored each other. Papa DiLeo, Tony, was retired now, having sold off the private-investigation business that he'd operated for decades. The sole survivor of a shooting incident that left three other victims dead, he was

never able to go back to work and now was content to live
on Social Security and spend his days futzing in the kitchen,
sometimes getting in Connie DiLeo's way, and improving
on cooking skills that had always been exceptional. He kept
a garden in their small backyard and raised his own toma-
toes—he never used store-bought. The gunshot wound to his
head had left him with sight, hearing, and balance problems,
but the hardy man seemed to get stronger as time went on.
Gina loved him—she loved them both. Odd how things have
a way of working out, she often thought. If Papa's life hadn't
been put in serious jeopardy—only to be incredibly saved
by Thorn—they might never have met.

After dining on a delicious antipasto, homemade lasagna
and Sambuca-laced espresso, Gina said good night to her
parents and left their Sheepshead Bay home at eight-thirty.
She navigated the Miata along the Belt Parkway, ran the
Gowanus, and moved through the steady traffic flow onto
the BQE. Driving faster than she normally allowed, Gina
could feel the little convertible vibrate on the rough roadway. She clutched the wheel with both hands. The day had
been tiring. It would be nice to shed her clothes, soak in a
hot bath, and get into bed. Dinner had run late. She hoped
Thorn hadn't called and become concerned. She exited at
Atlantic Avenue and sped through the green light at Hicks
before it had a chance to change. No sitting at red lights
tonight . . . Gina wanted to get home.

At Grace Court Alley, she clicked the garage remote and
waited as the overhead door slowly rose. Checking and
rechecking both sides for clearance, Gina carefully steered
the Miata into the well-lighted but tight garage. She
climbed from the car and moved quickly toward the kitchen
access door. Gina sensed something, a presence, almost as
if she was being watched. A shiver raced down her spine as
she tapped the wall-mounted control button and the over-

head door began its slow descent. She let herself through the kitchen door and entered the warmth and safety of the town house. Gina leaned against the door until it clicked tightly shut.

A sardonic smile further misaligned Robinson's grotesque features. He turned the key and the BMW roared to life. A broader, even uglier smile appeared as the car moved slowly away. He turned the volume up as a soaring Wagnerian passage reverberated through the car's sheet metal. The bass notes must have been audible for blocks.

Luther was alive with excitement. The long, watchful wait had paid off. He had the seed of a plan.

He would leave now . . . but he would be back.

# TWENTY-FOUR

**Thursday, April 27, 8:30 P.M.**

Backed into the dead end of Grace Court, his low-slung BMW concealed behind a Pontiac van, Luther Robinson had an unobstructed view into the entrance of Grace Court Alley on just the other side of Hicks Street.

Robinson had come prepared. He was ready for her, but she hadn't shown herself all day. Where the hell was she? Doesn't this bitch ever go out? he thought. His whole plan depended on her leaving the town house in that little convertible. He knew she was home; he'd seen the lights go on at eight o'clock. He checked his Jules Jurgensen watch again, and calculated he'd been squatting there, waiting, for eleven and a half hours.

A green Crown Victoria appeared on Hicks Street, an unmarked police car, no doubt. It slowed at the alley entrance and turned in to park in front of Number 8, the first town house on the right. A man got out: had to be a police detective. The guy was better than six foot and well built. He moved with the agility and purpose of a jungle cat. It was Savage, the rat-bastard cop who'd royally fucked Derek and who was crusading to totally destroy him. Shifting anxiously in his seat, Robinson felt the bulge of the 9mm at the small of his back. He fought a crushing urge to make a play.

The town house door opened. The Miata-driving bitch greeted the cop with a big smile and a kiss, and let him in.

The bastard was probably there to get a little poon-tang, Robinson thought. How fortuitous. I get to see two for the price of one.

"I'm having lunch with Morgana Feldman tomorrow," Gina said, leading Savage across the deep carpet of the living room into the kitchen beyond. He always liked to sit in the kitchen when they talked. It was a "Celtic thing," he always said. "I'm meeting her at Shelley's out in Bay Ridge."

"And?" he asked, seeming to know what might be coming, but wishing it wasn't.

"She's very excited about working with me on a fundraising campaign for Little Abe's college. She thinks she can get the approval of her committee right away. And she's sure we can get this thing off the ground inside of a month."

"Unnhh," Thorn replied in a descending tone that wasn't quite right. He sat heavily on a kitchen chair. She could tell by his voice that the only reason he'd stopped by was because he'd promised her last night that he would. Clearly he wasn't going to stay very long.

Gina stood silent, concerned by the reappearance of his spiritless attitude. She, more than anyone, had witnessed the roller-coaster changes in his mood in the past week. She knew he was suffering in silence, functioning marginally on the job but empty otherwise. He'd been denying his loss of appetite and inability to sleep, and for sure his sex drive had gone off somewhere on a road trip.

She put her arms lovingly about his shoulders and whispered softly, "Please don't worry about any of this. Let me take care of it. Besides, where can you possibly find the time, Thorn? You're working twenty hours a day now. You can only do so much, you know. Anyway, even if this fundraiser doesn't do what we expect"—she paused, and then guardedly continued—"we can tighten the belt and sponsor him to an education all by ourselves."

"What, we?" he snapped. "*We* are not gonna do that!"

"And why not?" Gina was incredulous.

"Gina," he argued, "try to see this from my perspective. I can't let you help. It wouldn't be right."

Shocked, she persisted. "Why do you feel that way?"

"Because I do. This is my obligation to Abe's son, not yours. So it must come from me, not from you or anyone else. . . . Don't you understand? It just has to be that way."

"Thorn, sometimes you are so damned stubborn. All I want to do is help. Can't I do that? Won't you let me help?"

"Can't ask you to do that . . ." He shrugged dejectedly. "I just can't." He was squirming in his chair, clearly anxious to leave.

Standing over him, she stroked the back of his neck. "I know how you feel. . . ." She held his face in her hands and kissed him gently on the lips. He put his arms around her and held her tightly. When he pulled away, she saw the redness ringing his eyes. It was time to change the subject. She sat on a stool at the breakfast nook.

"What's going on with the case?" she asked. "Have you been able to find out anything more on that ogre Robinson?"

"No. It's amazing," he said, preoccupied. "He's a shrewd bastard. And he must have his antennae up; he's just suddenly vaporized. We've got all the places we've known him to visit staked out, but he's not shown himself anywhere in days. We're still waiting to hear from Latent Prints on a possible match, but nothing yet. If we can't get a match on those prints, then it's gonna be back to the drawing board, and this thing is gonna drag on and on." He shook his head in frustration, and she could feel his despair.

"What about the art dealer?"

"We're gonna try to flip him, but I'm not betting on it. It's just an outside shot." Thorn stood and pulled on his jacket. "I just wanna be there when it comes time to snap the cuffs on Robinson . . . and *I* want to be the one to do it."

Gina heard the venom in his voice, and it worried her. "I really hate that you're leaving, Thorn. Good God, you've only been here for five minutes. Why don't you stay?" It was a plea.

"I can't, baby." He stood and gave her a tentative peck on the cheek. "I really gotta be going. Call you tomorrow."

As Savage steered across the Brooklyn Bridge into Manhattan, he knew he wasn't functioning right. Maybe if he got a good night's sleep he'd feel better in the morning. He'd have his wits about him again. He'd be able to concentrate again. He'd be back on the ball. He wished he could sleep away the crushing guilt.

He parked the Ford opposite his Sullivan Street apartment house and tossed the I.D. plate on the dash. Like a man toting a great weight, he trudged up the few steps to his building. He thought about checking his mailbox in the entry foyer, but decided no, it'll all be there in the morning. He let himself through the inner vestibule door and climbed the stairs to the second floor.

Why, he brooded, had he ever allowed Abe to go uptown alone that night? The chief was right: Thorn Savage should have damn well been there. Abe, forgive me.

Robinson ran his finger along the mailbox nameplates, stopping at Apartment 2, SAVAGE. He smiled when he saw the ancient lock on the inner vestibule door. He had seen the cop's face, and now he knew where he lived. A phenomenal plan was rapidly formulating. He couldn't wait to execute it. Luther Robinson slid back into the night.

# TWENTY-FIVE

**Friday, April 28, noon**

It was a beautiful day in the Heights. The late April sun was warm without being hot, and its brilliant rays splashed along the time-worn, uneven sidewalks, filtered through century-old sycamores.

The routine of the day had begun many hours ago. School children, book-bags strapped to their backs and still wiping sleep from their eyes, had started to appear from the apartment buildings and brownstones around eight. Suits on their way to offices emerged soon after. United Parcel and FedEx had already finished their dropoffs, and Sanitation had just completed its noisy pickups. The nannies with their charges were back too, steering strollers to the playground.

Luther Robinson stretched his mouth wide in a gaping yawn, shifted his weight, and repositioned himself in the form-fitting cockpit bucket. While trying to get comfortable, he never allowed his eyes to stray from the narrow entrance to Grace Court Alley. The bitch hadn't yet shown herself, but Robinson knew eventually she would have to. And when she did, he'd be there waiting. After following the hump cop home last night and then making a quick trip over to his penthouse to pick up the things he might need, he had sped directly back here and had been watching ever since. Come on, bitch, he thought, let's go.

Could he have missed her? he wondered. Maybe she slipped out when he took five lousy minutes to go take a goddamned leak. Possible, but not likely. The bitch was still in there.

At that moment the private garage door to Number 8 Grace Court Alley began to rise. The small red convertible backed out, driven by the good-looking white chick. Savage's ho. Luther started his engine and dropped the BMW into gear.

The Miata made straight for the Brooklyn-Queens Expressway, blending quickly into the midday flow. Luther was impressed by the aggressiveness of the driver. Almost losing sight of the vehicle as it merged into the Gowanus approach, he cut off three cars and used all the horses at his command to catch up, determined to keep it in view. The woman was setting a quick pace. "Bitch is tough to follow," he mumbled as he herky-jerked left-foot brake, right-foot gas, around and through the intervening traffic. She was tough, but he wasn't going to lose her now.

Gina checked the time and slowed her pace. There was no need for further speeding; she was back on schedule. Anyhow, Morgana would surely be late. She always was.

They usually met for their monthly lunches in Lower Manhattan near Gina's job. But since she had taken a week off to finalize some of the wedding plans—caterer, flowers, dress fittings—they would meet today at Morgana's favorite spot in Bay Ridge, Brooklyn.

Gina smiled as her thoughts turned to Morgana. They were as different as two people could be, and yet Morgana was the best friend she'd ever had. They'd known each other since P.S. 52 in Sheepshead Bay, and down through the years had become inseparable. Morgana was tolerant, generous, outrageous, and quite wealthy thanks to a terrific settlement from a terrible marriage. Dave Feldman was a complete lunatic with the Midas touch in business and the Tyson touch at home. The last time Morgana had her jaw wired, she also wired her attorney, and Dave Feldman took a monumental financial broadside. Since the divorce Morgana had devoted herself to fund-raising, and she sat on the boards of several charitable organizations.

By some miracle Gina found a spot on a meter on Fourth Avenue and, with backing skills any parking-lot jockey would envy, slipped the Mazda behind a navy-blue Toyota in one quick shot. It was a short half-block to Shelley's Café. She had just settled in at a small table in the corner when Morgana made her entrance.

Dressed in psychedelic yellow Spandex leggings and a swimmingly large cashmere sweater that billowed around her narrow hips, the maid of honor waved an armful of bangles in Gina's direction and "yoo-hoo"ed freely across the crowded restaurant. Three-inch heels clicking like castanets, she wound her way through the labyrinth of tables and threw her arms open for an embrace.

"Jeez, I don't believe it, I'm actually on time for a change." Morgana's voice was deep and throaty. Oversized Yves Saint Laurent sunglasses hid her dark exotic eyes and a smile widened her pretty face. "You look absolutely wonderful, Ms. McCormick."

"You're looking pretty fashionable yourself," Gina acknowledged, and then asked incredulously, "You've gotta tell me, Morgie, what color *are* those leggings?"

"Buttery Banana, silly. Absolutely the latest." She spun around, locking her head and arms at weird angles normally only achieved by department store mannequins. "I saw them in a window. I jammed on my brakes—almost got in an accident—and ran in and bought them. Just had to have them. Aren't they great?" She hung a hot-pink-and-gold tapestry tote over the back of an adjacent chair and sat down with a flourish. "What a beautiful day it is," she rambled on in typical Morgana Feldman style. "Don't you just love the spring?"

"I think it's the best time of the year," Gina agreed, smiling. "I think it even does something for my looks because I feel so good."

"You don't need nuthin' to help your looks, sweetie." Morgana winked. "When ya got it, ya got it. Know what I mean?"

Gina shook her head and handed Morgana the menu. "You're a pip, lady. Come on, let's have some lunch. I'm starving."

Luther Robinson looked on from Fourth and Marine, and then ducked into the entrance of Reuben's Shoes and surveyed the street. The Miata was a half-block away, parked on a meter right behind a blue Toyota. Turning his back to traffic, he did some impromptu window-shopping as a radio car cruised slowly by. He watched the reflection in the glass until the cops disappeared from view.

Gina ordered the shrimp salad—the best on the planet according to Morgana—and fresh melon slices. Morgana followed with another favorite: spicy chicken wings with celery and blue cheese. Gus the waiter scribbled the order, bowed, and left.

"So tell me," Morgana asked quietly, "how's Thorn holding up?"

"Not so good."

"Ohhhh. I'm sorry."

"He's been very quiet."

"You mean, more so than usual?"

"Yes. Much more. He's depressed. Acutely so, maybe.

You know how he is. He's intense, for starters. It's hard to tell what he's thinking most of the time. Abe was his best friend. It's gonna take a long time for him to recover from this. He carries things around inside, if you know what I mean."

Morgana listened, shaking her head sadly. "What did he say about the fund?"

"I don't think he wants us to do it. In fact, I'm sure he doesn't."

"So, what's the problem?"

"He's got this notion that he's somehow responsible for Abe's death."

"Guilt is a terrible thing."

"Yeah," Gina said. "I just don't know what to do."

"I still don't understand why he wouldn't want us to start the fund."

"It's because he needs to somehow be the provider here. And not turn any of the burden over to others." Gina shrugged. "If I can get him to change his mind, can I still count on your help to set it up?"

"Course you can," Morgana assured, raising her sunglasses and resting them atop her head. Her almond-shaped ebony eyes gave her a sensual Eurasian look. "I'd love to work on something for that poor policeman's boy." Then, instantly switching gears, she said, "So tell me about your dress, I'm dying to see it. It must be gorgeous."

"Oh, it's beautiful. It's silk brocade in ivory, with an Alençon lace collar. I went for the final fitting yesterday." A dreamy gaze settled across her face. "I can't wait for you to see it."

"It sounds positively gorgeous. I just know you're going to look like something out of this world." Morgana poured her Perrier and raised her glass. "A toast to your future and your happiness."

\*      \*      \*

Luther Robinson strutted up to the passenger side of the little Mazda as if he owned it. Again he summoned the skills he had honed as a young thief. With a quick eyes left, then right, he jammed the slim-jim past the outer felts of the passenger window. Another eyes left, then right. Slowly, sensitively, he moved the spring-steel tool through the door's innards. His concentration suddenly snapped as he realized that he was being watched. Looking over the convertible's top, he saw a woman motioning from behind the wheel of a stopped Oldsmobile. She wanted a spot and apparently thought he was getting ready to leave.

"Not going out. Sorry," he hollered. The disappointed old bag sneered and drove off.

Lifting and twisting the slim-jim, he probed blindly for the lock actuator inside the door. *Click,* the lock button popped. He checked over his shoulder, slid into the car, and closed the door. There on the shift console, where he had expected to find it, was the garage-door remote. His gloved fingers slid open the access hatch on the remote's backside. He examined the eight tiny toggles that determined the coded frequency combination and memorized their configuration. After closing the hatch, he carefully placed the remote precisely where he'd found it, with the Linear logo facing the dash. While relocking the Miata's door, Robinson picked up in his peripheral vision another radio car cruising the block. He made a show of digging into his pocket, and then cranked a coin into the parking meter.

The precinct car rolled past without giving him a look.

"Rings. Tell me about the rings," Morgana said.

"Plain gold bands. That's all we want."

"God, this is so romantic, isn't it?" Morgana was getting misty. "Did you arrange for flowers? Contract with the caterer? You know, everybody believes they've got to be married in the eyes of God. But us Jews believe you've also got to be married in the eyes of the caterer." They both broke out in laughter.

"There's going to be lots of flowers and lots of candle-light. Everything will be in spring colors. It's just going to be wonderful. I never thought I'd be this happy again," she sighed thoughtfully. "He's a terrific guy."

"You deserve to be happy, Gina. You're a good woman." Then, leaning across the table in a coy whisper, "So listen. You never told me, but . . . is he a good lover?"

"What?" Gina sputtered, choking on her water.

"Tsk. You know what I mean. Is he . . . ?"

Only Morgana, Gina thought. "He's wonderful," she replied succinctly as Gus arrived with their food.

It was Morgana's turn to pay the check. She left a gener-ous tip and walked Gina out of the restaurant. "Send my love to Thorn," she said, patting Gina's hand. "Tell him I was asking for him. Tell him I hope . . . you know, that he feels better."

After a quick hug, Gina turned and headed to her car. She could hear the click of Morgana's heels fading in the distance and chuckled to herself.

The rest of the afternoon should have been uneventful, but it wasn't. During the ride home, lightning began to flash in the heavens. What had been a beautiful day began to take a dark and threatening turn. Fast-moving, sullen clouds were draping the city like a pall. Gina increased her speed at the first crack of thunder, and her hands nervously twisted on the steering wheel. Another boom in the distance reignited her paralyzing childhood fear of electrical storms. She needed to reach the security of home. Fast.

\*     \*     \*

Savage finished reading the last of the fives turned in that morning by the four canvassing teams working the apartment buildings and tenements off Broadway in the One-fifties. The reports all read alike: nothing to report. Slipping off his glasses, he pinched his aching sinuses and gazed out at the dimming sky through the dirty windows of his temporary Manhattan North office. From the looks of the angry cloud formations that appeared to be converging on the city from every direction, what had been a beautiful day when he sat down with the fives was rapidly going into the dumper. Savage's thoughts shifted to Gina. He hoped the brewing storm wasn't going to be a boomer. She had a tough time with those.

He reached into his jacket pocket for a Wint-O-Green, but came up only with the cellophane-wrapped fortune cookie he'd been carrying around for days. He tore open the wrapper, cracked the cookie in half, and pulled out the fortune slip. As he munched the bland pieces, the phone on his desk began to ring. Pete Pezzano walked into the small office at that moment. Waving Savage off, he picked up the call.

"Homicide Task Force, Lieutenant Pezzano." Big Bird rubbed his bloodshot eyes as he spoke. "Yes, ma'am, hold on, he's right here." He held out the phone to Thorn. "A.D.A. Pankow."

"Thorn Savage. Tell me something good, Marilyn. We're running out of time."

"Wish I could, Sergeant. Just got off the phone with Kornbluth. It's the second time I've spoken with him. Just as I suspected, I've gotten nowhere."

"Ah, shit," Savage growled, again gazing out the window, thinking the Hamilton homicide investigation was going the way of the weather. "He doesn't want to deal?"

"Never even got to that. He's calling our bluff. He's

inviting the indictments, saying he can beat the conspiracy and money laundering charges at trial. He may be right."

"Yeah, but he's still got the bribery to worry about."

"Their position is if they beat the top two, the underlining bribery can't stand without the superior charges. I don't happen to agree with that particular assumption, and I truly don't believe Kornbluth really does. I think he's just jockeying for time—running the clock. As it stands now, at least, they're saying that they're prepared to go to bat."

"So you've not been able to personally interview Ogden?"

"No. Kornbluth won't allow it. Besides, there's no point in trying to squeeze them on Hamilton's murder, unless and until they're convinced they've got a big problem with the current matters. Right now they don't seem pressured at all. I gave it my best shot, but we're gonna need more."

"Will Ogden get bail Tuesday?"

"Almost assuredly. The judge'll set it high, but he will set it. He's not going to have much choice. What we've got so far isn't compelling enough for him to continue to deny bail. And Kornbluth knows that."

"Can't imagine that bastard getting back out on the street. We need a little more time to develop the connection between Ogden and Robinson. Once we can show that, I'm positive that Ogden's gonna want to cut a deal to save his own ass."

"Sergeant, have you guys been able to come up with *anything* more? Because without additional leverage, this guy will never talk. Without more positive incriminating evidence to carry us beyond prima facie, we may not be able to convict at trial. And they know it." Facetiously, she added, "He'll wind up pleading out downstairs to attempted overnight parking, or some other bullshit unclassified misdemeanor. He'll do a lousy thirty days, if that, and walk. Then we're all back to square one."

"I know you're right, but this guy pulls the strings on a homicidal maniac, Marilyn. Allowing him back on the street is like . . . enrolling Ted Bundy at Swarthmore. Real bad things are gonna happen."

"Well, you guys better come up with something fast. We've only got the weekend and Monday to tighten up our case against him. Otherwise . . ."

"Otherwise," Savage echoed dispiritedly, "he's out on bail. I can promise you we're eventually gonna have the solid stuff we need, but we're gonna need a little more time."

"I'll do what I can on Tuesday, but no guarantees."

"Thanks. I know you'll do your best." Savage hung up and looked across at Pete Pezzano, who had slouched even lower in the chair. "Terrific, huh?"

Pezzano shook his big head and exhaled hard through pursed lips.

Savage offhandedly picked up the fortune slip and read it.

*Life without love is not worth living.*

\* \* \*

The sky was charcoal. Storm clouds billowed above and several tentative drops of rain streaked Luther Robinson's spotless windshield. He pulled into the parking lot, closed the moonroof of his BMW, and strode with arrogant determination into Dyker Garage Doors, Inc.

"May I help you, sir?" The clerk's name tag was as big as her friendly smile as she greeted him from the far side of the showroom. As she approached, the smile drooped and she stiffened like a ramrod, just as he'd expected. As if on cue, a nearby clap of thunder exploded, shaking the metal building to its foundations and adding to the chill that must have been reverberating through "Joyce"'s backbone. The drooped smile morphed into a mask of alarm.

"I do hope so . . . Joyce," Robinson replied, knowing menace rode just beneath his velvet voice and dignified bearing.

Unconsciously, the woman placed her hand over the name tag.

"I've somehow misplaced the remote for my garage door. Do you handle Linear door openers?"

"Yes . . . yes, we do," she stammered, her glance falling away from his face.

Flustered, the woman knelt at a base cabinet behind the sales counter and fumbled around. After prying open several boxes, she turned and asked, "Is this what you need?"

"That, my dear Joyce, is precisely what I need." He was toying with her. "Oh," he added as an afterthought, "do install a fresh battery."

He paid cash from a wad, declined a receipt, and left as the woman darted to the office, no doubt to sit and catch her breath.

Back in the privacy of his BMW, he slid away the cover on the reverse side of the remote and carefully examined the series of eight switches. He set the first two up, the next two down. 5-6-7-8: up, down, up, down. He slid the cover panel back into place.

Earsplitting thunder cracked and a white-hot bolt of lightning, jagged and forked like a dowsing rod from Hell, flashed across the menacing sky. Huge drops of rain splattered his windshield. Within moments the deluge was in full force.

# TWENTY-SIX

Straining on tiptoe, Gina stretched to adjust the framed oil portrait of Millicent Kearney that hung in the front room above the mantel. The portrait of Harrison Kearney's late wife was one of his most cherished possessions. Startled by a sudden violent burst of thunder, Gina reeled stiffly backward into the center of the room. Frozen, hands clenched at her sides, she quaked in fear. Violent storms had always been her enemy. This one had been raging for hours, and she wondered when it would end. Surely it would let up soon. The ring of the telephone made her tense up again as she stood eyeing the picture, making sure it was level. Breathless, she moved in short anxious steps to the sofa and picked up the portable on the third ring.

"Hello, sweetie." Thorn's baritone came across the line. "How're you doing on this terrible night?" She relaxed a little at the sound of his voice.

"Okay, I guess," she said. "But I know I'd be doing a lot better if you were here. You know what these storms do to me." As she spoke, she parted the curtain behind the sofa and peered warily into the night. In the wash of the buffeting streetlight, the downpour was coming in rippled sheets, and she watched the gusting wind drive the rain sideways. A raw shiver momentarily possessed her.

"Gina, I'm gonna be stuck up here till well after midnight, and tomorrow I've got to be at the chief's office by eight. I've been ordered down there, and at the very least I expect a hellacious chewing out for the way this case is going."

"And at the very worst?" she probed.

"Don't know. Might have to get my uniforms out of mothballs. But I called to make sure you're gonna be okay. I know how much you hate these storms."

"I'm all right," she lied, releasing the curtain and curling her legs beneath her on the down-cushioned couch. "I guess I won't see you until dinner tomorrow? Neary's at eight?" Her resolve was stiffening.

"Right. Listen, Gina, are you sure you're okay?" He persisted. "I'll just take the rest of the night off . . . I could be at your place in twenty minutes."

Mustering her strength, she declined. "You really are sweet to be so concerned, but pretty soon I'm going to be a cop's wife. I can't be expecting my husband to come running home every time there's a little rainstorm." Gina strained to sound convincing. She probably wasn't, but Thorn acted convinced.

"Love you, Gina," he whispered. She loved to hear the words.

"I love you too, Thornton Savage." She clicked off the cordless phone with a rose-colored thumbnail and indulged herself with romantic visions of how different life would be when Thorn became her husband. For starters, there would be far fewer of these frightening and lonely nights. Her parents' reassuring presence had relieved the panic attacks when she was a little girl, and she knew that if Thorn could be there now, these unsettling, childish feelings would subside.

Gina uncoiled from the sofa, pulled the robe tightly about her, and straightened the curtain, which hadn't fallen properly back into place. Passing the gilt wall mirror that hung above an eighteenth-century pier table, she moved down the paneled hall to the first-floor bath. With a turn of the faucet, hot water began to stream into the deep old ball-and-claw-footed porcelain tub. The fixtures were very old. The room was from a gentler era, and bathing here transported her back in time, back to a time she often thought herself more suited to.

Studying herself in the cheval glass as the tub filled behind her, she opened her robe and let it fall from her shoulders. It gathered at her feet. Her thoughts turned to Thorn. She needed him . . . now. Closing her eyes dreamily, she arched her head back in a slow sensual sweep and imagined him kissing her long, yearning neck. Her breasts heaved as she sensed Thorn's powerful arms about her, his hands touching, searching, and caressing. Gina could feel his tender kiss driving her on and longed for his strong thrusts, which always brought her again and again to passionate heights and explosive release. She sighed deeply and looked again at the mirror, her naked image now stolen away as gathering steam obscured the glass, leaving only the vaguest suggestion of her form.

Sighing, she slipped into the tub and let the water envelop her.

The car moved slowly up the slight grade of Hicks Street, slogging through rain that was easily winning the contest against determined windshield wipers. Squinting to see into the alley, Luther finally discerned lights glowing in the town house; she must be home. The unmarked Crown Victoria wasn't parked outside, so she was alone. Hunched forward against the steering wheel, his face nearly pressed against the windshield, he struggled to see anything of the roadway before him. The BMW carefully crept north three blocks and parked around the corner on Pierrepont, just off Henry. Despite the incredible downpour, he would make his approach on foot.

The night was perfect for him. He loved this weather. The wild, gusting turbulence that blew the rain in every direction excited him. It played to his love of violence. As he leaned into it, he struggled to control the jerking umbrella that twisted and turned spasmodically in his grasp, like a trapped animal trying to break free from its bonds. He overtightened his grip and made it a game of domination. He could feel his adrenaline building, his whole body going on full alert. He would enjoy this night.

The heavens were raising Hell. Pitch-black alternated sporadically with surreal electric blue, as lightning arced wildly across Brooklyn and spent itself in the Narrows. The resonance of rolling thunder reverberated in and around the older Heights structures, hitting them like a phantom wrecking ball and shaking them to their brick-lined basements. A bolt grounded nearby, flashing night to day. He smelled the ozone.

As Luther turned into Hicks, he stopped short, stunned. A police radio car was parked directly in front of Grace Court Alley. What, he thought, was it doing there? It wasn't there a few moments ago. Interior lights burned bright inside the cruiser, and he could see two figures seated within.

"Hmmm."

Torrents of water cascaded from the umbrella's leading edge, splashing at his feet as he pondered his next move. It made no sense at all, he thought, for anybody to be driving around in this storm, and probably most patrol cars not on assignment would sit it out in some quiet spot. But why did those suckas have to park there?

"Dammit."

Twelve-hundred-dollar shoes squished and Armani

slacks clung to his flesh from the knees down. Standing there in the torrent, waiting for the cops to drive off, would surely call attention to him. He turned to retrace his steps and trekked to a bank of pay phones on Montague. It was twelve-thirty when he lifted the receiver and dialed 911.

"Emergency Operator 328. What is your emergency?" The voice was that of a young black woman.

"Dere's dis po-leece officer gettin' the shit beat out of his ass over here on Tillary Street at the corner of Jay. Y'all better send some help." In his best street voice, Robinson feigned excitement and hung up before the operator could ask anything further. He'd said enough. He turned again into the gusting wind that blew in from the harbor, and walked headlong into the storm back toward Hicks. He hadn't taken many steps from the phone when the flashing roof lights of the troublesome radio car came into view. It roared past him, siren wailing, its speed thwarted by the braking action of puddles in the roadway. He turned and watched as it passed, the sound of its siren fading in the distance as another roll of thunder crashed.

He swaggered. The unwitting sentries were gone.

Gina patted herself dry to the accompanying sound of bathwater gurgling down the drain. She could hear little of the storm in this windowless room, which was why she'd selected it for tonight's extended bath. Her hair turbaned in a towel, she sat, naked, on a velvet stool and, propping one foot at a time on the edge of the draining tub, applied a lightly scented lotion to her legs. Thunder boomed again nearby and her heart rate quickened as the house lights momentarily dimmed.

"Oh, Thorn. God, how I wish you were here." Her brows rose and she squinted in fear. She forced her thoughts to the upcoming wedding—beautiful flowers, sparkling crystal goblets, brimming punch bowls, and festive music. She envisioned friends dancing by, smiling in happiness for her and Thorn.

She stepped to the small alcove off the bath and slipped into a delicately embroidered cotton nightgown. Removing the turban, she shook her hair loose and ran the antique sterling comb through it. She could almost smell the white gardenias, arranged amid hundreds of small pink tea roses, mingled with baby's breath.

The darkly dressed figure with the black umbrella picked up his pace. His steps came faster, with purpose, those of a hungry predator that had selected its prey. Into the alley cul-de-sac he swept, rapid footfalls muffled on wet pavement. Homing in on the overhead door, he triggered the remote. The metallic starting clack of the mechanism was lost in the noise of the storm, carried off by swirling wind and rain. His footsteps perfectly timed, he again clicked the remote. The door lowered slowly behind him. Sidestepping the Miata, he collapsed the umbrella.

Gina stepped into a pair of satin mules and slid the gleaming solitaire back into place on her left ring finger. It was time for bed. Dousing the light, she left the bathroom and made her way back up the hall. She stopped opposite the staircase to give the grandfather clock seven more days of life. Bending before it, Gina rewound the heavy weights as the huge brass pendulum swung gently from side to side. It was there—in the pendulum's convex reflection—that she saw a dark specter looming behind her.

Spinning quickly, she found herself face-to-face with a monstrous visage, a gargoyle with a hideous grin. She was frozen. The specter took her in its arms and embraced her in a mortal pas de deux.

No words were spoken. Death made not a sound.

The icy blade made its fatal penetration. He released her, and she slipped to the cold slate floor as her knees gave way. Gina curled into a fetal ball, blinking in disbelief. She struggled for breath as consciousness ebbed. In a broken whisper, timid with fear of the unknown, she murmured: "Oh, Thorn."

Death knelt beside her. He was not yet finished with her.

# TWENTY-SEVEN

**Saturday, April 29, 1:00 A.M.**

"Jesus, is this storm ever gonna let up?" Red-eyed and weary, his size-twelve brogues propped heavily on the desk, Pete Pezzano stared contemplatively through the squad-room window at the relentless rain.

Savage sat opposite, rereading some of the original fives. Nothing new had developed since speaking with Marilyn Pankow earlier in the day. J. Harry Kornbluth would have little problem arranging bail for his client on Tuesday morning. Unless the People strengthened their case by then, Ogden would walk.

"Dammit." With swift and intense force, Savage batted the Manhattan phone book from the desk. The thick directory landed askew clear on the other side of the room. His sudden display of anger set Pezzano off.

"You know," Pezzano said, "in the old days we'd go down to the Culture Club and drag Robinson right out of there by his fuckin' nuts. And nobody would say a goddamned word. Why? Because we were doin' God's work, that's why. Day or two later we'd have a confession, and the case would be closed. Now we gotta sit around with our hands on our asses, waiting for Ogden and Robinson to voluntarily declare themselves murderers. We can't build a fuckin' case around any witnesses—they're all fuckin' dead. Killed by these two cocksuckers."

The few detectives still in the squad room sat silently as the boss raged on. Pezzano was losing it; exhaustion and frustration had taken their toll.

"They can play by any fuckin' rules they want," Pezzano continued, "while we gotta go by Marquis of Queensberry."

Savage nodded in sympathetic agreement, knowing the lieutenant would soon run out of gas.

"This is a fuckin' war with these sons of bitches. They're eatin' us alive and we can't fight back." Saliva dribbled onto Pezzano's jutting chin as he ranted, verbalizing his frustration.

"Pete, it'll all come together," Savage quietly interrupted. "We'll get these pricks." He kept his tone measured, not knowing where he'd parked his own anger.

"Ahhh, shit!" Pezzano hissed as his gaze drifted off somewhere into the unseen distance.

"Pete, you know we're expecting to hear something from Latent in the morning. I'm betting they've got something to report. Would you have someone check with them first thing?"

Pezzano's Saint Bernard head nodded. He was cooling off. "Consider it done."

Savage gave him a reassuring slap on the upper arm. "Thanks, Pete. I appreciate everything you're doing, buddy."

"Ah, Thorn . . . sometimes I just wonder. . . ." Big Bird's voice trailed off as he stood and headed to the coffeepot.

Savage glanced at the squad room clock. It was coming up on 1:15. "Well, I think we can call it a night, so I'm outta here. I'll call you from One P.P. in the morning. Right after my meeting with the boss."

"Howd'ya think that's gonna go?" Pezzano asked, raising his brow.

"Don't know. But I'm sure it won't be pretty."

"Worried about being flopped?" Pezzano asked.

Savage nodded. "Ever since it's turned out that Ogden and Robinson are the suspects in Abe's murder, the chief's been glacier-cold. I really wouldn't be surprised if I was flopped. Hell, as far as he's concerned, direct orders were disobeyed."

"There's no way anybody coulda predicted a thing like this," Pezzano offered in support.

"Hey, he warned against it," Savage lamented.

"Still. You shouldn't be held accountable," Pezzano said. "But if he does flop ya, you won't be the first fallen angel in this fuckin' job. And you sure as hell won't be the last, right? Anyway, if I know you, you'll land on your feet."

"Good night, Petey."

"Good night, Thorn. Careful driving home in this freakin' storm." Pezzano locked his desk. His exhausting eighteen-hour tour was finally over. "Wish this rain let up earlier. I'd have made the trip home and slept with my wife. Too late now. Looks like the dorm again tonight."

Savage paused at the station house door, surveying the slackening rain, grateful that his car was parked nearby. Jerking the collar of his Burberry full up, he made a quick dash out. Moments later he was headed downtown, toward home and sleep. He was wasted. The marathon had been going on forever, it seemed, and he'd been averaging only a few hours of sleep per night. Abe's murder had devastated him, sapping him physically and emotionally. But every ounce of energy he could find would be spent in the apprehension of his friend's killers. Until that was accomplished, everything else in his life had to take a back seat. It was good that Gina understood. Their wedding day was drawing nearer, and he couldn't wait until he could go home each night to her.

The Ford turned east and ran crosstown at 110th. He

slowed the speed of the wipers as he headed downtown again on Fifth Avenue, crossing the line dubbed the DMZ by cops. It was the point along uptown Fifth Avenue where graffiti-scarred buildings and trash-strewn vacant lots, emblematic of the ghetto, gave way to the opulence that is Fifth Avenue, below Mount Sinai Hospital. He sighed in relief, feeling less guilt for not breaking away from the investigation to pacify Gina. She could sleep well now. The storm was over.

The collar of his coat still turned up, Savage walked slowly to his building. Though the rain had stopped, rivers ran along the curb, converging on the overworked drain at Houston Street. Clogged with debris carried along by the raging stream, it strained, unable to swallow the incoming volume. As he walked, he breathed deeply. The air smelled pure. The incredible downpour had hosed off the filthy city, flushing out the crud that built up over time in its nooks and crannies. Water still dripped from building facades and awnings. We needed this, he concluded.

Pushing his way into the vestibule of the three-story brownstone, Savage emptied his overflowing mailbox. Most of the accumulated correspondence was junk. The remaining letters were bills. One from Visa—skydiving fees, he suspected. There was also something from the IRS that turned out to be a benign correspondence. Whew, he thought, it's amazing what those three letters can do to a pulse rate. Upstairs, he turned the key in the lock and trudged into the flat. Draped across the hump of the camelback, Ray blinked twice in cold acknowledgment before nodding off again.

Savage tossed the mail onto the cluttered kitchen counter, grabbed a carton of milk from the refrigerator, and raised the container to his lips. Gagging at the smell of the sour and curdled contents, he opted instead for a can of tomato juice. After filling Ray's food dish and water bowl, he reset the kitchen clock to daylight savings time and then slogged into the bedroom. His clothes landed in a lump on the floor. They needed dry cleaning anyway. He set the alarm for six and slid under the sheet, hoping to actually get some much-needed rest. His mind filled with the investigation, Harvard tuitions, and the a.m. meeting with Chief Wilson, Savage finally slipped into a tortured non-sleep.

The BMW sat idle. The driver watched as the lights went out in the second-floor apartment.

"Good Christ," Savage mumbled as he raised his head from the balled-up pillow. The pounding at the door was heavy. Enough to wake him from the deepest sleep he'd had in weeks. At first he thought he was dreaming, hearing things, but there it was again, a no-nonsense summons.

"What in holy Hell is this?" He sprang from the bed with an agility that belied his zonked-out grogginess. Heavily hooded eyes snatched a quick glance at the Westclox. It was four-thirty in the morning and, until his eyes could adjust, darker than the inside of a coal miner's mitt.

He reached for his robe and instinctively grabbed the .38 from the nightstand. The pounding at the apartment door started again. The thought *this can't be anything good* cycled repeatedly in his head. He groped his way through the living room and foyer to the source of the alarm.

In silence he peered through the door's peephole to see—nothing. Cautiously, he slid back the bolt and opened the door a crack. Nothing. Nobody. Puzzled and dazed, he stepped into the lighted hallway and looked down the long staircase. No one was there. It was quiet, not a sound. Something was very wrong. As he turned, he spotted the manila envelope that had been duct-taped to his door.

He stared at it. With cold certainty he knew it contained something terrible. Dry-mouthed, he slipped the gun into his robe pocket and began to pull the tape from the door. He pried open the rabbit-ear clip and tore at the envelope's seal. Despite the dread that squeezed his gut, he spread the envelope wide. The nail on the finger inside was finely manicured and rose-colored. The finger itself still bore a gold ring. Though caked with dried blood, the solitaire in the Tiffany setting was unmistakable.

His mind raced. His body quaked violently as his hands clenched into stone-crushing fists.

A wild man, Savage turned and crashed blindly back through the dark apartment, leaving a swath of tumbling furniture and overturned lamps until he reached the window that fronted Sullivan Street. He yanked the venetian blind, tearing it from its ancient mounts, and jerked wildly at the window sash, muscling it open with sheer brute force. Half naked, gasping in deep quivering gulps, he leaned from the open window, his mind overloaded with hatred and rage.

The street was empty and still. A *Times* truck waited for a green at the corner of Bleecker, but there wasn't a person within sight. He strained to hear, hoping to discern footsteps above the idling hum of the truck's noisy diesel. Looking north on Sullivan, beyond Bleecker, he made out a low-slung car lurching away from the curb. Floor-boarded, its wheels losing traction on the wet asphalt, the car raced toward Washington Square. It was impossible to make out the license-plate number or distinguish the make. But as the vehicle grew faint in the distance, Savage released a tortured primal scream.

Pinholes in the left taillight lens shone through the mist-filled night like thousand-watt kliegs.

# TWENTY-EIGHT

**Tuesday, May 2, noon**

The bumper-to-bumper cortege snaked along the narrow, winding roadway. It extended from the grave site clear back to the gilded-iron gates of St. Charles Cemetery in Pinelawn. Gina had a lot of friends, and it seemed that every one of them had turned out to say good-bye. Savage had a lot of friends, and it seemed that every one of them had turned out to offer support.

Morgana Feldman and Armand DeCaprio flanked Savage during the service. Connie and Tony DiLeo, devastated at the loss of their only child, sat in a fog of gloom on metal folding chairs graveside. Gina's father was inconsolable—the light of his life was gone. Even Maureen Gallo showed up. She expressed sympathy and support but then, like the lady she was, remained at a discreet distance, blending anonymously into the background.

Surrounded by rows of friends and supporters, Savage had never felt more alone. Unblinking eyes and a thousand-mile stare revealed him to be off on a very long walk down the dark streets of his own soul, looking in at the great hollowness that had taken residence there. As some priest conferred the unheard words of the final blessing, Thorn noted only how the sprinkled holy water beaded up on the crowned lid of the polished casket. He was stoic and silent—like a dormant volcano—and his distant expression never changed as his heart and soul was lowered into the muddy Long Island grave.

Thorn drew on every last molecule of self-control to conceal the fury that coursed beneath the surface. This wasn't over. This had only begun.

For the sake of Gina's memory, he remained graveside after the service, expressing countless "thank you's" for endless condolences. Despite the worried pleas of both Armand and Morgana, Thorn drove back to the city alone. He had much to do.

"Judge, the people request that the no-bail order currently in effect be continued in the matter of *People* versus *Ogden*."

"Has the case been presented upstairs, Ms. Pankow?" the judge asked, perusing the case jacket and leafing through Ogden's probation report. He didn't bother to look up at the A.D.A.

"No, Your Honor," she responded. "However—"

"And why is that?" the judge demanded with an irritated frown. At the defendant's table, J. Harry Kornbluth gave his client a knowing nudge.

"Scheduling difficulties with the arresting officer, Your Honor," she offered. "The matter could have been presented yesterday. However, the officer was unable to appear due to a family tragedy." She was bending the truth and knew it. But under the circumstances, who could prove her wrong? She'd read the newspaper accounts of the Mc-Cormick murder and was now an unannounced but very willing participant in the advancement of *People* versus *Ogden*.

"Judge Cooperman," Kornbluth interrupted, "the People have had more than enough time to present this matter to the grand jury. But the seven-day no-bail clock placed on them by Judge Cromartie has run out. Unfortunate happenstance notwithstanding, my client can't be expected to endure any further disruptions to his life while the People lollygag around. If they had a case, they should have presented it. Mr. Ogden is prepared to post whatever bail the court sees fit in order to secure his release. We steadfastly maintain his innocence and dare to say that the People will probably never be able to gain an indictment in this matter. For some unknown reason, they appear to be stalling. They're free to stall all they like, but not while my client rots in Riker's."

The judge scribbled notations on the case jacket and declared, "Bail is set at five hundred thousand dollars. Bailiff, call the next case."

It would be the last time Savage ever set foot in the town house Gina had loved so much. She hadn't owned it, but had always seen to it as if it were hers. With a hesitant push against the glossy black-enameled door, Thorn let himself in. He punched the five-digit code into the alarm keypad and expelled a sigh as his gaze fell fully on what had been her world.

He had come, he told himself, to collect belongings that had accumulated there during their time together: clothes, books, and some pictures. He'd come, he really knew, because he couldn't let go.

Flipping on lights, Thorn moved in a semiconscious daze through the deeply carpeted living room and dining area into her kitchen. There he looked aimlessly around— for what he did not know—and then moved reluctantly into the long hallway where she'd faced her killer. Heavily hooded, swollen eyes never glanced at the spot where she'd fallen. They could not bear to see the sum total of her life, now but a mere chalk outline on a polished slate floor.

Grabbing the newel post at the foot of the staircase, Savage began to take the steps, slowly, like a man in weighted shoes. Tired and weak, he clutched the hardwood balustrade tightly. The ornate railing was tough and strong, and it gave him needed support. The hall clock below startled him as it sounded the Westminster chimes and then gonged eight times. He trudged along the upstairs hallway that led to her bedroom. As he entered, the tight tourniquets of self-control that he had worn for days let go. All the emotional lacerations began to hemorrhage.

Taken on a windy day at the beach, the photograph in many ways was unremarkable. It was slightly out of focus, and in it her hair was tousled, as was his. They were smiling in a way that only happy lovers can. The candid photo revealed them at their best and somehow captured their essence. He crossed to her bed and sat, picking up the framed picture from the nightstand. He stared at her happy face. The photo blurred and became indistinct as he blinked his watery eyes to regain focus.

Thorn stared out through the west window, mesmerized by the steady stream of traffic on the spotlit Brooklyn Bridge. As if in a trance, he pondered the headlights of white juxtaposed against the taillights of red: the constant ebb and flow of the city that he both loved and hated. He looked down at the tirelessly moving river, thinking that some things just don't die.

A tear flashed down his cheek as his eyes took in the majestic old sycamore across the street, which had been Gina's favorite tree. It had been planted long ago by someone surely now gone, as Gina was now gone. Thorn studied it. The bright green leaves, similar to those of a maple, seemed to be painted on. They were motionless and drooping, as if in mourning. Come autumn its leaves would fall along with the golf ball–sized prickly seed pods; the kind he and his kid brother Brian had thrown at one another in mock combat as children so many years ago. But next spring the leaves would return, green and beautiful, bigger and better. Gina would not return. But Thorn knew he would forever feel her embrace when in the shadow of a sycamore.

Pulling the picture to his chest, he took one last look at the frilly, feminine room. He closed the door, made his way back down the flight of stairs, and headed for the den.

A brand-new bottle of Glenlivet beckoned him from the bar. Bewildered, unable to sort through where his life would go from here, he selected a glass, poured, and re-capped the bottle. He gulped down the liquor. Maybe, if God was merciful, the booze would numb the pain. She was gone. It was finished. Over. Good fortune like that, he thought, could never happen again within this lifetime. Be-sides, he would never want anyone but Gina.

He poured again, not bothering to recap the bottle.

Memories of her stormed through his tortured mind. Reduced to tears and bludgeoned by grief and sorrow one moment, he found himself overflowing with hatred and an urgent desire for revenge the next. Finally, despair and hopelessness completely seized him. Mentally exhausted, he collapsed on the sofa and fell into an anguished sleep filled with tormented and twisting dreams that kept leading him back to her muddy grave.

The grandfather clock was striking three when he came to. The bottle stood before him, empty and useless like his soul. The booze hadn't done a damn thing for the crushing pain. Standing, wobbly, he grabbed up the picture and a fresh bottle of whiskey, and stumbled away.

"It's only fitting that I do it there," he whispered in a be-sotted stupor. "That's where she'll be. She'll be waiting for me. . . . I know she will," he mumbled.

Tires chirped as the car skipped recklessly along the empty highways. During the entire wild ride, the emotional bludgeoning continued. He sucked long and often at the scotch, thankful he'd brought it along. Thirty-seven minutes after leaving the town house, the green Ford squealed into the deserted parking field at Oak Beach on Long Island's south shore and came to a sliding stop just before the dune line.

"God forgive me."

He wandered aimlessly along the moonlit beachfront. The wind was strong, almost a gale. Banked sand, storm-tossed and weedy, rose sharply at the shoreline, and he sat there cradling his .38 and looking out to sea. Inexplicably, he studied the back of his hands and, for the first time, noticed the silver hairs that had appeared there. He closed his eyes, recalling the young man he used to be, hair blowing freely in the breeze as he drove his first convertible on some carefree adolescent afternoon. His eyes fell open then and gazed hollow at the foamy surf as it pounded relentlessly against the passive shore. The crests of the biggest waves, backlit by the horizon-hugging moon, shone in a beautiful teal hue. In the distance, more waves crested and broke, exploding one upon the other. They were magnificent in their youth, but as they neared the shore they became less formidable. They finally exhausted themselves at his feet, their mighty strength spent and gone, diminished to a frothy foam destined to be blown to bits by the merciless and unrelenting wind. A gull sailed across the horizon, riding the current for all it was worth. In moments it was only a speck . . . and then nothing.

He licked at his lips. Did the salt come from the airborne spray that swirled about him? Or did it come from tears, windblown and smeared across his tired and lined face?

"Fight it. . . . Fight it, Thornton," he gasped. "Fight it long enough to have your revenge."

The .38 dropped into his pocket, his head into his hands. He wept.

# TWENTY-NINE

**Wednesday, May 3, 12:15 P.M.**

"Chief of detectives' office. Administrative Aide Dolan speaking."

"Darlene, this is Thorn Savage." His tone was brusque. He didn't want to offend her, but neither did he want any small talk. "Boss available?"

"Please hold, Sergeant." Her words, brief and businesslike, rode on a soothing and sympathetic tone. "I'll connect you."

Nude, except for the oversized Yankees T-shirt he'd slept in and a pair of two-strap Birkenstocks that Gina had bought him "for no particular reason," Thorn crunched the kitchen phone receiver between his ear and shoulder while he waited. He quickly popped three aspirin to kill off the pounding in his head, and then ran scalding hot water at the tap and rinsed the Mister Coffee carafe. The tarry gook congealed at the bottom was the dregs of a pot he'd made last week—in another life, before his world had forever changed. He opened the long pantry cabinet beside the stove and, ignoring his stock of ginseng, ginkgo biloba, and vitamin E, reached for the five-pound can of Maxwell House. There, next to the sleeve of coffee filters, was a recently opened package of tea bags. *Gina.* He slammed the pantry door, unable to remember—and no longer caring—why he'd opened it in the first place.

"Thornton?" The line suddenly came alive with Chief Wilson's voice. "Ray Wilson here. How're you bearing up, buddy?"

"Good," he lied, noting the informality of the chief's "Ray," and "buddy."

"If there's anything we can do . . . ?"

"I need some time off."

"Of course you do. You've got it. Take as much time as you need or want. You've been clobbered with two major broadsides. A leave from The Job is certainly in order."

"I've still got all my vacation days, and a lot of 'lost time' on the books. I'd like to lump it all together. I need a timeout," he said, realizing his voice was a lifeless monotone. He remembered accumulating this time for a honeymoon. Now it would be spent on a crusade.

"No problem, Thornton," the chief assured him, making no reference to the disciplinary meeting that had never come about. "You don't need to justify anything here. I'll have Darlene draw up a request for extended leave and I'll approve it today. If you have to exceed the amount of days you have coming, don't worry. We'll work it out somehow."

"Thanks, Chief. I'll stop down at my office in a little while and turn in my car."

"Thorn," the chief of detectives said, "you sure you're all right?"

"I'm fine, boss. Just need a little time."

Despite his scrambled state of mind, Savage knew he had to take the trouble to request the leave. If he just went AWOL, it would have been greatly out of character, and someone would come looking. The last thing he needed was interference from The Job.

His leave request approved, he had all the time necessary to accomplish what he had to do—what he would not do under color of the NYPD. That which anyone else, including the criminal justice system, would be powerless to do. His mind was made up. There would be no Marquis of Queensberry, no prima facie. He would give no quarter and expect none.

After pulling on a pair of faded Levi's and lacing up his favorite pair of Adidas sneakers, he slid the holstered Smith & Wesson into his belt-line. He was dressing for the gladiator's arena, and only he, or his opponents, would leave it alive. Returning to the kitchen, he found Ray sound asleep atop the Kelvinator.

"Still sleeping it off, eh, buddy?" He gently scratched the cat's battle-scarred head, face, and chin. His old friend, secure in his own little world, never moved.

Savage rinsed Ray's beer dish and swept last night's collection of empty Bud cans from the countertop into the kitchen pail. After deep-sixing the empty Dewar's bottle, he put what little was left of the Drambuie back under the sink and again reached for the phone and dialed.

"Paradise Motors, Eli speaking."

"Eli? Thornton Savage. How are you?" The car dealer's phone number was one of the oldest entries in Thorn's address book.

"Thorn, for crissake, where the hell you been? I was saying just the other day I haven't heard from Thorn Savage, must be a year. What's goin' on? You must be a fuckin' general in that police department by now."

"I need a favor."

"Listen." The old man's smoky voice was warm and paternal. "I read the newspapers. I know you got troubles, major-league troubles, as they say. Me and your old man was like brothers, ya know that, right? I loved the man. And somehow I always thought of you as a surrogate son. Thorn, if there's anything I can do to help, you got it."

"I need a car."

"What about that little T-bird that took up space in my shop for three years while you restored it from the ground up?" Eli grunted, surprised. "Whaddya do, get rid of it?"

"I need a very *special* car," Savage intoned ominously.

"You got the pick of the lot," the old man countered. Then with a sarcastic chuckle, he added, "Friggin' things ain't sellin' anyway. Whaddya lookin' for?"

"Nondescript, plainer the better. And it'll need plates."

"Funny plates?"

"You're psychic, Eli." Thorn had always marveled at the man's gift for mind reading. It was that facility which no doubt made Eli Clipper the phenomenal car salesman he'd always been. He could put Henry Ford in a Chevy.

"Yeah. . . ." Savage drawled. "It's gotta have funny plates."

"I got a nice set of Jerseys that came off my cousin Lou's old Merc."

"They can be traced right back."

"Yeah, so what? If anybody wants to talk to poor old cousin Lou, they'll have to dig him up."

"All right. But I also need the car to be untraceable. I don't want anything coming back to haunt you."

"Thorn, you're worrying me," the older man said with a dramatic sigh.

"Don't worry yourself. I'm gonna be okay."

"Get here around eight. I'll have something ready for ya."

Savage flipped ahead a few pages in the address book and dialed Dieter Krongold. Dieter was a defrocked plain-clothesman who ran a half-assed one-man detective agency out of Borough Hall in Brooklyn. He spent his days running down deadbeats and his nights getting the goods on unfaithful spouses. From Dieter he arranged for binoculars and a high-resolution night scope.

Before the afternoon was over, most of the pieces Savage needed were in place. He overfilled Ray's food and water bowls, not knowing when, or if, he would return.

The drive uptown was a blank. He parked the department Ford in front of the Thirteenth and rode the elevator to the third floor. The spring in his step was gone, his face devoid of feeling, as he stepped into the offices of Manhattan South Homicide.

"Boss! Jesus Christ, how are you?" Richie Marcus blurted from behind his cluttered desk in the large squad room. The ex-marine jumped to his feet and, in quick long strides, walked over to greet Savage. "We just got notified from downtown that you'd be taking a leave. That true?"

"True," Savage confirmed. His voice was soft and clear . . . and emotionless. "I'm gonna take some time off. Kinda get myself organized, ya know." Savage held out the keys to his department car and dropped them into Richie's open mitt. "I just stopped by to bring in 7146."

"What're you gonna drive?" Marcus asked. The husky, ruggedly handsome man with the slagheap voice looked at Savage with a disbelieving frown. "All you got is that souped-up little T-bird. If you drive that thing around the city, it'll get destroyed in no time, for crissake. That's if some son of a bitch don't steal it on ya."

"Nah." Savage shook his head, forcing a grin. "I won't be driving the Bird. Not going anywhere. What do I need a car for?" He shrugged his wide shoulders for emphasis. "If I want to go somewhere, I'll take a cab, or a bus. . . ."

Thorn moved slowly past Marcus but was stopped by the other cops from the unit who had clustered to greet him. They had converged to offer expressions of sympathy. He nodded and thanked them all individually, and then quickly disappeared into his office, closing the door behind him.

The first thing he saw was her picture on his desk, and

the already small office suddenly became smaller. The block walls seemed to be closing in. Internal pressures were building again. Savage sat, silently praying for the misery to subside. He had to make it out of the office with the same fortitude he'd displayed when he came in. There could be no breakdown in front of the troops.

While Savage struggled to regain his earlier impassiveness, Richie Marcus knocked on the office door and let himself in.

"Got a minute?"

"What's up, Rich?" Savage murmured.

Marcus closed the door behind him. This was to be a private conversation. "Thought I'd bring you up to date on a few things," he said, and quickly fired up a Winston.

"Shoot."

"Talked with Petey Pezzano a little while ago. Seems Ogden and Robinson have gone underground. None of the surveillance teams have been able to pick up on either one of 'em. They've just vaporized."

"What else?"

"Nothing more on an address for Robinson under either Lucy or Luther. I've checked with postal and every utility, including telephone and cable, going back five years. Even checked with the major papers for home delivery. *Nada.*" Marcus took a deep drag. "Got any idea of how many Robinsons there are in New York?"

Savage nodded. "Probably owns or rents under some other name."

"How long we know one another?" Marcus asked intently.

"A long, long time, Richie."

"How many times have you covered for me? Like in the days when I was too fucked up on booze, or too stupid to cover my own ass."

Savage shrugged. He stared blankly at the man but didn't answer the question. It didn't need to be answered.

"I know you, Thorn. I know how you think. You've watched out for me and saved my job more than once down through the years. I haven't forgotten that."

"The Swami never forgets, does he?" Savage quipped through a manufactured smile, wanting to diminish the heaviness of Richie's approach and put the man at ease.

"You're damn right! The fuckin' Swami *never* forgets." Marcus was suddenly bolder and, at the same time, more relaxed. He leaned forward across Savage's desk and spoke softly. "If it wasn't for you, I'd have put my papers in long ago. Or prob'ly better said, if it wasn't for you, somebody else woulda done it for me. Know what I mean?"

"I'm with ya," Savage said with an attentive nod.

"And you gotta know I loved Abe Hamilton. I knew him every bit as long as you did, from way back when in Street Crime. And you know I wouldn't have fucked with him all the time if I didn't love 'im—know what I mean? Besides, he could give it right back as good as he got it."

Savage nodded again.

"Now," Marcus continued, gauging his every word, "with what happened to Gina . . . and everything. And"— he sucked the cigarette again—"knowing you as well as I do, I know that you've got some kind of plan. I don't need to know what that plan is, but if I can help in any way, I'm here. I'm at your beck and call, night or day. You know where I live." The man leaned closer, and in a conspiratorial whisper added, "Anything!"

Savage cleared out the top drawer of his desk and transferred everything, along with Gina's framed picture, into a legal-size brief folder. He opened his locker and removed a full box of Remington-Peters .38 cartridges; he dropped

them into the folder as well. From this point on, there would
be no turning back. Savage knew the price he'd have to pay,
even if he was successful in the deadly quest. He would
probably be finished with the PD. He might himself become
a wanted felon. What difference? When it was over, either
he'd be with Gina, or he would be leaving the world a much
better place.

As he left MSH headquarters he saw Richie Marcus
erase 909 from the "In Service" side of the auto chart, and
chalk the department taxi up on the "Out of Service" side.
The Swami then removed the keys to the cab from their
hook on the pegboard. Thorn carried the duplicate keys in
the zippered folder.

It was precisely eight o'clock when Thorn steered the
Thunderbird onto the lot of Paradise Motors in Richmond
Hill, Queens. Finding one of the overhead doors wide open,
he pulled the little car inside the shop and parked it. He
found Eli Clipper seated behind his desk in the showroom,
enjoying his evening feed.

*"Jeet?"* The strange-sounding syllable was Eli for *Did
you eat?* "Gotta keep your strength up, you know." Eli
pushed the family-size tub of fried chicken across the desk.
"You don't look too good, Thornton. When's the last time
you got some sleep?" Eli's genuine concern for his goy surrogate son was reflected through eyes scrimmed by the
murkiness of age, the startling shade of blue that Savage recalled from his youth still discernible.

"Sleep! What the hell is that?" Thorn leaned over the
desk and clasped the old man's hand. "How are you, Eli?
Good to see you. And no thanks, I'm not big on KFC." His
words spilled out in the preoccupied monotone. He knew
that Eli, a master of the read, picked up on that right away.

"Then here, have some French fries. Fuckin' things are

delicious." Oily fragments of Original Crispy clung tena-
ciously to Eli's chin as he struggled to speak the words with
his mouth full. "C'mon," he urged. "Otherwise, I'm gonna
wind up eatin' it all."

Thorn wondered why this man hadn't had a massive
coronary long ago; he'd always eaten this way. As they
chatted idly, Eli ingested every possible greasy morsel.
Then, incredibly, he washed it all down with a diet Pepsi.

"When are you gonna give this up and retire?" Thorn
asked, struggling to make small talk. "You're here twelve,
fourteen hours a day. Eventually you're gonna drop dead
right in this goddamned showroom."

"Drop dead?" The man's face twisted sarcastically. "You
kiddin'? I can't drop dead. I owe too much fuckin' money.
Soon as I pay off all the cock-knockers and lice that I owe
money to . . . then, I can drop dead. Besides, if I wasn't
here selling cars, where would I be? Where does an old Jew
go anymore? Miami? With all them Cubanos talkin' Span-
ish, and all them designer people walking around half-
naked, it's like Carnival in Rio down there. Fuck it. I'll stay
right here, thank you. I gotta do what I gotta do."

Thorn forced a grin in response to Eli's patented cynical
diatribe and looked around the familiar office that his father
had often brought him to as a kid. Nothing seemed to have
changed; even the pictures along the walls were the same.
The old brown leather couch still sat in front of the huge
window that overlooked the lot. Eli's desk still faced out so
he could quickly spot a tire-kicker and pounce immediately.
Eli Clipper was one of the last of a dying breed—the
modern-day horse-trader.

"You know," the old man said softly, "I'm very sorry
about your fiancée. I know she must have meant a great
deal to ya. . . ."

Thorn grimaced and shrugged. "I don't know what this

is gonna cost, Eli. And I don't care. But this oughta cover it."

He set the T-bird's New York state title on the desk. He had already signed it over.

Eli waved him off. "Don't worry about it. I got this shit-box of a Buick out back that I was gonna cannibalize for parts. My body man spent the day knockin' off all the identifying numbers, even the confidential ones. If you should have to abandon it, it can never be traced." Studying Savage, Eli squinted from behind his wire rims.

"People don't change," Eli said. "You're just as head-strong now as you were when you were a kid. I don't know what you're doin', and I'm not gonna ask. But my mongrel instincts tell me I'd be a schmuck if I shouldn't worry about what you're up to."

Thorn, expressionless, did not respond.

Eli leaned back in his swivel chair, stretching, the motion highlighting dinnertime grease stains that dotted his half-knotted paisley tie. Running age-spotted hands through a crown of thinning silver hair, he expelled a deep breath and stood.

"Come on," he said, "let's get you saddled up."

# THIRTY

Savage tipped the container to his lips and dumped down the last mouthful of cold coffee, calculating it'd been three days plus since he climbed into the oil-burning Buick and began floating between the Culture Club, Ogden World Galleries, the Carlyle, and the one-time briefcase-exchange spot up on 204th. The silver coupe never showed at the Lenox Avenue nightspot, and Ogden's Bentley, released by court order from department impound, was absent from its usual spots on Madison Avenue and near his East Sixty-seventh Street hotel. Richie Marcus was right—the scumbags had gone underground. Thorn harbored no doubts, however, that his roughed-up Buick with the radically tinted windows and Jersey plates had been seen many times by the always-searching eyes of those concerned with such matters.

Only last week he had labored to *keep* Ogden behind bars in order to *get* Robinson behind bars. How quickly priorities can change, he thought. Now, more than anything else in the world, he wanted them out and about. He'd even gotten a handle on controlling the periodic strangulation of pent-up rage that came and tightened like a noose around his neck. The anger was counterproductive, so he channeled it into reservoirs of strength and energy. Every time he slumped, visions of the cocky pair sharpened and focused his mind, rejuvenating him.

Ogden's incarceration at the time of Gina's murder was the best alibi in the world. Ogden was probably right to be smug. Who could possibly testify to his culpability in Gina's death? Luther? Not likely. Anyway, convictions for conspiracy, even a murder conspiracy, weren't possible when the only evidence was the testimony of a co-conspirator. He knew that any attempt to prosecute high crimes based solely on vague threats, uttered in a holding cell, or on pinholes in fading taillights from a block and a half away would be a waste of time. In the eyes of the law, those factors alone might offer "reasonable suspicion," but would never reach the high bar of "guilt beyond reasonable doubt."

As the score stood, Derek Maximilian Ogden and his murder machine, Luther Robinson, had very little to worry about from the State of New York. But, he thought, they'd better be looking over their shoulders for the rest of their miserable lives.

Still, Savage had expected the pair to go into hiding and not be found at their usual spots—if anywhere—until things cooled down. But he also knew that sooner or later Robinson would have to visit the street retailers, if only to show them he was still in command. Robinson would no doubt make personal appearances in the BMW, eyeball everything, and move on. He would acknowledge no one, and no one would acknowledge him. But everybody would know that he'd been there.

"Where the hell is he?" Savage hissed.

For the tenth time in an hour, he checked his watch. The air was still and much too warm for spring. It was a humid New York City night. Roasting in the non-air-conditioned Buick, he lowered the windows for fresh air, covering his head with an old gray cap to conceal his face. Despite his disheveled appearance, street people could discern from a mile away that Savage was no junkie—his bearing was pure cop. His eyes, they could tell, were connected to a brain—unlike a junkie's, whose pupils were only dark tunnels leading to nowhere.

Although he could never be confused with a junkie, at the moment he felt like one. With each shift of his position he readjusted the sweat-soaked shirt that stuck to his flesh. His face bore sharp stubble and his chin felt like a wire brush. He rubbed the back of his wrist against it, satisfying a stubborn itch. For three days he'd called the Buick home, leaving it only to piss or fetch another container of coffee. He was rank; he needed to bathe. He blinked and stretched his red-rimmed eyes open wide. His body was demanding rest.

"How long since I've slept?" he said, talking freely to himself. He shook his head vigorously, fighting to stay alert.

"C'mon, dammit, c'mon," he muttered, hoping to will the big Bentley into an appearance. Followed, he hoped, by the BMW with the betraying bores in the taillight. "Where are those bastards?"

By three-fifteen, total exhaustion forced him to give it up. Though business was still booming on 144th, the big gray Bentley and the elusive BMW were again no-shows. He cranked up the Buick and slowly drove off. Loath to give in to his aching body's demands, Savage realized that his reservoirs had run completely dry; he had to rest. He would build back some strength and resume in the morning.

A hulk of a man in a brown derby emerged from the dark shadows of 144th Street. In seconds he was joined by two other equally large companions, also wearing derbies. They watched through tightly focused and unblinking eyes as the Buick with the New Jersey license plates headed down Broadway and faded from their view.

Having been lulled into feline dreamland by the hum of the Kelvinator's noisy motor, Ray was comfortable in the meat-loaf position on top of the fridge. At the sound of a key rattling in the apartment door, his ears spiked and his golden-yellow eyes popped open. He blinked twice and watched in silent assessment as the bone-weary human ran his hand along the wall in search of the light switch. Slamming the door behind him, the man crashed headlong onto the living room sofa. Ray recalled seeing much behavior of this sort, back in the days before his human had met the nice-smelling lady. But tonight was different: there was no accompanying aroma of booze. On silent pads Ray jumped to the counter, then to the floor. He lapped a drink at the water bowl and sauntered to the sofa. Preening his whiskers, face, and what remained of ragged ears, he curled up in the small of Thorn's back. They slept.

At 5:20, insistent ringing finally broke through Savage's near-coma. Stirred too, Ray stretched and yawned, then leapt onto the coffee table, down to the floor, and up to the windowsill to check out Sullivan Street and await the morning sun. Savage clutched the sofa's thick arm and dragged himself to a sitting position. He reached for the phone on the adjoining lamp table and picked it up on what might've been the fiftieth ring.

"Hello," he mumbled, only partially awake.

"Good morning, Sergeant Savage." The voice was not familiar. Almost cultured, it contained an unmistakable edge of arrogance.

"Who is this?" Savage demanded, buying time to clear his head.

"It sounds as though I may have disturbed your sleep. Tsk, tsk. But then, it is quite early, is it not?"

Savage sensed his blood pressure soaring.

"We understand that you're not getting much rest lately, Sergeant. That's too bad. We're very concerned about your health."

"Oh, yeah? I'll just bet you are." There was no hint of hesitation or surprise in Savage's casual response; he marched right into the game. Fury, like a third-rail short, surged throughout his system. Full consciousness had returned in a heartbeat.

"We have a message for you. . . ."

"We? Who's we?" Savage cut in, pretending to be coolly untroubled as he gently pressed the RECORD button of the PhoneMate, noticing at the same time that the machine was flashing to indicate a prior stored message.

"Come now, Sergeant. You know who we are."

Savage bristled. "No, I don't. Tell me."

"We're the same people who sent your sweet-ass bitch on her long journey into darkness."

The viciousness of the remark hit him like a Tyson uppercut. Reeling from the impact, Savage groped for an appropriate reply.

"Really?" he finally choked out lamely.

"She was only the beginning, the appetizer, as it were. You see, Sergeant, we don't like people who meddle in our affairs." The practiced voice paused for a gruff snicker. "Our sources tell us that you've taken a leave from the department. But alas, you just can't stop putting your fucking nose where it doesn't belong, can you?"

"No, scumbag, guess I can't," Savage snarled, still unable to convey his outrage at the bastard's boldness. Traffic noises in the background told him the call was originating from a public phone.

"Tsk, tsk, Sergeant, such common language for a gentleman of your station. One would think that someone who was about to marry some society slut would have some degree of class."

*The fucking* Times *ad!* The nagging question of *how* had just been answered.

"Let's not discuss my failings. Let's talk about yours." Savage tried to steer the conversation away from insults and taunts about Gina that he couldn't bear to hear. It didn't work.

"Oh, and by the way, your bitch had a real nice body, man. Nice and tight. An excellent piece of ass."

*Explosive, cataclysmic*—silence.

"What's the matter, Savage? Afraid maybe I had a good time with her?" Jeering laughter poured through the phone.

"You're a fucking dead man, Robinson. You've played all your cards. From here on in, it's gonna be my show."

"Robinson?" There was a falter in the voice. "Who's Robinson?" The arrogant edge had been blunted flat.

"Your call was designed to wake me and shake me, to keep me on the ropes. Right, motherfucker? I just thought I'd give you a little something to keep *you* awake. Sleep with one eye open, asshole."

"Shit! You make me laugh, cop. Don't try playin' mind games with me, fool: I wrote the book. I know every move you make."

"And I know every move you've made, Luther."

"Yeah? Like what moves you know about?"

"How about a cop that got dead in a staged stickup inside Matt's Bar?"

"They say that things come in threes, Savage." The voice faltered, the speaker momentarily losing his cool. "So

I guess you must be next. Apparently, you don't know who you've fucked with."

"I've heard that line before, asshole. Keep talking. I want to become familiar with your faggot voice." Savage forced the insults and bravado. Any sign of weakness had to be avoided. If he could somehow irritate the caller into staying on the line, the man just might say something impulsive or revealing that he could benefit from.

"You must have thought your status as a policeman would spare you from retribution. But now you see that your status means absolutely nothing. That's because you are nothing. You tried to hurt us and you failed. But we've been able to hurt you, haven't we? And we're going to keep on hurting you, Savage." The arrogant polish had given way to icy menace. "You're on my list, motherfucker!" Hideous taunting laughter, then click as the line went dead.

Savage held the receiver pressed to his ear until he heard the hum of the dial tone. He was certain a vessel was about to burst in his brain. The call had beaten him into an impassioned frenzy. Shaking and seething with anger, he cradled the receiver, stood, and suddenly unleashed a wrecking-ball right that crumbled plaster and underlying lath in the near wall. He collapsed inward, stoop-shouldered and empty, reeking in the same clothes that he'd put on three days earlier.

Ray weaved back and forth, bumping his chowder head against Thorn's legs, purring in high gear. Despite the intensity of the moment, Ray wanted breakfast. The flashing light of the answering machine finally got Savage's attention. He hit PLAY and listened to the unmistakable gravel-filled voice:

"Boss, Richie Marcus here. Listen, hope everything's goin' okay. Everybody's been thinkin' of ya. If there's anything at all that any of us can do for ya, please, just let us know. . . . Listen, I'm sorry to bother ya at home, but we've been tryin' to reach ya for days. . . . We've got some news that I'm sure you'll want to know about. We still got a No-hit from BCI and NCIC on the fingerprint exemplars Diane slicked from Robinson! Hard to believe this guy ain't been collared, even under an assumed name, since he was a juvenile. So be it. Also, Latent couldn't match any of his prints to anything found on Abe's paycheck, but how does this grab ya? They *did* find that same latex glove residue on it. Also, using those exemplars they're going back over Abe's gun, Matt's Bar, and all the murder cars we still have in impound, blah blah blah, et cetera et cetera. Also . . . they're going back over the crime scene at Gina's place. Like I said, sorry to bother ya at home. Just thought I'd keep you up to date. Take care. . . . Oh, I almost forgot. That thing that we, ah . . . discussed, can be found a block west of the Nineteenth. Nobody'll bother it there. It's all Police Vehicles Only parking. Stay safe. Call me if you need me."

After playing Marcus's message, the machine repeated the conversation he'd just recorded. He replayed it over and over again. The voice on the machine belonged to the man who operated the Culture Club, the man he'd watched make the money switch with the Nairobi Trio. It was Luther Robinson, no question.

Beyond any damning evidence that the official investigation might eventually reveal, Savage now had an incriminating taped threat—and admission—from an identifiable source. He knew there was now enough evidence to at least initiate a lawful prosecution. The system could move ahead.

"Fuck that!"

Savage looked down at the PhoneMate and pressed ERASE.

# THIRTY-ONE

**Sunday, May 7, 11:45 A.M.**

Derek Ogden's long strides easily outpaced the late-morning
pedestrian flow along West Fifty-seventh Street. Dark eyes
focused into tunnel vision, jaw tightly set, he marched with
military precision through the throngs of shoppers, tourists,
and street vendors, keen radar anticipating any necessary
sidestep or dodge. The great strides and strong gait were
customary. The pinched brow and strained countenance
were not. Also out of character was the fact that he ignored
the billboard announcements of upcoming performances as
he passed Carnegie Hall. One block beyond the concert
house, he turned into Petrossian. Declining the maitre d's
lead with a caustic shrug, he found his way to a side booth
and slid in opposite Luther Robinson.

"Lay it on me," Ogden said firmly. "What the hell is
going on?"

"He knows," Robinson answered with icy brevity.

"How much?" Ogden queried, his face wrought with the
question he really didn't want to hear the answer to.

"I'd say he pretty much knows the whole fucking deal."

"How did you find this out?"

"I talked to him."

"You talked to him?" Ogden couldn't believe his ears.

"Yes! I called him from a safe phone to fuck with his

head. I did such a good job of it he tipped part of his hand. It's a goddamned good thing I did; knowledge *is* power."

"Well, if he knows so much, how the hell come we're not in irons?"

"Because I think he knows more than he's told the police department. For some reason he's layin' back. The mother-fucker's got some kind of plan, and we damn well better get our shit together. And I mean now!"

"He knows about the bitch?"

"Well, that's a given. That was the whole idea, right?"

"Yes," Ogden acknowledged. "But what about the cop? Has he got us connected to that?"

"Oh, yes," Robinson said, slowly rolling a near-empty cognac snifter back and forth between open palms. "He'll never have enough to prove it, but he's got it."

Ogden drummed his fingers on the linen-covered table, and then slid the napkin onto his lap. "What's the word from uptown. Anything?"

"Atkins knows to use only safe phones. We must assume that most of our lines are hot. The Club, the gallery, and the Carlyle."

"What about your place?" Ogden pressed.

"No. They don't have my place. But if anybody dialed in from the Club, the gallery, or your suite at the Carlyle, they damn sure would."

"You and I'll just continue to use only the cells." Ogden contemplated that idea. "Maybe they're not even safe. You certain your place is still cool?"

"No question."

"All right," Ogden said. "You hole up there. I'll stay at my place."

"Everybody who is any-damn-body knows you stay at the Carlyle," Luther whispered with a disbelieving frown.

"I've been staying at the Pierre under an assumed

name," Ogden revealed. "And, I gotta say, it's a goddamned good thing we tucked those two cars away. Right now they're too high-profile. If you need to get around, get yourself a rental, a cab, or ride shank's mare. I'll do the same." Without missing a beat, Ogden motioned to the waiter and ordered the grilled sole. Robinson declined lunch, but ordered another Rémy.

"Have you got the basics in your apartment?" Ogden asked. "Food, drink, whatever?"

"If I'm going to be holed up there for a while, I could use a few things."

"I'll send Tommy Bruton over."

"He's out?" Robinson asked, surprised.

"I posted his bail. He'll be our legs. At least I can get room service at the Pierre. How much cash is still in your apartment?"

"Couple of bundles. Few hundred K. Give or take."

"I'll come by tonight and pick it up. Fucking Kornbluth is hounding the piss out of me for some cash. Everything we had in the Bentley has been confiscated by the city as evidence."

"You get that all back, right?"

"If we win the cases, I do."

"If you lose any of them?"

"Every last nickel of it gets absorbed into the city's general fund, and will probably go toward filling potholes or testing new birth control on the frigging park pigeons. If I take a fall on any one of the charges, Kornbluth says we can just kiss all that fucking bread good-bye."

"What are our chances?"

"Kornbluth figures we have an excellent chance of beating the money-laundering and conspiracy. However, he thinks the catch is going to be the bribery charge. That's why we've got to make this fucking Savage dead. You hear me, Luther? *Dead!*"

After an unsteady three-slice shave, Savage climbed into the steaming shower and stood hunched, like a beaten warrior, allowing the needles of hot water to work their magic. They helped soothe his sore and tired joints, but did nothing for his overpowering sorrow. If only the cleansing torrent could wash away the unendurable, the unbearable, as easily as it erased days and nights of grunge. Through eyes clouded in melancholy, Savage watched the grime disappear down the drain.

He rinsed and stepped from the tub. The clean clothes were a simple treat; the cotton, soft against his flesh, felt good, but the crushing misery would not subside.

He sat and scratched out a note to Mrs. Potamkin. He wrote that he "may be called away" for an extended period, and asked would she be kind enough to "look after" Ray in his absence. He folded the note into an envelope that he'd slide under her door on the way out. The old lady was Ray's surrogate human anyway. She would take good care of him—forever, if need be. Though the cat would probably never see another beer.

Though he was still exhausted, the few hours of intense deep sleep had energized Savage enough to resume. He knew he needed food for energy and strength, but had no appetite. He would survive on coffee. He finished dressing, said good-bye to Ray, and was gone.

Today he'd float the East Eighties, banking on Robinson living somewhere in that section of Manhattan. If the horrific-looking bastard wasn't going to come out and play, then Savage would just have to find where he lived and go call on him.

It was warm, and he welcomed the brightness of the

noon sunlight; it made him feel more alert. Thorn drove
with windows open, inhaling the freshness of the new
spring air as it circulated through the moving car. Hour
after hour, he threaded through the side streets of the Upper
East Side, hoping to spot any clue to Robinson's where-
abouts. Keeping an eye out primarily for the BMW, he
noted every off-street parking facility on every side street
from Seventy-eighth up to Eighty-sixth. He would visit
each of them on foot if he had to.

When the Buick's fuel gauge started bouncing off
EMPTY, Thorn headed down to the Mobil station in the East
Sixties to refuel. While in the neighborhood, he drove past
the Nineteenth Precinct to verify the Swami's phone message. The department taxicab was there, parked exactly
where Marcus had said it would be. Sipping his fifth coffee
of the day, Thorn slowly cruised back up First Avenue to
continue his search of the East Eighties. At Eighty-second
and First he stopped for a red light.

Barely visible among a mob of quick-moving pedestrians crossing in front of him was a stocky black guy carrying two large bags of groceries, one in each stubby arm.
Staring intently, Savage shifted in his seat, trying to get a
clear view of the man's face. No go, but he had absolutely
no neck. Savage watched him cross to the east side of First
Avenue and continue toward Eighty-third. There was something about his walk.

Within seconds, horns began to sound. Over the blare he
heard some guy holler, "Move it, for crissakes!" The light
on First had gone green. Savage pulled the cumbersome
Buick into the next bus stop, let the traffic behind him pass,
and continued eyeballing the toter of the overloaded Gris-
tede's bags. He bailed from the car and followed on foot for
another block until the man disappeared into the lobby of

the Southview, a high-rise apartment building at 400 East Eighty-fourth. He never got a look at the man's face.

The man was not wearing a black jacket or charcoal striped trousers, nor did he have a chauffeur's black cap on. But it was definitely Tommy Bruton, Derek Ogden's gun-toting driver, Savage concluded. He had close-cropped hair, no neck, and short thick arms, and, as Abe had put it, he "waddled like a damn duck."

From the corner, Savage keyed in on the Southview's ruddy-faced doorman, who was helping an older woman get seated in the back of a taxicab. Once this had been accomplished, the man slammed the taxi's door and tipped his cap. His hair was carrot-red, turning gray, and thinning. The unseasonable overcoat, festooned with brass buttons and epaulets, gave the diminutive doorman the appearance of a character out of *The Wizard of Oz.*

Here I am, Savage thought, looking for the Scarecrow, and I find a friggin' Munchkin. For the first time in weeks, a smile came to his face.

When the doorman about-faced and ambled back into the lobby, Savage returned to the Buick he'd abandoned in the First Avenue bus stop. A parking ticket decorated the car's windshield. The last thing he needed was to have his wheels towed away. With no proof of ownership, he'd never get the damn thing back. He slipped the "parker" up under the sun visor with the two others he'd gotten in the past few days, drove quickly to Eighty-sixth, between Third and Lexington, and found a stationery store.

Fifteen minutes later, Savage strode into the Southview's spectacular lobby toting a new clipboard full of official-looking printed forms. The doorman quickly cupped a lit cigarette. Staff here must be prohibited from smoking within public view, Savage thought.

"Sir. May I be helpin' ya?" The doorman eyeballed the

sneaker-clad Savage as if he were a bug in his soup. Thorn was glad that he'd at least shaved and showered that morning.

The man was clearly Irish, but Savage sensed the brogue was very much overdone. He couldn't stand professional Irishmen. The leprechaun, if he so desired, could probably speak in perfect accent-free Brooklynese. Flipping through the forms on the clipboard, Savage replied, "Perhaps. This *is* 400 East Eighty-fourth Street, is it not?"

The little Irishman nodded suspiciously. "Yes," he said, "this is the Southview."

"Good. I'm Inspector Thornton. Department of Buildings," Savage announced officiously. He jerked his driver's license from his shirt pocket and slipped it right back in with one easy motion.

"And just what might we be doin' for you, sir?" Irish drawled snottily.

"I'm here to ride the elevators. It's time for their annual inspection."

"Sir?" Irish was taken aback. "They were just inspected. Here, come look. You can see where the gentleman signed off on the inspection sheets inside the cars. He was here a week ago T'ursday, he was." Letting loose with a couple of gagging cigarette coughs, the man led the way to the bank of three elevators, still cupping the smoldering butt inside his closed palm.

"I know, I know," Thorn exclaimed, winging it. "They were inspected last week. But I've been sent here to do a follow-up." With a shrug, he added, "Orders are orders."

"This is a modern buildin', sir," the man argued. "These elevators are in tiptop shape. I can assure you o' that." The man's tone left little doubt as to the annoyance he felt at the municipal intrusion into his little domain. His already red and spider-veined face was beginning to go purple.

"Well, Mister . . . ?" Savage said.

"O'Brien." The man grunted, coughing twice. "Dinty O'Brien."

"Dinty," Thorn said, looking dramatically back over both shoulders, then adding in a confidential tone, "it may interest you to know that we're finding more problems and faults with these newer models than we did with the old K-60s. It's gonna take some time to get all the bugs out." Where the hell did that come from? Savage asked himself as he stepped into one of the mahogany-paneled elevator cabs.

Wide-eyed and haughty, Dinty responded in a voice dripping with Gaelic sarcasm. "Y'doon't say?"

"How many garage levels below, O'Brien?" Thorn took up the offensive by adding lots of attitude to his tone, deciding to verbally put the little prick in his place.

"There be t'ree of them, sir," Dinty uttered, still standing in the hallway, his look questioning.

Sensing the emerging suspicions, Savage decided to counteract the man's doubts by putting him on the defensive.

"Of course, you do know you'll have to ride with me, Mr. O'Brien."

"Excuse me, sir?" the doorman protested crossly, taking one giant step back.

"Building Department Regulation EI-86 states: 'A building representative must accompany the inspector while said inspection is being performed.' "

"Surely you jest, sir," Dinty objected. "I can't be leavin' the lobby. Are you crazy? I'm sorry, but I can't be goin' with ya. I've got an impartant job to be seein' to here."

Savage had hoped that by asserting the made-up rule, he'd somehow allay Dinty's dawning mistrust.

"Well." Thorn winked, as if doing the man a solid.

"From one Irishman to another, I'll just go ahead and say you did. How's that, Dinty?"

"Ah. Well . . . that'd be good of ya, sir." The Munchkin coughed twice again, turned, and walked off. Savage pushed the button for garage level 3.

Thorn's nostrils filled with the scent of tires, gasoline, and hovering monoxide: the familiar ambience of large-capacity indoor parking garages. Stepping into the expansive concrete bunker, he surveyed the area before him. It was a sea of automobiles, lined row upon row. This level was accessed by only two of the building's three elevators. An engine roared to life and moments later a small sedan moved through the right-side aisle. Its tires squealed as it turned onto the up ramp and disappeared. Seconds later, a horn sounded somewhere above. He wondered why tires squealed so easily inside garages. He decided to walk through each level clockwise until he'd viewed every vehicle on every floor.

He moved at a rigid pace until he'd completed the lower level. Momentum was constant as he power-walked up the main ramp, repeating the search process on the middle level, his eyes clicking left and right as he weaved through the aisles. Again, disappointment. With only one level remaining, he prayed that his earlier intuition wasn't just a case of wishful thinking. Arriving at the top level, he noticed that this floor had a third elevator and also offered several emergency exits to the street.

The purpose of the third elevator quickly became clear. PENTHOUSE ONLY was stenciled across its door, and instead of standard call buttons, it was commanded by a coded electronic touch pad. Pretty nice, he thought. One of the benefits of springing for the penthouse was that you got your own personal elevator. As he passed a massive support pillar, he stopped dead in his tracks.

Parked adjacent to the penthouse elevator, in adjoining spots reserved for PH ONLY, were two covered vehicles: one with the low-slung configuration of a sports job, the other a barge of Goliath proportions. He felt his ears redden as the sight kicked his pulse into overdrive. He did not need to roll back the elasticized hems of the custom-made covers to confirm the finds. In a guttural growl he said, "Gotcha, you bastards."

# THIRTY-TWO

Certain that the paranoid Robinson would have electronic
security monitoring his garage parking spots and the area
around his private elevator entrance, Savage scanned all the
immediate concrete walls and ceilings for telltale wires.
Seeing none, he eyeballed the overhead duct system. He
moved a quick dozen steps to the nearest louvered vent and
studied the darkness beyond its wide aluminum slats. Shifting into just the right angle, he spotted the telltale glint of a
small lens mounted several inches within. The area around
the penthouse elevator and both of its private parking spots
were well within the cleverly concealed camera's field of
vision. He returned to the house elevator. It was time to go
upstairs.

A pleasing chime sounded as the elevator opened onto
the chandeliered corridor of the thirty-second floor. Moving quickly down the hall of mirror and marble, Savage located and entered the emergency stairwell. Ensuring
egress, he used the clipboard's narrow edge as a thin
doorstop. With the .38 drawn, he started up the dozen steps
that led to the roof. Sliding his back along the stairwell
wall for support, he advanced smoothly and silently.
Halfway up, he had a complete view of the top landing.
The area was an electronic minefield. Two cameras covered every angle at the landing and stairwell, and there

were at least two infrared motion detectors. The steel door marked 33-ROOF/PENTHOUSE was laden with pressure and sound sensors. Even if he had been foolhardy enough to disregard the security and alarm systems, he knew the door would also be barricaded from the other side; he'd never be able to force it. Savage turned and retraced his steps. He gathered up his clipboard and rode the elevator back to the lobby.

Dinty O'Brien blew a shrill blast from a silver whistle attached to a braided lanyard and waved a white-gloved hand into Eighty-fourth Street. The doorman was fully occupied procuring taxicabs for a line of Southview haves queued behind him beneath the building's arched awning. Seizing the moment, Savage let himself into the doorman's cramped office off the lobby. The claustrophobic room smelled foul, as if somebody had just eaten limburger and then thrown it up into a bucket of crushed-out Pall Malls.

He quickly skimmed through a stack of manila folders piled atop the office desk, then spun a Rolodex through the *O*s and *R*s. Nothing: no Ogden, no Robinson. The desk drawer was a hodgepodge of thumbtacks, rubber bands, and single-portion packets of Burger King mustard and ketchup. Concealed at the rear of the desk's file drawer was a nearly empty fifth of Bushmills Irish. Pinned to the wall above the desk was a monthly work chart that resembled a calendar. The chart specified which doormen worked days, which doormen worked nights, and which doormen were off. On the shelf just above the schedule he found a small three-ring loose-leaf binder labeled TENANT ROSTER BY APARTMENT NUMBER. He poked his head from the office and took another glance out onto Eighty-fourth—Dinty was still blowing his little donkey heart out. Savage wetted his index and middle fingers and flipped quickly through the coffee-stained, dog-eared pages.

The listed penthouse occupant was a Mr. L. L. Robeson. The roster's penthouse page contained Mr. Robeson's telephone number, along with a boldly highlighted notation: UNDER PENALTY OF IMMEDIATE DISMISSAL, THIS NUMBER IS NOT TO BE GIVEN OUT TO *ANYONE*. The written instructions also detailed instructions for doormen to ring the apartment twice, hang up, and then immediately redial in the event of any situation, emergency or otherwise. Another note directed building personnel to deny entry to all, except those pre-approved by the penthouse occupant, Mr. L. L. Robeson. Listed beneath that warning was the name of the sole approved visitor: Mr. Derek Ogden.

With a felt-tip Savage scribbled the penthouse phone number across the back of his left hand, placed the seven-by-nine binder back on the shelf, and left the office. He rode the elevator back down to the garage and closely examined the four fire exits. Selecting one that opened onto First Avenue, he balled up a page from his clipboard prop and jammed the paper wad into the door's striker plate, defeating the self-locking mechanism.

As Dinty scrambled in abbreviated steps from taxicab to taxicab, the ersatz elevator inspector discreetly slipped from the Southview. The shrill blasts from O'Brien's whistle faded to nothing as Savage melted into the city bustle. Pumped by adrenaline, Savage jogged the two blocks back to the Buick. He took yet another parking summons from its windshield and slipped it under the sun visor. Then he gathered his gear and hurried back to Eighty-fourth Street.

At thirty-five stories, the newer Wimbledon House stood adjacent to Robinson's building from the east. Having slipped past the Wimbledon's doorman, Savage rode the elevator to the top floor and let himself onto the roof. He moved along the graveled surface to the roof's westernmost edge and peered over the side. The taller building looked down on the Southview, providing him with a clear, unobstructed view of Luther's inviolable sanctum. He estimated that Robinson's penthouse structure occupied about a third of the Southview's roof area. Other rooftop space held fenced-off sections of air-conditioning equipment and elevator machinery. Accessible from Robinson's apartment through leaded French doors was a rooftop garden and landscaped patio. Adjusting the lenses, he trained Dieter Krongold's field glasses on the apartment's easternmost windows. A black-and-white floor of polished marble defined what was probably the living room. He held the view for several minutes; nobody came into sight. All seemed quiet within. He slipped the binoculars back into their scuffed, chamois-lined leather case and waited.

Savage heard his own breath. The anticipation caused it to come in short, audible gasps. His anger, born of frustration with a flawed system he'd dedicated his life to, was deepening. He also knew his weakened physical state was contributing to the intense negativity.

Exhaling hard, he fought off all thoughts of the past and the horrendous events that had brought him here. He couldn't allow his psyche to go into the crapper now. He had to remain focused on the mission at hand. Taking several more deep breaths, he considered his next moves. For now, there was nothing to do but wait.

From his rooftop position he watched an American 737 begin a steep eastward bank in the clear sky above the Hudson. He fixed his gaze on the graceful bird as it lined up for its final approach into LaGuardia. His eyes followed the jet all the way in. Behind it, tracking in the same pattern, was another Boeing, a Delta, and behind it yet another. A thought stirred. He peered back over the edge and fantasized about a parachute landing onto Robinson's rooftop garden. It would have to be done on a clear night, but he knew he could do it. Hell, he'd landed in hula hoops from ten thousand feet, but . . . never at night. Besides, Armand would have to pilot him. He gave up the idea. He couldn't involve his friend.

Savage reached into his jacket pocket for his cell phone, wondering if Robinson was actually inside the penthouse. He had yet to see any sign of life from within. Both bastards could be in China, for all he knew. Maybe they were just storing their ego-gratifying automobiles in the Southview's basement.

Thorn considered calling the apartment on some bullshit pretense to see who, if anyone, answered the phone. Again fighting mental fatigue, he concentrated until it hurt. Was he giving the bastard Robinson too much credit for smarts? Or perhaps, even worse, not enough? He checked the back of his left hand; the numbers were still bold and clear. Calling now, he thought, would only serve as an alert. He placed the cell phone back in his pocket. Better to be patient. Once the interior lights went on in the apartment, he would have L. L. Robeson in a fishbowl.

Savage watched the sun dissolve into the western horizon somewhere beyond New Jersey, abandoning the city to a black, moon-forgotten night. His aching body yearned for something soft—a chair, a pillow . . . his own damn bed. Instead, he lay on unyielding mortar, brick, and gravel. From his perch, he marveled at the nighttime Manhattan skyline and its lacy system of bridges, which fed out like arteries leading from the world's heart. The lofty peaks of the city's most prominent structures, awash in accent lighting, glowed lustrous like slender tapers, awesome as they pierced the blackened heavens.

He tried to make an objective assessment of his physical status. Though he suffered no hunger, his coffee-saturated belly simmered like a bubbling cauldron. Though he was physically worn, his thought processes were still sharp and focused. Kneeling, he cushioned his knees on the sturdy satchel and propped his elbows on the parapet capstone. Committed to wait for however long it would take, Savage forced himself into a motionless, half-conscious, stamina-saving state of suspended animation. He barely moved for hours.

At fifteen minutes past three in the morning, the darkened penthouse came alive.

The newborn glow from within the apartment radiated trapezoidal patterns of light across the rooftop garden. Savage pressed the glasses to his eyes and fine-tuned the focus, achieving sharply defined images. The lights below shone brilliant at first, and softened as a dimmer was adjusted.

Robinson appeared first. He moved quickly through the living room and disappeared into a hall. Shortly afterward, Ogden sauntered into view and dropped heavily into a chair that backed up to the window. Savage focused in on the familiar bald spot. The development was far more than he'd hoped for—he had them both.

When Robinson reappeared, he carried a dark brown leather attaché case and set it on the floor next to Ogden. Savage watched as the two men laughed and conversed below. Revulsion rising in his throat, he popped a Wint-O-Green to keep from grinding his molars down to bloody stubs. He would give anything to hear what they were saying.

Robinson stepped behind a mirrored art deco bar. After washing his hands in an unseen sink, he dried them with a bar towel and poured two drinks from a bottle whose label Savage could not discern. Drinks in hand, both men stepped through the French doors into the night-shrouded rooftop garden and sat facing one another at an ornate wrought-iron table. When Ogden fired up a cigar, Savage saw him full-face. He could see only the back of Robinson's shiny head.

Groping through the satchel, Savage quickly unpacked Krongold's night scope. The Russian-made gadget amplified starlight thirty thousand times, and with its 3.2 magnification Savage could literally have counted the hairs in Ogden's nose through the total darkness; it also allowed him to read the man's lips. At that moment Savage became an invisible—if half-deaf—third party at the table. Though able to interpret most of Ogden's words, he strained his ears to catch any of Robinson's. But the sounds of the city streets, coupled with the whirring of a nearby rooftop ventilator, swallowed them up.

"Tell me, who lives better than us, Luther?" Ogden said, taking a deep puff on his fresh cigar. "There is absolutely nothing in this world that either one of us could possibly want and not be able to have."

"True," Luther agreed, and sipped from his glass. "But I'll be a damn sight more secure when that meddling cop is out of the picture."

"Savage is nothing more than an eager civil servant," Ogden said with great outer assurance, though inwardly doubting his own words. "And look how much his Boy Scout eagerness has cost him already—his jive-ass main man and his Brooklyn Heights bimbo. Hell," he added with a snicker, "ain't going to be no damn wedding bells for that motherfucker. You saw to that."

"Man is starting to worry me."

"He's nothing more than a mild inconvenience, Luther.

An inconvenience that you will eventually deal with, and then we can move on."

"Unh."

"I had better get going," Ogden said. He finished his drink and stood. "It's late and I've got a lot of arrangements to see to in the morning."

Savage switched back to the binoculars and spied through Robinson's massive windows as the pair returned to the lighted living room. He watched Robinson hand Ogden a small silver automatic. The older man tucked the weapon into his belt-line.

Directing his remark to the expansive heavens above, Thorn softly uttered, "Thank you, Jesus."

It was time. Savage tossed all his gear into the satchel and scrambled from the roof, reaching street level in bare minutes. Running full tilt from the white-brick building, he showed only briefly as a faint image before being absorbed into the shadows of the night.

Sketchy as it was, he had a plan as he piloted the Buick full throttle down York Avenue. He prayed for enough time to execute it. He knew it would take a lot of luck, a commodity he'd been out of for some while. Well-worn tires screamed for mercy as he laid the Buick into a high-speed ninety-degree right at Sixty-seventh Street and raced west. The streets were empty. Every light fell green for him. He thanked God for New York City's intelligent, progressive traffic-light system.

Prominent in the far-right lane of deserted First Avenue, silver whistle pinched tightly between his teeth and white-gloved hand visible like a beacon, the Southview doorman motioned to the oncoming headlights. The lone taxicab—heading uptown at a good clip—slowed quickly and steered into Eighty-fourth. At the doorman's direction it stopped before the awning-covered walkway. The uniformed man held the taxi's door for the balding black gentleman with the leather attaché.

"Good night, Mr. Ogden." The doorman tipped his hat as he closed the door. The yellow car lurched forward and quickly accelerated through the quiet side street.

"Hotel Pierre."

The cabbie, faceless beneath a floppy gray hat, nodded acknowledgment as he reached over with a gloved hand and punched the start button on the meter.

Southbound on York, then west on Sixty-seventh, the cab crossed Third Avenue and passed the Nineteenth Precinct station house. Ogden felt calm and relaxed. In minutes he would be home; the Pierre was now only blocks away. Midway between Lexington and Park Avenues the taxicab slowed and pulled to the curb beneath a POLICE VEHICLES ONLY street sign. It parked behind a beat-up car with New Jersey plates.

"Driver," Ogden demanded, "why are we stopping here?"

The driver pulled the key from the taxi's ignition and climbed from the car.

"Goddamned cab drivers in this fucking town . . ." Ogden said angrily, shaking his head in exasperation. How he missed the convenience of his Bentley and the dependability of Tommy Bruton. Suddenly, his door swung wide and he winced as a stubby gun barrel was jammed painfully into his right ear.

"Good evening, sir," the cabdriver croaked. "And welcome to Rollerball, where there are no time-outs, no substitutions, and we play to the death."

In a reflexive move, Ogden began to slide his hand beneath his jacket.

The cabbie pushed and twisted his gun, screwing its front sight into the side of Ogden's head. "No, no, Mr. Ogden. I don't think so. . . ." The driver reached down and quickly snatched the silver automatic from Ogden's beltline. "My, my," he said, dropping the small pistol into his own pocket. "What do we have here? Looks to me like criminal possession of a loaded gun . . . by a predicate felon, of all people. That's a minimum of a year, Mr. Ogden. Why, I'm surprised at you. . . ."

"What are you, a fucking cop?" Though surprised at what was occurring, Ogden maintained his poise and customary arrogance.

The cabdriver did not respond.

"What do you call this bullshit?" Ogden turned his head to see the driver's gun, now pointed directly at his face.

"It's what I call justice, Mr. Ogden. Did you know that justice delayed is justice denied?"

"Justice? Justice, my ass!" Ogden said. "What do you mean, justice? I demand to—"

The words were strangled as the cabdriver grabbed Ogden's collar and hauled him out onto the sidewalk. They were face to face. As the driver locked the taxi's doors, Ogden finally recognized the face beneath the floppy cap and took a hesitant step backward.

"Savage!"

Prodding with the muzzle of his revolver, Savage steered him to the car with the Jersey plates and swung the passenger door wide open.

"I want to call my lawyer. I want to speak to Kornbluth right fucking now, Savage."

"Get in," Savage snarled, jabbing his gun into Ogden's ribs for emphasis. Ogden complied. Savage slammed the old Buick's door.

"Savage, you bastard!" Ogden went ballistic as Savage sat behind the wheel. "I'll have your fucking job!"

"My *job*?" Savage laughed, though his smile quickly transformed into a look of glaring contempt. "Screw my job. I thought you wanted my life, scumbag."

"Why are we not going into the station house? Where are you taking me? This is against the goddamned law, Savage. I promise, not only will I have your job, but I'll also see you in jail, so help me. I can do that, you know. This is kidnapping. You're treading on very thin ice here, motherfucker."

Savage calmly ignored Ogden as he shifted the Buick's transmission lever into DRIVE.

"Now!" Savage began, looking at the man beside him in the front seat as they rolled slowly uptown on Park Avenue. "I'm going to read you your rights. First, you have the right to remain silent. I strongly suggest that you take full advantage of that right. Because if you don't, I will kick you to death."

Ogden made a tentative move to speak, but Savage glared him down.

"*Next,*" Savage continued, "you have the right to be obedient, and if you do everything I tell you to do, you have my word that I won't hurt you." The tone stiffened. "If you give me just the slightest excuse, however . . ." He stared across into Ogden's disbelieving face and raised the .38 he still held in his gloved left hand. "I'm gonna blow your fuckin' head off."

Five minutes later, Savage parked the Buick on East Eighty-fourth Street just west of First Avenue.

"Why are we back here?" Ogden asked.

"I told you to be quiet. *I* ask all the questions. Besides, you know goddamned well why we're here."

"What is it that you want, man?"

Reaching into the visor, Savage handed Ogden the parking summonses. "First thing, I want you to get fuckin' Kornbluth to take care of these for me."

Ogden shuffled through the tickets, glancing at each one, and then stared over at Savage, a look of disbelief on his face. "What the fuck are you talking about?" he snarled. "These are shitty parking tickets, for crissakes."

Savage snatched the forms from Ogden's hands and jammed them back under the visor. "What the fuck do you think I want?"

"Money?"

Savage felt his eyes tighten into menacing slits at the sound of the word, but he let Ogden continue.

"If it's money you want, all you need do is get that case that was left on the back floor of the taxicab you picked me up in. It's got well over two hundred thou' in it." The man was calm and persuasive. "There's really no reason that you and I can't do some business here. And don't forget, there's plenty more where that came from. Get with it, man. Hell, I'd just as soon give it to you as that Jew shyster, Kornbluth." Staring at Thorn with a suggestive shrug, Ogden's look was one of smug pragmatism. "Just name your price, man."

Thorn kept his voice eerily composed. "My 'jive-ass main man . . . and my Brooklyn Heights bimbo.'" He turned to stare into Ogden's suddenly uneasy eyes. "That's my price! Got enough to buy them back for me?"

The temperature in the Buick fell to that of a meat locker, and Savage fought an overwhelming urge to reach over and strangle the dope-dealing murderer. "Well, do you?"

Ogden, eyes shifting nervously, made no attempt at an answer.

"Tell you what we're gonna do, Derek. We're gonna wait for your boy, Luther—"

"Luther?" Ogden scowled. "Hell, I don't know anyone named Luther."

Ignoring the lame denial, Savage continued. "Then we're all gonna have a nice talk, okay?" He spoke down to the man as if he were a child, baiting him, watching him become more frightened with each passing moment.

"What . . . ?" Ogden gasped, his baritone cracking. After clearing his throat, he continued in a voice weak and subdued. "What are we going to talk about?"

"We're gonna talk about dope, money, and murder. And who did what to whom! And who's gonna go to jail for it."

"Murder?" Ogden spun in the seat. "Whose murder do you intend to pin on me, Savage? I never killed anyone. . . . You'll never prove a fucking thing; you oughta know that—"

"Put your hands out." Savage cut the man off in mid-sentence, producing a handful of nylon lock ties. He bound the man's wrists together, palms out. Looping a tie through the man's belt, then around the wrist tie, he pinioned the man's hands into his lap. More ties bound his legs at the ankles. A pair of early-morning pedestrians were typically New York blasé as they passed by, seemingly unconcerned with the curious actions of the two men in the parked car.

"I don't know what the fuck you think you're doing, Savage. But I've got to tell you, man, you're fuckin' up big time. Do you hear me? You missed the boat a few weeks ago. Tonight, again, you're pissing away the opportunity of a fuckin' lifetime. Don't be an idiot; I could fix you up for life . . . for ten lives, goddammit."

Savage busied himself with the ties, unmoved, hearing not a word.

As Ogden opened his mouth, apparently to try a new

tack, Savage sealed it closed with a wide strip of packing tape. Ogden, defiant, glared.

Thorn pinched the man's cheek and winked. "There, that oughta hold you for a while." Savage wiped sweat from his own brow. "It's hot in here, isn't it, Derek . . . ?" Thorn's demeanor was still baiting and sarcastic. "Oops, may I call you Derek?" He quickly answered his own question: "Of course I may. We're pals, right? I'm gonna show you what a thoughtful guy I am. I'm gonna leave your window open a bit, so you don't bake; this old car ain't got no AC. Can you imagine that?" Savage turned the car's ignition switch to ACCESSORY and tuned the radio to a country music station.

"You like music, right?" Thorn said. "I'm gonna leave some shit-kickin' on for your entertainment." Savage laughed; he was getting spacey. "I love baiting and torturing you, you prick."

Through the tinny radio, some nasal redneck was crying in his beer because of a "long-gone woman."

"Sad, isn't it?" Savage said contemplatively. "You know what the Chinese say: 'A life without love . . . isn't worth living.' "

He stuffed Ogden's nickel-plated automatic back into the hogtied man's pocket.

"Now, I don't want you bothering anybody, and don't try blowing the horn: I've disconnected it. I'll be right back. I'm just going into the Southview and see if we can't convince our boy Luther to join us." Savage patted the man on his bald spot. "I'll be able to see your every move. So you stay nice and still. Okay?"

Glistening sweat appeared across Ogden's brow, dripping into his eyes and causing him to wince. Savage slid from the car and in seconds was out of sight. Ogden wriggled, squirmed, and struggled with every ounce of energy he had to work free of the nylon bonds, but quickly accepted the futility of the effort. His wrists were already bleeding; his strength would give out long before the restraints would, no matter how hard he tried. He resigned himself to having no choice but to sit this one out and let the maniac cop play his stupid fucking game. After all, he thought, what could be the worst possible scenario? Luther Robinson might have to take the fall for a homicide or two, but *c'est la vie.*

Kornbluth would have Derek Ogden back on the street inside of an hour.

# THIRTY-THREE

Two sleep-jarring rings, then silence. Luther Robinson cracked an eye and glanced toward the digital clock. Black silk pajamas glided on ivory satin as he skimmed across the circular bed toward the ebony nightstand. He waited, wondering what Derek might have forgotten. In seconds, as expected, the phone erupted again. He picked it up on the first ring.

"Yes?" he said flatly.

"Mr. Robeson, sir? This is O'Brien"—*cough, cough*—"the darman."

Robinson bit down angrily at the corner of his lower lip and rolled his eyes. The tubercular brogue coming through the line had about the same irritating effect on him as chalk screeching across a blackboard. He disliked the grating little man. "What do you want, O'Brien?"

"Mr. Robeson, sir. I'm sorry to be wakin' ya at this ungodly hour, but I t'ought I oughta be callin' to infarm ya—"

"Inform me of what, O'Brien? That it's four-thirty in the morning? This damn well better be good. Let's have it, man."

"Beggin' your pardon, sir. But a shart time after your cump'ny left a bit ago, a suspicious-lookin' "—*cough, cough, cough*—"feller come into the lobby askin' me some"—*cough, cough*—"questions."

"Questions . . . ? Questions like what?"

"He . . . he wanted to know if you wuz in, sir."

Sitting bolt upright, Robinson reached over and jerked the lamp chain. "And what did you tell him, O'Brien?"

"I told him . . . uhh, *no*, sir."

"What else did you tell him?"

"I said you'd gone out, and usually don't be gettin' back till marnin'. I made that all up, y'know. I hope I dun right, sir."

"Umh . . ."

"Feller told me he's goin' to be watchin' the buildin' from acrarse Farst Avenue. He must be wantin' t'see you real bad, y'know. He give me a nice crisp fifty-dollar bill so I should signal him when you return."

There was a protracted silence on the line. Finally, clearing his throat to hide any hint of his unease, Robinson spoke. "Tell me, O'Brien. Exactly what did this man look like?"

"Well, since y'be askin' me, sir, I'd have to say he could easy pass as a damned flatfoot, y'know. For sure he was slender, but strarng-lookin' just the same. He was needin' him a shave, and he was wearin' this floppy old cap, pulled way down low, like he didn't want no one to be seein' his face."

"Can you make out where he is now, O'Brien?" Robinson asked, repeatedly winding the coiled receiver cord on and off his slender index finger.

"Well . . . yes. Yes sir, I can. He crarsed the avenue, he did, and got into a real beat-up old car." *Cough!* "A Buick, I believe it to be, sir. Still there, 'tis. Parked in Eighty-farth Street, on the other side of Farst. Would y'want me to be callin' the police now, sir?"

"No!" Robinson cried. "That is *not* what I want you to do." Again he cleared his throat. "Listen very closely to me,

O'Brien. You never made this call. Do you understand? There'll be a considerable bonus for you this month. . . . And I mean considerable."

"Yes sir! Thank you, sir! Mum's the word. Glad to be of serv—"

Robinson slammed the receiver back into its cradle and silenced the sot's cloying voice in midsentence. Nostrils flaring, he charged barefoot through the sprawling apartment to the front room that overlooked First at the corner of Eighty-fourth. He carefully parted a blind in the darkened room and peered down across the avenue into the side street. O'Brien's description was right on.

"Shit . . . shit . . . ! Goddamned shit!"

Sliding out of the silk pajamas, leaving them lying in shiny clumps where they fell, Robinson stormed back through the apartment to the master suite and into the bath just off the large closet and dressing area. His well-ordered world was in jeopardy, possibly about to completely unravel.

At times like this he wished Aunt Lucy was still with it in the head. Whenever beleaguered, he would go to her and she would protect him, console him, and help him see things clearly. Aunt Lucy had always been the cool hand on his fevered brow. She could no longer come to him. However, Luther reasoned, he could still go to her.

He would skip town for a while, he decided. Now that the crib that he'd so fastidiously protected from the prying eyes of the world was completely blown, it was the intelligent thing for him to do. He would fade for a few days, relocate, and—with Derek's input—properly plan what needed to be done. Savage would have to wait to die. It would be at a time and place of their choosing, not the cop's.

Staring deeply into the eyes reflected in the wide mirror

above the twin-sink vanity, Robinson opened the tap and ran water into one of the black onyx basins. He had to overcome the welling within his loins. He knew the driving rush, if not checked, would soon become an overwhelming compulsion, a compulsion he would be powerless to resist. There was only one way to relieve the pressure.

Fantasizing of the moment when he would stick his gun in Savage's ear and dispatch the bastard to pig heaven, Luther steadily stroked himself until he ejaculated into the sink. Spent, and feeling the immediate relief of a great load off, Robinson moaned loudly in satisfaction and watched the results disappear down the gurgling drain.

For the moment, at least, the irresistible pressure to act had subsided. He adjusted the water temperature until it flowed as hot as his flesh could tolerate. He dispensed squirt after squirt of antibacterial liquid soap into his open palm and repeatedly scrubbed his hands, wrists, and forearms. Then he bathed and dried his genitals.

The closet had once been a large den; now it was a miniature Brooks Brothers. Row upon row, rack after rack, it was organized by color—degrees of black and shades of white—and style groupings. Robinson picked out a black turtleneck and charcoal slacks and quickly dressed. He grabbed his pre-packed Gucci overnighter from the top shelf and his dark windbreaker from the hook behind the door. Stepping back into the bedroom, he knelt beside the mammoth circular bed and reached under the mattress until he felt the cold steel. Along with Derek and Aunt Lucy, the nine was his true friend. None of them had ever let him down. Checking the ammo clip, he jammed the Glock into the windbreaker's specially tailored oversized pocket.

With long rapid strides, he left the penthouse and boarded his personal elevator. Its security monitor was black. The small screen showed nothing, not even a test pattern. The system's indicator light was glowing red, showing it was on. Twice he hit the reset—no response. He worked the directional joystick that controlled the garage camera—no results. For a long second he contemplated. Coincidence? Perhaps, he thought. Those screens had gone down before. He dropped the Gucci bag to the floor, removed the Glock from his pocket, and pressed the call button for the garage. During the slow ride down, he hit the light switch, blackening the dragonfly lamps.

When the elevator offered a gentle bounce, signaling its arrival at the parking level, Robinson jacked a round into the 9mm's chamber. As the door slid open, his unblinking eyes scanned the well-lit, quiet garage from the concealing darkness of the elevator box. From that vantage point he quickly eyeballed the overhead air duct that housed the security system's camera. No wonder his monitor screen was black; the aluminum louvers of the ventilation grille had been tightly closed. The wide directional slats could only be adjusted manually, he knew. Finally, after allowing several minutes to elapse and hearing not a sound, he made his move. Glock in hand—finger poised on the trigger—he picked up the overnighter from the floor and moved quickly from the blackened space toward the BMW.

At that hour of the morning the roads leading from the city would be wide open. Robinson envisioned Savage's beat-up Detroit iron straining to stay with his fleet Bimmer. If the cop was fool enough to chase him, he thought, it would be the tortoise and the hare all over again, except this time the hare would blow his fucking doors off.

As he reached his car, the Gucci bag slipped from his grasp and his mouth fell agape. In stony silence he circled the covered coupe. The BMW wasn't going anywhere. Not on four flats. He lifted the edge of the cover on the Bentley. It too sat on its rims, its massive Denmans razor-sliced through the wide white sidewalls. His angry glance fell on a scrawled note pinned to the BMW's cover:

*You were right. Things do come in threes. . . . Maybe you're next?*

Robinson's jaw tightened into a crushing vise. The killing machine was emerging again. And this time there was nothing he could do to prevent it. He wrung the note into a tightly packed ball and flung it across the garage.

"That motherfucker! The *balls* of that motherfucker . . . It's got to happen eventually . . . it might as well be now."

Bakery trucks, just starting their day, and fareless taxicabs, just finishing theirs, were the only things rolling at that hour just before dawn. Straining to stifle a yawn, Savage rubbed his tired, burning eyes. Redoubling his concentration, he again narrowed his focus to the Southview's lobby entrance. No one had come or gone from the building in the last twenty-five minutes. Sensing Derek Ogden's hostile vibrations beside him, he turned and gave the trussed-up man a condescending wink. The gesture elicited a muffled expletive. Savage allowed himself a malicious chuckle.

Concealed behind a block-long phalanx of tall sidewalk evergreens, Robinson slipped from the Southview's garage level through the fire-exit door nearest Eighty-third Street. Obscured by the urban greenery, his dark figure moved along the building line to the corner, where he quickly slipped across First Avenue. Circling the block, he entered Eighty-fourth from Second. He stopped momentarily to get his bearings.

As always, his approach would be made from the rear on the driver's side. His skill, honed many times, was unques-

tioned. He was the master. The lord high executioner.
Twisting the cap from the small glass vial, Robinson took a
quick blow of coke and, silent in Vibram-soled shoes,
moved off along the street's south side. All was quiet. He
maintained a steady, implacable pace. His predatory instincts had never been so keen. Forming a mental still of the
entire scene, his street-brilliant mind studied it, searching
for the slightest pitfall. There was none. No cars were moving through the block. There was not one person on the
street. The intensity, the anticipation, the sensuality of the
moment was almost more than he could bear. He sucked in
a deep breath, held it, and then let it out slowly.

Up ahead, barely distinguishable in the dim available
light, was a shabby Buick with the Jersey plates—the
derelict car that had been seen all week floating past the
Culture Club, hanging near the Carlyle, and squatting on
upper Broadway near 144th.

Robinson crossed on a diagonal to the street's north side,
picking up his pace, closing. Coming alongside the Buick,
past the point of no return, he was fully committed. How
accommodating, he thought. The fool in the floppy hat even
left the fucking window open for me. Listen to the crap this
jerk's got on the radio. *Country!* Damn, how can anybody
possibly listen to that pathetic shit? Smoothly drawing the
nine from its special pocket, he took two more measured
steps. Supporting the gun with both hands, he squatted into
a partial crouch and pushed the barrel of the Glock past the
open driver's window. He fired twice.

Chunks of brain matter, fragments of scalp, and bits of
dirty gray cap splattered the passenger compartment. The
tinny cowboy music, uninterrupted by the hellacious car-
nage, wailed on. Luther, erect and smug, released a moan
from deep in his belly. Smiling contentedly, he tucked the
smoldering gun back into his jacket and looked around at

the empty sidewalks. He was in the clear—*end* of Savage, *end* of fucking problem.

Taking only a half step in the direction of First Avenue, Luther froze. A figure, tall and broad-shouldered, stepped from a recessed doorway, blocking his intended path.

"Ahh, bee-jeez-us, now!" the figure said in cloying brogue. "Look what you've gone and done, Mr. Robeson, sir. Seems you've blown away a pillar of our fine community. *Begosh* and *begorrah*."

The voice was that of the half-pint Irish doorman, O'Brien, but the figure uttering the words was too damn tall. His mind boggled, Robinson stared as the figure moved from the shadows into the wash of the streetlamp.

"If you be wonderin' about O'Brien now, the little feller's not workin' tonight. He won't be back on the door again till T'ursday."

It all came home in an instant. Robinson gaped through the Buick's brain-spattered windshield and stared at what little remained of the face behind the steering wheel. Disoriented and gasping in disbelief, he yanked at the car's curb-side door. It was locked. He reached through the open window and jerked up the lock button. With both hands he grabbed the outer door handle and yanked again; the door opened.

Interior lamps flooded the grisly scene. Derek Ogden's head was mangled. His left eyeball, blown from its socket by the hydrostatic force of high-velocity bullets crashing into his skull, dangled ridiculously against his blood-drenched cheek; it stared into oblivion. Incongruous twangy *yahoo*s pulsed from the radio.

*"I've cried my eyes out for you, my darrr-linnn'* . . . *since you up 'n' went a-wayyy."*

With a mewling cry, Robinson backed away in spastic jerks. Overwhelmed by the sudden avalanche of panic, hatred, sorrow, and anger, he shot a tentative yet frigid glare at the rat-bastard cop who stood not twenty feet away.

"Seems you've also gone and left your wee mittens home tonight, eh, Mr. Robeson?" Savage said, still speaking in the damnable brogue. He was displaying a small revolver held tightly against his chest. His hands wore white surgical gloves.

Luther's mind was racing; to where, he did not know. Aunt Lucy's gentle face flashed through his thoughts.

"Should have asked to borrow mine," Savage said. "Lord knows, you must have put a whole bunch of your fingerprints all over that Buick by now."

Robinson dropped to a defensive crouch behind the Buick's open door and ripped the still-smoking 9mm from his jacket pocket. When he looked up again to take aim, Savage was gone . . . disappeared . . . like the wraith in *Hamlet*.

His survival instincts screaming, Robinson clambered to his feet and opted for a hasty retreat back through Eighty-fourth Street. Looking over his shoulder with each step, he quickened his walking pace to a jog. The jog soon became an all-out sprint. He had to get to Scarsdale.

Savage opened the Buick's passenger door, leaned in, and silenced the tinny radio. He turned the ignition switch to OFF, and then right back to ON. He made sure the collection of parking tickets he'd gathered all over the city were still stuffed in the visor above the slumped Ogden's head, and then stepped back and slammed the door. He pulled the fresh surgical gloves from his hands, slipped the gloves into his pocket, and took up the chase.

# THIRTY-FOUR

**Monday, May 8, 5:00 A.M.**

The city that never sleeps was rolling over on snooze for a few more of those precious moments before eight million alarms signaled the beginning of another day. However, on the still-darkened concrete sidewalks of the East Side, a game of life and death was already in progress.

Luther Robinson darted into Second Avenue and nearly got tagged by a barreling southbound M15 bus. He thought of trying to flag it down, but knew the driver would never pull over except at a marked bus stop, and who the hell knew where one of those might be? He continued running west on the sidewalks of Eighty-fourth and checked quickly over his shoulder. His pursuer was a full half-block behind.

The idea of fleeing from Savage was despicable. The thought of not facing the miserable bastard who had coldly engineered Derek's bloody murder—at *his* hands—was mind-numbing. But as Derek had always taught, logic and reason should always call the shots. Luther dug down and turned on more speed, giving it everything he had. He would live to even the score another day.

At Third Avenue, Robinson saw that the cop had narrowed the gap to less than half a block. Where was the son of a bitch getting his speed from? Robinson wondered. He concentrated on keeping up the flat-out pace.

At Lexington, with the first glimmer of dawn beginning

to bleed into Manhattan's avenues, Robinson realized he could no longer maintain the incredible pace he had been setting. The dogging cop wasn't cutting him any slack, either; the gap had closed to a quarter of a block. If Savage kept coming on at that rate, Luther calculated he'd never make the concealment of Central Park before the cop was on him. He decided to shift direction. Running southbound on Lex, he moved with the light flow of early-morning vehicular traffic. Lexington was always a good avenue on which to hail a cab, even at that hour. But not too many cabs were going to stop in the dark to pick up a frantically running black man with a fucking gun in his hand.

Savage watched Robinson head downtown on Lexington. He felt his calves beginning to burn from the intense pace and knew he had to close the gap before his legs gave out. *Fuck it!* He'd run his legs to bloody stumps before he'd quit this race. Luther Robinson, the soulless killing dynamo, was going to get switched off.

Crossing a dozen side streets down into the lower Seventies, Savage managed to stay with the younger man. The earlier flat-out pace had slowed considerably, and then even more, but Savage's legs were weakening; he was unable to close the gap any further. Apparently, Robinson's reserves were dwindling too—at about the same rate as his own. He wondered if he'd ever see a goddamned radio car cross his bow.

Gulping for oxygen, his heart about to explode through his heaving chest, Robinson could not take another step. He staggered to a stop at the corner of Sixty-fifth, leaned against a mailbox, and puked his guts out.

\*     \*     \*

Savage slowed to a strength-renewing walk, his willpower concealing his own exhaustion. As Robinson looked up from his retching, Savage's watchful eyes seemed to peel another layer from the man's veneer of ill-gotten dignity. Savage was slowly narrowing the gap, marching implacably.

Robinson felt the power of the approaching man's fixed, resolute look. It radiated from the cop as he moved forward in steady steps. Robinson could take no more. A cluster of traffic droned by as he turned from the daunting stare and made another break.

Down Lexington into the East Fifties Robinson slogged, his once easy, fluid sprint reduced to a sloppy, rambling quick-walk. He realized that despite his greatest efforts, he'd been unable to widen the gap between himself and that crazy bastard, Savage. Fortunately, though, the tenacious pit bull of a cop had been unable to close it. Desperate, frustrated, and angry, Robinson again decided to make a stand. He took cover amidst a row of empty cars parked at the curb next to Bloomingdale's.

"Let's do it here, motherfucker." Hands trembling from exhaustion, Robinson propped the automatic across a Ford fender for stability. Pouring sweat burned his eyes as he struggled to target the oncoming blur. He fired twice, a silencer muffling the sound.

Savage dived behind a streetlight stanchion as one round slammed into its aluminum base and another ricocheted off the sidewalk. Separated from Robinson by sixty feet of no man's land, Savage struggled for breath and renewal. His chest was molten and his contracting calf muscles verged on crippling spasm. His food and sleep deprivation were finally catching up with him. His engine was out of fuel—running on fumes of misery and intense hatred.

Thorn's mind suddenly conjured up agonizing visions of Gina: choking, gulping for breath, her life-sustaining blood pumping from her chest. She was dying all over again in his mind, butchered by the animal only yards away. He couldn't give up. He would never give up. He would run Luther Robinson to death.

With each difficult gasp, Robinson felt a resurrection of strength. Keeping his gaze locked on Savage's trapped position, he uncorked the vial of magic white powder. In seconds, the rejuvenating effects began. He needed to kill the cop soon or greatly widen the breach that separated them. Suddenly, in cocaine-induced bravado, he yelled across the divide:

"Hey, Savage. Want to know how many times I stuck it to your woman . . . ?"

There was no response.

"Hey, cop!" Robinson continued. "Your bitch could suck a mean dick. Know what I'm sayin', man? Just before I cut her fuckin' heart out, I made her suck me dry." He roared with uncontrollable laughter. "What are you gonna do about that shit, motherfucker?"

The taunting words pierced Savage's chest like a fiery spear. He fought the impulse to take the bait. Street smarts and years of discipline exercised shaky control. Swallowing pride and as much air as his burning lungs could handle, he glared across the breach. But he would not be lured into gun sights.

Visions of the slain Derek Ogden made him seethe with venomous anger, and Robinson took another hit from the

vial. Despite the chemically produced euphoria, he read
Savage's rapacious glare. Analyzing it, he understood the
cold-blooded, determined look. He pushed away from the
car.

Spurred by Robinson's taunts about Gina, Thorn found
his own last stash of strength and took up the chase. Block
after block, lost in a vacuum of single-minded hatred, he
matched Robinson's every step. At the sudden appearance of
a Seventeenth Precinct patrol car, he cool-breezed into casual nonchalance. The cruiser had stopped briefly for a light
on Forty-sixth at Lexington. The late-tour uniforms inside
were obviously unaware of what they'd driven into, and of
the silenced shots that had been fired by Robinson only minutes before. Savage considered hailing the cops and ending
the madness, but Robinson's words echoed. The game had
been irrevocably changed.

Robinson had all he could do *not* to signal the police car.
On the green, he looked back and watched as it rolled slowly
through the intersection and disappeared, heading toward
Third. Once the car was out of sight, the deadly game resumed. At Forty-fifth, Robinson left Lexington. Turning
west, he stumbled a short half-block and disappeared into
Depew Place, a narrow, little-known service street that ran
beneath the northbound side of Park Avenue.

If only he could just get inside, anywhere, he could bar-
ricade himself and keep that fucking pit bull at bay. He
lunged onward, past loading docks and randomly set
Dumpsters, with the kamikaze cop only twenty yards behind and slowly closing. Stumbling, with every last drop of
energy he could muster, Robinson ran into a small alley that
appeared at the end of Depew. He was boxed—there was no

way out. He turned to see Savage appear at the alley's mouth.

Savage was intensely aware of the new morning light at his back. He was in mild silhouette. Advantage Robinson. Advancing by Braille, he worked himself along the soot-covered brick wall, groping mortar-joint recesses with one hand and squeezing the grips of his Smith & Wesson tightly in the other. Thorn knew the short alley. He'd always surmised that once upon a time—very long ago—it had been Forty-third Street, before being truncated during the creation of Grand Central Station.

Above the expected smell of urine and vomit from this outdoor toilet for the homeless was the additional stench of a decomposing animal—a cat possibly, or a dog. Debris was everywhere. Fifty-five-gallon drums, dented and rusty, stood randomly among piles of overflowing trash bags. It was a foul-smelling and dense grove of ankle-twisters, hiding places, and deathtraps. His vision slowly adjusted to the minimum light, yet Savage barely avoided kicking an empty wine bottle that lay in his path. A noisy clink might be all Robinson needed to zero in.

On end, near the alley's back wall, were three refrigerator-size cardboard cartons. Waterlogged from many rains, they stood there like soggy, tilting, monolithic sentries nearing collapse. Thorn concluded, inhaling deeply, that Robinson *had* to be behind one of them. There was no other place, except inside the trash piles, for him to be. Expecting shots with each passing second, Thorn wondered if he would actually hear them. He didn't care if he died there, as long as he didn't die alone. Musing that death lurked behind one of the three huge boxes, his exhausted mind remembered *Let's Make a Deal*, the old TV game show where contestants selected fortune or failure from behind one of three curtains. In a nanosecond, a variant of the game played in his mind:

*Okay, Mr. Savage, is the grim reaper behind carton number one? Carton number two? Or carton number three?*

Thorn stifled a fear-choked breath, swung his arm violently, and battered the carton nearest him. Allowing no time to think, he hit the next. Both boxes collapsed into soggy heaps. Ignoring the terror that could easily consume him, he drew the revolver tightly into his waist and kicked the third box over, tensing defensively as it too collapsed into a soggy heap.

Nothing.

Confused, he turned, checking his steps. Could he have missed something in his fatigue? There was really no other place a man could hide in there. Then he saw it. A rusted steel door. Hiding in plain sight, it blended perfectly into the age-darkened brick wall. It was ajar. Robinson had found an escape hatch.

"God help me," Thorn muttered. How much longer could he go on before dropping in exhaustion?

The oversized door swung smoothly on well-greased hinges. Passing through it, Savage found himself on the top landing of an iron staircase. With the .38 at high port, he moved down into the bowels of Grand Central Station.

Down too, he was certain . . . into hell.

# THIRTY-FIVE

The century-old iron stairs had narrow treads and tall risers that made them hazardous to descend, especially in the puny light provided by the bulbs screwed into high sockets at every other landing. Savage traced them quickly down through a silo-like shaft, lined in heat-blistered brown brick. The difficult stairs could never have been designed with fare-paying customers in mind. They were, Savage decided, a means of egress for track workers, or access for emergency crews. At a point he estimated to be five stories or more beneath street level, the silo bottomed out at yet another steel door. *Behind curtain number five . . .*

Before venturing on, Savage reached up to the lone anemic bulb that barely lit the final landing and backed it off a turn, swamping the area with darkness. Damn thing's wattage was so low it wasn't even hot. He cracked the door an inch and gazed into the eerie dimness of a train tunnel whose tracks had long ago lost their gleam. After allowing his eyes to adjust to the new level of darkness, he slipped beyond the door, closed it silently behind him, and became one with the rough-hewn tunnel wall. He quietly inhaled a long, deep breath and held it, shutting down the clangor inside as he listened intently for any sound.

It was quiet . . . quiet like a grave.

But Savage knew Luther Robinson was there. Savage

sensed his menace, felt it in the rising hairs on the back of his neck. He read it too from the internal sensors that savvy street cops develop over time. Somewhere in the dimness of the ancient tube was his enemy. His prey. Savage was ready; every nerve in his body had clicked onto full alert.

The time of final reckoning had arrived. One way or the other, it would all end in this long-forgotten cavern beneath the waking city. Savage knew, surer than Christ, that only one of them would walk out of there. Mulling that certainty a fraction longer, it dawned on him that neither of them might ever again see the light of day.

*So be it.*

Robinson, after all, was not going to surrender. Robinson was not going to simply turn over his weapon, weep, and say he was sorry for all his fucking mayhem, and then march obediently off to death row. Savage knew that Robinson was going to fight to the finish. But it was okay. One way or the other, he'd soon be able to rest. For a split second, his tired mind considered the irony of his life's finale possibly occurring inside a train terminal: it truly being the "end of the line."

His eyes finally fully adjusted to the new low level of light, and with silent partners Messrs. Smith & Wesson on point, he began to grope his way forward.

Compared to the partially flooded rail bed, the old passenger platform was high ground. What Robinson needed, and what he found, was even *higher* ground. Concealed in the man-space between the twin-sided timetable posting board, eight feet above the midpoint of the platform, he popped the magazine from the nine and checked the remaining ammo. He still had twelve rounds—way more than enough. He laid the weapon in his lap and tapped the coke vial for another quick snort. He had never felt more pumped. Never been more eager for the kill, or as thirsty for blood. Although having to concede that Savage was nobody's walk in the park, he recalled how he'd outwitted and beaten similar wily types before. Savage, after all, was just another humbug civil servant—no match for the lord high executioner.

Here he was, Robinson mused, sensing the chemical's beginning rush, about to do deadly combat with the bastard who'd undermined his perfect life. Who'd unearthed the money-spewing network that had taken years to organize and who had disgraced Derek before the *entire fucking world*. Derek, God! His thoughts swirled through anger, hatred, second-guessing, and chemically induced paranoia. The revered, darkly handsome face of his mentor suddenly appeared in a fog before Robinson's fully dilated pupils. He reached out his hand to touch, to feel, to stroke the perfect features of Derek's scar-free countenance. Upon his touch, the vision quickly morphed into a butchered, blood-dripping death mask.

"It wasn't me," Luther pleaded. "It was him; it was that fucking Savage. I . . . I didn't know."

The mask hovering before him spoke. "Avenge me, Luther. Take his heart out." The strong baritone was unmistakable.

"I *will*! I . . . I swear to you."

The specter evaporated as quickly as it had appeared. Luther tried, but could not recall a vision ever accompanying the voices he'd heard so frequently since he was a child. But then again, never before had he known this intensity of anger or this all-consuming need for vengeance.

"You took Derek from me, you bastard," he murmured. "Why do you keep coming?"

As the coke hit evened out, he sensed impregnability. "I'll see you dead, moth-er-fuck-er. . . ." he snarled. Then abruptly, as if a switch had been thrown, he began to laugh. The laughter grew until it became maniacal. When it finally subsided, Robinson climbed eight more iron rungs and slipped behind several huge conduits gnawed by age and oxidation. Overlooking Track D-14, he had now fully taken the high ground. "You're a dead man, Savage," he muttered. *"You are a dead fucking man!"*

Moving in dense silence, Savage inched along the rail bed to the mouth of the tunnel, which opened onto a vast, long-deserted platform area. He ran his hand along the jagged stone wall, touching the deep scars left by steam shovels and picks, the primitive tools used to gouge the cavernous area from Manhattan bedrock. He'd read somewhere that in its glory years the terminal's eighty-three underground tracks had handled as many as seven hundred trains a day. Angry at his lapse of concentration, he pulled his wandering mind back to his task.

Should he wait Robinson out? Stay tucked away at the mouth of the tunnel and hope for Robinson to show himself? Or should he make the first move and hope to draw fire? Suddenly, wild, insane laughter came at him from every direction. The unnerving sound echoed, reproducing itself exponentially against the cavern's myriad jutting angles. The laughter finally rose to a crescendo and vanished into the silence as suddenly as it had begun.

Savage hesitated to do anything that might give an advantage to his cunning adversary, but he had to do something, soon. While his adrenaline reserves still existed. Could he stay safely stashed between the old pillars of the tunnel and hope for Robinson to step into his crosshairs? No, Robinson wouldn't make it that easy.

Thorn edged out along the rail bed, deserting the relative safety of blackness. Ankle-deep in standing water, he moved in a crouch, his head well below platform level. Hunkered down on the rails, he soon discovered the source of the small flood as droplets formed and fell from a corroded flange above. The leaking water main was one of a system that coursed overhead and disappeared into the blackness of the converging tunnels.

Anxious, he raised his head and sighted along the surface of the platform, hoping to see, hear, or feel anything that might guide him. Illumination of the vastness came from wattage-starved bare bulbs, their dingy half-glow enveloped in pale yellow halo. Lit randomly throughout the cavern, they created more shadow than light.

The platform of Track D-14 probably hadn't been used in forty to fifty years. Dust had settled and remained undisturbed through the decades. Once bustling, the platform was now quiet, forbidding. Squinting, Thorn imagined leggy women in 1940s-era Joan Crawford fashions, and scores of cigar-smoking, barrel-chested men in fur-collared overcoats.

Thorn knew that many levels above, men were pouring from sleek silver trains that brought them from the calm and security of Westport, or some other backyard community, to Grand Central Station. Non-police men. Men who toted briefcases to work—not handcuffs, not guns, not bullets. Safe in the vacuum of their mundane existences, completely oblivious to the deadly drama now in its final act down on old Track D-14.

The total silence of the ancient station was broken only by the steady drip of water. The sound was oddly soothing. Squatting on his heels, he took several deep breaths as he tried to coordinate his wandering thoughts. Visions of Gina began to dominate his mind. She died alone, he remembered, with no one to hold her. All that he'd ever wanted in a woman, taken away, slaughtered by a beast who lurked somewhere just beyond his grasp.

He rose again to peer down the lengthy platform. Nothing. There was no way to summon help. Help, he thought, was unacceptable anyway. If ever he was to have any self-respect . . . if he ever wanted a night's sleep . . . he must kill Robinson . . . and he must do it alone.

Gently, almost inaudibly, the plummeting droplets splattered onto the outer rail in a haunting, hypnotic tempo: one-two-three . . . one-two-three, lulling him. His eyelids, weighted and heavy, pulled downward. Helluva time to be runnin' outta gas, he thought with a disbelieving sigh. Unable to stave off the inevitable, Thorn let his head fall forward in a sudden involuntary nod. Needing a morsel of total rest, his eyes stuttered shut.

He was with her; they whirled in an eerie hologram to something Viennese. She was dazzling in white lace and satin; he clung, praying the image would not abandon him. They moved entwined, eyes locked, spiritually connected. Gina was a dancer, Gina was his lover, Gina was . . . *gone!* His heavy eyes snapped open; he was back in the now. Gone was the dream. Seething hatred radiated through him like an electric current all over again.

Robinson was nowhere in sight. Where could the beast be?

He struggled to stay alert. But again he drifted into a dreamlike state, transfixed by the background patter of waltz time. They danced, two karmas in perfect tune, the tempo she loved so much indelible in his heart and mind. Step-two-three . . . step-two-three.

Lowly discord suddenly invaded the soothing reverie. The rhythm was off. The beats and rests were syncopating. The droplets that seduced with metronomically perfect waltz time were changing tempo. They fell at a faster rate, staccato. It was a signal, a signal that Gina herself was sending. Robinson was on the move. He was overhead, on the straining water pipe.

Adrenaline rushed through Savage.

Careful, Thorn. Don't betray that you're aware of him.

He displayed no reaction to the telegraphed approach. Narrowing his vision to stare into the liquid mirror that surrounded him, he focused on the reflected image of the ancient conduits above. All sensory perceptions became magnified—the sound of the telltale drip; the pounding in his chest. The beast was only moments away. Timing . . . that's the key. With a quick, violent snap of his head, he cleared away another untimely attack of fatigue. He needed but a few more seconds of absolute concentration.

He lusted for Savage's blood, and sadistic fantasies flitted through Robinson's mind. The fear and confusion that had plagued him earlier had passed. His greatest concern now was that Savage might succumb to initial wounds that he would inflict, and thereby not be conscious to suffer the tortures of hell that animated his cocaine-saturated mind. Tortures he would deliver as painstakingly and cruelly as he had to the stray cats and dogs and grounded birds as a child. And he would do it here in the privacy of this providential dungeon that he'd somehow stumbled into. He was feeling the rush, big time.

Emotionally and chemically supercharged, Robinson moved forward, silent, hidden, safe within the suspended snarl of bulletproof tubing. Owning the high ground and having the clear advantage, he moved, snake-like, toward his hated objective. The squatting cop beneath him was a duck on a pond. Grinning at the metaphor, he thought: Only inches to go and that son of a bitch will be a dead duck.

\*    \*    \*

Thorn detected the almost imperceptible: a subtle, momentary change in the reflected picture. Robinson had arrived at his vantage point. Ignoring all instincts for self-preservation, Thorn made no move for cover. That, he thought, would only delay the final contest. Don't give it away now, Thorn. Hang in there, man. Don't let him suspect that you know. Be cool, but focus . . . focus.

The muzzle of an automatic pistol appeared in the reflected scene. It began its tilt downward, toward him. To carry out its mission the gun had to be accurately aimed. Wait . . . wait for the horrible face to appear.

"Just say die, cop!" Luther snarled, unable to resist the taunt as he squinted behind the sights of the well-aimed Glock.

Savage whirled and planted his back against the platform wall. Supporting the .38 with both hands in classic combat style, he pushed it out at eye level. Instantly, he dialed in a sight picture of a gnarled face mostly obscured behind a poised weapon. Five faultless squeezes of his trigger claimed all remaining concentration.

It was over in less than a second. The terrible sound of gunfire echoed throughout the cavern, reverberating in a hallelujah. The .38s had found their mark.

For a split second Robinson must have known defeat. Crammed into the maintenance crawl space, unable to dodge the deadly fusillade, he had to have known he'd lost. Geysers of red spurted from his gaping head wounds. They faded to a trickle when the monster's heart ceased to beat.

The cancer had been excised. Robinson was DOA.

Whatever had sustained him was fast ebbing. Dropping to his knees, Savage let his arms fall limply to his sides, the dirty water in which he knelt quenching the smoking snub nose of the Smith & Wesson.

Staring into nothingness, he was lost in himself, trying to make a connection with the old Thorn, the pre–Gina McCormick Thorn. The Thorn Savage who'd coped with life by insulating himself from pain with an inner strength, an emotional circuit breaker that had kept the joy of loving—and the inevitable pain of losing—at arm's length . . . until Gina. Could he ever find himself again?

The days of the previous weeks had all congealed into a mélange of anguish, fear, and hate. Unable to recall even what day it was, he forced his mind to concentrate.

Strength slowly returned and he struggled to his feet. Shaky, reaching out to the platform edge, he supported himself with both hands. His saturated pants legs dripped into the blood-tinged pool at his feet. He decided that only he and the tunnel rats would ever know what had happened here, and where Robinson lay. He knew that he would never tell.

Slogging the length of the long, sealed-off platform, he came to a fire door, behind which he found a staircase. Painfully, he ascended the steps to street level. The emergency door at the top landing opened right at the terminal's Lexington Avenue entrance. The brilliant morning light was harsh, forcing him to squint his flame-red, watery eyes. All around, revolving doors consumed humanity at an incredible rate. Buses roared by, belching their sooty miasma. Taxis cut from lane to lane, ever attempting to advance a few additional inches. New York City was awake. He dissolved into the human hubbub, deep in thought.

Above the din of blowing horns, he heard the wail of a police siren somewhere in the distance, or was it an ambulance . . . ? Did it matter?

A bespectacled, middle-aged executive clambered from a taxi, sweeping past Thorn as if he were invisible. The man disappeared into the terminal: a worker bee.

Thorn's thoughts flashed to his elderly, eccentric upstairs neighbor. Mrs. Potamkin had probably wanted happiness and contentment as a young married woman in Hitler's Germany, and all she got was a tattooed serial number, and a life of agonizing over her young husband, Julius, whom she'd last seen in October of '39, being herded with hundreds of other men into slatted cattle cars. Talk about the end of the line. But Mrs. P went on.

Could he accept the truth? Could he go on, knowing that his dedication and beliefs had so little impact on anything? Life, he knew, would go on with or without him. The world would continue to be what it was, a place of good and bad, heroes and scumbags, predator and prey. Life was a game and he was just a minor leaguer, an aging one at that. Damn, did his existence make any difference to anybody?

Savage pulled himself into the waiting cab and sat preoccupied as it forced its way into the city's arterial flow.

"Where to?" the driver said.

The digital display on the meter triggered thoughts of another cab parked on Sixty-seventh Street, and of the contents of the briefcase on its backseat floor. Thorn patted his pocket. He still had the keys to that cab.

A warm sun lit the sky, boasting of the advent of a new day. His eyes had adjusted, and a feeling of acceptance settled in. There were things he yet had to do. He was here, in this world, for a reason. Life would deal him whatever it may, but he must go on.

An ironic smile settled slowly across his haggard face. Abe's kid was going to attend Harvard after all. And he was going to go first-class. An anonymous benefactor was about to make a tremendous cash endowment to ensure just that.

"Take me home, driver," he said resolutely. "Gotta feed

my cat and then get some sleep. Tomorrow I'm due back at
work."

"Whaddaya do?"

"I'm on The Job."

# East Side

# –

# West Side

. . . and all around the town,
Sgt. Thorn Savage
prowls the dark streets of Manhattan
in pursuit of justice.

Look for John Mackie's next
two novels of the NYPD,
coming soon from
New American Library.

Read the first in the series
featuring Detective Thornton Savage and his
homicide task force

# MANHATTAN SOUTH

## By John Mackie

When Candace Mayhew's husband travels for
business, she joins her Gambino-mob boyfriend for a
clandestine meeting...
With a tap of a trigger, the lovers lay dead.

Later that same morning, Andric Karazov plays with
his toy Napoleonic Calvary and thinks about the
less-than-perfect job he just completed, while a
senator in Queens contemplates his run for the
presidency as his wife enjoys another
rendezvous with her Russian lesbian lover.

As Savage soon realizes, all of these people are linked
to Candace Mayhew—it isn't long before he closes in
on the assassin and his life
is threatened

0-451-41045-9

Available wherever books are sold, or
to order call: 1-800-788-6262

# FIRST AVENUE
## By Lowen Clausen

Written with compelling authenticity by a former Seattle police officer, this debut novel is the powerful story of a Seattle cop who can't shake the image of the abandoned, dead baby he finds in a seedy hotel—and who can't give up on finding the truth until those responsible are brought to justice...

**"*First Avenue* is as moody as Seattle in the rain, and just as alluring. A skillful, memorable first novel."**
—Stephen White, *New York Times* bestselling author

**"I loved this book...[it] has an authenticity only a real cop could convey."**
—Ann Rule, *New York Times* bestselling author of
*The Stranger Beside Me* and *And Never Let Her Go*, and
a former Seattle cop herself

0-451-40948-5

Available wherever books are sold, or
to order call: 1-800-788-6262